Dial 323 L O V E

By: C.M. Arnold

Printed in the United States of America

For information about special discounts available for bulk purchases, sales promotions, and all other inquiries, email cmarnoldwrites@gmail.com

ISBN 978-0-9997132-0-4 (paperback)
ISBN 978-0-9997132-1-1 (eBook)

LCCN: 2018901859

Books in this series…

1. Dial 323 LOVE
2. Descension *(spring 2018)*
3. Affliction *(coming summer 2018)*
4. Redemption *(coming fall 2018)*

CHAPTER ONE

Maggie Hunter never considered herself a criminal. She is, by all technical standards, an entrepreneur. A businesswoman. A smart woman. An exquisite concoction of allurement and intimidation, simultaneously capable of drawing people in and shutting them out. If cunning and calculating are undesirable traits, she doesn't wish to be desired. But oh, she's a beautiful woman, born with the natural ability to turn heads. Well into her forties, and unlike many of the other ladies in her zip code, she hasn't been under the knife once. Her features are not surgically altered; her looks are not courtesy of Botox; her blonde hair is not a shade that can be bought in a bottle and applied over a sink. The aura she produces intoxicates without acquiescence. Her persona says come to me. Her smile says trust me.

Her eyes say everything else.

Through two perfectly placed slate grey spheres, she possesses the uncanny ability to convey exactly what she wants in explicit detail without the hassle of words. Eyes that pick up on potential, sign deals, and sell dreams. You see, Maggie is a woman well-versed in the art of manipulation, painting persuasion with every purposeful move she makes. She is also a woman who knows her worth, but more than that she's a woman who knows others' worth. And, most of all, she's a woman who knows what those so inclined are willing to pay. Power is a personality flaw in no need of correction; success something measured with her own personal ruler.

This particular mid-May morning is just another day to her. She carefully applies a red lip in the mirror, then single-handedly zips up the back of her demure couture dress. She crosses the expanse of her bedroom to take a seat on a perfectly made California King, where she pulls on a pair of red-soled stilettos. Her penthouse apartment is open, high-end, and contemporary, furnished with only the finest top of the line accouterments. Ample glass provides panoramic views of West Hollywood, her elevation so high that the tops of palm trees are nothing more than peons in her peripheral vision.

She gives herself one last look in the mirror, running a manicured hand through her perfectly curled locks. She smiles, satisfied, and grabs her Fendi bag off the quartz island. By the door a set of brown Louis Vuitton luggage is waiting.

Out in the hallway the elevator doors open and she steps in with her bags. It's an elaborate square with a glass mirror on the back wall and an attendant in the corner. She looks over at the old, kind-faced man in the little uniform and smiles.

"Good morning, Barney." She presses L for the lobby and the doors close.

"Good morning, Miss Hunter," he replies, returning her smile. The numbers start ticking down as they stare ahead. "What's on the agenda today?"

"On my way to the airport."

"New York? Miami?" He inquires as if he knows her. To some extent, he does.

"Memphis."

"Memphis?" He sounds surprised. "Is this business or pleasure?"

She knows he's just making small talk, but she smirks to herself anyway, the irony being that the two are interchangeable to her even if he doesn't know it. "An old friend of mine is performing his first solo at a blues club down there."

"Oh. Well that sounds like it should be fun," Barney muses in his usual, upbeat way. "Shall I page the valet and have him call you a town car to LAX?"

"Just tell Julio to pull the Benz around," she replies. "I can drive myself."

"Yes, ma'am."

She can hear the familiar static hissing of his walkie-talkie being activated before he speaks into it. "Julio? Yes. Bring Miss Hunter's car around front. She's on her way down."

At the final *ding* of the elevator she pulls down her Chanel shades. The doors open and she struts out, crossing the lavish lobby with long strides. A bellman is waiting, holding open the door for her. She thanks him as she exits out into the world. Her Mercedes is parked right at the curb like she knew it would be, its glossy white paint glistening in the SoCal sun. Julio is holding open the driver's side door for her, revealing its red interior. Symbolism at its finest.

"Good morning, Miss Hunter," Julio says with a wide smile.

"Good morning, Julio," she replies, returning his smile as she slides into the sporty coupe.

He hands her the keys and she hands him a fifty. He accepts it excitedly.

"You have a good day now."

"Thank you. You have good day too. Be safe."

She winks at him. "Always."

The door closes, the top goes down, and she speeds off with one hand on the wheel.

Forty minutes later Maggie is removing her jewelry and putting them in a bin with her bag. She gives the bin a push down the conveyer belt and attempts to proceed through security. But then there's a young TSA agent stepping in front of her, preventing her from going any further. She looks up into his slightly vexed but profitably cute face. He fits the typical twenty-something transplant role to a tee, with that new California cultivated glow. Pale skin that's a little tanner, brown hair that's a little blonder, and oh, that vain 'I wanna be somebody' body. The boy probably went to the gym three times a day just to maintain. *How splendid*, she thinks. He doesn't have a clue what she's thinking; he hasn't been taught to read minds just yet. He just knows she's yet another person who's making his menial job more difficult.

"Ma'am," he says. "Your shoes." He points with his eyes to her feet. His voice carries that note of annoyance almost all people have who work with the public on a daily basis. She doesn't fault him for it. Instead, she looks down at her stiletto-clad feet and lets out a little laugh.

"You'd think I had never done this before." She reaches down and removes them, putting them in a bin. "It's just that I always keep my heels on."

It's not said any certain type of way—she doesn't even change her tone or give him a look—but the line still has the young man's ears turning red. She gives him a second glance, taking note in how his little mock-cop uniform hugs him so well, then continues on her way. Once she's grabbed her crate at the other end; her shoes and jewels back on, she fishes her billfold from her purse and takes out a card. She fans the little nondescript piece of parchment between her fingers as she turns back around.

"Oh, young man," she coolly beckons.

He glances around nervously, either in sheer disbelief that the gorgeous, first-class flying cougar who keeps her heels on is actually calling for *him*, or because his subconscious senses the imminent trouble associating with her will naturally lead him to be in. Maybe it's a little bit of both. Either way, he walks straight to her.

"Yes, ma'am?"

She holds out the card to him.

"Call me if you get tired of feeling people up for minimum wage."

Austin Edwards is confused, but he's also curious. That latter almost always trumps the former, and it's no different in this instance. He takes the card, watching her sashay away to her gate without another word. Intuition is something that has always eluded him, but a few years down the road he might just wonder what his future would've looked like had he not put himself in her path.

~

Later that night Maggie finds herself in Memphis, sitting by herself in the back of a dark, smoky bar sipping a glass of Moet et Chandon. It's a tight space lacking any real kind of ambiance, jam-packed with people she neither knows nor cares to know. One could easily choke on the second-hand fumes, and the hazy filter makes it damn near impossible to see the stage clearly. However, it's awfully hard to miss the burley woman with the banjo, currently singing a tepid rendition of "All I Could Do Was Cry." Maggie is almost positive that Etta would not approve. The woman finishes; the crowd claps. *Southern hospitality*, she thinks. The announcer comes back on stage.

"That was Miss Cheryl Grange from the Chattanooga Bay, y'all. You enjoy the rest of ya time in the city, momma." He pauses, then incites the crowd. "She had a beautiful voice, didn't she?"

They coo their approval. The microphone crackles, then calms.

"Now our next performer," he starts. "He ain't no stranger to these parts. Please give a warm welcome to Memphis' own, Mister Marvin Brown!"

The crowd erupts in applause as an older man carrying a saxophone case comes out from backstage. Maggie grins. He looks quite a bit older than he did when he left Los Angeles; there are more than a few wrinkles on his weathered face and the wiry hair on his chin is almost all gray. But he still moves with that same swagger she remembers. She watches as he sits down on the stool in the middle of the stage and takes out his golden sax. The announcer puts the microphone in front of him and then backs off.

"Thank y'all for comin out tonight." His smile is cut from the same cloth as Maggie's, and once he flashes it at the crowd they are instantly under his spell. "Most of y'all know me. Thought I'd bless y'all with some of this blues music of mine if ya don't mind." He pauses, looks out into the crowd, scanning the sea of faces for hers. He finds what he's looking for. She doesn't have to see his eyes to know there's a glint in them. "First, though, I wanna give a shout out to an old friend of mine—Miss Maggie, fresh in from the city of angels. She's on the back row over there. Likes to keep a low profile."

He winks. She smiles politely and raises her glass.

He begins to play.

After Marvin's set has finished, he and Maggie and a couple of his buddies sit around a table in the back smoking cigars. Marvin had known better than to try to hand her a Newport from the crumbled carton he keeps in his back pocket, but he also knew if someone were to bring a box of Cubans around she'd put one between her pretty lips, puff away, and not cough once. So he'd had it arranged.

"Back in the day me and this girl right here use to run LA," he brags to his friends.

Maggie glances over at him out of the corner of her eye. The mix of the liquor he's been drinking combined with the rush from his recent performance has his lips a little loose. But she lets him have his fun; the two sixty-something corduroy-wearing drunkards he's telling his story to hardly seem like a liability. She imagines that one is a barber, and maybe the other one owns a hardware store.

"Don't be spilling all of my secrets now, Mr. Brown," she warns before taking a drag.

His friends begin to file out, congratulating him one last time as they go. Soon they're all alone.

"Just so you know, I've since upgraded," she casually informs him, inhaling just as casually. He watches her, transfixed. She exhales a sinuous string of smoke. "I now run Rodeo. Melrose. Beverly Hills. Bel-Air. Calabasas. Mulholland. Multiple cities, actually—I've taken it on the road."

He raises an eyebrow.

"Rafael goes down to Miami every so many months. After a weekend in South Beach he brings back…well…let's just say it's a lucrative amount. And I send Theo to New York occasionally, since he knows his way around those streets like a pro. Sometimes I'll go with them if I need to get out of LA for a while, it depends."

"Wow. So you still got Theo working for you?"

"You sound surprised."

"I just figured he'd eventually tire of playin somebody that he ain't."

"Sometimes he gets to be who is," she replies simply. Then she adds, a smile in her voice, "I cater to all demographics, cultures, and orientations.'

"But still." He takes a puff. "Anyway, he gotta be into his thirties by now," he says, giving her a knowing smirk. "I thought you liked to keep 'em in that 20-29 bracket."

"If you still look good, do good, and are making money it doesn't matter how old you are." She takes her last hit then puts it out. "And he's thirty-three."

"So that would make you…forty-three?"

"Ok."

He grins. She's so predictably poker-faced.

"How bout we get outta here? I'll treat you to some of the best barbecue chicken in the city."

"As long as you're treating," she replies as she stands, reaching for her bag.

He shakes his head. "You don't ever change."

She smiles.

~

Andrew James Brooks does not—nor has he ever—considered himself a sex symbol. He has always been more concerned about his education, and literature, and the future than being some kind of Casanova. He is content with his girlfriend of three years, Grace, and has every intention of marrying her once they graduate. Though he errs on the upper side of average—with his lean body, thick dark hair, and piercing green eyes—it is not the end-all-be-all handsomeness that would cause an oppressive ego. And his ego is not. He is a humble young man with just enough southern charm to not be introverted. He is simple in the most complex of ways, the iridescent naivety of youth shimmering just under the acquired wisdom of an intellectual. A combination that college cultivated twenty-two-year-olds pull off so well.

The boy has dreams, too. As the only child of a housewife and a part owner of a truck dealership, he knows his apple landed somewhere left of the tree. But he doesn't mind that he is the only one in his circle thinking outside of the square. His mother wants her baby to be safe; his father wants his son to be practical. Grace wants the canine, the two point five, and the white picket fence line. As for AJ, well, he just wants to become an acclaimed writer and to appease them all in the process. It is probably that natural inclination to please.

To him this particular mid-May evening seems no different than any other. If there is pandemonium pending, he doesn't sense it. He gets into his outdated powder blue Ford Escort; his last class just let out. He puts the key in the ignition and twists it once to let it do its thing and die. Then he twists it twice and holds it, listening as the engine finally comes to life with a hoarse growl. He smiles and puts it in gear. As he maneuvers out of the parking lot and onto the highway he fumbles with the radio dial, flipping past the static and the commercials until he hears a familiar riff. He manually rolls his window down halfway. The air is heady with the scent of spring; flowers and rain and imminent change. Soon his fingers are unconsciously tapping to the rhythm on the rim of the wheel. He makes two rights and a left, then slows down and pulls in and parks. The commute is short and he doesn't even get to finish the song. He cuts the engine off and reaches around to the backseat to grab his grease-stained apron. He pulls it on over his plain grey t-shirt and ties the strings behind his back with nimble dexterity. Before he gets out he takes a quick glimpse at himself in the visor mirror just to make sure he's presentable. He sees nothing wrong in his reflection other than an errant curl that he quickly tames with a little spit. Good to go.

He uses the back entrance into the kitchen. Pots and pans clang and something sizzles in the background. The familiar aroma of spices and smoke and soapy water flood his senses. A round-bellied man is lifting a batch of fries out of the grease pit and a pimpled-faced teenager is hand-washing a stack of dishes. They both look up when the cool breeze that's been let in hits their back.

"AJ!" They both yell simultaneously.

AJ returns their welcoming smiles. "What's up, guys?" he says as he delves further into the kitchen, swiping his card on the time clock in the back of the room.

Tim, the teen, turns off the water at the big steel industrial sink and dries his hands on a discolored towel. "So I'm sorta gonna fail two classes this semester," he tells AJ, his voice meek and somewhat hesitant. "I got the same teacher for both English and Lit, and she's a real bitch. My counselor says if I don't retake them and pass, I can't walk with my class next spring." He puffs out his bird chest in an act of faux indifference. "I don't really care if I walk with those douchebags or not, but my mom will be pissed if I don't."

AJ knows better. Tim is a good-hearted and self-conscious kid who probably cares *too* much about what those douchebags think. But AJ doesn't contradict him; he just continues to listen diligently.

"Anyway she wants me to get tutored over summer." He pauses as his timidity returns. "Seeing as you're really smart and like an English major and stuff I thought, I don't know, maybe you could help me. I'd pay you of course."

"You don't have to pay me, man," AJ tells him. "I've got some free time on Thursdays, would that work?"

"Yeah, that'd be–"

Their conversation is cut short when the door from the dining room swings open. Emerging from the adjoining room is a high-strung young woman with hair that looks like it's pulled back a little too tight. She wears a black ball cap that says "Wing Shack Team Member" in offset white letters and a black polo with a gold "assistant manager" nameplate pinned to it. Tim cowers back to his post at the sink. Meanwhile, she directs her anxious eyes on AJ.

"I need you out on the floor tonight instead of in the kitchen," she declares hastily. "Katie called in," she adds, punctuating with an eye roll. "Again."

"Okay cool," AJ concedes without argument. "That's fine with me."

"We've been swamped, like, literally all night," she continues pointlessly, getting a Dasani out of the fridge. "It's just been me, Tim, and Miguel in the kitchen." She collapses onto a stool and holds the cold bottle to her forehead for a beat before unscrewing the lid. "Susie *was* on the register, but she just *had* to leave at five." She takes a gulp and swallows. "Really, she could have stayed later. Anyway. Madison's been the only one serving since then, and she wants to go home. So you're going to be by yourself because I need to be in the kitchen, Miguel's leaving in an hour, and Tim doesn't have good interpersonal skills."

"That's fine."

"I mean it's not like we're busy anymore. It's practically dead out there now. I seriously doubt you'll have the magnitude of problems we had earlier."

"Really, Karen, I don't mind serving," he assures her.

"Good because you really don't have a choice." She hops off the stool, hands him a little pad of paper with a pen, and walks off texting.

Miguel looks over at AJ out of the side of his eye and shakes his head. AJ just laughs, clicks his pen, and heads out front.

~

A bell chimes. Marvin holds the wood framed door open for Maggie who trails behind him. She stands in the doorway and briefly surveys the situation. He's waiting for her snide commentary about how plain of a place it is, waiting for her to turn her nose up at the burnt undertones of greasy fried food and the remnant scent of cheap cigarettes. But instead she surprises him and marches across the now empty dining room to the table of her liking. He stands still in his spot, looking at her like she's both a piece of art and a piece of work.

"Yanno, most people just order at the counter," he says, only half-sarcastically.

"I'm not most people." She shrugs her stole off and places it on the back of the chair. "Don't worry," she assures him as she sits down. "Someone will come to us."

So he follows suit and takes a seat across from her. His phone buzzes in his pocket. He takes it out and looks at it, then shakes his head and returns it to his pocket without answering.

"That could be the money calling," she chides facetiously. "You're not going to pick up?"

"It's just one my girls. She somehow got herself all the way ta Nashville and now don't know how to get herself back. Wants me ta come get her."

Maggie sits quietly for a beat, with her legs crossed and one foot jostling just a little.

"You know I'll never respect what you do," she says.

He scoffs with a snort. "Excuse me, but last time *I* checked we was both in the rental car business." He leans back and leers at her greasily. "Only difference is mine are automatics and yours are stick shifts."

She smirks. "Yes, but I look so much more classy while doing it." Her shoulders arch airily. "I'm inconspicuous. Me? I just look like a businesswoman. You?" She shakes her head. "Subtlety was never your strong suit, in pastel suites and dyed alligator boots, draped in gold from head to toe with one of those little top hats—all of which you probably bought at the corner store. It's obvious you're selling the corner, and what's more whatever scantily clad female you have standing on it."

He looks down at the table and ruefully shakes his head. He can't help but smile; she may be talking shit but she's also speaking the truth.

"Plus," she adds. "Just as a woman, I can't respect it. However hypocritical that may make me."

"Hey, I'm better then alotta these dudes out here. I cut my girls their little checks. They get their money. And I don't ever put my hand on em," he informs her matter-of-factly to justify his actions. "Not even when they're late with it."

She smiles ever so slightly.

"Shoot," he says. "You probably beat yours if they don't come home with the right amount. Probably got em all shook."

She snorts, choosing to ignore his comment. "I'm looking to hire a couple new guys. Lost one of my longtime employees to Universal Studios. He finally landed his first lead role in a feature film."

"I sure hope he thanks you in the acceptance speech for keepin him afloat all them years he was *aspiring*."

"I want my boys to succeed. I'm never mad when they reach their dreams." She sounds sincere when she says it but then she sighs. "It just leaves me with spots to fill."

"You said you had two spots ta fill. What happen to the other guy?"

She sighs again and crosses her arms. "He got too caught up in the lifestyle. Got a little money in his pocket, made friends with a few high rollers, and started making some not so good decisions."

"Them fast broads in Beverly Hills got him on that stuff, didn't they?"

She nods with her lips pursed. "And we can't have that." She stares off into space as she thinks about the workers she's recently lost and, more importantly, the money she has lost because of this. She thinks of Brent's bright grin when he told her he got the part. She thinks of Caleb's blown out, blood stained nostrils when she told him he was fired. She thinks of the twenty or so clients she's had to reschedule in the last month and what that's cost h–

"Can I get you two something to drink?"

The unfamiliar voice breaks her train of thought and she looks up into the greenest, most unforgettable eyes she's ever seen.

"Gimme some of that E&J on the rocks, AJ," Marvin says to the server, who he clearly knows. He laughs when he notices what he's said and turns to Maggie, who is looking at AJ like he's a piece of real estate she wants to put a bid in on. "Gimme some of that E&J, AJ." He nudges her "That was cute, wasn't it?"

She looks at him blankly. "They serve liquor at the Wing Shack?"

"This is Memphis, baby," Marvin tells her, as if that's explanation enough.

"Well. In that case." She trains her eyes back upon the young waiter. "I'll take a glass of Courvoisier. Neat. And a water on the side, no lemon."

"Yes, ma'am," AJ replies. "I'll be right back with your drinks."

He's not a drop-dead hunk, she thinks to herself. But there's something about him. He has that something.

"Oh, by the way," Marvin quickly interjects before AJ can get away. "This here is Mister Andrew James. Andrew, this is Miss Maggie Hunter."

AJ smiles politely. It's the kind with the potential to induce butterflies and raise pulses. She adds it to the list of pros she's making in her head.

"Nice to meet you," he says, extending his hand to her.

They shake. She smiles.

It's the kind with the power to make a secure man sell his soul and a wise man sign on a dotted line.

"Likewise."

"He takes the mike at The Blue Café every now and then himself," Marvin tells her off handedly.

"Oh, you're a singer?" She sounds intrigued; not only that but interested.

AJ opens his mouth to answer but Marvin gets there first.

"He recites poetry."

"So you're poetic," she muses rather than asks, tilting her head at him ever so slightly. "Maybe even some would say a little romantic?"

AJ can't decide whether or not he's really supposed to respond to this and is relived when Marvin just keeps talking.

"He's been workin' here, what?" He looks at AJ. "Three years now?"

"Going on four," AJ says, finally getting a word in.

"He's bout to graduate from the University of Memphis," Marvin informs Maggie. "He tryin' save up and go to one of them fancy graduate schools out where you're at." He looks back to AJ. "Which one is it now, UCLA?"

"USC."

Marvin turns back to Maggie, who hasn't taken her eyes off AJ the whole time. "USC. He wants ta be a film writer."

"Oh honey," she tells AJ. "You're too pretty to be a writer."

AJ blushes, patiently waiting for them to stop talking to him so he can leave.

"Take offense ta that blatant objectification, AJ. Us artists don't need to be classified by our looks," Marvin tells him.

AJ simply smiles and tells them that he will be back and then slips away.

"Nice smile," Maggie says absently once he's gone.

"Don't."

"Don't what?" She looks at him like she doesn't have a clue what he means and bats her eyes innocently.

"He's a good kid."

"Good for him."

"He's got a girlfriend."

"And most of my clients have husbands. And I've got two feet and two hands and the sky is blue when the sun is shining what's your point?"

He cocks his head at her and scolds her with his eyes. "Try ta have some morals."

"Says the man with a limp and a cane," she retorts, smirk on her lips.

"Hey, maybe I got osteoarthritis. You ever think about that?"

She laughs. Even though she doesn't respect what he does, even though he's trying to stop her right now from doing the exact same thing, he's always able to make her laugh. AJ comes back with their drinks and sets them on the table, pulling out his notepad and his pen.

"Are you all ready to order?"

"Well you see, I'm not really a chicken wing connoisseur," Maggie begins, inconspicuous of her agenda. "So I'm finding it hard to choose." The truth is she hasn't even so much as glanced at the menu. "In your professional opinion, what would you recommend?"

AJ thinks for a minute. "Well. I know Marvin and his friends really like the extra spicy," he offers. "But a lot of the locals like it Sweet Memphis style. It's usually done to pork, but we do it to our chicken, too."

The smirk that curls her lips says that her filthy mind has latched onto something innocent and is taking it way out of context.

Marvin mumbles to himself, right hand rubbing his face.

"I like the sound of that," she says to AJ. "I'll take an order of Sweet Memphis Style."

AJ nods and smiles, writing down what she wants without really knowing.

About thirty minutes later two plates have been completely cleaned off, and Maggie and Marvin are leaning back in their chairs looking uncomfortably full.

"That was actually pretty good," Maggie admits.

"See, your fancy little ass needs to come down a couple of notches every now and then." He leans in and gives her a sultry look. "You wanna go to the club?"

She lifts an eyebrow at him. "Don't you think we're a little old for *the club*?"

"Hey, a wise woman once told me if you still look good, do good, and are making money it don't matter how old you are."

She smiles subtly. "Alright then. Let's go to the club."

AJ comes back to the table to check on them. "Did you enjoy your chicken?" he asks Maggie.

"As a matter of fact I did. Excellent recommendation."

"Good," he smiles, starting to collect their dirty plates. "I'm glad I could be of service."

"Yes," she utters unassumingly while staring at him wickedly. "Well." She tears her gaze away and looks over to Marvin. "I'm going to go to the powder room and freshen up before we go, I'll be right back."

"Ok," he says, draining the last drop of liquor out of his glass.

She gets up and heads towards the restrooms. AJ waits until she's out of earshot and then turns to Marvin.

"Was she flirting?"

"Nah," Marvin says. "She was scoutin'."

AJ doesn't know what this means, but when he goes back to bust their table after they've left, there's a one-hundred-dollar tip and a business card waiting for him. Maggie Hunter Management—no street address, simply Los Angeles, CA and a number. On the back she had written, "Call me after graduation."

CHAPTER 2

Three weeks later AJ sits alone in the tiny kitchen of the tiny duplex he and Grace rent. There are two matching tassels hanging from the ceiling fan above and they twirl over his head counterclockwise. Laid out in front of him on the unvarnished oak table are Maggie's business card and an opened black box with an engagement ring in it. It's not an overly flashy ring, just a simple diamond and simple band. He knows Grace isn't the type of girl who would feel comfortable walking around with a huge rock on her hand, even if he could afford to give her one. She's more modest than material, more sentimental than showy. He knows she wants to wear her grandmother's white lace wedding gown. He knows she likes October as a month—not too hot, not too cold. He knows that her favorite colors are orange and pink, and that Shania Twain's "From This Moment" makes her tear up. He knows she loves him, and likes the name Gavin for a boy, when the time comes, of course. She's told him all these things in passing, over early morning study sessions or late night in bed, and he's kept mental track of it all.

He knows her well. They began dating the first semester of their sophomore year at UofM. He wanted to write screenplays and novels and such, and she wanted to be a registered nurse and heal people. They somehow had two classes that corresponded with both of their majors and they had been together ever since. Three years. There were never any "breaks" or "taking of space" because those were just outs and they were both in. For the last year they have been living together contentedly in the left half of a three hundred square foot duplex. He knows marriage is usually what comes next in these kinds of natural progressions, and so he bought a ring.

Now here he is, indecisively looking between the ring and the card and feeling an unaccustomed sense of confliction that he would soon learn to just ignore. He had called after graduation just like her stylistic, cursive handwriting told him to do. He waited until all the festivities had died down, after he had attended three of his classmates' parties and had gotten back home were Grace proceeded to pass out half on the bed and half off after having had one too many Straw-Ber-Rita's at the last stop of the evening. While she slept it off he snuck out back and dialed the number.

She answered on the eighth ring, after his heart had already relocated to his throat and his palms had begun to sweat. The second her cool, eloquent voice came over the line he felt like everything would be alright, that all his stars were destined to align. What were the chances that a Hollywood agent would walk into his place of employment, sit down in his section, and take an immediate interest in his mundane little life? This had to be fate, he thought. And oh, fate is such a hard thing to ignore. He told her who he was and she said that of course she remembered. She told him she was very interested in managing his writing career; even though she hadn't read anything of his, which should have been a red flag but somehow wasn't, she was still willing to take a chance on him since he came so well recommended by her dear friend Marvin. As it turned out, Maggie was also a firm believer in fate. She just had a *feeling* about this, at least that's what she told him. She also told him if he really wanted this, if he really wanted to be taken seriously, he would need to move to Los Angeles. Because nothing can be done in Tennessee. This he knows to be true. Like she knew the best way to validate a misfit was to tell them they were meant for more than wherever they were currently stuck. Before she ended the conversation, she told him to call her when he got into town. He told her that he would if he decided to come. She smiled then, but he couldn't see it.

AJ hears Grace's car pull up outside and quickly closes the box with the ring in it and slips it back down into his pocket. The screen door slides open and she shuffles in with multiple grocery bags in hand.

"Hey, honey," she says, struggling but smiling all the same. She heaves the groceries onto the Formica countertop, catching her breath as she swipes a strand of strawberry blonde hair out of her face.

"Did you buy out the store?" he jokes as he gets up to help her. He grabs the milk and the eggs and heads to the fridge.

"Well, you know, I started that couponing," she reminds him, gathering up the canned goods. "And guess what?"

"What?" He amuses her.

She looks at him, beaming. "I saved twenty-seven dollars and sixty-one cents!"

"Whoa."

"I know," she says, taking out some box-mixes. "And I got all the ingredients to make that chocolate cake you like so much."

"Sounds good." He closes the fridge. "Listen, Grace, I need to talk to you about something."

She immediately stops what she's doing. "Oh my God. What happened?"

"Nothing," he says quickly to comfort her. Maybe he had made his tone a little too serious. "Nothing bad, I…I got an offer."

She lifts a brow. "What kind of offer?"

"Kind of like a job offer."

"What's kind of like a job offer?"

He takes a breath and takes a seat back at the table, patting the chair next to him for her to join him. She does.

"This woman from Los Angeles came into my work a few weeks ago," he starts, unsure of how this is going to go or sound. "She's an agent and I told her I was a writer and she left me her card."

Grace is staring at him in an ungrasping kind of way.

"Anyway," he continues. "I called that number a couple of days ago and talked to her…and she said she'd represent me. She wants me to move out there."

Grace's face remains unreadable and unchanging.

"Say something."

Her freckled nose furrows and her eyes fill with bemusement. "What," she grapples. "Well what about us?"

"We're still us," he assures her.

"I thought…I thought we had decided to stay here," she says in a voice that makes her sound both annoyed and authoritative. "I thought that we had decided tuition was too much for graduate school and we'd be better off saving our money and staying here. Save up, move out of this duplex, and get our own place. Remember the house on Rose Street? With the 2.5 acres and the cute little shed? I'd go to work at Memphis Memorial and you'd go to work at your dad's dealership? What happened to that?"

"I don't want to work at the dealership," he states plainly. "I don't know the first thing about selling a semi or fixing a semi or the parts of a semi…"

"Didn't he say he'd send you to a business class at night for a few weeks and you'd be good to go?" This is how she counters, and under her breath adds, "Since that English degree really isn't going to do anything."

He doesn't say anything, but just crosses his arms.

"And you don't have to know how to fix a semi. It's not like I'm askin' you to be a mechanic. You'll be a salesman. You just have to know how to make a sale."

"I don't want to be a salesman." His voice hinges on cold now. "And you're really starting to sound like my parents with that *English degrees are useless* crap."

"I didn't say that."

"You implied it."

"Well, you are still working at The Wing Shack," she states with a huff. "I know it don't take a degree to do that."

"The Wing Shack," he retorts. "Where had I not been, I would have never met an agent." He sighs and then takes a gentler tone with her. "Do you know how big of deal this is, Grace? People struggle for *years* to land an agent, and I do it overnight. What are the odds of that? I mean, even if it is a sham or a scam or turns out to be a total bust if I don't take this chance I'll always wonder. You know? I'll always wonder if this was my one chance."

She just sits there in silence for a moment and stares at him like she's trying to understand. He knows she doesn't. But at least she tries.

She looks down. "You know if you go, I can't go with you." After a while she looks back up and meets his eyes. "I've worked my butt off in college for the last four years. I just got offered a full-time RN job at one of the biggest hospitals in the state. I can't pass my chance up either."

He gives her a meek smile. "You know there are tons of hospitals in LA. Top hospitals. All of which probably have open positions for an RN."

"Yeah, but I don't really like LA."

"You've never been there."

She wrinkles her nose. "It just seems so fussy. And congested. And the traffic. You know I don't even like commuting to downtown Memphis."

He leans back a little and takes a breath. "Then I guess we'll have to do the long-distance thing."

"Do you think those really work?" She asks honestly with eyes full of doubt.

He meets those doubtful eyes even though he's doubtful too, and strips any waver from his voice. "We'll make it work." He leans forward and takes her hand in his. "I'll make it work."

She's softening slowly with each assuring word.

"I love you," he tells her. "And you love me, right?" He doesn't want to be that guy. The guy who uses the L word to assuage his girlfriend's fears. But every guy has to be that guy sometimes. And it's not like it isn't true.

"Of course I love you, AJ," she answers. "More than I think you know." She takes a breath and then pushes on. "And enough to let you chase this crazy lead of yours halfway across the dag-on country without me."

He smiles, relived and appreciative. "Then you have nothing to worry about." He leans back again. "And, realistically speaking, there's a good chance that this crazy lead of mine won't work out, and I'll be back in Tennessee in a month."

He can tell she wants to smile at the prospect of his dreams not panning out. But she doesn't. She forces her supportive face on.

"What will you do in LA?" She asks. "I mean this woman, she's just an agent. She's not going to provide you with a life…"

He shrugs, unsure himself. "Look for a cheap apartment to live in, a decent restaurant to work at." He flits over any other possible options in his head but at the end of the day all he can add is, "And wait."

~

Anjanae Collins is waiting at the bottom of a winding grand staircase. She looks both impossibly tired and terminally bored as she crosses her arms and leans against the intricately carved railing. Her glossy jet-black hair is pressed straight to perfection. It's only a quarter after eight but her makeup is already done, even though she doesn't need it and probably never will. She attempts with no avail to stretch the skimpy white silk robe to cover more of her skin; it's a chilly morning in Bel-Air. The robe was a present from her husband for her twenty-seventh birthday the month before. He had sent it priority from Dubai, or Ibiza, or wherever it was he had been at the time, along with a matching white Swarovski-crystal embellished thong. *More for him than me*, she had thought upon opening it.

Her eyes stare crossly at the luggage that's been left on the last step. Footsteps follow the sound of a door being closed on the floor above and then he appears on the landing. Julius Collins descends the stairs in his affluent attire: Ralph Lauren sweater fitting snugly around his mildly round middle, collar and cuffs of a corresponding dress shirt peeking out from underneath, complete with creaseless slacks and suede loafers. He's got his bespoke readers on his nose and one of his many gold Audemars around his wrist and yet another bag in his hand.

"You do plan on coming back, right?" Anjanae asks him dryly.

"I'm going to be in New York for eight days, dear. Do you want me to run out of clean clothes?" He grabs the handle of his suitcase when he reaches the bottom and rolls right past her like she's not even there.

"Of course not. That would be tragic."

"Don't be crass," he says, pausing in front of the mounted mirror in the hall to adjust his collar. "I told you it's not becoming on you."

She looks down at the marble floors submissively.

"I left the keys to the Porsche out. You know, should you want a change from the Range." He smooths a comb over his short hair. "But don't touch the Lamborghini," he states with a note of enhanced importance like a parent reciting house rules to a preschooler who couldn't possibly know better. "And remember," he adds, walking over to the nearby Venetian table to pick up some sort of equipment bag. "If you want to go out in the Rolls, you need a driver."

Something suddenly dawns on Anjanae and she looks up with confusion etched across her face. "Hold up," she says. "Did you just say a minute ago that you was gonna be gone eight days? I thought y'all was only spose to be gone for four?"

He laughs derisively. "Uh. There's that ever so charming southern twang that only presents itself when you start to get wound up."

She ignores his patronization since she's damn near numb to it. She's damn near numb from it. However, her silence still speaks volumes. He finally looks at her.

"Now what is it, Anjanae?"

"The opening of that new art gallery in West Hollywood is Saturday," she says simply, already not expecting much. "You promised two months ago you'd go with me."

He looks down and sighs. It's more for effect than out of actual guilt, but still, he can lay it on thick when he wants to.

"What can I do to make it up to you, Anjie baby? I can't have you moping around the mansion with those sad eyes all week." He holds up a finger as a thought strikes him. "I know. I'll send Roscoe over to Fifth Avenue when we arrive to fetch you something stunning that you can wear to the event in my absence. Will that make it better?"

He doesn't give her time to answer because no sooner has he said it is he giving her a quick, curt kiss.

"Be good," he tells her like he always does with his hand on the door. And then he's gone. And she's left standing there all alone in an empty mansion. Again.

~

AJ is in his beater with the windows down, cruising along freeway lined with palm trees. Its noon on Monday, and as luck would have it he seems to have missed out on that all-day gridlock everyone talks about. He wears a smile that is a mile wide and worth more than a million dollars. As far as his eyes can see there's not a cloud in the sky. It's been a week and a day since his conversation with Grace and a week since he had the same conversation with his parents. He had gone over to their house after his dad got off work, sat them both down on the couch, and told them his plans to move to California as gently as possible. He had waited while his mother took a slow descent into hysteria; shocked silence that turned to stuttering, stuttering that turned to sniffling, sniffling that turned to sobbing. His father had just shaken his head and gotten up, mumbling something about fruitcakes and queers into his beer as he left the room and the conversation. AJ had put his arm around his mom and told her everything would be all right, and that *he'd* be all right. Then he grilled steaks for the two of them and they sat and had dinner out on the patio like they had so many times before. By the time he left around nine, and long after his father had "retired" for the night, his mom had calmed down but her eyes were still coated with the same fear. He reminded her that he had never given her a viable reason to worry about him. She agreed and said that he had always been a good son and a smart kid. And then proceeded to plead him not to leave anyway.

It had taken him two hours to find a cheap apartment online and two days to make the drive. All of his belongings are there with him in his little car, one box with all of his clothes in it and another box with a used microwave and toaster he got from a neighborhood yard sale, plus one box of utensils and cups and plates he had purchased at one of those stores where everything is a dollar; one box of miscellaneous kick-knacks and notebooks, a box of his favorite books he couldn't bear to leave behind, and a travel case with the slightly outdated MacBook his mom got him for his eighteenth birthday. That was it. That was all he had and all he needed. He left before the sun came up on Sunday and drove all day, only stopping once to eat and twice to fill up the tank.

When nightfall came and his eyes got heavy he pulled over at an out of the way motel somewhere in Nevada and slept in his car. He was up again bright and early the next morning and had been making great time ever since. There had barely been any weather the entire trip. He was coasting through the calm.

He takes the Wilshire Vermont exit and glances over at the time on the car radio. It's a quarter past twelve and his GPS is telling him he's within five miles of his new home, and in three hours he's going to have his first official meeting with Maggie Hunter. He couldn't be more pumped. He makes his way into Koreatown, finally spotting his street sign. He pulls up and parks in front of an old, lackluster brick building. It's about five stories high and the main level seems to be split between a restaurant and a pawnshop. The chunky yellow and green painted letters on the Plexiglas of the restaurant side read REEH AND WOO KOREAN BARBECUE with all of the foreign symbols directly underneath. There is a big tacky banner hanging higher up on the building that says ROOMS FOR RENT with a number he's already called. He shuts off the engine and hops out of his car.

Being that it is lunchtime the restaurant is fairly busy. Men in suits sit alone on barstools, having something light. A group of college-aged kids sit together at one of the long tables by the window, sharing a hodge-podge of varying dishes. There are families in booths enjoying entrees and full course meals. He stands in the doorway looking around, but for who or what he's not really sure. A young Korean waitress tries to seat him, but he politely declines and asks where he could find the owner. She points to an older Korean man in a white chef's outfit who is standing back by the kitchen door. He thanks her and goes to him.

"Excuse me, sir," AJ says to him. The man is not taller than AJ but his eyes still seem to be looking down on him. "I was wondering if you knew about the apartments upstairs? I called and spoke to someone about them earlier in the we–"

The man cuts him off and hastily speaks to him in Korean. AJ suddenly feels the need to apologize.

"I'm really sorry about the inconvenience, I just need to get in contact with whoever the landlord is so I can move my–"

The man cuts him off again and continues on in Korean. He sounds very much annoyed. AJ doesn't know what to do. This scene gets the attention of a young Korean man busting a table across the restaurant, who puts down his rag and goes over to intervene.

"I got this, Mr. Woo." He puts himself between them and says something in Korean to the man, who proceeds to throw his hands up in the air and walk away. Jae then turns his attention to AJ.

"You must be the new tenant renting 4B upstairs," he says to AJ.

"Yes," AJ replies, relieved that someone finally knows what he's talking about. He holds out his hand. "Andrew Brooks. You can call me AJ."

He shakes his hand. "I'm Mr. Reeh's son. Jae-sun Reeh. You can call me Jae. I recently dropped the sun because being Jae *sunray* was getting to be a little too cheery for me to handle, quite frankly."

AJ laughs. Jae looks to be about his age. He's thin with straight black hair that lays flat against his scalp. His mildly awkward mannerisms remind him of Timmy back at The Wing Shack.

"Come on," Jae says, and gestures to the back. "I'll show you up to your room."

"Okay. Great." AJ re-gathers his bags and follows Jae. The staircase is in a dark nook behind the counter and to the right of kitchen. There's no elevator insight. Jae leads the way and bounds up the first flight with ease. AJ trails behind, lugging his luggage up each step with a heave. The dusty, old wooden planks under his feet creak and moan in protest. "So your dad owns the place?" he asks breathlessly.

"Yeah, he runs the restaurant with Mr. Woo—who you were talking to—but does the renting part himself. That's why Mr. Woo didn't know what you were talking about."

"Yeah," AJ mutters to himself. He finally makes it to the third floor and takes a breath before continuing to trek on to the fourth. "You speak English really good, by the way," he comments idly to Jae, not thinking in the moment that it sounds offensive.

"I speak English really *well*," Jae corrects, not offended and still twelve steps ahead of him.

AJ reddens, thinking to himself that being on the road for so long has killed off a few brain cells and affected his grammar and sensibility. Because here he is, a recent college graduate with an English degree, getting a lesson from someone not even originally from this country, whom he may have just unintentionally insulted by acting surprised that he spoke so "good." And then he's corrected again.

"I was born here in Los Angeles," Jae informs him. "My parents migrated from Seoul in the early eighties."

They reach the fourth floor and Jae fishes out a key from his pocket. He unlocks the first door on the left and looks back at AJ.

"Here you go."

AJ steps into the small studio and his immediate thought is that it feels very empty. The lighting is poor and the paint scheme is drab. There's a box spring mattress and the simplest of couches, plus a microwave, a plain white 1950's style refrigerator, and one little chair in the corner.

"This is one of the nicer ones," Jae muses. "Fully furnished."

AJ takes it in. It is an awful lot to take in, and at the same time not very much at all. But it will have to do.

"So I didn't ask. Where are you moving from?"

"Memphis," AJ answers. "I'm a writer and–"

"Oh," Jae says. His voice is a little lofty now and he almost rolls his eyes, not needing to hear anymore because he already knows. "One of those."

AJ's confused. "One of what?"

"One of the aspiring writer-actor-singers. They come and go," he imparts sagely. "I've lived here all my life, so I know. Anyway," Jae smiles, and then says more pleasantly, "Welcome to LA. I'll leave you to your unpacking." He turns to leave.

"Wait!"

He turns back around.

"You work here, right?" AJ asks.

"Yes." Jae eyes him skeptically. "Why?"

"You think your dad would give me a job?"

Jae just laughs, like he finds the naivety of new transplants truly comical, and then walks out the door. "Have a good day, AJ."

AJ can still hear him chuckling in the distance.

~

When AJ drives up on the address Maggie gave him the first thing he notices is that there is no business name or sign of any kind on the building. The only indication he has that he's at the right place is the street number, 360, plastered boldly on the illustrious navy blue header. For reasons not yet made obvious, the glass windows and doors are tinted and there are no noticeable indicators that anybody even works there. He parks out front on the rather inconspicuous Hollywood street and gets out. It's quiet; unlike all the hustle and bustle he passed coming down "the boulevard" only a few blocks away.

He walks through the door and there's what appears to be either a lounge or a waiting area where a couple of guys are hanging out. He doesn't get much of a chance to take it in because he is quickly being whisked away. A tall and elegant black man with high cheekbones and smooth skin has taken hold of his arm. There's a door to his left and he's being led to it. As he gets closer he sees that it's actually a glass-enclosed office. He sees her. She's wearing a bright royal blue blazer that's opened with a black top tucked in underneath; matching royal blue pants that are stylishly slim. She's prominence epitomized, he thinks to himself. When he enters the room she immediately stands like a businessman would when the lady he's courting comes to the table. Her heels have to be at least six inches high.

"Andrew!" She exclaims with her classic smile, coming from around her desk to kiss him twice on each cheek like Parisians do. But French she is not. At least he doesn't detect an accent. "Welcome to my office."

It is a fairly unassuming office, nothing out of the ordinary. He notices a bookcase on the back wall with an array of miscellaneous novels arranged on the lower shelf, plus two unlit candles that say *Magnolia Blossom* sitting on the top. There's a file cabinet in one corner and an oriental vase in the other. There are no framed pictures of family or friends. But there are two framed degrees mounted on the left wall. One is from Berkley Haas School of Business and the other is from MIT Sloan School of Management.

"Have a seat."

He does as he's told and takes a seat at her expansive mahogany desk. It's neat and slick and all clean lines, just like her. There's no clutter or messy paperwork to be had—not even a landline phone—just a computer, a calculator, and a coffee cup stained with red lipstick. He catches a whiff of her perfume as she goes back behind her desk; it smells expensive and formidable and not at all like anything Grace or his mother ever wears. She sits down across from him, still smiling cordially. Her eyes meet his for the first time on her turf. And for the first time since he arrived in California he feels very, very far from home.

"I do hope you found it okay."

He nods with a smile. "Yes."

"That's Theo, by the way," she says as she gestures with her eyes to the man in the corner who brought him in. She smiles warmly at this

Theo. "He's kind of like my personal assistant, been with me forever. Theo, this is Andrew Brooks."

The two men exchange nods of greetings. Maggie focuses her attention back to the matter at hand.

"I'm so glad you decided to come out to Los Angeles, Andrew. How are you liking it so far?"

"It's nice. I'm glad to be here." He swallows the lump in his throat and smiles nervously. "I just wish I spoke Korean so I could get a job in my building." He thinks about it and then adds, "But I'm going to put in some applications today while I'm in Hollywood, and Downtown, too. So hopefully–"

"That won't be necessary," she interjects nonchalantly.

"What?"

"Getting a job. That won't be necessary."

His face contorts in confusion. He must be misunderstanding something. Surely she hasn't already landed him a gig without having even seen a writing sample; that's thinking way too optimistically. "I don't...I mean how am I going to support myself?"

There's a knock at the door and his question goes unanswered.

"Come in," Maggie says.

A strapping man walks in with a Gucci duffel bag. The top three or four buttons of his white silk shirt are unbuttoned, revealing his tan, toned, and waxed chest. A Hermes belt holds his fitted black slacks in place. His red eyes suggest that maybe he's missed more than one night of rest.

"How was the scene out in South Beach?" She asks him.

The man starts to speak rapidly in Spanish, using hand gestures just as quickly to accentuate his presumed annoyance and distress.

Maggie holds a hand up. "Rafael, do you see a Rosetta Stone sitting on my desk? English please."

He sighs and starts over.

"I think I threw my back out. I am in traction and going to need chiropractic visit. The fifty-million-mile car ride back to LA did not help the situation."

AJ eyes the man curiously while trying to piece together just who he is and what his role is here. Rafael seems not to be concerned with who AJ is at all.

"Darling, we've been over this before," Maggie tells Rafael in her artificially sweet voice. "You know you can't fly. You don't have a green card. Immigration will take you."

Rafael rolls his eyes dramatically.

"I'll set you up an appointment with my chiropractor," she placates. "Now how did we do?"

Rafael unzips the bag. "You tell me."

He turns it upside down and multiple stacks of money come tumbling out onto the desk wrapped in rubber bands. AJ is astonished and doesn't have a clue what to think. Maggie on the other hand looks only mildly impressed.

"Well it certainly looks like it was worth the trouble."

Rafael nods wordlessly. "I am going home now to sleep and shower," he says on his way to the door. "I'll see you tomorrow."

"Don't forget you have a client tomorrow night!" She calls after him.

His audible sigh can be heard from the hallway.

AJ is still speechlessly staring at the money when she turns her attention back on him

"Look, Andrew, I'm just going to give it to you straight, okay?"

He looks up and meets her eyes.

"This town has the ability to exploit you," she starts. "Use you to its advantage, eat you up, spit you out, defy you and defile you all for the sake of a dollar." She shrugs. "So why not just let me do it first?"

He's still staring at her, still speechless.

"Because at least I'm going to be honest about it," she continues. The nonchalance in her voice is mystifying. "Plus, I pay well. Way better than a dollar. Way better than any of your alternatives."

He's ten miles past conflicted. He thinks he knows what she's implying and he thinks he knows what she's going to say next, but his mind refuses to wrap around it. So he just lets her keep talking.

"You'll be making money while you're making contacts. You get to live in the city that puts you in line with all the people and opportunities you need to achieve your dreams. But unlike all the other dreamers living here, you will never have to worry about how you'll support yourself while waiting for that big break that may or may not ever come. Because you will *always* have me."

He sits there quietly with his hands gripping the armrest of the chair till his knuckles turn white. He knows he should get up. He should get up and walk out the door and never come back. But he can't. It's like he's been shell-shocked into immobility. He's transfixed now, and even though he doesn't want to…he wants to know more.

He watches as she pulls open a drawer and takes out a folder.

"This folder entails first tier job duties." She hands him the folder. He puts out a hand and pauses before finally taking it. "You know, the basics," she says as he opens the folder and begins to peruse its contents. "Escorting a lady to dinner. Being someone's date for an event. Pretty much just evening arm candy."

He looks up and nods. He feels like he's having an out-of-body experience, floating above himself and looking down and watching in horror as he continues to not get up and leave. Then she pulls out another folder.

"Now this folder entails second tier job duties." She passes it to him. "And what each…duty…costs."

His eyes are growing wider with each line he reads. She glances over at him and he can practically feel her reading his apprehension.

"Of course you'll see that second folder deeds have a much bigger pay out." She hesitates briefly before getting even more ballsy with him. "You do all of that, don't you? You're not one of these guys who says, 'I don't do this or I don't do that,' right? Because in order to work for me you have to do it all."

"Yeah," he replies faintly. "I do all that."

She flashes him her pearly white teeth. "Great."

He hands her back the folder.

"So," she implores. "What do you say?"

He doesn't say anything. He's still stuck in that hesitative pause, on the precipice of plunging. He still thinks he's in control; thinks his feet are still firmly planted on the ground, and that he can backup. But he can see it in her eyes; leaned in too close to the edge to ever regain balance. One more little nudge and he'll be going over. One more little nudge and the deal will be closed.

"I don't want to corrupt you if you don't want me to," she tells him, sounding calm and honest and like it wouldn't really affect her life one way or the other if he got up and walked out. "Marvin told me you were a good person, and I believe that," she continues in the same manner. "But I also believe that you'll be very successful here. You just have to know how to separate your personal life from your business life. And then it's just another job, AJ."

She's so nonchalant. He doesn't know how a person can be so nonchalant. Hearing her tell it, you'd think she was just a branch manager at Burger King or KFC, interviewing for her next fry cook. Acting as though this were at all normal. Acting like she does this every day. He supposes she does. He supposes she's half right, too. He saw the money on the table; he saw the prices on the paper. And he knows even after she takes her cut it will be way more than he's ever made. He could live comfortably. Until he found something better. Until he could make it as a writer. He would just do it for a while.

No. He can't.

Could he? Nobody would have to know. He's miles away from home with no way of it getting back. And he does need a job. And hell, women do this kind of thing all the time, right? Except that their situations are often cheap. They have to service grimy lowlifes and cheating husbands, not provide company to lonely Beverly Hills housewives. This wouldn't be like what they did at all. Their bosses are sleazily abusive men, not some elegant unassuming woman with an actual office. This would be different. This would high-end. This would only be temporary. Just until–

"So are you in or not?"

He looks up.

"I'm in."

She smiles but she doesn't seem surprised. If there's anything Maggie has learned over the years it's that money talks, location is everything, and dreams are detrimental. If she grants the first two and exploits the last control is hers to have.

She shakes his hand to seal the deal, then stands up. "I apologize but I must be going, I have a benefit event in Brentwood at five," she says as she heads for the door. "Report back here at 9 a.m. tomorrow and we'll have orientation, okay?"

She doesn't wait for an answer. She's gone. He doesn't move. He just sits there while trying to insert logic into what he's just agreed to and wondering what orientation could possibly entail at a job like this. For the first time in nearly fifteen minutes he becomes aware that Theo is still in the room.

"So," AJ utters tentatively, staring blankly at the desk in front of him. "Agent is code for…"

"Madam." Theo answers his question without any ado; the jig is up after all.

"And that would make me…"

"Well," Theo waxes nostalgically, leaving his spot in the corner. "In the olden days you'd be called a gigolo. But I suppose callboy suffices now." He tilts his head at AJ when he passes the desk. "Prostitute if you're being blunt, escort if you're being demure."

The real words make AJ uneasy, even a little queasy; he swallows down the lump that's formed in his throat. Theo is about to leave. AJ finally looks at him.

"And you're…"

Theo pauses in the doorway and throws AJ a look over his shoulder. With a wink he says, "The best and most requested."

He calls Grace that night once he's back in his Koreatown studio and settled in a little bit more. After his misleading meeting with Maggie Hunter he went out and bought a new mattress and sheets. It seemed like the right thing to do. He then stopped at a nearby grocery store and bought the bare minimum of lowest-assembly-required foods to sustain life. Half a ham sandwich and one bottled water later—because low-pressure and the off-brown stuff coming out his sink still had him suspicious—he finds himself staring at the four walls of his apartment; they all feel far too close together. Panic blooms in the pit of his stomach and he has to remind himself that this is what he wanted.

She answers on the second ring and sounds ecstatic just to hear his voice. He asks about her day, and she tells him with great excitement all the details from her first shift as an RN. He listens as she goes on about catheters and IVs and all the other things one can insert—literally and figuratively—in a twelve-hour shift. He lets her brag about the fact that she doesn't have to wipe as many butts now and revel in her new, more important responsibilities. When she finally takes a breath he tells her he got a job. She sounds relieved. Also surprised, but he dismisses that. He tells her he's a server. At the restaurant attached to his apartment. It's the first lie in a long line of what he gets the feeling will be many. Though she tries to hide it he can tell she's not impressed her boyfriend went halfway across the country to be a waiter. But he dismisses this too because at least she *sounds* proud of him. She cares about him and that's what matters, and before she goes, she asks him why he sounds so nervous. He says something about starting a new job and cliché jitters and all that. She reminds him that it's nothing he's never done before. He agrees with her that she has a point.

~

The sound her heels make on the glossy wood floor reverberates off the walls and echoes in his ears. She's walking the expanse of the in-house gym as she talks. There are two elliptical machines, two treadmills, multiple yoga mats, a bench with a dumbbell, a cart with weights varying in size, and a few other contraptions that AJ doesn't know the proper names for.

"Cardio is Mondays, Wednesdays, and Fridays. Weight training is Tuesdays and Thursdays. Pilate's every day," she casually informs them. "And yes, gentlemen, I said Pilates. You have Sundays off." She takes a sip of her low-fat latte, and then as an afterthought adds, "So you can go repent should you feel the need."

AJ is standing next to Austin, the former TSA agent Maggie plucked from LAX, taking it all in. The dark blonde boy looks just as wide-eyed and out of his element as AJ feels. This gives him mild consolation. He's not alone.

"The shower room is to your left." She stops walking and looks at them. "You all can strip down in there, and then we will proceed."

The two boys exchange wary looks but do as they've been told

A few minutes later they file out in the Calvin Klein and Ralph Lauren briefs that were left for them to put on. Her eyes scrupulously run up and down their bodies. With her it's hard to tell whether or not she approves of what she sees.

"I do random physical inspections to make sure you still look good naked," she says while circling them like a hawk stalking prey. Though her eyes will never give her away she is quite pleased with her latest selection. Their stomachs are taut and their arms and thighs are toned. And perhaps the most important attribute—seeing as there would be no remedying it if were less than satisfactory—is that their designer undergarments are *well* filled out. Luck is on her side. She stops circling.

"I also do random drug tests," she says seriously. "So don't test me."

They both nod, too exposed to speak.

"Come," she motions. They follow and she leads them into a large walk-in closet where she proceeds to dress them in suits and take their measurements.

"I provide your uniforms," she tells them as she stretches her tape measurer from AJ's pants leg to his inseam. "Usually Armani or Tom Ford. When you're working out on the town or at a public event, you always wear your uniform." She stands back up and has him relax his arms at his side and then puts the silver tipped end at his shoulder blade. "You keep it on until someone tells you to take it off." She stretches out the tape. "You are not circa 1980s Patrick Dempsey and this is not a pizza parlor. We dress to impress." She retracts her tape and moves on to Austin.

AJ takes a moment to check out his new look in the 360-degree mirror. He had never seen himself look this way before; so dapper, so elegant. He could count the number of times he had worn a suit on one hand. Twice. Once at his cousin's wedding and once at his grandfather's funeral. Those had both been rented; he had never personally owned one. Looking at himself now he didn't know why. He looked good in a suit. He looked damn good. Maggie catches him admiring himself and smirks.

Thirty minutes later and back in their regular people clothes AJ and Austin are sitting at Maggie's desk. She fans out a colorful array of prophylactics in front of them.

"You always use a condom. Every time. No matter what."

Both boys are looking down in amazement at all the different sizes and colors and textures. Never in his life has AJ worn a purple condom. Much less a ribbed, extra-lubricated, extra-large, gold wrapped purple condom. Wouldn't even know where to find one. He supposes you really have to go the extra mile with these rich California women; plain white Trojans were probably *so* last season.

"And I still want you checked every other month. I set up the appointments, you go. You don't have an option."

AJ and Austin exchange looks again.

"As for the clients, you go to them. Their house. Their hotel room. You never bring them here or to your place. Understood?"

They both nod.

"Also, you yourself do not make arrangements. Every client must go through me." She opens her drawer and takes out two phones. One black. One white. "I have two separate phones with two separate numbers. One is my personal phone, which each of you will be privy to having the number to. The other is my work phone. It is only used for work."

Austin looks between the two phones. "Which one is the work phone?"

Maggie looks at him like he's slow and holds up the black one. "*This* is the work phone. If you meet a prospective client while you're out, you give them my work number, and I will set up a date. This phone is very important. It holds all of my clients' names, numbers, and personal information. High profile clients. You do not touch the black phone." She thinks about it, then adds, "Matter of fact, don't touch the white phone either. Don't touch any of my stuff, follow the rules, and I'll be the best boss you've ever had." She scans their dismayed faces. "Any questions?"

She's met with silence from AJ. But Austin, endearingly ignorant Austin, has that confused look on his face again. She waits for it.

"So…nothing's done online?"

"What, did you think I was going to take out a post on Craigslist?" She asks him facetiously. "Put up a nice headshot, maybe even a peek at the goods. Write a cute little bio about how you're an aspiring actor, low on funds, looking to 'have some fun.' Just so everyone's *clear* on what we're advertising. And then I'll give out my contact information to every perv with a penchant for pretty, corn-fed, Midwestern boys and a halfway stable Wi-Fi connection."

Austin looks off to the side and rolls his eyes as he realizes a little too late that he's once again asked the wrong question.

"No," she says definitively. "That's how you get sodomized and I get arrested."

"I just thought that would be the eas–"

"That *is* the easiest way. The Internet is the easiest way to do anything, but the Internet is also incriminating. It leaves a trail ten thousand miles long back to you that can never be erased. So we handle business in person over here. That means you're going to have to know how to be flirty, charming, and convincing face to face." She looks right at Austin now. "That means you're going to have to have an actual personality."

AJ briefly glances over at Austin to see if he received the jab but it seems to have gone over his head.

"What I'm saying is," she concludes, "should things ever go left, for whatever reason, there will be no proof. Unless of course you get yourself tracked by someone's crazy husband, and for God's sake don't. Because otherwise talk is just talk. It's your word against someone else's. There'll be no scandalous text messages, no old online ads, no pictures, nothing in no one's inbox…do you all understand what I'm saying?"

They both nod without hesitation.

"Good," she says, pushing back her chair. "Follow me."

She takes them out to the rec room where all the other guys are lounging around on their downtime. There's a huge flat screen television mounted on the wall and a large black leather couch and matching leather recliner, a pool table, a mini fridge, and a bar cart with a big bucket of ice with multiple glasses and just about every kind of top shelf liquor you could imagine. It's the type of set-up every man wishes he had in his house. Two men are playing a game of pool and two are sitting on the couch watching TV.

"Attention," Maggie says. They all stop what they're doing to face her. "These are the two newest members of Maggie Hunter Management, AJ Brooks and Austin Edwards." She turns to the newbies. "AJ, Austin…this is Garrett Hill…"

Garrett is a typically attractive, baby-faced twenty-something with the type of silkily perfect blonde hair you'd find on a boy band member. Garrett smiles un-enthusiastically and nods to the new guys.

"What's up, mates," he mumbles with a noticeably English accent and immediately turns back to the TV.

"Dominique Davis…" Maggie continues.

Dominique is working the bad boy angle, with tattoos covering much of his exposed skin. He is also twenty-something, with lean muscle and a lanky frame. And though the tats say tough, the rest says otherwise. His hair is meticulous and acutely shaped up with well-maintained waves. His face looks perpetually mischievous and the dimples do nothing to help this fact.

"Y'all can call me Double D or Nique the Freak," he says. "Or," he adds with a lecherous leer then, "Mister 'if you got a girl don't bring her around me.'"

"Call him Dominique," Maggie says. She then looks to Rafael, who AJ has already kind of met. "And of course my dear Rafael Sotolongo."

Rafael gives a curt wave and then goes back to playing pool.

"Why he get ta be *dear* though?" Dominique asks, offended.

"Because I am the best."

"Homie I'll take all your clients and have a four way," Dominique snaps, quickly sitting up straight from his slouched position. "Get it? Cause you only got like three clients. Shit, I'll take ya women that ain't your clients. I'll take ya main chick, ya side chick, ya mamacita. Shit, I even take ya grand mamacita." He pauses. "Except," he says, cocking his head contemptuously. "They still gotta pay." He locks eyes with Rafael and leers. "And I bet they do."

Rafael says something snide-sounding in Spanish under his breath.

"The fuck he just say to me?" Dominique asks no one in particular while getting even more riled up. "What's that mean? Was that a *threat*? Cause where I'm from we don't take kindly ta *threats.*"

"Yes, we all know you're from Watts" Rafael retorts tiredly while rolling his eyes. "You're so gangster and scary." He puts his pool stick down and looks at Dominique. "Lemme tell you, back in Havana you'd be eaten *alive.*"

"Back in Havana, back in Havana," Dominique mocks from his spot on the couch. "I swear sometime I feel like I'm listenin to a Cuban Rose Nylund."

Garrett raises an eyebrow with a smirk. "You watch *The Golden Girls*, aye Nique?"

"Shut up, blondie. I don't wanna hear it from you. Them girls got me through some things. Aight?"

"While simultaneously preparing him for his future career of servicing old white widows," Theo says, not bothering to look up from his book.

Garrett and Rafael both snicker.

"Oh y'all got jokes now, huh?" Dominique asks rhetorically, and then shakes his head with pursed lips. "Y'all don't want it with me, man. I swear I ain't the one."

"Everyone settle down. You are all equally dear to my heart," Maggie soothes. Dominique grumbles a little more and then turns back around. Maggie turns back to AJ and Austin, who have said nothing during the introduction process shenanigans. They both look culturally and morally shocked. "You two better go home and get some rest," she tells them. "You both have your first clients tonight. I'll text you the addresses where you'll be meeting them later."

With that, orientation is over. She goes back into her office and shuts the door.

AJ and Austin are quiet as they walk to their cars. AJ doesn't know why, but there's something calming about seeing Austin take out a key without a clicker and manually unlock an old rusty white pickup. It could be that it's the only other non-pretentious vehicle in the parking lot besides his; the kind of cars people drive say a lot about them. The back window of the truck is covered in Buckeye decals. The bed is littered with mashed cardboard boxes and discarded Mountain Dew bottles. And when he opens the door some trash falls out onto the pavement. But he picks it up.

"You from Ohio?" AJ asks casually as he fishes out the key to his own clunker.

Austin looks up and smiles; AJ notices how lopsided and boyish it is.

"Sure am."

AJ nods. "I've been to Ohio a couple of times. My uncle, he actually lives out there."

Austin's eyes light up at even the mere connection. "Oh yeah?" he says. "You ever been to Aquilla?"

AJ acts like he's thinking for a second even though he knows he's never been. The truth is, probably nobody had been to Aquilla; if they had, they probably wouldn't have remembered it. But Austin looks so hopeful and AJ doesn't want to disappoint him. They're both just fish out of water looking for someone to relate to on dry land.

"No," AJ finally says. "I don't think so, anyway. Could have been, though."

"Yeah," Austin says, looking down. "It's a pretty small town. It's 'bout four hours from Cincy, two to Columbus." He wads up the fast food bag in his hand and tosses it back inside his truck. "What about you?" he asks. "Where 'bouts you from?"

"Memphis."

This seems to please Austin, as he gets a big shit-eating grin on his face. "See," he says. "I knew you wasn't one of these Cali assholes."

"No," AJ laughs. "I actually just got here yesterday."

"It's been about three months for me," Austin offers.

"Do you like it?" AJ asks honestly.

"Shoo. I don't know, man. It's different. Real different." Austin shakes his head warily. "I came out here 'cause I flunked out of college. Had to do something, you know? People always been telling me that I look good and that I should be in movies and stuff. Fuck, I started to think why not. I could be an actor." His lips turn up as his hand unconsciously goes to rub the back of his neck. "But trying out for auditions and not getting them *sucks*. So does payin' eight-hundred dollars a month for a shitty apartment two-blocks from Skid Row." He thinks about it and then adds optimistically, "The chicks are pretty hot, though. But you gotta pick and choose cause some of them are just fuckin nuts. I'm tellin you, man, there are a bunch of weird ass people out here."

AJ nods. "Yeah, I think we just met a few." This cracks Austin up. AJ smiles then adds, "I think we're about to be a few."

"Dude," Austin laughs, trying to catch his breath. "What did we get ourselves into?"

AJ is laughing by this point too. "I don't know but it sure isn't what I had in mind when I moved here."

"Shit, me either. My old man would flip if he found out."

"Yeah," AJ wipes the laughter-induced tears from his eyes. "I don't even want to think about it."

Their laughter quiets down after a beat and then Austin asks seriously, "Do you think we're gonna regret this?"

"Hey," AJ says. "If it turns out bad, we can always walk out."

"True," Austin agrees.

"I didn't sign my life away, did you?"

"Nope."

"There you go then. We still have choices."

Austin looks down and nods.

"If I want to quit, I'm going to quit," AJ adds defiantly.

"Shit, if you quit, I quit."

"Deal."

"Deal."

They both get into their cars feeling a little bit better than they did before. Austin cranks down his window and leans out.

"Knock em dead tonight," he yells jestingly over the noisy engine.

AJ smiles. "Bach atcha."

The dented, dirty pickup backs out and pulls away, leaving a cloud of black diesel smoke in its wake. AJ restarts his own car for the second time.

CHAPTER 3

AJ has never dined at a five-star restaurant before, much less one off of the famed Rodeo Drive. He's so far out of his element and his new cologne he has on smells nothing like his usual regimen of soap and Old Spice. He's at the best table, per request, seated across from Mrs. Kelly. He's in his Armani "uniform" and she's in a dress whose price he couldn't begin to guess. She's over twice his age, wears pearls, and looks like she's had extensive work done. He feels like people should be staring, but they're not. He's ungodly nervous but masks it to the best of his ability. The plates are square and the petite-portioned food seems to be more for decoration than nourishment. The bottle of champagne cost her a grand, and he feels bad that he hasn't even been able to finish one glass of it. The lavish liquid tastes foreign on the back of his tongue, and the sparkling carbonation only serves to tie his stomach in further knots. She's on her third glass; he assumes it's an acquired taste. He can feel her hot objectifying gaze on him as he pushes a piece of green garnished escargot around his plate.

"You know," she remarks in an accent that wants to be British but isn't. "At first I was so upset to hear that Caleb was no longer with Miss Hunter."

The way she looks at him makes him feel like he belongs in these places even though he knows he doesn't—also a bit like prey about to be taken down.

"He was a blonde," she muses, taking another sip from her glass. He watches as she swallows and then trains her eyes dangerously upon him. "But I think I'm starting to come around to brunettes."

AJ forces himself to smile, blushing slightly.

"And those green eyes," she adds lustily.

The maître 'de comes back to the table at long last. AJ wonders if he's thinking things about this arrangement, or if he sees this type of thing all the time. It's surely not an odd sight to see an older man with a younger woman, especially in Los Angeles, but what about the other way around? Was it a double standard? Were red flags going up? He wants to ask the waiter what he makes and where he can fill out an application and when could he start, when technically he hadn't even made it to–

"Can I interest you two in dessert?" The maître 'de asks.
"Crème Brule, Chocolate Mousse, a slice of Cheese–"

"No thank you," Mrs. Kelly quickly cuts him off. "We're ready for the check."

AJ swallows harshly.

Mrs. Kelly's bedroom is bigger than AJ's entire studio. His natural instinct doesn't know whether to be impressed or intimidated; regardless, he's here now and it's too late to back out. The bed is huge, with four intricately chiseled pillars at each corner to support the overhead canopy. It is perfectly made as if never been slept in. A Cavali duvet is pulled back halfway to reveal crisp white sheets that probably had something like an eight hundred thread count.

The ride from the restaurant up into the hills had been short and chauffeured. She had kept her hand on his knee the entire time, but hadn't tried anything else. Maybe to maintain decency in front of the driver, he didn't know. But now, in the privacy of her room, decency is out the door. She heads straight to the vanity dresser.

"Let me get your money out before I forget," she says with her back to him, opening her clutch and taking out a few big bills. She lays them aside, and then he sees her pull out a little vile. She proceeds to pour out white powder onto a mirror that she had lying flat on the surface of the vanity, almost as if waiting at the ready. He watches as she arranges it into a nice, neat line. And then continues to watch as she rolls up part of his proceeds, bends down, puts it to her nose, and snorts every last bit of it up. AJ tries to keep his jaw dropping; he doesn't know what to think or how to act. She sniffs as she recomposes herself, wiping her nose, and then she turns to him.

"You want some?"

"I'm good," he quickly answers.

A devilish grin overtakes her face as she slowly walks to where he stands rooted in the spot. "We're about to see."

The second her lips meet his neck his senses flood with the thick aroma of Chanel, an ever-present reminder of her affluence and age. If he focuses hard enough on the feeling of her skilled mouth on his skin, biting down and then chasing the sting with her tongue, he can feel the familiar hint of desire start to burn at the base of his spine. He concentrates on this, repeating in his head for the fifteenth time that she's just a woman and he's just a man and that this is nothing out of the ordinary. The flame melts the fears slowly.

Mrs. Kelly drops to her knees and begins working on his belt. From this vantage point he has a clear view of her gray roots, as well as the fake Double-D's that poke provocatively out of the top of her dress. Suddenly, in that moment, AJ understands the mission of his job: to make her feel like the woman she wants to be. The prettiest woman. The youngest woman. The only woman. In that moment, AJ understands he is simply the fantasy that compliments the façade. When she gets his pants open she meets his eyes with mischief and stands back up. He gently places his hands on her waist, wordlessly turning her around. She complies. His hand goes to the zipper on the back of her dress. He drags it down the barest inch, and then leans into her until his mouth is right next to her ear.

"Now this is my first night," he murmurs lowly. "So I'm going to need you to tell me what you like." He takes her earlobe into his mouth, but only briefly enough for her breath to hitch. "And what you want me to do to you." He starts moving her zipper further down, going down with it, kissing the skin on her back as it is exposed to him. "And while I'm doing it to you, I want you to tell me if I'm doing it right."

She grins to herself and then whispers back, "Baby, I think you're going to be all right."

An hour later she's smoking a Virginia Slim and smiling. He dresses, takes the money, and leaves. It's perhaps the oddest he's ever felt.

~

In another bedroom on the other side of Beverly Hills, Theo is lying in bed next to another woman whose name he can't remember. Her blonde hair is in mild disarray from their recent romp, and her delicate fingers stroke his skin. He's propped up on one elbow and staring down at her lovingly, feigning attentiveness as he does so well.

"God, you're a beautiful man," she remarks as her hand roams over his smooth scalp and then down further to cup his chiseled jaw. "And so much better of a lover than that ex-husband of mine."

He smiles kindly, if not just to amuse her.

One of those nightly entertainment news shows has been playing on the plasma screen T.V. across from them, long forgotten in the background. But when the newsgirl begins to talk about the upcoming premier of a highly anticipated new movie, their attention is suddenly piqued. Her hands stop stroking him, his eyes stop roving her, and they both fixate on the screen.

"The Los Angeles premier of *Evaders* staring two-time Academy Award winner and Hollywood heartthrob, Troy Langham, is this weekend at Grumman's Chinese Theater..." Says the dolled-up reporter as pictures of a handsome, dark blonde, middle-aged man on previous red carpets flash on the screen behind her head. "Langham has been doing press in New York all week leading up to this weekend's premiere. Meanwhile, the actor's wife, the phenomenal Patrice Grove, has been in Europe promoting her new movie *The Disgraced*. Talk about a power couple."

The newsgirl's voice fades and the nameless woman focuses her attention back on Theo. But Theo's attention is still on the screen. She strokes his jaw and then kisses his neck.

"What do you say we go to that premiere? I hear it's going to be huge. Plus, that Troy Langham is just *so* gorgeous." She pauses, batting her eyes for an effect that is lost on him. "Of course not as gorgeous as you."

Theo chuckles as he rolls out of bed and gathers his clothes.

"And ever since the divorce I don't have anyone to go to these things with and I simply cannot be seen out by myself. That is the epitome of pitiful." She pouts her collagen-injected lips the best she can and shoots him a longing look. "You do that type of thing too, right, dear? I mean you're a male escort, I assume you'll escort. I'll tip graciously, of course."

He smirks as he finishes buttoning his shirt. "Yes. I do that type of thing, too." He walks over to her full-length mirror and checks himself. "And no need to tip me," he adds. "I wanted to see the movie, too."

She smiles, thinking of the jealous grimaces on all of her fake friends' faces when they see her with her younger, handsome, black date. *My*, they'll think, *how marvelously she rebounded.* Seeing the glee on her face makes Theo smile, too, knowing exactly what she's thinking and thinking *if only they knew.* He grabs the money off the table and tells her that he'll see her Saturday at seven.

~

The guys are all lounging around the rec room the morning after when Maggie walks in. The signature click of her heels announces her arrival. She's got a coffee cup in one hand, her bag thrown over her shoulder, and her big sunglasses pulled down over her face.

"Austin." The way she says his name lends to displeasure. Austin looks up, his expression that of a dog who's made a mess on the floor. What's worse, everybody else looks up, too. And she's going to say it in front of all of them. She lifts her sunglasses and locks eyes with him. "I talked to Mrs. Roosevelt this morning. You did not get a good review."

Austin swallows. "We get reviewed?"

"Hell yeah, bruh," Dominique interjects. "Think of it as gigolo Yelp. You gotta show out for them stars every time." He looks over at Maggie and lifts his brow. "How many stars he get?"

"One."

Austin's cheeks turn crimson against his will. "Well what did she say?"

From the corner of the coach Theo just shakes his head, not even bothering to look up from his book. He can't decide if the boy's a masochist or simply a dumbass.

Maggie smirks coyly, not at all concerned about sparing him any dignity, and then says curtly, "I believe the reoccurring adjective was *quick*."

Snorts and tempered chuckles can be heard around the room, except for Theo, who continues reading, unbothered, and AJ, who genuinely feels bad for Austin and who secretly fears that his own public shaming may be up next. He quickly glances over at his fellow fresh-faced coworker and sees him focusing on the floor in embarrassment.

"Quick movement; quick finish," Maggie continues. "No rhythm; no stamina."

"White boy problems," Dominique interjects.

"Well my women never complain," Garrett intervenes.

"That's cause you look like God took his time when he was in the workshop craftin your ass. He broke out the chisel and the file and went in. They too blinded by your beauty ta bitch."

Garrett rolls his eyes.

"Do the hair flip," Dominique goads. "Go on and do it."

"Fuck off."

"Look," Maggie says to Austin, ignoring the other two's antics. "I understand that Mrs. Roosevelt is very attractive for an older woman. I don't know if you were only preparing yourself to screw fat homely woman who couldn't possibly ever get laid on their own, or if you even mentally prepared at all, but that most certainly will not always be the case. Sometimes you are going to be with women who are visually appealing, who are going to turn you on. Of course I'm not stupid, I realize that physical attraction has little to do with men's physical reactions, because you all can derive pleasure from absolutely anything and anyone regardless of appearance, but this isn't about *you*. And FYI, five minutes of fast, bland, back and forth pumping is only going to do it for *you*."

Austin nods that he understands. He can feel her stern gaze on him, even as he continues to focus on the floor, even as he attempts to blend in with the back of the couch and pretend that he's somewhere else.

"If they wanted to be done like a feral cat in spring they'd do their husbands or a hobo or any random person with a dick. They call me for quality. They pay for satisfaction. You're representing my brand when you're out there doing what you're doing and if you can't do it right you *will* be cut from the team. These aren't your little hometown high school girlfriends who faked it for you in the back of your Chevy to salvage your ego. These women don't care about your ego. They're going to complain. And when they complain, they're going to be complaining to me."

"I'm sorry," is all Austin can muster. He doesn't know what else to say, he's never been so humiliated.

"Sorry doesn't cut it. I'm sending you for a session with Theo. He's going to teach you some technique and how to move your own body. You're twenty-three, it's about time you learn."

Theo flips the page in his book. "Some talent can't be taught."

"Well try," Maggie tells him, heading for her office. But then she pauses, and looks back over her shoulder. "Oh, and Andrew..."

AJ's head shoots up. He's almost scared to know what she's about to say.

"Good job." She gives him the smile. "Mrs. Kelly has already called and requested you for next Tuesday night." And then she gives him the look. "She obviously liked that Sweet Memphis Style."

He smiles meekly, his own cheeks getting a little hot, and lets out the breath he's been holding in since what feels like last night. Maggie goes into her office and shuts the door.

"Go on then, AJ. I see you," Dominique praises. "Puttin it down in the 90210 for all the white brothas back in Memphis."

~

"You're from Ohio, right, Dallas?" Theo asks Austin. It's later in the afternoon and all the other guys have since cleared out, leaving the most experienced and the least experienced alone in the rec room.

"Austin," he corrects timidly. He doesn't know why, but being left alone with Theo makes him a little uncomfortable. Austin has always prided himself on being a gym rat with a nice body that girls liked to stare at, but in this room none of that matters. In this room he isn't the tallest, the most muscular, or the most experienced. Theo is physically more of a man than him in every way, despite the fact that he swishes his hips when he walks and wears diamond studs in both ears. That's where it gets real confusing.

"And Ohio," Theo muses, walking over to the bar cart and pouring himself a glass of Grand Marnier. "That seems like the type of place where people put on those tacky foam fingers and paint their faces—always some non-complimenting colors—in support of their favorite sports team." He takes a sip of his drink without grimacing and then turns back around. "Is Ohio a sporty state, Austin?"

"Ye…yes," Austin stutters, unsure of where the conversation was going.

"And what kind of sports are big over there? Football, basketball, rugby, hockey…."

"Just about everything," shrugs Austin.

"Well what's your personal favorite?" Theo probes further, taking a tone that makes it seem like he really wants to know the kid.

"Football," Austin answers after thinking a second.

"What's your favorite team?"

"The Buckeyes."

"And who are some of the Buckeye's most famous players?"

"Well," he starts, considering the question. "There's Archie Griffin and Eddie George…Chris Spellman, Troy Smith…"

"When was the last time they won a big game?"

"They won the NCAA National championship in 2002…"

"What about the time before that?"

Austin thinks for a second. "1970."

"And the time before that?"

Austin's forehead furrows and his eyes squint as he mentally runs through the sports trivia in his head. "1968," he finally says, assuredly.

"There you go," Theo says, raising his glass. "You just added at least two to three minutes onto your time." He takes a drink as Austin stares at him in confusion. Theo swallows. "After you're done with football stats, circle back around to basketball. Then baseball, then hockey, till you've given them a good solid thirty minutes."

Austin is flabbergasted. "Does…does it really work?" He finally asks. "Thinking about sports, I mean…"

"That's what I hear," Theo replies, refilling his glass a little more. "I don't know. I'm not really into sports."

"Then what do you do when you're trying not to…you know…" Austin implies, and then whispers. "When you're *with* a woman."

"It really helps that I'm not into women either."

Austin is rendered speechless. Theo peeps the look on his face and smirks, secretly taking pleasure in making the green country boy squirm.

"You can go ahead and wipe that homophobic look off your face. This isn't small town Ohio; it's time to get caught up with the times," Theo tells him, picking up his glass and walking over to the pool table. "Plus," he adds lowly as he passes him. "With a little body like that, the boys in this town will be all over you."

Austin is quickly turning red again. He gulps.

"Of course, Miss Hunter won't make you take their offers. But they do tip well, if you ever feel so inclined." Theo glances over at him again, and tries to hide his smile at how thoroughly horrified Austin looks. He drains his glass and then braces his hands on the pool table. "Now, let's teach you how to roll those hips." He looks back at Austin over his shoulder. "Watch and learn."

~

The sun is high in the sky and shining brightly over the Santa Monica shore. Anjanae has a perfect view of the ocean from her table by the bay window in the little bistro where she has brunch every Wednesday and Sunday. Annabelle and Christine are with her as usual. Annabelle is a blonde—by bottle not biology—who has a running bit at dinner parties about her and her fifty-something husband's May December romance. The real punchline, which of course is never revealed, is that May and December are only seven months apart, much like her and her husband. Annabelle's husband is an entertainment lawyer to many a talent, one of which being Anjanae's husband, Julius.

Christine is a brunette who has been thirty-nine for five consecutive years, who prides herself on her ability to throw a good banquet, and who carries an overweight Pekingese in a Prada purse. Her husband is a highly successful banker who belongs to the same country club as Julius. All three husbands have golf outings often, where they drink Scotch by the sifter, discuss their many *deep* thoughts, and trade crudities with class. All three women are housewives, which is pretty much where the similarities end as far as Anjanae is concerned. Still, it's brunch every Wednesday and Sunday. Because who wants to be friendless?

Three mimosas sit on the table next to each plate. On Anjanae's plate are Belgian waffles topped with strawberries and bananas and big decorative dollops of whipped cream. On the other two women's plates are bran muffins.

Christine stares longingly at Anjanae's food. "My God I wish I could eat like that."

"Do you want a bite?" Anjanae offers, moving her fork aside as if the woman would really eat off her plate.

"No," Christine sighs with an air of fostered jealously. "I'll just watch you eat it and live vicariously."

"Her metabolism will eventually stop working," Annabelle adds. She takes the smallest possible bite of bran muffin that she can, and then pats her thin lips delicately with the cloth napkin. "And then she'll blow right up like a balloon." She quickly looks over at Anjanae. "No offense, dear."

"Oh yes," mutters Christine. "I forget she's not our age."

"I forget we're our age," Annabelle replies exuberantly. "I swear juice and botulin has completely changed my life." She puts her hand on her heart and then waves it outward dramatically. "Totally reversed the aging process. I look twenty-two."

Anjanae avoids looking at Annabelle when she says this because her eyes always give away her thoughts. And right now she's thinking, *this bitch couldn't pass for twenty-two with five facelifts and a fraudulent birth certificate.*

"She's using the word botulin because she thinks it sounds like a holistic healing experience and because she thinks you probably don't know what it really means but it means Botox," Christine tells Anjanae, like she thought she really had to explain it. "She gets Botox."

"Oh everybody does," Annabelle assures, peeling the last bit of muffin from the foil and licking it off of her French-tipped finger. "Anjie won't have to, of course. Black doesn't crack."

"Annabelle!" Christine gasps, and then whispers in a lowered voice. "That was racist."

"That wasn't racism. That was a compliment."

Anjanae isn't really paying them any mind; in fact, she's zoned out a little bit, pushing a strawberry around her plate.

"Honey, what ever is wrong?" Annabelle finally asks her. "You have hardly said a word and have barely touched your waffles. You usually scarf them down with a fervor."

Anjanae looks up. "I'm fine. Really." She forces a smile as to not look how she feels. "I'm just not very hungry today, I guess."

Christine reaches into her bag, past the Pekingese, almost like she had it planned. "Is it because of this?" She tosses a tabloid onto the table and turns it to a dog-eared page.

There in the spread is a picture of Anjanae's husband with his arm around a young blonde starlet. Anjanae can just barley glance at it before Annabelle snatches it up off the table.

"Huh! Trollop!" Annabelle declares with affirmation as her eyes scan the contents. "It says she's twenty-one. They're having a liaison in New York." She abruptly closes the magazine and sets it back on the table. "How cliché." She rolls her eyes. "They might as well take it to Paris."

"She's the lead actress in his movie," Anjanae rationalizes. "They have to be around each other."

"Whatever you have to tell yourself, dear. But just know it's the nature of the beast, they all do it," Christine consoles half-heartedly.

Annabelle holds up her hand. "You know what I'm going to do for you, Anjanae? Because I'm such a good friend?" She takes out her wallet. Anjanae and Christine watch as she thumbs through her many cards, and finally pulls one out. "I'm going to give you this special number." She smiles sinisterly as she passes it to a confused Anjanae.

"And just what is that?" Christine asks Annabelle, looking over Anjanae's shoulder to get a better look at the business card.

"A male escort service."

"Oh," Christine grimaces. "That is so vulgar."

"Hey, if he's getting some on the side, why shouldn't she?" She glances over at Anjanae. "Only occasionally, of course. You don't want to become a full-fledged slut."

"How do you have this number?" Christine beseeches.

"Because I use it."

Christine sits back, hand going to her pearl clad chest. "Oh you're not serious?"

"Why not? I get tired of screwing the same Viagra popping old man. Don't you, Anj?"

Anjanae says nothing. She's still staring at the card in shock, wondering to herself if this topic ever came up over anyone else's midmorning meal, and making a mental note to try and meet more mentally stable, morally grounded people.

Annabelle gets a cheesy smile on her face as she reminisces. "Mine goes by the name of German Chocolate."

Christine turns her head and lets out a high-pitched, piercing cackle.

"I swear to God it was the best sex of my life," Annabelle continuous. "That man did things to my body that my body didn't even know about! He rendered me *totally* speechless."

"Well that's a phenomenon in and of itself, isn't it?" Christine says under her breath, elbowing Anjanae.

"I completely understand now why the people say, *once you go black you can never go back.* I am here to tell you it is not an urban legend!" She looks at a still stunned Anjanae. "Well you're black, Anjie, you must know. I'm sure you've lain with a plethora of young virile black men." She takes a sip of her mimosa. "You know. Before you got chained to the one old one. Tell Christine."

"I wouldn't call it a plethora..."

"I'm going to need another drink," Christine says. "Waiter!"

As if on cue, a young man outfitted in white quickly rushes to her beckoning.

"I need a freshening," she tells him. "Less orange more champagne this time."

"Yes, ma'am," he replies, scurrying off to fulfill her wish. Christine slips her dog the rest of her bran muffin, which he snuffles up so fast that he loses his breath and starts making God-awful snorting sounds under the table.

Annabelle looks back to Anjanae. "Seriously, call the number. Her name is Miss Hunter and..." Punctuating with finger snaps. "She. Will. Hook. You. Up."

"Oh you can tell she's gotten a little bit of black inside her," Christine smirks.

"Honey, it wasn't a little."

The two older women fall into cackling. Anjanae thinks, not for the first time, that they sound like hyenas. She pushes the card back across the table.

"I appreciate the offer, but I don't think I'll be needing this."

"Oh, don't be a prude," Annabelle says. "Keep it. Just in case you change your mind."

~

When AJ stops by headquarters the next day he's relieved to find that no one is there except Theo, who sits with his legs crossed at the end of the couch reading a book called *Bad Feminist*. AJ pauses in the doorway. He doesn't want to bother him, but he needs…well, he doesn't know what he needs. He wants advice, he supposes. Advice. Guidance. Something. But he doesn't know how to go about it. Much like he doesn't know how to go about any of this. All he knows is that he hasn't felt like himself in two days. He doesn't know if this is where he should be. And he wonders if he's made a mistake, or if it's a feeling that will eventually pass in time. He tentatively approaches the couch. Theo senses him, and looks up.

"I heard you had a successful first night on the job."

AJ smiles wearily. "Yeah." He sits down on the edge of the couch, hands on his knees.

Theo studies him. "So how does it feel?"

"You mean how does it feel selling myself for sex?"

Theo snorts.

"Okay I guess. Kind of weird. I don't know." He thinks about it, then shakes his head. "I know I'm a guy and that this should be a dream job and all but…"

"The first time is always the hardest," Theo tells him. "You become numb to it. Pretty soon it'll just be routine."

AJ's silent for a while. "It must be difficult for you," he finally says, treading with caution. "Having to…I mean…." He chickens out at the last minute, not knowing how to finish his thought.

Theo closes his book. "I take it you talked to Austin."

AJ doesn't say anything. He had talked to Austin, and he feels ashamed now for discussing Theo's private proclivities and even laughing at some of the ill-informed things Austin had said.

"It's just going through the motions, Andrew. That's all that it is."

AJ nods.

Theo looks at the young man beside him. All he sees is an acutely self-aware, observant young man who just happens to be blessed with good looks. He's different in the simple fact that he cares, and Theo can tell he's not the type of person for whom a simple explanation will help sleep at night.

"My dad was born and raised in Harlem," Theo starts. "My mom was an immigrant from Kingston, Jamaica. She left the country at eighteen in search of a better life." The look on his face says she didn't find it. "She wound up in New York, married my father. It was hard times. He enlisted. I was born on a base in Germany, lived there for eight years with my mom while he served."

AJ turns his head to look at him.

"Once he got discharged we moved back to America. A little ramshackle project house in Jamaica Queens—I'll never forget it. I had a hard time making friends. I didn't act like the other kids in my neighborhood, being raised in another country and all that. They didn't get me, so they didn't like me. Plus, I always just felt different in general anyway." He shakes his head. "We never had nothin. No car, no money for bus fare. I'd have to walk home from school—always scared, always looking over my shoulder after an eight-hour day of being bullied and beat up—and come home to a father with PTSD that never got treated and a mother who never learned how to handle life so she turned to the pipe. It wasn't a good life. And at nine years old there's not much you can do about it. That was difficult."

The life Theo speaks of is a life he knows nothing about. And he wonders, perhaps naively, how someone who seems so normal and so grounded could have derived from such mar.

"I ran away from home at sixteen," Theo continues. "For two years I was a transient, going from once vacant street corner to another, one man to another, one couch or underpass to another. Doing anything, *anything* for a dollar. Doing anything to get by. That was difficult." A nostalgic smile suddenly comes to his face. "I met her when I was twenty-three. She was working on Wall Street."

"Miss Hunter worked on Wall Street?" AJ asks, shocked. "Like she wasn't *working* Wall Street, she actually had an office job…"

Theo smiles. "Those degrees on the wall ain't for show. They're the real deal."

AJ looks impressed.

"She didn't drive back then—she walked. Everywhere. In six-inch heels. I always admired her. She was always walking past me; I had a little makeshift stand at the time on the same block as the building she worked in. One day I tried to sell her a dress. She told me I was too pretty to be selling fake Gucci out of a garbage bag."

AJ smiles, having heard a similar line not that long ago.

"She wrote me a letter of recommendation, not even knowing me, and I got a job as a maître 'de at this nice little bistro in Chelsea. She would come in on her lunch break and get whatever the special was. I would try to take my fifteen when she was there and we'd talk. About how much she hated her job and her boss and her landlord, and I'd talk about one or two of my ninety-nine problems. We'd discuss what it would be to live someplace sunny and not have to walk in the rain or trudge through the snow. What it would be like to wake up and know we're in control. Of our futures, our finances, our lives." He glances at AJ. "Female patrons were always hitting on me—visibly whenever I was working, subtly whenever I was seated with her because they thought that she was my girlfriend. But she always noticed. She notices everything. Remember that." He looks back away and sighs. "Anyway, she concocted this crazy plan to get us out of our stagnant lives. She pitched it to me, I caught it, two months later we were on the opposite coast and she had upgraded from associate to CEO."

AJ sits there in silence, amazed with the new insight he has. Amazed at how people get to be who they are.

"She saw something in me," Theo says, and then smiles reminiscently. "This Queen from Queens that she met on the street. And from that point on I was never alone." He shrugs. "I figured I was better off with her than I was without her. And I'd like to think of her as more of my partner in crime than as my boss. I don't know if that's how she sees me…but whenever the self-deprecation starts to kick in, whenever I start to feel used…I just think how I don't have to want for nothing and haven't in a long time. I think how smooth that silk Versace feels on my skin. How good that gold Movado looks on my wrist. How I have more than my parents ever had, probably way more than any of those kids from that neighborhood in Jamaica Queens came to have, and then I don't feel so bad. For bein a sellout. For sellin myself. My self-value might be a little low sometimes, but my street value sure is high."

AJ considers it all, looking from Theo to the floor.

"This isn't difficult. This is what you make it." He stands up. "It helps to have a couple of drinks beforehand if you're feeling the nerves. Maggie will pick you up and drop you off." He gives AJ a parting smile, then leaves him to his thoughts.

As he slides behind the wheel of his BMW, Theo wonders if he did the right thing. Many boys had come and gone, and he knows without a shadow of a doubt AJ could and probably would bed more women than any of them had. Because along with his unassuming allure, he possessed a perceptiveness that the others would never be able to emulate. He knows Maggie saw it. And as he pulls out of the parking lot, he knows he should have told the kid to quit.

CHAPTER 4

The night falls at 360 Hollywood Place and AJ is pacing. It's officially his second night on the job; he's dressed in a nice pair of slacks and a button-up dress shirt. He looks at his watch and then over at Maggie's glass enclosed office. She's supposed to be taking him to his date tonight but it's not quite time. He's been told there will be no restaurant prelude this time; she's dropping him off at the door of his client's house. He decides at that moment to take the advice he sought and saunters over to the bar cart. He pours himself a glass of bourbon and throws it back.

In Bel-Air, Anjanae throws back her second glass of bourbon. She doesn't know what she was thinking when she dialed that number, and it's all becoming a lot less clear. The little low-cut black spaghetti strap dress she's wearing doesn't do much to cover her; it hits about mid-thigh, if not a little higher. Originally she'd had on another, slightly more demure dress. But after her first shot, looking classy when you were about to buy sex suddenly seemed counterproductive, so she changed into something a little more appropriately inappropriate. She looks at the clock on the stove, then begins to pace. She stops, pours herself another, throws it back. Her face scrunches up as the heat of it hits her. She shakes her head and continues pacing the expanse of the kitchen, wondering for the tenth time since she dialed the number what she was getting herself into.

Five minutes later a big black Lincoln Navigator pulls up to the luxurious mansion. AJ opens the passenger side door and gets out.

"Be safe," Maggie instructs from the driver's seat. "Don't behave. And I'll be back outside in an hour."

He nods and shuts the door. The SUV pulls away and he trudges up the walkway. God it's a huge house. He can't imagine living in a house so huge. He gets a little dizzy just looking up at it; then again, that could be the bourbon. He presses his finger to the doorbell and hears it echo grandiosely on the other side. A few seconds pass, and then there's a slightly drunk woman opening the door. She's pretty, he thinks, and younger than he expected.

"Welcome," she says, hearing the nervousness in her own voice, despite trying to sound sexy. "I'm Anjanae."

She steps aside and he enters. The door is closed behind him.

He smiles politely. "I'm Andrew. Or AJ, if you want."

They shake hands, which is somewhat of an awkward thing to do in such a situation, but still seems necessary to the both of them. As soon as she lets go of his hand, she turns her back and heads off into the house, swaying slightly as she goes.

"So this is the foyer," she says in a voice reminiscent of a tour guide.

He looks up at the chandelier hanging above, then follows her. They make their way into the large, elaborate kitchen.

"The living room is to the left. The guest bath is at the end of the hall."

She still has her back to him. He watches her, amused by her tipsy time-buying antics.

"And this is the kitchen." She finally turns around to face him, laughing at herself as she does. "I don't know why I'm giving you a tour."

He gets to take her in now. One strap dangles dangerously off her bare right shoulder; he doubts she's aware, but he is. He finds his eyes being drawn to the elegant column of her throat, her defined clavicle, and the smooth skin of her chest. He can make out the clear outline of her nipples under the sheet fabric of her dress. Her breasts are small, but perfectly shaped and not in need of support. His gaze travels down past her slim waist to her shapely brown thighs and slender legs. The heels she has on just accentuate everything. He doesn't know what type of man would leave her here like this and why she would think that she ever needed to pay, but one thing he's sure of is that he plans to make it worth her while.

He meets her chestnut eyes, perhaps her very best feature, and gives her a charming smile of reassurance. "Well unless there's another place in particular you want to show me, I've seen all that I need to see."

She flushes slightly. "You have?"

He nods. His hand grazes the countertop as he slowly saunters towards her. "And I like what I see." He momentarily breaks eye contact to glance about the darkly lit room. "You have a very nice kitchen."

She looks down, avoiding his darkening eyes once they are back on her. "It's kind of a waste, really," she begins to ramble nervously, drunkenly. "I don't even know how to cook, I'd probably burn down the entire house if I tr–"

"Do you want to put it to use right now?"

She looks up. "You mean…"

He simply nods, a mischievous grin slowly taking form on his face. "It shouldn't go to waste."

Her expressive eyes meet his as the corners of her lips quirk upward into a little mischievous grin of her own. The smile dissolves as he closes the distance, but the look remains the same. Soon they're breathing in each other's air, so close and statically charged that a shiver runs through her in anticipation. It's a tentative lean, and then his lips meet hers. What starts off slow escalates frantically. He easily lifts her up and sets her on the countertop. Glass shatters in the background but goes unnoticed as they feverishly go at it with a passion surprising them both. She bites at his lips as she kisses him, and in turn he sucks her plump bottom lip between his teeth. He can feel her smile against his mouth. Her fingers make quick work of the buttons on his shirt, and then she's pushing it off his shoulders. When her hands make contact with his skin, a shiver runs through him. And when his hands run up her legs, lifting the skirt of her dress till it's gathered around her waist, he feels like there's nowhere else in the world he should be.

~

While Dominique is getting ready for a date, the others are lounging around the rec room. Garrett and Rafael are engaged in a game of pool, Austin is watching the flat screen, and Theo and AJ are reading on opposite ends of the couch.

"Garrett, Austin, Andrew," Maggie calls as she exits her office. "New client has just moved into a brand new mansion in Beverly Hills and wants to have some fun. Her name is Fereshteh Abdollah and she apparently has a thing for white boys." She looks amongst the three. "I don't know if it's a fetish or what, but which one of you wants to take her on tonight?"

"I've got an appointment with Mrs. Tate in an hour and she always wants a round two. Sometimes three. A right addict she is for all this," Garrett tells her cockily, unintentionally doing the hair flip in the process. "So clearly I'm occupied for the night."

Austin and AJ exchange looks.

"Austin you look nervous, I don't like that." She looks at AJ. "You can handle this, can't you, Andrew?"

"Yeah," he says, still a hint of nervousness present in his voice, though he tries to mask it. "I can handle it."

"Good. Ten sharp. I'll get you the address."

Dominique pokes his head out of the bathroom. "Be careful," he tells AJ. "That sounds like the name of a Sultan's wife. Don't get yourself killed."

"Thanks, Nique," AJ says. "I appreciate the reassurance."

~

Fereshteh is a fairly attractive woman, with long dark hair down her back and a sun kissed complexion. AJ thinks she's probably in her forties, although it's hard to tell. She stands in the middle of her ornate bedroom, wearing nothing but a silk slip, speaking in a language he doesn't understand. If he had to guess, AJ would say it's either Farsi or Persian, but again, and especially with no *real* experience in Middle Eastern dialects, it's hard to tell.

"I'm sorry," he says, politely. "I don't understand."

She keeps going, undecipherable hand gestures and all.

"I don't…I don't know what you're saying," he tries again, attempting hand gestures of his own and looking at her apologetically.

It's clear she doesn't know what he's saying either. She stops talking and sighs. The look on her face is pure frustration, mixed with a little lust and a lot of confusion. She starts talking again and then it's AJ's turn to sigh. He's starting to feel as though this is a hopeless situation.

"What do you want?" He asks her gently, searching her eyes for any indication of anything, *anything* to latch on to. But she just keeps rattling off instructions that he can't comprehend. "What do you–" He decides then to claim defeat on the language front, calmly putting his hands up in a show of surrender. "Okay."

He starts unbuttoning his shirt. He gets it off, tosses it to the side, and then removes his belt. She's stopped talking. He moves over to her and carefully places a hand on each side of her waist, well above her hips.

"Is this okay?" he asks, looking into her eyes. He knows he's not going to get a verbal reply that he can decipher, but he's not going to do anything without permission.

She smiles. And then she starts touching. He lets her have free reign to do as she pleases, never moving his hands from where he's safely placed them as he feels her hands go from his hair, to his shoulders, and then down his back. He doesn't protest as her explorations take her from his backend, which she gives a little squeeze, back around to the front of his pants. She slips one hand under the waistband of his briefs, and looks him lecherously in the eyes as she takes hold of him.

Seeing as they had finally found a language that they were both fluent in, AJ decides to proceed. With a slow roughness he runs his hands up her body, taking the little negligee with him. Now that he has her naked, he swiftly spins her around and bends her over the bed. She gasps in surprise, but it's quickly followed by a sly smile of approval that she throws back at him over her shoulder. One of his hands holds her in place while other wanders expertly. He leans into her, putting his lips to her ear.

"Is this okay?"

She murmurs something sexy sounding into the bedding, pushes her ass against him, and nods as his nimble fingers continue to strum her. He smiles to himself.

"Good."

He pushes his pants down and rolls on a condom.

Later, when he's walking through the door of his apartment, Grace calls. Even though it's three o'clock in the morning in LA and he's dead tired, he answers. As he listens to her tell him about her rough night at work, he catches sight of one particularly prominent claw mark etched in his shoulder.

~

The next morning AJ and Rafael are alone in the rec room shooting pool while the others are either already out working or still in bed recuperating from the night before. Which is what AJ should have been doing, but he never was one for sleeping in.

"My client last night left me a five-hundred-dollar tip in addition to my fare," he says as he stares down the stick. "She was Iranian or Pakistani or something. I don't know. I couldn't understand a word she said." He shoots. "But she must have liked what I did."

Rafael walks around the table. "I have an old white woman who insists on calling me Ralph. I don't know if she has trouble comprehending or if she has beginning stages of the dementia." He leans down and points the stick. "Like doesn't she know my real name is so much sexier?"

Rafael shoots. Maggie pokes her head out of her office.

"Oh, Andrew," she beckons him. "Would you come to my office, please?"

AJ goes. Maggie has taken a seat back at her desk and she looks somewhat displeased as she turns her chair to face him.

"Mrs. Collins has called and requested you again," she tells him.

AJ thinks back to that night in that lavish kitchen, a scene still very fresh in his mind, and feels a wave of almost giddiness wash over him knowing that she had called again. He'd be lying if he said he hadn't wondered if she would. And he's relieved that she did. So much so that he has to work to hide his smile.

"Oh she did," he replies, feigning nonchalance.

"Yes, and now I don't usually do this, but she insisted that she speak to you personally to set up your next encounter." She grimaces disgruntledly. "She's a persistent, demanding little thing."

This causes him to blush as a thought is evoked somewhere in his mind.

"So here's the black phone," Maggie sighs, handing it to him. "Go stand over there in the corner where I can see you. I've already hit dial."

AJ takes the precious phone and goes to the other side of the room. It rings a few times, and then her familiar voice comes across the line.

"Hello?" She sounds unsure.

"Hey," he says, trying not to sound too eager. "It's me. AJ. Andrew." Then smoothly adds, "You wanted to make another appointment?"

"Yes. I did. I do. But..." She hesitates and then starts to ramble nervously, like she does. "Can we...can we meet somewhere public? But private. Like a restaurant. But a low-key one. Can we just...go out to dinner?"

"We can go wherever you want and do whatever you want."

"I want to go out to dinner. *Just dinner*. Somewhere out of the way. I'm thinking a quaint, quiet, undiscovered type of place."

"I know just the spot. I'll have Miss Hunter send you the address."

He hangs up with a smile. Maggie doesn't miss it. He catches her disapproving gaze and quickly wipes the look off his face and hands her back the phone. He continues to the door, avoiding further eye contact.

"This isn't going to become a problem is it?" He hears her ask before he can get out the door.

He turns back and gives her his best look of composedness. "Miss Hunter," he says reassuringly. "I'm good."

She keeps her stern stare on him for a good four seconds more, but then she smirks. "From all the phone calls I've been getting, I assumed as much."

With that, she turns back to her computer, wordlessly dismissing him.

CHAPTER 5

AJ is standing outside in front of his apartment building when seven o'clock rolls around. The sun is setting and the fluorescent lights from the open sign in Reeh & Wooh Barbecue's window glow brightly. Since moving in almost a week ago he has eaten multiple meals there. Jae had been kind enough to teach him all the names of the waiters and waitresses, as well as how to pronounce certain difficult dishes on the menu. AJ thinks he's actually starting to pick up a little Korean.

He watches as a platinum-white Range Rover pulls up to the curb and parks. Despite not being able to see clearly through the tinted glass, he knows it's her before she gets out. And when she does, his breath catches in his chest. She's just as pretty as he remembers. It has only been a couple of days, but the mental images were hazy and collected in the bad lighting of a too dark kitchen. Still, they have been playing on a reel in his mind ever since. But seeing her in reality again is so exponentially better. Her attire is much more casual tonight. In the back of his mind he thinks the flowing sleeveless top, cropped boyfriend jeans, and simple sandals compliments her just as well as the lusty little black dress and heels had.

"Hey," he says with a smile as she locks her car and steps up onto the sidewalk with him.

"Hey," she replies, tentatively.

He leads her inside and walks her to a table for two in the back corner. He notices her looking around skeptically as he pulls her chair out for her.

"Is this a safe neighborhood?" She asks, sitting down.

He goes around the table and takes his seat across from her. "I mean…I think so."

A waiter approaches the table. "You ready to order?"

Anjanae looks at the menu and then at AJ. Helpless.

"Do you trust me to order for you?" He asks her.

"I guess," she grumbles, closing her menu. "Because I don't know what any of this is."

AJ looks up at the waiter. "My usual times two." He looks back to Anjanae. "What do you want to drink?"

"Just water."

"And two waters," he says to the waiter. "Thanks, Joon."

Joon nods and then leaves. AJ's eyes turn to her. She's looking down, toying with the edge of the tablecloth, well aware of his eyes on her. He knows she's unsure, and he wants nothing more than to cure her of her doubt. She finally looks up.

"So," he says then. "We meet again."

"I just want to talk. That's all," she says straightly in her best serious tone. "I don't want you to have any expectations."

"It's not my job to have expectations."

"I just wanted to say…it's just that…well…I'd never done that before."

"You mean pay for sex?" He asks, tone sarcastic but playful.

She blushes slightly and looks down, shaking her head in dismay. He smiles.

"No worries. I only recently started turning tricks myself," he says light-heartedly. "You were just my second client."

"Well. Doesn't that make me feel extra special."

"It should."

"Anyway," she continues. "I just didn't want you thinking things about me, because that person you met the other night…that wasn't me. I was drunk…and the things I said and did don't ever happen and *won't* ever happen again."

"Then why are you sitting here across from me right now?" He asks her coyly, and then before she can answer, adds, "And why would you think that I would think things about you? I've got no judgment."

She avoids his eyes. "I just don't do things like that."

"Things like cheat on your husband?"

Her head immediately shoots up at this. The waiter drops the drinks off and then disappears again. She crosses her arms and sticks up her nose, trying her best to appear offended.

"And why would you assume I'm a married woman?"

"Because you have a piece of work on a particular finger that you could cause blunt force trauma with." He smirks as he takes a sip of his water. "Should I leave you unattended in this *unsafe* neighborhood."

She tries not to smile.

"Plus," he adds. "My boss refers to you as *Mrs.* Collins. I may be from the south, but I'm not stupid."

"That's why I picked you."

He's not sure what she means by this. "Because I'm not stupid?"

"Because you're from Memphis. Or at least I assume you are as your...services...are advertised as," she does air-quotes, "Sweet Memphis Style."

He tilts his head to the side, amused. "So...after one dials 323-LOVE-ASAP..."

She snorts.

"Then do you get hit with some pre-recorded automated message? Like..." he pauses and then continues in a mocking tone, "Welcome to Madame Hunter's House of Whores, where fantasies are brought to life and fetishes are fulfilled. Press two to hear your options."

She takes a sip of water. "Not as forward, but something like that."

"So what's your thing with Memphis?"

"I'm from there," she says simply.

This surprises him. "Are you really?"

"Born and raised."

"Where abouts in Memphis?"

"I grew up off of South 4th Street. Near Crump Boulevard, if you know where that is."

He leans back in his chair and gives her a look. "And you're jittery about being in Koreatown?"

She looks down, smiling slightly. "Maybe I've lived in a gated community a little too long."

"You know, I would have never guessed you were from the South. You don't have a drawl at all."

"Maybe I've had elocution lessons," she replies jokingly. But he doesn't know if she really is. She takes another sip. "Besides. You don't either."

"I work hard at it," he answers honestly. He leans forward, intrigued. "So tell me," he says. "How does a young girl from Memphis meet a Bel-Air Billionaire?"

She hesitates, debating on how much of herself she should reveal. Her fingers begin toying with her discarded piece of straw paper. "I moved out here when I was nineteen," she starts. "I didn't want to be an actress or a singer or anything like that; I just wanted a change of scenery. And California...it sounded nice."

He nods.

"I was a hostess at this fancy restaurant in West Hollywood. Well-to-do people would come in often. It was nothing new. But one day this man I'd never seen before comes in. I could tell he was somebody…he had this air about him. And he just strikes up a conversation with me." She pauses, and then with a wry smirk says, "He asked me out like he knew he could get me. And he did." She shakes her head. "I don't know. I guess it was like fate. I was in the right place at the right time."

AJ studies her, taking note in the flimsy white piece of paper in shreds between her delicate fingers. "I get that."

She watches him absently run a finger up the side of his glass, collecting condensation, and wonders to herself if he really does.

"Do you like Los Angeles?"

She shrugs. "It's different. I've been here for almost eight years now and it's still hard to make friends. You meet people. You make acquaintances. But…"

"But it's hard to tell if any of that's really real," he finishes her thought.

"Yeah."

"I get that, too."

She thinks, maybe he does. The waiter delivers their food.

Thirty minutes later they are both leaning back in their chairs, bellies full and plates empty.

"So," he asks her, smiling because he already knows the answer. "What did you think?"

"That was the best barbecue I've had since leaving Memphis," she admits without a fight.

"See. Not that bad. What do you say we continue the night on a good note?"

She gives him a look that's intended to put him in his place. "I told you, just talking."

"Well," he adds optimistically. "If you change your mind, my place is right upstairs."

"Your–" she briefly glances up, ungrasping, and then looks at him. "You live in this building?"

"Mmhm," he nods.

It's about the size of my walk-in closet, she thinks as he holds the door open and she steps in. "So this is your place," she muses idly as she looks around at his small, empty studio.

He goes to the fridge and grabs a beer. "You don't sound impressed."

"I just assumed a high-end hooker like yourself would at the very least have a balcony and a view."

He pops the lid. "I have a fire escape and a view of the building across the street..." He takes a swig. "And I got a restaurant in the lobby that you just recently remarked had the best barbecue you ever had."

She smiles.

"I know it's not Bel-Air with marble counter tops..." He pauses to give her a playful look. She gives him a stern one back. "Were they quartz? It was dark, I couldn't tell." She rolls her eyes and he smiles. "Anyway," he says. "Give me time. I'll get there."

She sways in her spot, arms crossed, looking elsewhere. "I guess you plan on doing a lot of business."

He ignores her comment. "Why don't you take your shoes off and get comfortable."

"No. I should head out."

"Why? We're just talking, right?"

She looks unconvinced.

"Look, there's only three pieces of furniture in this room and I'm assuming you don't want to sit on the bed. So you can have the whole couch to yourself and I'll sit all the way over there in the little chair, okay?"

He waits for her to concede, and she finally does, warily taking a seat on the yard sale couch Jae had helped him carry up the stairs the day before.

"You want something to drink? A beer? I've also got an unopened bottle of bourbon I brought from home. My dad gave it to me on my twenty-first birthday. It's like...I don't know...a special edition or something. You want some?"

"I'm fine."

"You're afraid to get tipsy around me. You don't trust yourself."

She rolls her eyes again at the assumption. He has to admit, he likes it when she does that. He may very well be provoking it at this point.

"That's fine," he continues. "I made a pitcher of sweet tea this morning. You're from the south, I know you like sweet tea."

"You make sweet tea." It's more of an observation than a question.

He lifts the pitcher from the fridge and then kicks the door shut. "Yes. I brewed it, even added some sugar and ice and a lemon wedge."

He grabs a plastic glass from the cabinet and pours it to the brim. "It was real hard work. Definitely not a task for the weary."

She masks her smile as he hands the glass to her. He then goes over to the chair he's been relegated to. He crosses his legs, getting more comfortable, seeing her do the same. He decides to pry a bit more.

"So you never said what your rich husband does."

Surprisingly, she doesn't flinch at the infiltration. "He's a director producer."

It's as if the dots are just now beginning to connect in AJ's head. "Wait," he says, appearing to be having a revelation. "Your husband...your husband is Julius Collins, isn't he? *The* Julius Collins. I was...that was..."

"Yes, those were Julius Collins' countertops," she finishes his line of thought for him with a smirk. "I take it you're a fan."

"I'm familiar with his work," he replies, trying to be cool. The truth was AJ had seen almost all of Julius' films, even the amateur ones, and had long admired his work as cinematographer.

"Well now you're familiar with his wife."

"He's like..."

"Twice my age, yes, I know." She takes an agitated drink of her tea and swallows. "I know what it sounds like."

"What does it sound like?"

"Like I'm a gold digger. But I never intended...I didn't want..." She takes a breath and gathers herself. "You get to this point where you wonder if you'll ever have any more than what you have. When you're working double shifts as a waitress to pay rent on a studio smaller than this one. When you realize that art degree you have really isn't going to get you anywhere and that you're no happier in your new town than you were in your old one. When you can't sleep at night for worrying about your future...you get tired. And when you're tired you make mistakes." She then quickly adds, "Not that I'm saying I made a mistake or that I ever make mistakes...I'm just saying."

"What kind of art do you do?"

She's thrown by the question. It surprises her that this is what he held on to, no comment or judgment for the rest. "I paint," she says after a second.

"I write."

"Oh I see," she says in a tone of sarcasm. "You ironically become entangled with a producer's wife as soon as you get to LA. How very convenient, Mister I Write."

"Hey," he retorts, putting one hand up. "You picked me out of the lineup. You pressed three or four or whatever number Sweet Memphis Style is." He takes a sip of beer. "Plus, I haven't been here long enough to completely have my morals rearranged just yet. I don't use others to get ahead." He smiles good-naturedly. "I use myself."

She can't hide the smile that happens this time.

"How did you even find out about Maggie?" He asks her.

She leans back into the sofa, slipping her feet out of their sandals and bringing her legs up to her chest. "On Wednesdays and Sundays I have brunch at the Belvedere with two of my girlfriends." She stops herself. "Well. I don't know that I'd actually call them friends. It's more of a passive aggressive, arranged socialite circle of ladies who lunch together because we don't have anything better to do on Wednesday and Sunday mornings type of relationship."

AJ smirks as he listens.

"Julius introduced us. They all have husbands in the business. Anyhow. Christine not so subtly insinuated this Wednesday that I have marital issues and low-and-behold Annabelle had the perfect suggestion. Instead of worrying about who my husband is hooking up with while he's out of town, I should just hire a hooker." She takes another sip of tea. "These rich white hussies are really a bad influence on me."

AJ shakes his head. "Peer pressure's a bitch."

Anjanae laughs to herself. "She kept going on about the man she got. Said it was the best sex she had ever had. He went by German Chocolate."

AJ smiles knowingly to himself as he takes a swig of beer.

"What?" She asks.

"Nothing. It's just that…well, Theo should be winning Academy Awards for his performances."

She still looks confused.

"He's gay."

Her jaw drops. "Annabelle has sex with a gay man?" If he's not mistaken, she sounds almost pleased. "The best sex of her life was with a gay man?"

"Now don't be going and telling her the ingredients that make up that German Chocolate cake she's been indulging in. You'll spoil it."

They both end up cracking up, and as the laughter slowly fades into a silence that's a bit more comfortable than it was before, AJ gets a little gutsier.

"So just how old is Julius?"

"He's fifty-six," she says matter-of-factly.

"And you are?"

"Twenty-seven."

"Mm," he says considering this. "So technically now you're not only a gold-digger, but a cougar also."

"What? You're like the same age as me. Close to the same age." She scrunches up her eyebrows and quirks her head at him. "How old are you?"

"Twenty-three in two months."

She does half of a headshake, feigning a sad look of pity.

"What?"

"Twenty-two and a prostitute," she says grimly.

"I'll have you know that up until this week I had only ever been with five women." He thinks about this. "She probably wouldn't have hired me had she'd known that."

"So that makes me lucky number seven."

"You know, I was just sitting here thinking I should have you a shirt made that says just that." He makes a big spanning hand gesture across his chest. "Lucky Number Seven."

She laughs. He smiles. Then there's a static silence. It stretches until it breaks.

"It's late," she finally says. "I should get going." She gets up and opens her purse, pulling out a small, pre-counted wad of money. She places it on his counter. "The price of an escort to dinner." She then takes out a couple more bills. "And the cost of company." She smiles wearily and then continues to the door. He's conflicted on what to do, because if she walks out, she may not come back. And for some reason foreign to him, that possibility creates a hollowing sensation in the pit of his stomach. He decides then to bend the rules. If just this once.

"You know..."

She pauses at the door.

"It really is ridiculous that you have to go through all the rigmarole with my boss to get ahold of me. You should have my number." He gets up and looks for something to write on.

"I...I don't think I'll be needing it. It was nice meeting you, and you're a nice person and all...but like I said, I don't do this type of thing."

He jots it down on the back of a Mattress World receipt. "Take it anyway. Just in case you change your mind." He hands it to her, and, reluctantly, she takes it.

"Goodnight," she says definitively.

"Goodnight, Anjanae."

She closes the door behind her as she leaves. He stares there for a moment, shakes his head, and then gathers their empty glasses.

~

When Saturday night rolls around and the regular working world is coming out of their cubicles to begin the weekend, Maggie's men are just getting ready to clock in. Theo is standing in front of the full-length mirror doing his tie. Tonight is the movie premier with his Wednesday night woman. Or is she Tuesday? He can't keep track. This will be Austin's second attempt breaking from the gate; he sends up a silent prayer that he doesn't stumble this time. As he bends down to lace his leather dress shoes, Rafael emerges from the bathroom and walks by him with nothing but a white towel wrapped around his waist. Austin almost falls over trying to get away. Rafael pauses in front of the TV to grab a bottle of hair gel off the ledge.

"Get out of the way, fool," Dominique grumbles from the couch.

Rafael gives him the finger as he squirts a dollop of the liquid into his hands. He careens around Theo to get a look in the mirror as he massages it through his wavy black hair. AJ is perched on the armrest of the couch reading a novel. He's still in his own casual clothes, not yet knowing whether he will end up having a date tonight or not. As if on cue, Maggie exits her office.

"I haven't gotten any calls today so it would seem you have the night off," she says to him.

AJ nods as he closes his book and gets up, totally fine with the idea of going home to his own bed.

"Enjoy it," she tells him. "You had a great first week, Andrew. I'm very proud."

He smiles, focusing on the fact that she's pleased and not that he's slept with three women in five days, and leaves.

"

~

As AJ passes through the restaurant on his way to his apartment, Jae pokes his head out from behind the counter, apron tied around his neck and a plate of food in his hands.

"Hey," he says. "I saw you and your date last night."

"Yeah," AJ replies with a nervous smile. He remembers what Maggie said about not bringing clients where you live. Except it's not like he's going to bring every client around.

"She was hot," Jae adds.

AJ relaxes a little. It's clear that Jae thinks Anjanae is just a girl he's seeing. Which, honestly, is how he'd like to think of it too. She's doesn't feel like a client to him. He knows that if Maggie knew this it wouldn't be good.

Regardless, he nods his head with a smile. "She's...she's something."

"In LA for one week and you're already getting girls." Jae shakes his head. "I'm jealous, man."

AJ looks down, smirking inconspicuously. Jae goes back to work and AJ heads upstairs.

No sooner does he make it to his room his cell phone begins to ring. He hopes it's not Maggie, calling to tell him that she found a client for him in the short time he was on the road from the office to home. But when he looks at the screen, it's an unfamiliar number. His heart races at the mere prospect and he answers with a hopeful hello. The voice on the other line puts a smile on his face, because not even two days after she said that she wouldn't...she changed her mind.

Speeding down the freeway on his way to her, all he can hear is her voice in his ear telling him that her husband would be back from his business trip soon, but that they would have the entire night to themselves.

He plans to prolong every minute of it.

They make it upstairs and to the bedroom this time. AJ takes his time undressing her. The last time had been fueled, frantic, and full of heat. He wants to take his time tonight; he wants to savor her. The last time garments had been left on or pulled to the side. Now she lays propped against the pillows, completely naked on the bed before him. He pauses before joining her, taking a moment to marvel her from a distance. He wants to tell her that she's beautiful, but he fears it's too early for such sentiments, that she'll think he's simply saying it to be saying it. She blushes under his darkening gaze. It only serves to make him want her more.

"Come here," she tells him, barely above a whisper.

He listens, lifting the sheets and moving over her. Limbs shift to accommodate, bare skin touches bare skin. For a while they just kiss, mouths molding and tongues caressing, because time is something they both have and want to enjoy. Her hands are in his hair, fingers threading runnels through his thick locks. His hands are moving with languor up and down her sides, one slipping under the small of her back to bring her body even closer to his. A shiver runs through him at the feel of her breasts pressing against his chest, and when he breaks apart from her mouth to kiss her neck, she grinds against his erection in response.

He bows his head, ghosting over a pert nipple with the faintest touch of his lips, only taking it into his mouth when he's sure he's driven her properly crazy. Only after he's given the other the same attention does he slowly begin to descend her body. Open-mouthed kisses are placed down her taut stomach as he goes; she's quivering now, he can feel it. When he takes his place between her legs, he locks eyes with her and places a single kiss to her right inner thigh. His hand that has been rubbing her other thigh slides along toned flesh to the underside of her knee, and carefully hitches her leg over his shoulder. She holds his gaze until he disappears out of view, and then her head falls back.

He loses track of all time as he works her over with his mouth. There's nothing but her, and he mentally catalogs her every reaction for future reference. How she whimpers softly and keens when he sucks on her gently. How her legs tremble against him when he slips his tongue inside. And as he paints his full name with his tongue on her clit, he revels in the fact that her fingers have found their way back into his hair. He can feel her pull on what he assumes are her favorite letters; The R and W in Andrew, the M in James, and the S at the end of Brooks. When he feels her stiffen, he keeps with the same steady rhythm. Seconds later he hears her breath catch, and then she sighs. His hands at her side hold her in place as she shakes, and he continues to lick her through it, lapping at her gently till the last of the aftershocks have subsided.

Once he's kissed his way back up her limp body he just stares at her. She's staring back with the sane shared intensity, pupils blown. The way his tousled curls fall into his emerald eyes makes her smile. She pushes them back with her fingers, and then takes his face in her hands, pulling his mouth back down to hers. As they kiss, she slides one hand down to grasp him. His lips falter against hers and he has to take a breath to keep his composure. She removes her hand and wraps her legs around his waist. He kisses her again, and in one fluid movement slides into her to the hilt. They both moan in each other's mouth at the feel. He holds still, letting her adjust to him. With his hands resting on either side of her head, he moves the sweat slicken strands of hair out of her face. He dips his head to explore the column of her throat and her collarbone that's he's long admired, and as he sucks on the skin covering her clavicle, he allows himself to slowly start moving.

The rhythm is set to slow. She keeps time with him, lifting her hips to meet his. He plunges and retreats, careful to catch every glimmer of pleasure that crosses her face. They take turns teasing each other, a sensuous game of who can retain their sanity the longest. She squeezes around him and smiles when he has to pause for a second. But he keeps his poise, hitches her legs up higher on his waist, and speeds it up. He drives hard into her, thrilling at the breathless little gasps leaving her lips beyond her control, nails digging into his back for dear life. And then just as quickly as he had taken the tempo up, he slows it back down. She whines and arches and wordlessly pleads for more, as he barley moves in shallow strokes. Her hands roam lower to wantonly grip his ass in an attempt to pull him further into her. He stills, withdrawing to the tip. It's his turn to smile now, as she quivers beneath him biting her plump lower lip. He knows she won't beg—not now, not yet—and she doesn't need to. He wants to give her all of him. And he does just that.

When he starts to roll his hips is when Anjanae loses her ability to comprehend. The voice she hears, *her* voice, sounds foreign and far off in her ears. It sounds strained and husky and needy as she moans nonsensical mantras of *fuck* and *yes* into the crook of his neck. The friction of him grinding against her while circling from within is enough to send her spiraling again. In the midst of it all she hears him groan against her as she contracts around him. Moments later she feels him shiver and shift. The sting of his teeth sinking into the skin of her shoulder that exact second sears itself to her memory.

~

In another bedroom, Theo lies naked amongst rumpled sheets in a chic hotel suite. Water is running in the background. Theo is in the spacious bed alone, relaxing in a pose of contentment with one hand behind his head and the other resting on his chiseled abdomen. Clothes are strewn haphazardly across the room. The shower shuts off in the conjoining bathroom.

"I have to say," Theo muses from his spot on the bed. "The movie was pretty good."

"I'm glad you thought so," comes a man's voice from the bathroom. Steam seeps through from the open door.

Theo looks over in that direction, impatient to objectify that piece of fine art once more. Then the two-time Academy Award winner and star of said movie, Troy Langham, emerges, plush white towel wrapped low on his waist.

"I put a lot of effort into the role."

Theo runs his eyes over the gorgeous actor on display in front of him; the damp swath of blonde hair, the glistening tan skin, the firm pecks, and the rippling six-pack that goes all the way down to a tantalizing v-cut where the towel so rudely intercepts his view. Theo feels himself stir under the blankets, despite having just had it all such a short time ago. He forces himself to look away, grabbing his discarded glass of champagne off the bedside table.

"So how long is that wife of yours going to be in Europe?" He asks, taking a sip.

"Only two more days," Troy frowns.

Theo puts his glass back down and turns to face him. "Then you best drop the damn towel and bring some of that effort over here," he says slyly.

Troy smiles that Academy Award winning smile, the one that gives girls and women all over the world hot flashes, and does as he's told.

~

Late the next morning AJ is about to go downstairs to see if Jae is hanging around and wants to grab some lunch with him, when his phone buzzes on his bedside table. He looks down at the screen and smiles. This time he knows whose number it is. He made sure to save her name in his phone after he returned home in the wee hours of the morning.

He picks it up. "Hello," he says casually, the way you would to someone you have an intimate rapport with.

"Hello." She returns it in the same tone. But then she takes a breath and attempts to address him in a more removed manner. "I was just calling to tell you that you forgot your money on the nightstand."

"Oh, did I?"

"You did."

"What are you doin?"

She's momentarily thrown by his question. She hasn't done this in a while. And what *this* is, she's not sure. "I…" she starts, and then continues more composed. "I'm sitting here in my bathrobe trying to muster up the motivation to get in my car and face the perils of Los Angeles traffic."

"Mm," he muses. "Well you answered what my second question was going to be. Nothing but a bathrobe, huh?"

She snorts.

"And what is a wealthy woman like you doing driving?" he kids her sarcastically. "Surely you have somebody for that."

"Yes, but I drive faster than him."

AJ laughs, sitting down on his bed. "So where is your impatient butt breaking speed limits to get to?"

"Oh just Santa Monica."

"For passive aggressive Sunday brunch with Christine and Annabelle?"

She's silent at first on the other end, surprised. "You remembered?"

"I don't *forget* anything."

Anjanae realizes what he means, and in doing so, realizes what *this* means. AJ knows she's gotten his drift.

"Have a mimosa for me," he says with a smile before ending the call.

CHAPTER 6

Garrett Hill has been working for Maggie for two years. He moved to LA from London at twenty, originally working at the Hard Rock Cafe on Hollywood Boulevard, not far from her office. At first, at least to a European transplant like himself, the restaurant seemed like the perfect spot to get "discovered." That was until he quickly realized that ninety percent of the patrons were tourists who knew even less than him about the business. After one year of living in a LA, numerous failed auditions, and money not well spent, he knew something had to give. Sure, he made decent tips batting his eyes at out of state women and calling them *darling* in his accent, but not enough to afford the life he thought he should be living. He was supposed to be an actor. Actors didn't struggle to pay rent on studio apartments. Actors didn't push hamburgers and souvenir cups. Actors didn't accidently max out their cards on clothes and empty their wallets on cover charges, because around every corner is a boutique and a bar. Actors didn't have to deal with this shit. Actually, they did. But all Garrett knew at the time was that he had been running in place for a year, and that was far too long for him.

Garrett always fancied himself a little better than everyone else, though he tried to keep that persona under wraps in order to come off as likable. From a young age he had known he had won at the gene pool. As a little kid, grown women were always coming up to him and grabbing his cheeks, fluffing his mop of blonde hair, and telling his mother what pretty blue eyes he had. His mum took it to her head. Back then, as a single mother trying to stay afloat, she had entered him in pageants and contests in an attempt to make a little extra money. She was the first person who put the idea of being an actor in his head. She was the first woman who made him feel that he could float on his looks alone. But she wasn't the last.

In primary school, his female teachers would always favor him, and he was the common crush among the little girls in his class, way before he could even appreciate their interest and attempts. At the end of the school year, when it was time for students to clean out their desks, his was always filled with wadded up notes, "yes, no, maybes," and glittery valentines. As expected, in secondary school he was quite popular. He went to prom all four years; the first two years with upper-class ladies, much to the chagrin of the guys in his grade. Then the last two years when he got to do the picking, he plucked the prettiest underclass girls. He was on the court twice; king once. In his spare time, he went to parties with the popular kids and collected virginities in the back of the props department from the multiple drama nerds who fawned over him. He hadn't even wanted to take stupid drama class, it was almost as bad as band for one's social status, but his guidance counselor advised him that if he really wanted to be an actor one day, he needed to. Garrett really wanted to be an actor. Despite not even wanting to take the class, and despite being far from the best actor in the class, he was cast as both Romeo and Pippin in two consecutive plays put on by his school. The same counselor who advised him on this advised him to apply to universities. But Garrett knew that would be a waste of time; he was clearly destined to be an actor, and acting didn't take a degree. When graduation time rolled around he was awarded no scholarships. But he was voted best looking.

One evening while he stood outside on the boulevard during the dinner rush, handing out flyers for the newest cocktail on the menu and bitching to the Hard Rock waitress next to him about how much life sucked, he got discovered. To his left a tall black man wearing Balenciaga was standing on Kevin Costner's star, flanked by two French tourists who seemed simply smitten with him. Garrett noticed the man glance over at him, but only briefly. A taxi pulled up to the curb, and the man with one arm around each woman walked over to it. The ladies got in, the man held up a finger to the driver for him to wait, and then he walked right up to Garrett. "I couldn't help but overhear you lamenting," the man had said with a smirk. He then handed Garrett a card and told him to "Take a little trip across the street, two blocks over, and one turn left. And tell Miss Maggie that Theo sent you." Garrett had watched as the man sauntered away and got into the cab with the two tourists, going where he didn't know. Then he took his fifteen-minute break and never came back.

Two years later and he still hasn't had his big break. However, his bank account looks like he's had at least a little one. If he's being honest with himself, he's getting a little tired of going down on retired gold diggers and making lonely ladies feel special. Come to think of it, those were never really things he fancied. What keeps him in check is the simple fact that he can sort of live like the star that he's not.

As it is, another middle-aged woman had her way with him last night, and he is in major need of some caffeine. It's currently nine o'clock and the line at Starbucks is out the door and around the corner, and he's at the end of it. As he waits he plays on his phone, checking Instagram to see how many likes the shirtless pic he posted last night (before that bitch had marred him with her claws) has gotten since the last time he checked. Three hundred and counting. Four people are in his comments telling him how much he looks like Justin Bieber, one (probably jealous) dickwad says he looks like Ruby Rose, and a girl he had shagged back when he used to work at the Hard Rock (before he had to simulate "love making") is telling him to put his shirt back on. Aside from those there are about eighteen comments that read something like "Hey cutie" or "Damn sexy" with little kissy face and heart emojis at the end. Some leave their numbers for everyone to see; he already knows those are too messy for him to mess with. Others ask him to DM them his number. He'll sift through these profiles later. First he'll separate the women from the girls, and then he'll go through their Instagram accounts in search of pictures of them on holiday on private islands, or wearing designer shoes, or sharing five-star food porn. Once he narrows down which ones he thinks can actually afford him, he'll forward Maggie the links and let her handle the rest.

Maggie usually forbids doing business online. If she had it her way none of them would have social media accounts of any kind, but she knows Garrett will have his Instagram for his own vapid self-appraisal, regardless. And he's been with her long enough for her to trust that he's not going to slip up and get her in trouble. Plus, she might as well let him reel in the fish that swim right up to his line.

After five minutes of not even moving forward an inch, Garrett glances up to see what the holdup is. It seems some girls are fawning over a supposed celebrity who is at the front of the line. *What rubbish*, Garrett thinks, and he cranes his head to see who the pretentious asshole is keeping him from his cappuccino. If they're that big of deal, couldn't they have sent their assistant? *That's what I'd do*, he thinks. Through the swarm of groupies and people simply wanting their morning jolt, he catches a glimpse of a good-looking blonde guy who's at the center of attention. Their eyes connect at the same time, both surprised to see the other.

"Garrett?" The blonde heartthrob says. He quickly excuses himself from his pawing fans and makes his way to Garrett. The two embrace in a brief man hug.

"Brent, what's up, mate?" Garret says with a smile.

Garrett hasn't seen Brent in six months, when he quit Miss Hunter's to star in a movie that was setting up to be a box office smash. He still looks the same, but rumor on the blog-o-sphere is that he just recently closed on a 30,000 square foot mansion in Calabasas. There were pictures of it online with a bright red Ferrari parked out front. It had been confirmed on IMBD that he had already landed his next leading role in a movie set to start filming in fall.

"Man, long time no see. How's it been? Here, let me help you out." He turns his head in the direction of the front counter. "Hey, Stacey…"

The young girl at the cash register blushes that Brent Calloway's called her by her name. Not that it isn't pinned to her shirt or anything.

"This here is an old friend of mine. Can you go ahead and get him his drink?" He continues charmingly. "He's a very busy man and I'm sure he could use the caffeine." He gives Garrett a slug to the shoulder and chuckles knowingly. "Am I right?"

Garrett looks at the line of people who have all turned around to give him, not Brent, a sour look. "She doesn't have–"

"Of course, Mr. Calloway," the cashier quickly says with a toothy grin, not giving two fucks about the other plebeians in line.

"What ya want?" Brent asks Garrett.

"A grande cappuccino," Garrett consents.

"Two grande cappuccinos," he calls back to Stacey. "Make mine bone dry, babe. Thanks."

Numerous people in line moan and protest.

"By the way," Brent says aloud. "Everyone in line right now, your orders are all on me this morning."

Their demeanors change and the crowd quickly bursts into cheers and applause. Brent turns and smiles at Garrett, who's a bit appalled by it all.

A few minutes later Garrett and Brent are sitting at an outdoor table drinking their cappuccinos and catching up.

"So how you been doin?" Brent starts. "You still workin for Miss Hunter?"

"Sure am," Garrett replies dismally. He takes a sip and then after a beat of silence smiles. "I don't have to ask how you're doing. Can't drive down Hollywood Boulevard without seeing your bloody head blown up to fifty times its regular size on the sides of buildings." He takes another sip. "Don't let it actually get that big."

Brent chuckles and takes a sip of his own drink. "Nah, man, I'm humble. When I got the role I had no idea it was going to turn into all this." He leans back in his chair, looking more thoughtful than he really is. "You spend a few years fighting for commercials and guest spots on soaps, doing what you gotta do to make ends meet." He briefly glances at Garrett with a smirk and then looks back away. "And then one day the right person sees you, you read the right script, land the right role…and the next thing you know your face is on a billboard."

"I've seen the promos," Garrett says supportively. "It really does look like a smash."

"I hope so. I feel like I've done everything but sell my soul to the devil to make it."

Garrett looks down, twirling the mixer in his coffee. "I dunno," he says under his breath. "Sometimes I feel like I've done that as well." He looks back up and sighs. "I'm about to just throw in the towel. Accept that my fate is to be a piece of meat. It makes me right good money. I shouldn't complain."

"Now don't be talking like that," Brent tells him.

Garrett stares him dead in the eyes. "I've been here three years and had Burger King and Listerine, mate. Burger King and Listerine." He holds his cup back up to his mouth. "Two commercials and about two hundred women."

They sit in Garrett's drab silence for a moment.

"Look, I'm going to give you some inside info because you're my boy," Brent tells Garrett, who immediately perks up. "One of the soap operas I had a recurring role on is having private auditions for a guest spot this afternoon. I'll text you the address and put in a good word."

"Seriously?" Garrett replies, looking more hopeful. "I'd really appreciate that."

"No problem," Brent says with his star smile. "And I'm gonna get you, Miss Hunter, Rafael, Nique, and T tickets to my premier."

"Cool," Garrett says, mentally drifting into a daydream where he's already got the part. He's picturing the people he'll meet and the connections he'll make. The right people with the right connections can change your whole life. Who knows where he'll be a year from now. Maybe he'll be the one starring in movies and buying Ferraris and gracing the front of billboards.

Maybe.

~

It's three days after AJ purposefully forgot the money on the nightstand. Anjanae's husband has since returned from his trip to New York, so she has to come to him. She barely makes it through the door before she's on him and he's on her. They go from the wall to the floor to the bed in hot succession. And then they come crashing into the bathroom, kissing feverishly; a mess of tangled limbs, slick skin, and sex. She breaks apart long enough to glance around.

"God, your bathroom is so little and plain," she breathes out.

He seals her mouth shut with another kiss and maneuvers them towards the shower.

"Wait," she laughs.

"What," he mumbles against her mouth.

"I need something." Kiss. "To put over." Kiss. "My hair."

He pulls back the shower curtain and turns on the water, not comprehending what she means.

"AJ sto–"

But then he's hoisting her up, entering the shower with her, pinning her body to the wall. She ceases to care about her hair. Her protests dissolve into a heady moan as the spray of water cascades around them and she guides him back to where he belongs.

Thirty minutes later AJ is lying on his rumpled bed, clad in only a pair of plaid boxers. He's staring across the room at Anjanae. He can't remember the last time his eyes left her. She's sitting in his lone chair, wearing only his button-up shirt and her underwear. Her usually very neat, well-done, straight hair is now a wild mess of curls. She looks less than enthused about it as she nurses a glass of bourbon with her legs tucked under her.

"I think it's cute," he tells her.

"It's not cute."

"No really," he says sincerely. "You should wear your hair natural more often." He's being honest. How she looks right now, in his shirt with the top few buttons undone, makeup washed away, and hair in buoyant coils…well, he thinks she's prettier than she's ever been. But he can see she doesn't see it that way. "I'm sorry," he adds nervously. "I didn't know that was going to happen. I've never dated…I mean I haven't ever been with…until….." He's stumbling over his words now like an idiot and he wishes he could just shut up.

But she knows what he's trying to say. Her expression softens as she looks down. "Me either," she says, and then makes a nervous hand gesture. "The other way around."

"It's not going to be a dead giveaway is it?" He asks, hoping he hasn't inadvertently got her into hot water. "Your hair, I mean."

"I'll just tell him that I had a really intense spin class, sweated it out and decided to just wash it. Or that the sauna messed it up or something."

"It's that easy? You just pick a place and tell him that's where you were? He doesn't ask what you do during the day?"

"He doesn't really care," she replies, taking a sip of bourbon. "I can probably just call Turquoise and she'll come make it all better." She tilts her head to the side as she considers this. "Of course, then I'll have sit under the dryer for the rest of the day, but he's been staying late on set so I'll probably still make it home before he does."

AJ lifts an eyebrow at her. "Turquoise?"

She shoots him a look. "She's my hairstylist. I would die without her; don't be making fun of her name."

"Would you say she's your friend?" He softly pries.

She shrugs. "I don't know that I'd consider her a friend. She works for me."

"Do you consider me a friend?"

There's a brief coy glance right before her mouth connects with the lip of her glass. "I don't know *what* I consider you."

He smiles mischievously. "Why are you all the way over there on that damn chair?"

She tries not to smile as she looks over to where he's at on the bed. A bed she was all over not too long ago. His dark hair is in complete disarray, and she takes pleasure in knowing she's partly to blame. She doesn't know why, but for some reason she can't seem to keep her hands out of it when she's near him. Her eyes travel over his body. She can make out the fine outline of his abs, the definition of his chest that is smooth save for a few dark wisps, and the subtle muscles of his arms that are more noticeable when he is engaged in action. He isn't as buff or as brawny as what you'd assume a coined "hunk" would be. He's lean, agile. Her eyes unconsciously rove lower, following the thin trail of wiry hair that leads from his navel and disappears under the waistband of his Hanes. Through the thin fabric she can make out his indentation. He isn't the biggest man she's ever been with, but he's still quite nice in both length and girth, nonetheless. And the knowledge of what he can do with what he has, well, it's enough to keep her awake some nights replaying scenes from their stolen moments in her head. She quickly looks back up, but he's already caught her and is smirking wickedly. Yes, that innocent face with trouble written all over it is what really undoes her. How quick he can go from cute to concentrative, how quickly his bright green eyes darken to the color of a gemstone and then he has her in the zone. *Those eyes.* Earlier, when he'd had her careening over the ravine, but holding her right on the edge, he had told her to look at him. She'd silently refused. He still let her go. And as she arched and moaned and splintered into a million pieces under him she kept her eyes squeezed tightly shut. She's scared to look at him when he has her like that, when he has her so completely and utterly open. She's scared she could forever lose herself in those eyes.

She gets up from the chair, but walks in the opposite direction of the bed. Instead she goes over to his closet. "It's just…when I think about how many miles that mattress probably has on it," she starts semi-sarcastically. "The chair just feels safer."

"For your information," he says. "it just had its first mile put on it about an hour or so ago. I don't bring clients to my place."

She opens the closet door. "I'd say that was more than a mile."

He smiles to himself as she begins to peruse the contents of his closet.

Upon first glance, she can immediately tell where he ends and Maggie Hunter begins. There's a small corner with a few pairs of well-worn Levis and plain Hanes t-shirts piled on top of a suitcase. Hanging above the suitcase is a couple of long-sleeved, waffle-knitted Henleys and a few flannel button-downs, along with a University of Memphis sweatshirt that looks exceptionally comfy. The rest of his crammed closet is one designer piece after another, hung on heavy wooden hooks, some with bags over them for safekeeping.

"You realize you have like sixty grand worth of designer apparel in a six hundred dollar a month apartment?" She says to him. "Does she provide all of this?"

"They're my uniforms. Quote, unquote."

"You have a suit jacket in every color," she muses as she thumbs through them. "Black, grey, navy. I'm assuming the white one is for when you do South Beach. Very Miami Vice."

"I'm a beginner so I haven't gotten my wings to fly just yet," he kids. "But I assume she'll eventually want me to take the show on the road."

Anjanae looks down at the shoes lining the floor. "Are those Ferragamos?" She asks in awe, and then proceeds to pick up the particularly glossy, patent leather loafers. "She bought you Salvatore freaking Ferragamo shoes." She shakes her head and sits them back down next to a pair of weathered Converse sneakers.

"Why don't you consider me a friend?" He asks her out of the blue.

"Because." It's not much of an answer. She moves on to his dresser and opens the first drawer like it's hers.

"I like you," he says simply.

"You're a prostitute." She's sifting through his selection of ties now.

"Male escort. And that's just a job," he tells her. "And you are not my job. I don't consider you a job." He pauses and then adds playfully, "Although, you definitely are work."

She finally turns away from his things to look at him. She smiles, but then she sighs. "Andrew," she says, using his unabbreviated first name. "I'm married. And you? Your job is to sleep with women. How am I supposed to…" She struggles with her stream of thought and her sentence strays. "It's just too risky. In every way."

"If you knew all the precautions I have to take," he tells her, shifting onto his stomach. "All the rules."

She looks amused. "There are rules?"

"Of course there are rules. Plus, like ninety percent of my clientele are old Beverly Hills housewives."

"You can't pay chlamydia off, you know?" She slyly chides as she starts walking back to him. "Herpes doesn't have a desired zip code. Syphilis doesn't care who you know or what your last name is."

"I don't think they're getting down like that, Anjanae." He lifts up on his elbows and peers at her through his curls.

"Do you not think these women's husbands don't have the same means and inclinations?" She asks him seriously. "Except when men are shopping for hookers, class usually doesn't figure into the equation. They sleep with a Hollywood Boulevard bargain and then go home and sleep with their wives, their wives call you over for a more satisfying session the following day, and then the next thing you know there's an outbreak in the hills."

"I don't think they go home and sleep with their wives. I think they are in sexless marriages. That's why they're hiring hookers."

She doesn't look appeased.

"I have to wear protection every time, no matter what, and get checked every other month," he says straight forwardly to her. "Those are the rules. That, and Pilates every day."

"You do Pilates every day?"

"I do."

"*I* do Pilates every day."

"See," he says with a smile as he sits up. "This is why we're good together."

She immediately looks away and grabs her jeans off the floor. "I should get going," she says as she tugs them on.

He sighs and leans back against the bedding, crossing his arms. "Fine. Go. Get out of here." He watches as she takes off his shirt and pulls hers back on. She sits down briefly on the chair to slip her shoes on, and then she's back up in motion. "You've been here over three hours. Your poor little Range Rover is probably up on blocks by now. You know. This dangerous neighborhood."

She swats him with his shirt as she passes by the bed and then tosses it to the floor. He smiles. She grabs her purse and sunglasses off the counter, and does a quick sweep of herself in the mirror of her makeup compact. "Am I presentable enough to walk through the restaurant?"

He looks her up and down in her casual couture with her big hair. "You look like Donna Summers about to embark on a world tour. Someone may stop you for an autograph, but other than that you should be good to go."

"Shut up," she says with a smirk. Her hand is on the doorknob.

"Let me take you out tomorrow night."

"No."

"Give me one good reason why not?"

"I'm married. You're a prostitute."

He gives her a cocky look. "Then why do you keep coming back?"

She's halfway out the door and stops to sigh, looking up at the ceiling.

"Thursday night is an inconspicuous one," he continues. "Less people out, less chance of being seen."

"And you don't have to work tomorrow night?" She sounds almost shrewd when she asks.

"As a matter of fact, I don't." He gives her the grin she can't ignore. "I'll pick you up at the bottom of the hill outside the gate. Seven sharp. I'll honk twice to let you know I'm there. Get your alibi together."

She shakes her head to herself. "Goodbye."

It may not have been a yes, but it wasn't a no. And he didn't miss the grin she was trying to hide.

Later he dresses and goes downstairs. He pauses at the bottom of the stairs when he hears someone yell. AJ quietly creeps around the back of the counter. It's two in the afternoon so the dining room is empty, and Jae and his dad are standing in the middle of the restaurant having it out. Mr. Reeh is holding a piece of paper and waving it in the air as Jae tries to grab it.

"What is this?" The older man asks angrily. "What is this?"

"It's not your business," Jae retorts, reaching for the paper again. His father snatches back out of reach.

"You live in my house. You are my son. It is my business!"

Jae slams his hands down on the table in defeat. "It's an application for an internship at a culinary school in Paris."

"No," Mr. Reeh says definitively. "You not go to Paris." With that he turns to go back to the kitchen.

"That's it?" Jae asks, heat boiling up in his voice.

Mr. Reeh turns back around. "Yes. I am your father. I say that is it, then that is it. You go to medical school. I paid for first four years of your college so you could be doctor not some–"

"Oh do not act like you paid some huge price for me to go to school," Jae interrupts him. "I went to public school all my life, that was free, and I got scholarships for my college! I *earned* scholarships! You didn't do anything."

"You do not speak to your father that way!" Mr. Reeh snaps.

AJ watches as Jae immediately becomes submissive and looks down at the floor ashamedly. "Dad," he says meekly. "This is what I want to do. This is my dream. And now I have this chance…"

"I did not raise you to be some sabbatical taking, self-seeking, dream-chasing drifter like these ignorant Americans you see moving here every day. That is what you would be in Paris. I raised you to be realist! I raised you to be educated and to make educated decisions! I give you better life and bigger opportunities than I had. You want to be cook rest of your life? Fine. You be cook here. Dream accomplished."

Jae storms out of the store. AJ quickly follows him, rushing past Mr. Reeh. He swings through the door out onto the street where Jae is stalking off angrily down the sidewalk like he's trying to outrun his urge to either scream or cry.

"Hey, Jae! Wait up!" AJ yells, running after him.

"I've gotta get out of here," Jae mutters, not stopping. "I've gotta get out of his house. The constant rules and shaming and expectations for twenty-two years. I can't do it anymore."

"So save up and get your own place," AJ says simply, sidling up next to him and falling into stride.

"I am trying. Best believe me I am trying. But to save I have to work and I have to work with him!" He abruptly stops walking and faces AJ. "Hey, where do you work? You think I could get a job there?"

AJ is totally thrown. His mouth moves for a few seconds without words actually coming out. "I…I work nightshift at a gas stations in Hollywood," he finally stammers out. "You wouldn't want to do that."

Jae stares at him a beat and AJ fears he hasn't been believed. But then Jae starts walking again. "You're right," he says. "I wouldn't. Those places get robbed all the time and I'm of a very delicate frame. I'd be an easy target."

AJ lets out a quiet sigh of relief as he walks alongside him.

"So I saw that girl sneaking downstairs about an hour ago," Jae says after a while. He shoots him a look. "In the middle of the day though, AJ?"

They both share a laugh.

Two days later Jae moves out of his father's house and into the cheap, vacant studio apartment across the hall from AJ's…in the building his father owns.

CHAPTER 7

Maggie is driving through Beverly Hills in her black Lincoln Navigator. She's got one hand on the wheel and her dark wayfarers pulled down over her eyes, in business mode. She never considered herself the type of person who needed two vehicles, because who really does? When she lived in New York she hadn't even owned one, but in Los Angeles you have to drive. So when she moved she bought a Mercedes, naturally. About every three years she goes to the dealership and trades in her old one in on a new one. Then one afternoon a couple of years ago she and Theo had gone to a car show at one of the convention centers Downtown on a whim, and she had fallen in love with the new line of Lincoln SUVs. Theo had a deep big belly laugh over it, and told her she might as well get an Escalade if she really wanted to fully embody the cliché. But she couldn't be deterred; she bought one with all the bells and whistles that very day. She adored her little Mercedes coupe, but there was something intoxicatingly empowering about driving something so big and so sleek.

Austin is riding shotgun on this particular afternoon, slumped down in the spacious passenger seat. He looks uncomfortable as usual, one hand scratching at his blondish-brown hair like he's got a dandruff problem and the other tapping the door handle like he's got some kind of nervous tick. She glances over.

"For Christ's sake," Maggie says. "Why are you lying low like that?" She focuses back on the road. "Straighten up. You act like we're riding down Rosecrans. This is *Rodeo* Drive," she emphasizes.

Austin does as he's told, sitting up and stilling his hands. "Am I supposed to know what that means?" He asks her meekly.

She sighs like she's in distress. "The innate inability of you fly over state people to recognize regal when it's right in front of you never ceases to sadden me."

He shifts in his seat, not knowing how to respond. The heated leather makes him feel like he's wet himself, and the lofty way she speaks makes him feel dumb.

"Rodeo Drive is the pinnacle of privilege in Los Angeles County," she educates him. "It is what Fifth Avenue is to New York, what Baal Harbor is to Miami. No one should be on this road unless they're rich." She takes an annoyed breath. "Of course you've still got your tourists poking around thinking they're going to purchase a souvenir when in reality they can't even afford a scarf in these stores. And then you've got that guy over there trying to sell his mixtape, who really needs to go back to the boulevard with the rest of the miscreants…but nonetheless. It's still the perfect place to prowl."

"Oh," he replies simply.

She rolls her eyes behind her shades. Austin isn't much of a conversationalist, and to let his first client tell it, not even a good fuck. Which is unfortunate because he has both the body and the face. And, from what she'd seen when she had him stripped down to his briefs during the fitting, he is extremely well-endowed. It is sad that the knowledge of what to do with it eludes him, but Maggie is ever the optimist. She believes she can shape him into what she wants him to be; something that every woman would want, again and again. He does at the very least seem highly malleable, and that is a positive. They ride in silence until she spots what she'd hoped she'd find.

"Cougar in a red convertible Mercedes at five o'clock," she says, eyes presumably straight ahead.

"Where's five o'clock?" He asks, careening around in all different directions.

"It's a euphemism. She's approaching in the right lane, roll down your damn window."

Austin looks to his right, and sure enough there's a sixty-something in a bright red six-speed convertible roadster coming up on them. "How did you even see her coming?" He asks as he quickly hits the button that rolls the window down.

"I have excellent peripheral vision and rear view mirrors," she chides dryly, slowing down slightly as the little red Mercedes approaches.

The older woman driving it looks up and takes immediate notice in Austin.

"She's smiling at you," Maggie says, still facing forward. When Austin doesn't react, she adds, "Smile back," through gritted teeth.

Austin gives the lady in the right lane his very best charming smile, even throwing in a wink for good measure. The woman looks pleased by a younger man taking interest in her. Maggie speeds back up a little. She pulls out the black phone and passes it to Austin.

"What do you want me to do with this?"

"When we get to the stoplight up here you're going to ask her for her number and put it in the phone. Make sure you get it right."

Austin used to consider himself a laid back guy, calm and cool. But Maggie Hunter makes him nervous. He supposes it's because there weren't too many women like her back in Aquila, Ohio. Women like her didn't exist where he was from. In the past week, he's caught himself thinking about home often. He tries to imagine his mother—who he suspects is very close in age to Maggie, though it's hard to tell— shopping on Rodeo Drive in high heels and dropping thousands of dollars like it's nothing. He tries to picture his mom saying some of the things Maggie says, speaking with an airy arrogance, usually with no regard for who she's talking to. He tries to picture it but he can't. His mother is a soft spoken, God fearing, casserole-making woman who wears whatever's on sale at Wal-Mart and is nice to literally everyone. She's the polar opposite of Maggie Hunter.

His dad had called Thursday. They discussed the Cleveland/Lakers game from the night before, the raise in wages his dad was finally getting after laying asphalt all across the state for thirty years, and how hot it was in Ohio while LA was still a cool seventy-two. His pops had asked him what was new, and he'd said same old same old, purposefully leaving out the part where he quit his airport job to work for a Hollywood madam. He had never lied to his pops. Austin is the youngest of three siblings, and his father's only son. They have the type of relationship that kids with absent fathers envy. His dad is the type of dad who played catch with him every night as a kid till the sun went down. The type of dad who never missed a game from t-ball to varsity. The type of dad who helped him and his friends work on their cars and trucks nightly. The garage outback was always filled with old Camaros and Mustangs, good old boys and the girls who chased them; the mini fridge filled with off brand cola and Bud Lights, country music playing in the background. People looked up to his dad, and he did too.

His dad had taken off work when the scouts came to his high school to watch him practice one sunny afternoon. Every time he hit the ball out of the park he could hear his pops' lone scream from the empty bleachers. His dad was there to celebrate with him when he got a full ride scholarship, and he was there to sulk with him when he flunked out six months in. When he went to his dad one day and told him he wanted to become an actor and move to LA, his pops didn't give him some spiel about that being the stupidest idea he had ever heard, even though by the look on his face it was. No, his dad didn't object or try to talk him out of it, he let his son make his own choices. A month later his pops helped him load all of his belongings into the back of a U-Haul, and then drove across the country with him to California. They made a trip of it, stopping at old battlegrounds and national parks, little roadside diners and popular sports stadiums. They'd had a great time. And then they reached their destination, a sketchy apartment complex with an alley entrance two blocks from Skid Row. Austin could tell Los Angeles was his pops least favorite part of the whole journey. But he still didn't try to dissuade his son, and when Austin dropped him off in front of LAX two days later, his pops had simply wished him luck like he always did.

That being said, there was not a doubt in Austin's mind that his dad would disown him if he found out what he was doing. His pops was a man's man through and through; a beer drinking, sports watching, union working, Republican voting man. He had Fox News influenced morals and old school views. In no way would his father approve of him working for a woman who essentially facilitates infidelity for a living and sells men for a seventy percent cut in her favor. His pops would *hate* Maggie. Austin had been thinking about this all week; he even considered quitting. But then he stopped by the office on Sunday. And she handed him his check. Even with just two clients under his belt (the first of which being a total flop, but he still got paid) and even only getting thirty percent of what they gave him, he had made over twice as much as what he would have at the airport.

For that price, Austin decided he could lie to his pops.

~

The sun is streaming in through the blinds of one of the penthouses at the Beverly Wilshire. Rafael has been in this particular room (although "room" is putting it lightly) multiple times with multiple women. It's a client favorite, with its sprawling living area, enormous bed, glamorous décor, and great view. It would really be much more practical to get a motel five miles or so further down Wilshire that rents by the hour, but he's not complaining because he's not paying. These women are the Richard Geres to his Julia Roberts; they have excessive needs, a few of which he'll cater to, otherwise he's just along for the ride.

He sits on a plush chair with his shirt already off as he waits for Mrs. Daniels to finish in the bathroom. He can hear her clamoring around in there, trying to make herself pretty, he supposes. He rolls his

eyes at the thought. There's nothing she could do to that painfully
pinched face, pale wrinkling skin, and those disastrously red corkscrew
curls that would make her appealing to him. She's probably his very
least favorite client, with literally no endearing qualities about her. His
imagination has to go to great, vulgar lengths for him to even manage a
halfway decent erection with her. Sometimes he thinks about borrowing
a Viagra from Theo's stash before he goes to see her, but he never does.
The side effects scare him too much. He can just imagine what the
Beverly Hills first responders will think when they have to retrieve an
undocumented foreigner with a debilitating hard-on from the top floor
suite that smells suspiciously of old lady perfume and sex.

His phone buzzes in his pocket, snapping him out of his
thoughts. He takes it out with a smile "Hello? Ramira?" He answers.

"Yes, my love," the woman on the other end says warmly. She
speaks in Spanish, the only language she knows. This helps him to keep
her in the dark.

"How are you?" He asks, speaking back to her in their native
tongue. "Did you get the money I sent you?"

"Yes, I got the money," she replies. "The construction business
must be doing very well."

She's oblivious. Completely and totally. But he loves her.

"Yes, I've been getting a lot of work." Technically that wasn't a
lie, he thinks to himself. "How is my princess?"

"She is good. She misses her father," Ramira tells him. "I bought
her a new dress and shoes with some of the money. She was so excited."

Rafael beams. "When she gets home from school today tell her
that I love her. Okay?"

"I will."

"And how are you?" He asks her.

"I am fine," she says somewhat solemnly. "I miss you. You
know how rough it is here with you being gone…" She takes a wistful
breath. "I can't wait to come join you in America."

"I can't either. And I miss you, too. So very much." He takes a
beat so she knows he's serious about that last part, and then asks her
playfully, "Have you been being good?" He knows he doesn't have a
right to ask, doing what he's been doing, but he does anyway.

"Yeess," she giggles. "Have *you* been being good? No other
women?"

"No, no other women."

There's a knock at the door. Rafael quickly goes to answer it. It's room service with a cart of champagne and strawberries.

"Where would you like it?" The little man asks.

"Over there by the bed," Rafael replies in English, which again, Ramira doesn't understand a word of.

The man nods and rolls the cart towards the bed.

"Who is that?" Ramira asks, having heard someone else.

"Oh just the milkman," Rafael lies, knowing how dupable his wife is and using it to his advantage, though he hates to.

"The milkman?" She repeats.

"Los Angeles is a very nice community," he continues to lie through his teeth. "They bring your milk right to your door."

"Oh, that is sweet."

So sweet. So culturally sheltered. So dupable. He takes the phone away from his ear as he walks over to the closed bathroom door.

"Mrs. Daniels," he says loudly. "Do you want to come out and tip room service?"

He waits a beat. No response. He rolls his eyes and shakes his head.

"She is freaking deaf," he mumbles to himself, walking over to the couch where she's thrown her designer clutch. She doesn't have a ten so he takes a twenty out—she won't miss it—and hands it to the little man. "Thank you," he says, quickly ushering him back out of the room. He returns the phone to his ear. "Sorry," he says. "I was giving him some money for being so nice and delivering the milk."

"You are so thoughtful," Ramira compliments, smile in her voice.

He hears rummaging in the bathroom.

"Listen," he tells her. "I have to go to work and bulldoze this old house down now. I will try to call later. I love you."

"I love you, too," she says.

He ends the call with a smile that quickly fades when the bathroom door opens. Mrs. Daniels emerges wearing nothing but a slinky white slip.

"Ralph, will you be a dear and poor the champagne, please," she instructs as she heads for the bed.

He begrudgingly heads over to the cart. He expertly pops the cork on the bottle while sneering at her. She doesn't notice. She's too busy fanning herself out over the sheets in what she thinks is a sexy pose.

"And then I need you to promptly strip and come ravage me. My husband expects me back in an hour." She smiles smugly to herself. "If he only knew I was screwing a Mexican. The thought is enough to thrill me on its own."

"Cuban," Rafael corrects as he pours her glass.

"Cuban, Mexican; potato, patatoe," she says flippantly. "It's all the same."

He bites his tongue and pours himself a glass.

"Oh and Ralph," she adds. "I heard you outside the door speaking in whatever language that was. When you do me, can you speak in that language? I won't have a clue what you're saying, but it just sounds so sexy."

He smirks to himself. "It would be my pleasure."

Yes, Rafael is married. Yes, he loves his wife. No, this wasn't the original plan. The original plan was for him to move to America first, make it big as a male model, and then move his wife and daughter out of Cuba. The original plan didn't work out. The Miami manager he had met while still in Cuba turned out to be a bust. He learned this after much hassle, danger, and risk of entering the country illegally. The fraudulent manager only booked him on one shoot, took his money, and then left him high and dry. Rafael stayed in Miami a year before moving to Los Angeles, where people who couldn't help him told him he'd have better luck with his career. Kind of. But not really. He went on many a "go-see," landed a couple of ads, and even got a few catwalk in. But he quickly learned that being an averagely booked model was not as glamorous as TV would like you to think. Lacking options, he got a job working construction with some guys that were also from Cuba and who also spoke his language: no need for identification, and money under the table. It wasn't much money, though.

One hot afternoon he was up on some scaffolding, helping to renovate a building for rent in Hollywood. He had taken his shirt off and tied it around his waist while he worked. A blonde woman walked out of the office next door, paused in front of her Mercedes, and then turned around and looked right up at him. It wasn't the first time he had gotten ogled from the ground by women, but when he got back down to the truck, all the guys were grinning and making kissy faces. She had left her number. He hadn't planned to call; he usually tried to be a good husband. But she was awfully good looking, and when you haven't seen your wife in three years, advances get awfully hard to turn down. He dialed. It wasn't what he'd expected, but it was exactly what he needed. No identification needed, money under the table. A lot of money.

Rafael, of course, wanted his family with him, but if his family was with him he couldn't work for Maggie. And if he couldn't work for Maggie, he couldn't provide for his family. At least not the way he had been. So what was the point? He and Ramira had been teen loves, both growing up in the same poverty stricken, violent village in Havana. They had always talked about their big dreams to make it to America. When he finally got the chance to go, they were both so excited. That was seven years ago, his daughter had been four and he had been twenty-three. Now he was thirty with the prospect of being a model gone in the rear view. Cuba was harder to immigrate from than just about anywhere due to the country's conflict and it would be difficult and dangerous for them even if he told them to come. He had never obtained citizenship himself, how could he be expected to help them do it right? How does one do it right? He doesn't know anymore. But he knows he's sent them enough money over the years to get a better house in a better neighborhood, and nice things that they would have never had otherwise. Even though he may have selfishly settled for the easy way, he can sleep at night knowing that they're well taken care of. And because of Maggie, so is he.

CHAPTER 8

AJ pulls up and parks outside the gate at seven like he told her he would. He turns off his lights and then honks the horn twice. There are about eleven or twelve houses in the secluded subdivision. The private road winds up a hill; Julius Collins' home is the last mansion at the very tiptop. It's a quiet neighborhood, but he wonders if she can even hear him from way up there. Why hadn't he considered this before? The other two times she had buzzed him in, the gate had opened and he had been able to go right up to the house. But her husband was home now, and he was waiting at the bottom of the hill hoping that she was still going to come down. What if she had changed her mind? He turns in his seat to peer in all directions, searching the darkness for her. He settles back into his seat and glances at his watch. Disappointment washes over him; she's not coming. Still, he honks one last time, doing so nervously. He waits a beat more, and right when he's about to put his car into drive, he sees her form appear out of the shadows. He immediately smiles, and it grows bigger as he watches her struggle to shimmy over the lowest part of the fenced off property in a dress and heels. She makes it over the fence and then over to his car. He gets out and opens the passenger side door for her.

"You honked three times, are you trying to alert all of Bel-Air to his affair?" She asks him with a deadpanned expression as she knocks loose leaves and twigs from the bottom of her dress.

"Yeah. Well. I didn't think you were coming."

"I just hiked two miles downhill in heels through the shrubs so the neighbors wouldn't see me and wonder what the hell I was doing. Excuse me if it took me a minute."

"I certainly hope no one saw you jumping the fence," he jokes with her. "That was a real cute move."

She scowls at him, though her eyes are smiling, and gets into the car. He gets back in and they drive off.

"So," he says once they get back onto the main road. "Where would you like to eat? Scarpetta, Urasawa, Mastro's…"

"You certainly know your swanky restaurants, don't you?" She realizes only after its left her lips just how condescending she sounds. Like she's his girlfriend, which she isn't. And like she's jealous, which she…well she wishes she hadn't said it.

"I wanted to take you someplace nice," he offers honestly.

"I can't go to any of those places," she replies in a more reserved tone. "I've been to them with Julius. It would be…"

"Risky?"

"Yeah."

They ride along in silence for a while. This is new and awkward and complicated for the both of them.

"And really," she says after a beat to break the ice. "I'm tired of eating sushi and escargot and things that I can't properly pronounce that aren't even cooked. I…I could really go for some Reeh and Woo barbecue."

He smiles to himself. "Yes, ma'am."

He merges on to the main fairway, leaving the luxuries of the Westside in the rearview for a little bit of normalcy in Koreatown. He looks over at her and catches her smiling.

"What?"

"Oh nothing," she says innocently. "I'm just having trouble getting past the irony of an escort driving an Escort."

He snorts, looking back to the road. "Destiny."

"You'll lose clients if they see you driving this thing. No offense, but you cost more than your car does."

"I plan on upgrading. I'm saving up. I made three thousand dollars this week." He looks over at her again. "How many people do you know that make three thousand dollars in a week?" He quickly remembers whom he's talking to. "Forget that I just asked you that," he says, looking forward. "The people you know probably make three million in a week."

She doesn't comment on this. "What kind of car would you want?" She asks him instead.

He considers it for a second. "Lamborghinis and Ferraris are definitely nice and all, but they've never really been my thing. Plus, I've always thought the men that drive those types of vehicles probably have some sort of complex or insecurity that they're expensively compensating for with half million dollar cars."

Anjanae bites her lip to stop the knowing smirk.

"I'd want something classic," he says definitively. "Classy, not flashy. Like a vintage GTO or something."

She's intrigued by his choice.

Forty minutes later she's pushing her empty plate back and sighing. He gazes across the table at her adoringly. He doesn't know what it is, why every little thing she does, every little thing about her entrances him. Like how she's not afraid to eat in front of him, and then rip off a paper towel from the roll provided on the table and dab away the little bit of barbecue sauce at the corner of her mouth. The way she rolls her eyes petulantly and all the times she tries not to smile but fails. How she has to keep pushing one rogue tendril of hair that has fallen loose from her perfect ponytail back behind her ear. She has it straight again, but it's slicked back, her beautifully expressive face on full display.

"Better than escargot, right?" He asks.

"Definitely."

"So." He takes a sip of water. "Where does he think you're at tonight?"

"At supper with Annabelle."

He nods. "That's good. She has a date with Theo tonight."

Anjanae looks momentarily confused.

"German Chocolate."

"Right, right." She takes a drink. "It wouldn't have mattered what I told him. He wasn't really concentrating while I was lying. He's flying back to New York to shoot this weekend, so he's busy packing." She pauses before unsurely adding, "Meaning I'm going to have the house to myself again…"

"I have to work this weekend." He sounds sorry, and he genuinely is. He can see her remembering what he does for a living after having allowed herself to forget for a while, and just like that, the metaphorical walls rise again. "Only at night, though," he quickly adds. "I can come over during the day. If…if you want me to."

"Relax, AJ," she covers coolly. "I wasn't suggesting anything."

He mentally kicks himself and Maggie. Then he spots Jae coming out of the kitchen.

"Hey, Jae, come here!"

Anjanae quickly shoots him a look as if to say *what are you doing?* He gives her a reassuring look back.

"Relax," he tells her quietly. "He's ok."

Jae comes over to the table, smiling pleasantly. "What's up, AJ?"

"Jae, I want you to meet Anjanae." He looks over at her. "Anjanae, this is Jae-Sun Reeh. His dad owns the place and he works here. Does some of the cooking. Mild culinary genius."

Jae reaches out his hand to shake hers. "Nice to meet you. And the *sun* is silent." He gives AJ a look. "I told him that."

"I don't know," she says with a smile. "I kind of like it. It's very…cheerful."

"A little too much so," Jae replies. "Plus it messes with the whole alliteration thing we've got going on here. Jae. AJ. Anjanae. We could be a trio on a variety show if we could sing."

She laughs. "You're funny. And AJ said you do some of the cooking…did you cook tonight?"

Jae blushes smugly. "I did."

"Well you're a fabulous chef. Have you ever thought about going bigger than this place?"

"All the time," he replies.

"He wants to go to culinary school in Paris," AJ tells her.

"You most definitely should," she tells Jae.

He blushes again and shrugs bashfully in an *awe shucks* kind of way. "So how did you two meet?" He asks them.

"I met her at work," AJ answers almost immediately, assuredly.

Anjanae looks scared.

"You know," AJ continues slyly. "At the gas station."

She relaxes with a smirk, leans back and crosses her arms like *do tell*.

"One day this little Range Rover pulls up to slot seven," he says, recounting their fake first encounter. "I was like, *oh, who is that? I have to meet her*. So I pumped her gas for her. Then I was too afraid to ask her for her number afterwards, so I gave her mine."

"And you called him?" Jae asks her sarcastically. "Must have left a good first impression."

AJ and Anjanae exchange glances. "Must have," he says.

"Well you must be special," Jae says to Anjanae. "He hasn't brought any other girls here."

She looks down and smiles. That means more than Jae knows. Because what she knows and Jae doesn't, is that he has ample opportunities.

"Well, I better get back to work," Jae says. "It was nice meeting you, Anjanae. I hope to see you back at the R&W sometime soon."

She nods. Jae heads back to the back. She waits until he's safely tucked away in the kitchen, and then lifts an incredulous eyebrow at AJ.

"You pumped my gas?"

He grins.

"Was this at the full service station you work for?" She asks, trying to not break out laughing.

He shrugs. "It sounded legitimate, didn't it?"

"So I'm assuming that he doesn't know what you really do."

"No." He takes a drink and shakes his head. "He does not."

"Doesn't he think you dress a little...I don't know...dapperly to be working at a gas station." She picks a fry off his plate and plunks into her mouth.

"I usually get ready at the office."

"So you don't really consider him a friend then?"

"I mean–"

"If he's not your friend then why introduce me to him?" Her smile is that of a coy smartass.

"He is my friend."

"But he doesn't really know you..."

He sighs. He knows she's giving him the run-around to prove a point. The point being that he doesn't have anyone he considers a close friend in LA either.

"He doesn't need to know me that well." AJ sits back and crosses his arms, giving her a placating look. "And I introduced him to you because he *is* my friend, and because he works here and I'm starting to think that this is our place."

"It is so conveniently located." She glances up after she says it.

"Don't get any ideas," he tells her with a twinkle in his eyes. "We're not going upstairs. In order to get you to stop seeing me as a prostitute I've gotta stop letting you use me like one."

She stares him down disbelievingly. "*Use* you?"

"You heard me."

"So what are you saying? You're cutting me off, first base and everything?"

"For a while."

Momentary silence.

"That's ok," she says. Then takes a sip of water. "I can run my own bases."

His ears redden at the thought, but he keeps his cool. "What about the anticipation of two and three?" He asks her, leaning forward on the table. "You're just skipping straight to five all alone. Where's the fun in that?"

She laughs. "Honey, there are only four bases in baseball."
She lifts her eyes at him over her the rim of her glass as she takes
another sip. "We can tell who *wasn't* a jock in high school."

"Yeah whatever," he smirks as he re-crosses his arms.

"Oh, that's right. I forgot you're a writer. You were probably
hiding in the dugout writing poetry."

"Ok, now you're really not getting any."

She laughs. It's easily one of his favorite sounds.

After AJ drops her off at the gate and she trudges back up the hill,
Anjanae unlocks the front door and lets herself in. It's quiet. It's always
quiet. The only time when it's not quiet is when Julius hosts one of his
private viewing parties. Then the foyer and the kitchen and the entire
living area is filled with Hollywood execs, movie critics, his former film
friends from his days at USC, Bel-Air billionaires from the club and
their snobby socialite wives, his favorite actors and actresses, and a few
privileged others of elite notoriety. Those nights she's forced to rub
elbows and make small talk and smile for what feels like hours on end
until everyone is ushered into the home theater to watch a movie that she
already knows the ending, alternate ending, and future sequel to. There
are, of course, those that hang around after the credits roll and the
standing ovation has long passed, hob-knobbing, brown nosing, and
drinking some more. And she doesn't get to crawl into bed until a
horribly indecent hour, by which time he's so loaded on Scotch and
compliments that his ego's at an all-time high. And then she still doesn't
get to sleep. She hates those nights even more than the deafeningly quiet
ones.

The sound her heels make on the marble echoes emptily
throughout the mansion. It has always felt empty to her, even when it's
filled with hundreds of his friends and fans. She was impressed by it
when she was just barely twenty and he first moved her in, but now it
seems entirely too big for two people who could create palpable distance
in a double wide. She removes her shoes and walks barefooted up the
stairs to their bedroom. The door is ajar, she pushes it the rest of the way
open and enters. He's lying on the bed in a white t-shirt and grey
joggers, engrossed in the manuscript spread out across his lap. He
doesn't acknowledge her and she doesn't acknowledge him. She
wordlessly grabs a sleep shirt from the drawer and begins to undo her
dress as she disappears into the conjoined master bath.

This gets his attention.

"How was your dinner?" He asks her from the bed.

"It was fine," she replies back to him as she turns the hot water on in the sink.

"Where did you girls go?"

"Some new place in Los Feliz," she lies, slipping out of her dress. She quickly pulls her favorite ratty old t-shirt over her head. It's big and grey, with the words *Santa Monica Community College* etched across the chest in faded navy. She grabs her face cloth off the towel rack, and just when she's about to reach for the soap, he walks in. He's wearing a stupid grin and holding one of his highfalutin cameras.

"Babe, I'm trying to wash my face," she tells him tersely, knowing what he's trying.

"Leave your makeup on for a little while. You look so pretty." He moves in to touch her face. She lets him. It's all so cold and procedural. He brings her mouth to his and kisses her. "Why don't you change out of that frumpy old t-shirt and put on one of them sexy little negligees that I bought you," he says lowly.

She pulls back and moves past him out of the bathroom. He follows her scantily clad bottom with his camera back into the bedroom.

"Come on," he persists.

She turns around, covering the lens with her hand. "I'm not in the mood."

He lowers the camera in disappointed defeat. "You're never in the mood," he says accusatorily.

She sits down on the bed and starts to lotion her legs. "We had sex not that long ago. Don't act like I deny you."

"Not in over three weeks." He cuts his eyes at her condescendingly. "I'd be scared of losing me if I were you. You're not married to some average man, darling, but you yourself are *very* average. I put up with you not putting out outta respect for our marriage but don't get it twisted, with my kind of clout I could walk out this door and pull all kinds of pussy if I wanted to."

She wonders if other successful men talk like this. She wonders if he ever hears how utterly pompous and pathetically absurd he sounds. She gets up, grabbing a book off the bed stand. "I'm going downstairs to read for a while. Don't wait up."

~

Maggie waltzes into one of her favorite Beverly Hills restaurants the next day. It's early evening and she's dressed in her casually chic business attire, posing as a professional with a nine to five. The well-altered pantsuit, nude pumps, and feminine Rolex lead the average onlooker to believe she's probably a businesswoman meeting a client for drinks after work. Which, in fact, is exactly what she's doing. To the naked eye she might be a lawyer, or an accountant, or a real estate agent. Her father told her at a young age that things aren't always what they seem. To say she took it to heart would be an understatement. She was never what she was.

The maître 'de smiles as soon as he sees her. "Good evening, Ms. Hunter. Will it be just you tonight?"

She smiles back politely. "Actually, I'm meeting someone."

She glances over his shoulder. The restaurant is one of those small, quaint, romantic types. The type of place where, if you were a no-name pedestrian, you had to make reservations two weeks in advance because there were so few tables. She spots her next business venture at a table in the back corner.

"Oh, there she is."

The maître 'de nods and lets her pass.

She walks by the tables of happy couples having early dinner and sentimental small talk over candlelit centerpieces and bottles of Bordeaux. They're of no use to her. No, the older woman wearing a compilation of Chanel and Gucci, with a blonde wig so believable it deserved compliment, sitting in the back with only a glass of white wine for company is her woman. The lady with the red Mercedes.

The woman quickly looks up with eager, misty blue eyes when she senses someone rounding the table. And when she sees Maggie, she looks as though she was expecting to see someone else.

Maggie just smiles and extends her hand. "Maggie Hunter."

The woman warily shakes it. "Isabelle Bronstein."

Maggie pulls out a chair and sits down across from her. Isabelle Bronstein looks very confused. A waiter appears at the table before questions can be asked.

"Can I get you something to drink, ma'am?" He asks Maggie.

"Cognac. Straight up. Courvoisier if you have it. If not, whatever's on the top shelf will do." She looks at the befuddled Mrs. Bronstein and smiles again, full of fake warmth for the waiter. "And another glass of your finest white wine for Isabelle. Put it all on my tab."

"Of course," he says, then disappears to get their drinks.

Maggie doesn't speak first; instead she waits to see if the other woman will make a fool out of herself. They always do when they think they've yet to be figured out and are still full of the idea of themselves. Before they realize they've been spotted as a pawn and are about to be put into play. As if on cue, Isabelle crosses her arms in a show of defense and frowns the best that the Botox will allow.

"I must admit I was more than a little concerned about coming here this evening. I'm not accustomed to getting text messages from random numbers requesting a meeting," she says in a snooty voice, glaring sternly across the table. "Just how did you get my number, lady?"

"Do you not recall giving it to a young man at a stoplight on Rodeo yesterday?"

Isabelle's face immediately flushes guiltily, her whole demeanor changing. The waiter comes back and sets the drinks down. Once he's gone, her mouth goes agape and she starts to stammer.

"I...I'm sorry. You must have been the woman driving. Forgive me...I just assumed you were his mother."

Maggie puts on a fake grin, taking a sip from her glass. "Well. You know what they say happens when you assume."

"You must be his girlfriend. I apologize," she says sincerely. "I didn't know."

She's still as clueless as she was when she thought a gorgeous boy of twenty-three would be into her sixty-something self without a catch. *Silly woman*, Maggie thinks. There's always a catch.

"I'm neither his mother nor his lover," Maggie sets her straight. "And there is no need to apologize. I'm here to facilitate, not altercate. That is if you'd like me to...*facilitate*."

"Facilitate what?" Isabelle asks, furrowing her face up in a way that not only makes her look haughty, but ugly.

"A meeting. An arrangement." She shrugs one shoulder simply.

"I...I'm confused. If you're not his girlfriend...then what..." She gets to thinking and then it dawns on her. "Are you his *pimp*?"

Maggie shrugs again. "The politically correct title would be madam since I'm a woman. That is if I am what you're suggesting that I am. Which, make no mistake, am I in no way saying that I am."

Isabelle Bronstein looks astonished, then disgusted, then judgmental. Performance emotions; Maggie's seen the show before. She knows the next line before it ever leaves Mrs. Bronstein's thin, pasty, pink lips.

"I don't know what kind of woman you think I am that I would engage in such boorish antics, but I should have you arrested for solicitation."

"Did I?" Maggie asks coolly, locking eyes with her. "Solicit you?"

"You most certainly did. I was just driving down the road when–"

"When you saw something you liked."

Isabelle doesn't have a quick come back this time.

"Look, Mrs. Bronstein…" Maggie starts. "It is *Mrs.* Bronstein, right? That's what the diamond on your finger is telling me. Anyway. I don't *think* you are any kind of woman. Quite frankly I don't care what kind of woman you are. I'm not in the business of judging."

Isabelle has gone totally silent and completely red.

"I am, however, in the business of giving people what they want. Any way they want it, all night every night, or on an as needed, strings free, always professionally discreet basis." It's her turn to sit back and cross her arms. "Now. Do I have something that you want?"

Maggie watches as Isabelle contemplates the possibility. When she throws back her glass of wine like it's a shot, Maggie knows the verdict. Checkmate.

She strolls back into the office thirty minutes later with a carryout container in hand and a pleased look on her face. The rec room is empty, but the unmistakable bass of gangsta rap can be heard blasting from the gym. She goes to investigate. Dominique is running on the treadmill in a sweat-soaked white t-shirt and polka dot Nike shorts, and Austin is doing shirtless pull-ups on the steel bar. She cuts the surround sound with a flick of the dial.

"Oh, Austin," she says with a smile. "Guess who landed you the lady in the red Mercedes?"

Austin lets go of the bar with heave, dropping back down to the ground.

"Oooh. The *lady* in the red *Mercedes*," Dominique muses with a pant. He pushes a button and the machine slows him down to a walk. "Go ahead then, Austin."

"Really?" Austin asks, somewhat surprised. He grabs his bottle of water off the weight bench, takes a gulp and swallows. "Just like that?"

"Well," she hesitates with a smirk. "She did take a little bit of an attitude with me." She looks over at Dominique. "One of those that *threatens* at first."

Dominique grins. "She don't know 'bout us."

"She didn't, but she learned." She looks back to Austin. "Anyway. You need to shower and dress. She wants you to meet her at ten in MacArthur Park. I know, it's not the Beverly Wilshire, but she's going to be one of these ones who thinks she can only cheat in covert locations."

Dominique steps off the treadmill, dabs his forehead with his towel and then wraps it around his shoulders like a prizefighter. "Hit it out the park," he says to Austin on his way to the showers. "And while you're hittin'," he adds lowly, "don't forget them baseball stats, playboy." He winks.

Austin flushes and rolls his eyes angrily. *Stupid Theo*, he thinks.

Maggie walks up to him and pats his rock hard abs with her palm. "You're looking good," she tells him. "You'll do fine. Try not to worry." She smiles reassuringly, then turns to go back to her office.

"Hey, you wanna feel mines?" Dominique asks her as she walks by, lifting up his shirt to reveal his own six-pack. "They're better."

"Put your shirt down and stop being a show off."

"Don't front," he calls out after her. "You know you like this, Miss Hunter."

She winks over shoulder at him and then goes into her office. No sooner does she sit down at her desk, the door swings back open. Garrett comes barreling in looking like an excited little golden retriever puppy that's about to get to play fetch, all swooshing yellow hair and happy-go-lucky grin. He pants before speaking; he's out of breath. She wonders if he drove here or skipped. He looks like he just got done skipping.

"Hey!" He says a little too loudly after he gets his breath, and then does the hair flip unconsciously. "I need off tomorrow."

"Excuse me?"

"I had an audition this afternoon and I just got the callback," he blurts out in one breath. "And not just any callback. I got offered the part! I was bloody brilliant I tell you. They loved me. I was simply blinding. I even said my lines in a little hokey American accent. Killed that shit. I was like...on fire. And they want to start shooting the scene I'm in tomorrow so–"

"You want off Saturday."

"I'd sort of like tonight off too so I can prepare..."

She stares at him incredulously. "Dominique has already asked for tonight off to go sing for some record exec. Now you want to take our two busiest nights off? You've got to give me some notice, Garrett. Appointments have been made."

"I'm sorry. It was last minute. I ran into Brent this morning and–"

"You ran into Brent and now he's going to pull you over the barrier with him. And I'm going to be stuck having to find yet another dirty blonde who can flip his hair for all the old freaks that are into the pretty boy persona."

His eyes plead with her. "It's just one guest spot. I'm not quitting."

She sighs. "I suppose I can send AJ to Mrs. Van Buren's house tonight after he drops Ms. Richardson off from the red carpet premier, she didn't request a night cap so he should be good to go as soon as the movie lets out at ten."

"Thank you," he says as he quickly scurries to the door before she can change her mind. "I promise, I'm not quitting!"

"You better hope Vera doesn't care that I'm sending a stranger to screw her tonight!" She calls after him.

He yells back at her from the hall, "AJ can handle it! I got faith in the chap!"

AJ handled it. He pulls his pants back up after the act. An older woman with fair skin and silky hair the color of fading gold sits on the bed in a white robe watching him get redressed. The lines under Vera Van Buren's light blue eyes show her age, sixty-five, but she still retains the beauty from her younger years. She has a slender frame, delicately defined features, and a French accent.

"What did you say you do?" AJ asks her as he pulls up his zipper.

"I run an art gallery out in Westwood," she replies. "Have been for about a decade now, ever since my husband passed away. It was his business; he was an art dealer." She takes a sip from her discarded glass of champagne. "It's really quite fulfilling, more so than what I did before. Which was sit around playing housewife all day. I like to have something to do. And it's a very interesting job."

"So you know a lot about art?" He asks, buttoning his shirt.

"You could say that. Why do you ask?"

"I have a friend who paints," he starts. "Well, she used to paint. I don't think she has in a while. But let's say she wanted to get back into it…"

"Okay."

"Where would be the best place to get supplies and that sort of stuff?"

"Well," she says after considering it a bit. "There are plenty of places around Los Angeles that sell art supplies. Very nice places. But there is this one particular boutique in Santa Barbara that is really worth perusing if you don't mind the drive." She sets her glass down and opens her nightstand drawer. "Here, I'll jot the address down for you."

He smiles as he straightens his collar. "I'd appreciate that."

CHAPTER 9

That same night while Austin is getting acquainted with Isabelle in the back of her luxury car, Theo is ravishing Annabelle in her upscale bedroom. Her husband has been gone all week at a golf retreat in Palm Springs; this is the second night this week that Theo's been called over.

She lets out a climatic shriek and throws her head back against the wall where he's had her pinned for the last fifteen minutes. She's paid for an hour but it never takes him that long to finish her; he's a master at masquerading. Her breathing is ragged, and when he unhooks her legs from around his waist she practically melts down the wall. He immediately goes to pull his drawers back up.

"Are you good?" She asks him throatily, eyes still glazed over. "Did you…"

He didn't. But he hopes the fact that he's already going limp will lead her to believe that he did.

"Because if you didn't…" She looks up at him lustily and moves to get on her knees.

He gently pushes her away. "I'm good. I'm fine." He puts on a good-hearted smile following the lie. "Remember, I'm here to service you."

She stands back up with an insatiable smile. "Well then," she says lowly. "I'm ready for round two."

She turns her back and saunters over to the bed in her corset and get up. He has a momentary look of doubt, but she misses it. He hikes his open pants back up.

"Ok. Just give me a minute, babe," he tells her as he heads to the bathroom.

"Take your time," she says as she sprawls out across the bed.

He shuts the door behind him and locks it. Theo takes a deep breath and stares at himself in the mirror for a moment, the slightest glimmer of reproach in his eyes. He then reaches into his left front pocket and retrieves a little blue pill from its depths. He's thankful that he remembered to grab one from his stash before leaving the office. Sometimes he forgets, and then when things don't work the way they should, he's up a creek. He turns on the sink and holds his head under the faucet, getting some water in his mouth. Theo then pops the pill while thinking about the date he's going to have with Troy Langham the following night at the Chateau Marymount. He's not sure which works first, but he's ready to go in no time.

It's actually not a "date" date because Troy can't be seen out in public with a man seeing as he's married to a woman, not to mention they're *both* A-listers who the paparazzi follows religiously. This means their encounters are relegated to secret places; room reservations made under fake names, sneaking in and out at late hours. Still, they make the most of their time together. They order room service. Theo opens the door while Troy hides. They both always have a laugh about it later. Because they order much too much food for one person, and the delivery boy who pushes the full cart into the room is surely suspicious, but he will never know. After the room service attendee leaves, Troy remerges, and they arrange the spread out on the table neatly. It's a five-star meal free of spectators and complete with strip steaks, lobster, roasted fresh vegetables, decadent desserts, and champagne. Even though they both keep themselves on strict diets, they sit down and thoroughly enjoy every bit of it, slyly joking of how they will work it off later. A plate of strawberries and chocolate is specifically saved for after *the later*.

Troy has been a client of Theo's for two years now, and over those years Theo has not only gotten to know him carnally, but personally. Troy told Theo that he'd known he was gay from the time he was a teen. But his desire to be a famous actor trumped all other desires. He caught his big break at just seventeen, and was immediately marketed as a sex symbol. Male sex symbols adhere to a female audience, and it's hard to keep the female audience hooked when they know you're not interested in reeling them in. Troy always thought this was crazy. Just because Mary Beth from Chattanooga puts that she's his biggest fan in her Twitter bio doesn't mean he's ever going to know she exists. Him being straight isn't going to make them magically cross paths and fall in love. So what does it matter? But it did matter, and he knows it matters. Troy knew it would matter before he even mattered, and for this reason he never told any of his managers or agents his secret either. He already knew what they would say: women are unfortunately fickle and their fantasies of you can be easily ruined as soon as they get a mental picture of you sucking dick. Which he also thought was crazy because gay men, on the other hand, can still lust after their favorite actor knowing all good and well that said actor prefers a pussy. His manager might not outright tell him not to come out if he knew, but he would certainly advise him against it. And even if Troy didn't want to come out, knowing he liked men would make his manager a nervous wreck. So he kept him and the rest of the world, minus Maggie and Theo, in the dark.

Troy had never slept with a man before Theo. He'd had a brief tryst with his gay manager at the Taco Bell where he worked in Montecito before being discovered. It was all very PG13; casual flirting, kissing, and a couple hand-jobs. Still, he was haunted that even *that* would come out one day. He feared that his former fast food liaison would be so hard up for money one day that he'd call the number on the back of an Enquirer and "leak" a statement about the "confused" sixteen-year-old Troy Langham, and then his whole career would go up in flames. That had been over twenty years ago, and of course nothing had ever been said, but he was still paranoid. So, being that he was so paranoid, he only ever slept with and dated women. He even went through a purposeful "player" phase. In his early twenties there was always a new photo of him with a new girl getting cozy at the club: a starlet here, an up and coming singer there, a lucky groupie. He changed women like he changed clothes, until he started dating Patrice Grove after they starred opposite each other in a box office hit. It only took him three months to propose, the engagement was quick, and they got married on a beach in Barbados where glamorous photos were taken that ended up on the cover of multiple magazines. The relationship was highly romanticized by the public, being that they were young, successful, and beautiful. He always knew he wanted to get married as soon as possible, because at least then he'd only have to feign interest with one woman and he could drop the ladies' man charade. That had been when he was twenty-five. He was now thirty-seven. He was still married, still famous, still unfulfilled. That was, until he met Maggie.

He'd heard her name whispered in closed circles before. It was always women talking about her men, her *talented* line up of *men*. He wondered. He wondered a lot. To say he hadn't been tempted over the years would be a huge lie. Gay fans would approach him occasionally with offers, stylish men in the Gucci store would flirt with him shamelessly, backstage at fashion week he'd get hit on, and he would always politely turn them away. Sometimes he thought about going to a seedy down-low spot and just getting himself a gigolo, if not just to scratch the itch, but he didn't want a disease and he definitely didn't want to be caught. But these women he heard talking about Miss Maggie

Hunter, they were well-to-do women. They were women who wouldn't want their affairs leaked either. So he had his assistant do some digging under the premise that he wanted a new agent and had heard she was a good one. Which, he ironically learned later from Theo, was one of her favorite disguises. He got the number, waited until he was home alone, locked himself in the bathroom, and dialed. Two days later he met Theo.

Theo had always thought Troy was attractive, way before he ever knew him personally. He never thought about Troy being gay. There was never any telltale signs or speculation stories being written about him in the tabloids, as there are with almost every male celebrity at some point. Of course, Theo knew there were quite a few closeted actors and singers in Hollywood; he'd slept with a few of them. Because discretion is key and discretion is what Maggie majors in. In ten years, up until Dominque's recent scare, none of her clients have been caught—by husbands, wives, paparazzi, friends, foes, or otherwise. So when Maggie told him he would have an A-list celebrity client who was very much in the closet, he wasn't surprised. However, when he went to the agreed upon hotel room and Troy Langham opened the door, he was surprised.

Being that this was his first male lover, there was a lot of trust Troy needed from him, and Theo did his best to put him at ease. He felt a certain level of empathy towards the man who could never be who he truly was. With him, he could be. While there was always an exchanging of money, the things they did were more reminiscent of a two-way relationship than they were of one-sided acts of illicitness. Even though Theo's job was to service, reciprocation occurred often with Troy. One of the things Theo liked most about Troy was that once trust was had, nothing was off limits. They were two open-minded individuals with electric chemistry. There were no set roles. No definitive dominant or submissive. No perpetual top or bottom. They took turns with everything, pleased and were pleased. Theo had been "seeing" Troy for two years now, and he still got butterflies in his stomach every time he saw his name on his schedule. Troy was a very busy man juggling a highly successful career and a wife, so there would be periods of time when their encounters would be few and far between. By the next time that they got to meet Theo would be more than ready for a reprieve from the forced and faked fornication of his day-to-day life. Sure, he had other male clients, but there was an unspoken comfortableness between him and Troy. After sex, Theo would catch himself not rolling out of bed fast and redressing, like he usually did. He caught himself lingering.

They would stare at each other, caressing and conversing.
Sometimes they'd flip on the hotel television and watch whatever was
on, feeding each other what was left of the room service they'd ordered
and drinking the very best bubbly. Nine times out of ten, if Theo
lingered long enough, they'd end up having sex again. Sometimes Theo
stayed the entire night. The overtime money is nice, but the company is
nicer.

From time to time Theo fantasizes about Troy when he's alone,
and it's not always sexual. Theo has never really had a significant other,
someone who was his and only his, something that was monogamous
and true. He'd never dated. He'd always just had sex. From seventeen
on, romance was reserved for those who could afford it. His body and
sexuality were simply a means to monetary advancement. It was sad,
when he thought about it, but he didn't let it get him down. Theo isn't a
naturally depressive person; he's a naturally positive person who has
taught himself to appreciate what he has. For a while now he's had quite
a lot. So what if he didn't have someone to share his life with? That's
just one thing. He has so much else—especially compared to his past—
to be grateful for. Still, everyone wants to be loved, and really he's no
different. He thinks back to when he was teenager, before his ideas of
love had been marred by money and manipulation. Back when he was
around fourteen, when the halls of his high school were filled with
puppy love and before he personally knew anyone else who was gay.
Those days when his classmates made out with their girlfriends against
lockers, he would daydream about a boyfriend for himself that he made
up in his head. A nice white boy with luscious blonde hair and beautiful
blue eyes, he'd be both handsome and sensitive. They'd make out
without anybody staring and make each other laugh and stay up late
having pointless conversations, and it would be everything. He's
realized that this illusion, this figment of his imagination from years ago,
is not far from Troy. And that the reality is far better than he ever
imagined at fourteen. Of course, Theo has been in the game way too
long to be foolish. He realizes that he's *not* a regular person, that he
can't have a regular relationship, and that *this* is far from a regular
relationship by any means. He's a male escort. Troy is one of his clients.

But that doesn't mean he can't dream.

CHAPTER 10

The next morning Anjanae is back standing at the bottom of the staircase as her husband comes down carrying his many bags. He is more dissolute about his departure this time, as he's still crabby about their riff from earlier in the week when she had denied him his husbandly rights. He avoids looking at her as he grumpily rattles off the rules.

"Be good. Don't touch the Lamborghini. And remember that you need a driver for the Rolls."

"Of course," she replies.

He gives her a half-hearted kiss and then walks out the door. All the while she's smiling.

Thirty minutes later AJ is standing out front in the driveway with her, staring in astonishment at the Phantom Rolls Royce in front of him.

"Anjie, I can't drive this."

"Of course you can," she says, tossing him the keys.

He watches as she goes around to the passenger side and opens the door. It swings out in the opposite direction of the types of cars he's used to driving.

"You said you wanted to go to Santa Barbara. For that long of a trip, this is the most comfortable car to take," she tells him matter-of-factly.

"It's only like an hour away…"

"The seats are plusher and made out of only the finest material. There's also a mini bar in the back and pull out tray tables."

"Is all that really necessary?" He asks her.

"Yes, now get in the car."

He sighs and does as he's told, opening the backwards door and sliding behind the wheel onto buttery soft leather. The interior is simply amazing and it still smells brand new. It smells better than brand new; everything about it screams money and unattainability. He runs his hands over the wood grain absently. She watches him and smiles. Then she grabs the little black hat off the dash.

"Here, put this on until we get out of the city limits," she tells him.

He looks at the chauffer's hat in her hand and then looks at her incredulously.

"You've got to be kidding me."

She tries not to break out grinning and to keep a serious face. "Go on," she says. "Put it on."

He starts the car and puts it in drive. "I'm pretty sure these windows have Presidential tint. I don't think I need a disguise."

She puts the hat down and pouts. "You're no fun."

"We'll see about that," he says with a smile as he steers the car down the long driveway.

"Are you really not going to tell me where we're going?"

"You trust me to drive this car, trust me to take you somewhere in it."

She sits back and crosses her arms. "Fine."

They drive in silence for a while with AJ taking extra care to mind all speed limits, and not only red lights but every yellow light as well.

"This feels so weird," she says.

"What?"

"Riding in the front seat. I usually ride in the back."

"You sit in the back of your own car?" He asks, appalled.

"It's a Rolls thing."

"Oh ok," he replies with an eye roll. He takes his eyes off the road just long enough to look over at her and grin. She grins back.

~

Being on the back lot is everything Garrett imagined. Seeing all the little trailers with the actors' and actresses' names on them, crew members jetting around on the back of golf carts, and the constant calls for hair and makeup; it all serves to intoxicate him further on the thought of fame. Even though it's just a soap opera, even though he only has one line, he's still a part of the process. He's still going to be on TV. And nothing can ruin that high for him.

Garrett watches the magic happen just off set. He's wearing a waiter's outfit and holding a pad and pen, waiting for his cue. The stage has been made up to look like a diner. The focus is on a table where a blonde is sitting across from a silver fox. He's watched both the actress and the actor on TV before, and now he's watching them from ten feet away. It's unreal.

"I don't know if I can do this anymore, Antonio," the blonde says.

"But I love you, Jeanette," the silver fox replies, taking her hand. "You're who I really want, not her."

Garrett enters stage right, heart racing under his mock white smock. He stops in front of their table.

"Can I take your order?" He asks in an American accent.

"Yes," replies the blonde. "I'll have scrambled eggs with a side of bacon."

"Cut!" The director yells. He shakes his head. "Kasey, you sound way too upbeat with that breakfast order. You're in the process of ending your secret love affair with your mother's third husband. It's not a cheerful moment."

"Do you know when the last time I ordered bacon was?" Kasey shoots back at the director. "Excuse me if my inner excitement seeped through. You have no idea the work it takes to maintain this body, Jeff," she tells him, waving her hands dramatically down her size zero silhouette. "This body that has been making *you* money for the last ten years." She throws up her hands then. "You know what, I can't take this constant nagging. I'm going on break."

She gets up and storms off set. Garrett stands there not knowing what to think. He knows some actresses have a rap for being temperamental, but he didn't think he'd be witnessing an outburst on his first day. Jeff exhales exasperatedly.

"Ok everybody. Take ten," he says, getting up from his chair. "And somebody get that bitch some bacon."

Kasey Franks swings open the door to her trailer and smiles as soon as she sees him. Theo is laid back relaxing on her couch, casually reading one of her scripts. He's shirtless, wearing a pair of snug fitting white pants the contrast artistically with his smooth, dark skin. He glances up.

"I thought you didn't get off for another hour?"

"I'm trying to get off right now," she tells him, undoing her jeans and quickly pushing them down her narrow hips.

He smirks and puts down the script. "Alright then."

He stands up and she is immediately on him, tugging at as his belt.

"I've only got about fifteen minutes before Jeff comes looking for me," she says, getting his pants open and shoving them down. "So this is going to have to be a quickie."

Theo pauses with his hands on her hips. "You're still paying for the full hour you requested though, right?"

Kasey stares at him panting. "Of course."

He smiles and then springs back into action, picking her up in one fell swoop and crashing back down on the couch with her. "Then it's no problem, baby," he answers against her lips.

"Antonio Alonzo has nothing on you," she moans as his hands slide her lacy underwear down her legs

He sits up and pulls her onto him, making her gasp. "I don't know," he replies lowly into the shell of her ear. "He's a pretty good-looking man."

~

Garrett is standing around the craft services table with some of the other actors on break. He notices most of them bypass the more scrumptious looking options for small pieces of fruit and crackers they merely nibble on. He follows suit, plopping a few green grapes onto his plate. He notices Richard Rodriguez, the actor who plays Antonio, talking to one of the directors a few feet away. Soon Garrett is staring and unable to look away, like a child who is blinded by rays while trying to steal a peek at the sun.

Garrett isn't attracted to men, but he can admit that Richard Rodriguez is an attractive bloke. He just radiates Je Ne Sais Que. The full head of wavy hair graying in all the right places, the swarthy dark complexion, the properly primped face; he is dashing in a very old Hollywood way. Richard Rodriguez is a star and not just in the soap sense. He'd had a few big movie roles in his heyday that were shot in the soap's off-season; a seductive young drifter who wanted to be a Latin singer, a high rolling poker player, and a loveable villain in an action trilogy. That had all been years ago, though. His last two movies had gone straight to Lifetime (they were of the Romantic Comedy variety). It didn't matter, though, because his real claim to fame is, was, and always had been *The Moments of Our Hearts*, better known as *Moments*, the long running soap. He would always be Antonio Alonzo. And that's all that really mattered.

Garrett becomes suddenly aware that Richard has stopped talking to the director and is walking straight towards him. His mouth goes dry.

Richard reaches out his hand. "Hello." He smiles, not a single tooth is crooked or discolored. It is the type of smile that is both practiced and paid for. "I'm Richard Rodriguez."

"Ye...yes..." Garrett stutters, trying to get his words to work. He smiles and shakes Richard's hand. "I know who you are."

He wasn't going to tell him that when he was a kid he used to watch the soap all the time. His mother loved American soap operas and would tape them while she worked the register at the local chemist's shop and Garrett went to school, then around six she'd thaw out two frozen dinners and they'd both plop down on the couch and watch the day's recordings. Garrett's mother loved "her stories," and being that they only had one Telly, he was forced to adopt the love. He knew half of Antonio Alonzo's storylines. All the wives, ex-wives, lovers, and children that came and went. All the times he had almost died but didn't.

"Today is your first day?" Richard inquires.

"Yes...yes, it is," Garrett replies, still smiling deliriously.

Richard smiles. "I could tell."

"That obvious?" Garrett asks nervously.

"You just seemed a little flabbergasted by it all." He shakes his head and makes a shooing motion with his hand. "Don't pay any attention to Kasey Franks. She is a dramatic. Thinks because she's been on this show for ten years she runs it." He grabs a handful of blueberries and then leans back against the table coolly. "I've been on this show twenty-five years, since its inception." He nudges Garrett. "And just between you and me," he says lowly, like it's a real secret. "She's been one of my least favorite leading ladies." He drops a blueberry into his mouth. "Horrible kisser."

Garrett laughs and Richard smiles.

"You know what," he says. "You're about the age I was when I got my start. What are you, twenty-two, twenty-three?"

"Twenty-three," Garrett says. He's still in disbelief that Richard Rodriguez is even talking to him.

Richard nods thoughtfully and pops another blueberry. "I've seen a lot of new actors come and go on this show. Some of their careers take off and some of their careers flop. But you've got that look, kid. You've got the *it* factor that everyone talks about but not everyone has."

Garrett smiles with a blush. "Thanks. Thank you so much. That means a lot."

"What did you say your name was?"

"Garrett. Garrett Hill."

"Hey, Rich!" Jeff calls from down the hall. "Come over here for a minute, I gotta talk to you."

Richard smiles politely. "Excuse me," he says to Garrett and then turns to leave. Halfway down the hall he looks back. "Find me after we wrap tonight, Garrett. Let's do drinks."

"Ok," Garrett replies faintly, both awestruck and star-struck. He watches as Richard disappears down the hall with Jeff to discuss a change in dialogue or something else Garrett isn't privy to knowing as a guest actor with one line. But he isn't just a guest actor with one line; he is a guest actor with one line and *the look*. And that's all that really matters.

~

AJ slows down as they come to a strip of stores and boutiques facing the ocean. He parallel parks the boxy car with ease in front of a little place that reads ART AND ECETERA. Anjanae looks at him, then out the window at the boutique, and then back to him. Her eyes glisten with intrigue.

"What is this?"

"Get out and see for yourself," he replies simply, smiling confidently.

They both get out and step up onto the sidewalk. He holds the door open for her, then watches as she stands there in shock for a moment, taking in all the blank canvases and brushes and eclectic knick-knacks. Her entire face lights up with excitement. Her smile curves upward into her high cheek bones, creating dimples under her sparkling eyes that give her the childlike quality of a kid in a candy store. He grins, knowing he's brought her to the right place. A kind-faced older woman pokes her head out from behind the counter.

"Is there anything I can assist you two in finding today?"

"I…" Anjanae starts, she's still in shock. "We're just looking, I think."

"Have you been here before?" The woman asks.

"No," Anjanae answers, her eyes still dancing from one corner of the store to the other, wanting to see everything.

"Ok. Well my name is Layla. Why don't I just show you around then?" She comes out from behind the counter. "What are you into? Drawing, painting, sculpting…"

"Painting," Anjanae answers. "I paint." Then second-guessing herself, "Well…I used to paint."

"Oh honey, there's no used to," Layla tells her. "Once you realize you're an artist you're always an artist."

Layla puts her arm around Anjanae and ushers her back to where the paint supplies are located. Anjanae looks over her shoulder at AJ. He smiles and nods for her to go on.

"Go ahead," he tells hers. "Take your time."

She smiles and lets Layla lead her away.

Thirty minutes later they emerge from the store, Anjanae carrying a couple of bags. AJ had tried to pay for the stuff she had picked out but she wouldn't let him. As he starts the car he hears a grumbling sound, but it's not coming from the engine. He looks over at her.

"Is that your stomach?"

"Maybe…" she replies, a little embarrassed.

"Are you hungry?"

Silence. And then, "Yes."

"Well let's do lunch then," he says, taking out his phone. "Do you know of any good places around here? I can put it in the GPS on my phone."

"The car has GPS…"

"Right. Of course. It's got bulletproof glass, why wouldn't it have GPS."

"I know a couple of places," she says tentatively. "But we can't go to them."

"Why?" He asks. And then remembers.

Those are places she's been with her husband.

"Right," he replies, looking down. Then he looks back up. "Well I can work around that. What are you in the mood for? Hamburgers, chicken, Chinese, Pizza…"

She picks a fast food chicken chain that they only have in California. He's never been, and she tells him that he has to try to it because it's the best and because all the ones in LA are in the ghetto. He just laughs and takes her word for it. But when he gets there and pulls into the drive-thru lane, she gets that nervous look again.

"What are you doing? We can't go through the drive-thru. I just ate here like three months ago. The workers know my face."

"Do you want me to go in and get it?"

"No. Never mind," she says after thinking about it. She shuffles in her seat. "Let me just get down and hide."

She maneuvers so that she's leaned over with her head down.

"You're creating a way more incriminating snapshot right now than had we just been seen seated at a table together," he tells her with a smirk.

She straightens back up and shoots him a glare.

"Alright," he sighs. "I'll put on the hat. Get in the back."

He stops a few feet shy of the drive-thru window and she shimmies over the console into the back seat. He grabs the little black hat from the dash and puts it on. As he puts the car back into drive he glances up into the rear view and shakes his head at her. She's grinning from ear to ear.

They park somewhere off the beaten path with the shore still in sight, and sit in the back together with the air conditioning on and the tray tables pulled out. They have their fried chicken with a bottle of chilled Rosé they find in the in-car mini bar.

"I feel like such a rap cliché right now," she says as she finishes off the piece of chicken that she's been so eloquently eating with a fork. "Eating fried chicken and drinking champagne in the back of a Phantom."

He wipes his hands off on a napkin. "I feel like the guy who rolls the weed."

She laughs. He smiles.

"More bubbly?" He asks. She nods and he pours a little more of the luscious pink liquid into her fast food paper cup. He's only had a couple of sips of it. He still hasn't developed a taste for the stuff yet, and more importantly, he doesn't want to be impaired when driving a million-dollar automobile.

"Cliché or not it was refreshing, "she tells him. "This little backseat picnic thing."

"Hey," he says with a smile as he sits back against the plush leather seats. "If your car's got tray tables, use em."

She smiles coquettishly and takes a sip of champagne. "So am I still on punishment?"

"Are you serious? I went from being a hired hooker to driving Miss Daisy. You are *definitely* still on punishment." He smiles playfully at her. "Until you learn to respect all of this…" He waves his hands down is body. "You're going to have to beg for it if you want it."

"Well," she replies, crossing her legs. "You can forget that. I don't beg."

Ten minutes later she's on her back with her eyes squeezed shut. Her shirt and jeans have since been discarded, and AJ lies between her legs placing kisses down her bare body. He licks along the lacey rim of her panties. She lifts her hips, wordlessly telling him what she wants. He stops and raises his head to study her face. After a beat she opens her eyes. The look he's giving her is lecherous as he slowly runs one finger from top to bottom over the dampening material that still covers her.

"What do you say?" He asks her.

She squirms beneath him, her eyes pleading with his. "AJ..."

He lowers his head back down and kisses all around her waist and thighs, but never where she wants him, all the while keeping an eye on her.

"Anjanae," he repeats lowly against her skin. "What...do you say?"

She forces out a breath. "Please," she finally utters, voice thick with desire.

AJ pulls her underwear down her legs, tossing them somewhere over his shoulder. He gets into position, but then he pauses. His eyes flick up to meet hers again as his mouth hovers just over her sex. "Please what?"

She groans at the sensation of his breath ghosting over her. She closes her eyes again, and that's when she feels his mouth on her. He kisses her so slowly, so sensuously, that her resolve slips at the mere thought of him stopping.

"*Please*." It comes out more wanton than she'd planned, but she's past caring about propriety. "God. *Andrew.* Please don't stop."

And he doesn't.

They take the Pacific Coast Highway home, watching out the window as the sun meets the shore and paints the sky a mural of mauve. It's dark by the time they reach Bel-Air; AJ parks the Rolls in front of the fortress in the exact spot he found it. He gets out and goes around to open her door.

"This concludes the round trip tour of Santa Barbara with complimentary meal, sex, and service to Bel-Air," he says in mock tour guide voice, holding out his hand to her. "Watch your step and proceed with caution to the right."

She laughs as she steps out of the car with her bags from the art store. Her clothes are mildly rumpled and her hair is a bit of a mess, but no one's home to take inventory of her appearance tonight. They both stand there in silence for a while, smiling at each other and swaying in their spots.

"I had a really nice time today," she tells him, looking into his eyes. "It's been a long time since I've been out and actually enjoyed myself. I…" She looks down at the ground. "Thank you. Thank you for today."

"It was my pleasure," he replies honestly. "I'm glad you had a good time. I had a good time, too."

She looks back up, smirking slyly. "I hope I didn't wear you out. I forgot you have to work tonight."

He smiles slightly and shakes his head. "I'll be alright."

There's a fleeting look of something on her face, and then she's looking behind her to the mansion.

"Well," she says, a hint of terseness in her voice. "I should let you go."

He senses the shift; he's starting to get accustomed to it. But still he tries. He'll always try to stop the walls from going back up.

"Do you want me to help you inside with your bags?"

"No." She gives him a placating smile. "I've got it."

"Ok. Well." He dangles the keys between his fingers and looks at her hopefully. "Till next time then?"

She holds out her palm and he drops them in her hand. She turns and starts walking up to the house. He waits. She stops halfway there.

"Till next time," she replies without looking back.

He grins, satisfied, and gets into his dusty little blue Ford. She shakes her head with a cynical smile and continues on up the steps to the front door.

~

Back at 360 Hollywood Place a dejected Dominique is splayed out on the couch with a half empty bottle of Paul Masson in his hand. Theo comes through the door and immediately stops in front of the full-length mirror to examine himself. Dominique takes in the other man's appearance and gives him the side eye. Theo is still wearing the same tight-fitting white pants from earlier in the day, but he's since returned a shirt to his body; it's bright pink and tucked in to the white pants neatly. The top few buttons of said shirt are undone, revealing a single gold chain that goes along with the multiple gold bracelets and rings he's wearing. He also has his pink diamond stud in his left lobe.

"Where you comin from?" Dominique asks him.

"A client," Theo replies, wiping a red lipstick stain off his face.

Dominique raises an eyebrow. "A female client?"

"Yes a female client."

"You come through the front door lookin like that?"

Theo shoots him a look and then turns back to the mirror. "Nah," he says sarcastically. "I came through the back door."

Dominique grins dirtily. "Kinky."

AJ walks in carrying his suit for the night over his shoulder, oblivious to the conversation going on.

"Real men wear pink, AJ," Theo tells him. "Remember that."

"Gay men wear pink," Dominique mumbles under his breath.

"You sure seem to know a lot about gay men, Nique," Theo retorts. "You're not thinking about dabbling on the other side are you?"

"Hell naw," Dominique says, taking a swig from his bottle. "Never that."

AJ heads back to the bathroom to get dressed. He's still thinking about Anjanae and wishing he hadn't had to leave her to go to some dumb dinner with yet another woman he's never met. At this point, Dominique and Theo are just background noise in his head.

Maggie walks out of her office and takes a seat in the chair next to the couch. She looks over at Theo, who is now stripping off his shirt again.

"You've got a date with Mister Man tonight, don't you?" She asks, using her little nickname for Troy Langham.

Theo nods.

"Damn," Dominique says. "Front door, back door, side door, trap door…"

"Yes, it's just a revolving door, isn't it," Theo replies, reaching into his pocket and taking out a wad of money. He hands it to Maggie. "I've got to take a shower before I go over there," he tells her. "Even then I'll probably still smell like that damn woman. She was wearing an atrociously fruity perfume."

"You don't like fruity?" Dominique jests.

Theo shoots him another look as Garrett comes bounding through the door. He's got the whole golden retriever puppy look going on again.

"Can I have everyone's attention?" Garrett exclaims excitedly. "Set your DVRs for 1 P.M. next Friday because my episode is airing!" He's so wound up he has to take a breath before containing. "I just wrapped filming at the studio."

"Oh, I thought I saw your car there," Theo says nonchalantly and then disappears into the bathroom.

Garrett looks confused. "What does he mean he thought he saw my car there?"

Dominique shrugs and takes a sip. "I guess he means he was breakin off some actress. Do any of your co-stars smell atrociously fruity?"

Garrett moves Dominique's feet aside and sits down on the couch to consider this. *Kasey Franks did seem to be in an off right chipper mood after her self-mandated fifteen-minute break*, he thinks to himself.

"Hey," Dominique says, looking over at Maggie. "How come it is that Theo gets all the famous clients?"

"Because Theo has been in the business the longest and has proven himself to be extremely discreet and trustworthy," she replies simply.

"I ain't discreet?" He asks, hurt. "I ain't trustworthy?"

"You spend too much time bonding with your best friends Paul and Remy to be trusted not to get loose lips," she says, pointing with her eyes to the bottle in his hand.

"Hey, I hold my liquor well."

"Are you telling me if I gave you Halle Berry as a client you wouldn't immediately go run and tell your homies that you banged her?"

"Iono," he replies. "Are you tellin me Halle Berry a client?"

She smiles cheekily. "That's none of your business unless she's yours, and she's not."

"Man, I'm finna be pissed if I find out Theo's bangin Halle. He can't even appreciate it!"

Garrett stands back up. "Alright well I'm off then. Richard Rodriguez invited some of the new guys to the private club he owns for drinks and such."

"Drinks with Richard Rodriguez," Maggie chides sardonically. "How romantic. Maybe your off screen chemistry will result in a progressive new storyline and you can stay on longer as one of Antonio's many lovers."

"Be happy for me," Garrett tells her while grinning. "I'm a blossoming star."

"More like a blooming idiot," Dominique mumbles into his bottle.

"Jealously is a such an ugly trait, Nique," Garrett says as he walks to the door.

Dominique takes a big gulp then grimaces. "I could neva be ugly."

Garret leaves the same time Austin and AJ come out of the bathroom, dressed to the nines in their date night attire.

"Look at chu two," Dominique muses drunkenly. "All three-pieced out and shit. Y'all some fly ass white boys, I ain't even gonna stunt."

"How'd it go with Mrs. Bronstein the other night?" Maggie asks Austin as she stands. She gives her purse to AJ to hold while she pulls her coat on over her dress.

"Good," Austin replies, buttoning his blazer. "She should be callin' you. She wants to set a standing appointment for Thursday nights. That's when her husband thinks she's got book club."

"Good boy," she tells him, taking her purse back from AJ. She throws a set of keys at Dominique. "Lock up when you're done wallowing," she tells him before walking out the door.

Dominique cranes his neck over the side of the couch to look at Austin without having to get up. "So Mrs. Bronstein, that's the lady you was meetin over at the park? You fuck her on like a picnic table or somethin?"

Austin shakes his head. "No," he says, dabbing some cologne on his neck and wrist. "In the back of her Benz." He smiles over his shoulder and leaves to go meet his next client.

And then it's just Dominique and AJ.

"That's some future top forty song title shit right there," Dominique says to no one in particular. "*Back of the Benz*. Or maybe *Mrs. Bronstein's Benz*." He takes another sip, and then starts to half rap half sing. "In the back of the Benz. Me and all your friends. I fuck you while da rims spin. Let's get it in."

AJ glances over at Dominique as he adjusts his tie, smirking skeptically.

"Shut up," Dominique tells him. "You know I'm fire."

AJ faces the mirror again. "I didn't say anything."

"Yeah but you looked at me like I ain't shit."

AJ watches out of the corner of his eye as Dominique tilts the bottle upside down, damn near chugging the brandy now. He glances at his watch; he's got another thirty minutes before he has to meet his client.

"Are you alright?" AJ asks Dominique seriously, plopping down on the couch next to him.

"Man, whatchu care?"

"I wouldn't ask if I didn't care."

Dominique's features are fixed in a stern expression; the face of someone too hard to be hurt; a front. He silently studies AJ, trying to gauge a motive for his concern. Finally, he takes another sip and looks back away. "I auditioned for a record label last night," he mumbles almost inaudibly. "One of my clients hooked me up with a meeting."

"How did it go?"

"How the fuck do you think?"

AJ doesn't push or ask him anything else. After a beat Dominique swings his legs off the couch and puts the bottle down. He sits there contemplatively with his elbows on his knees and his head in his hands.

"They said my voice was nice, but all I had ta present was covers I'd done of other singers' songs. They told me I need ta put together a demo tape of my own stuff. But comin up with lyrics and all that just ain't my thing. Plus, I don't know no producers or beat makers." He looks at AJ then, staring at him with the seriousness of a self-doubter needing a believer. "I can sing, though. I can really sing."

"I believe you," AJ tells him.

"Yeah," Dominique says dryly, raising the bottle back to his lips. "I got the pipes, but was obviously only meant ta lay the pipe"

AJ feels bad that Dominique feels that way. AJ had searched for and found Dominique's YouTube channel last week. He watched every iPhone-recorded video of Dominique singing timeless covers a capella, and he was simply amazed. Not that he had ever doubted Nique could sing, but Nique could *sing*. It was refreshing in the days of banal radio R&B to hear someone with real God-given talent, and pleasantly surprising to hear such a beautiful voice coming out of somebody who puts off such a tough vibe.

"I wrote something," AJ says gingerly.

"What, like some poetry shit?" Dominique asks uninterestedly.

"Kind of." AJ gets up and retrieves his knapsack from the floor. He takes a notebook out, flips to a specific page, and lays it down on the table in front of them.

After a second Dominique looks down at it. Then starts reading it. Then picks it up in his hands as he reads even more, facial expression changing. "Damn," he says quietly. He finishes reading what's written on the page and, without putting the notebook down, turns and looks at AJ. "You sing?"

"No," AJ says quickly, shaking his head with a smile. "No, I write."

"This song heat, though," Dominique replies, looking back down at it. "What you gonna do with it?"

"I…well…you can have it if you want. If not, that's cool, too. It was just something that popped into my head one night and I tried to put it together on paper. I understand if it's not what you're looking for. I–"

"I can have this?" Dominique asks seriously, cutting off AJ's self-conscious ramblings. His eyes are hopeful.

"Yeah," AJ replies eagerly. "Yeah, you can do whatever you want with it."

"That's what's up." Dominique tears the piece of loose leaf out of the notebook, carefully folds it, and puts it in his billfold right next to his money and his condoms. "Thanks, bruh."

AJ smiles to himself; secretly ecstatic that someone genuinely liked what he wrote. "No problem." He stands, straightens his collar, and leaves to meet his date.

CHAPTER 11

The next day is Sunday. And Sundays have become AJ's favorite day.

He watches as she reaches into the little toothbrush holder where there is one blue brush, one pink, and one odd little purple brush. It's a lazy Sunday; Anjanae is wearing a pair of loose fitting silk pajama bottoms and a tank top, hair pulled back in a messy bun. It hadn't even been a day, but he couldn't stay away. Julius was still gone, so there he was, standing in the mansion's master bathroom with her. She hands him the purple toothbrush and a tube of paste. He rolls his eyes.

"Just so you know," he says as he squirts a line of blue gel onto the bristles. "I brushed my teeth before I came over. I always do. And my client last night wasn't even that kind of client," he tells her truthfully. "She just wanted a date to a diner party, no second tier folder shenanigans."

"I don't care. It puts my mind at ease." She makes a hand gesture at him. "Go on. Brush."

He gives her a look as he begrudgingly puts the toothbrush in his mouth. She smiles happily. He's wearing one of her favorite pieces of clothing, a simple crewneck waffle-knit Henley with the long sleeves rolled up slightly, exposing his forearms. It's black, coinciding with his dark hair and making him look especially handsome without intention. The pair of well-worn medium wash jeans he has on fits him well too, and she has to tear her eyes away before she loses sight of her priorities. She reaches under the sink into the cabinet and retrieves a bottle of Listerine.

"Think your husband ever wonders why there's a third toothbrush in the holder," AJ mumbles, looking in the big mirror as he brushes.

Anjanae screws the top off the bottle of Listerine and fills it with the blue iridescent liquid. "I doubt it," she says. "He probably doesn't even notice."

"Must be nice to be that oblivious," he mumbles again, mouth foaming at the corners slightly.

"Yeah," she agrees, somewhat solemnly.

AJ leans over the sink, spits and rinses. When he comes back up he puts the toothbrush back in the holder with the other two, and takes the Listerine shot from her without protest. He throws it back, swishes, then spits into the sink basin again. He rinses the sink out and then looks at her inquisitively.

"Am I good now?"

That mischievous glint returns to her eyes. "Perfect."

She grabs him by neck of his shirt and pulls him to her. He smiles against her lips as she gives him a proper kiss. When they pull apart, he exits back out into the master bedroom. He kicks his shoes off and sits down on the perfectly made bed.

"So I thought maybe we could have a movie day. Stay in and see what's on T.V. Order a pizza," he says. "That way we don't have to sneak around or get into disguise."

Anjanae walks around the bed and grabs a remote off the nightstand. "We can do that." She presses a button and a huge T.V. comes up out of the dresser across from the bed.

"Wow," AJ says, watching in amazement. "It's just like being in the theatre."

She appears to be looking for something, rooting around in one of the armoire drawers, bending down to do so. He shamelessly catches himself watching her perfectly shaped, firm derriere. She stands back up, holding two different remotes. He trains his eyes back on her face.

"There's like eighty-nine remotes that work fifty-two different things in this house." She throws the remotes at the bed. "I don't think either of those works the T.V. but you can try." She opens up another drawer, looks inside, and re-closes it. "It's like he purposefully hides them to make my life more difficult."

He watches her open a drawer that appears to be her underwear drawer. She digs deep in it and pulls out a particularly inconspicuous pair of panties. She unfolds them to reveal a little key. She smiles victoriously as she walks past him, dangling it on her finger.

"Lucky for me," she says. "I hide things, too." She walks over to the door in the corner and unlocks the conjoined room.

"That…that's his office?" AJ asks. "Like where he keeps all his…"

"Heavily classified documents, state of the art equipment, and unreleased scripts?" She finishes his thought. "Yes. Do you want to read one?"

AJ looks like he's seriously considering it, but ultimately shakes his head. "No. No, I shouldn't go in there."

"Suit yourself," she says, disappearing into the room.

AJ scoots back on the bed till he's against the pillows, getting comfortable. He picks up one of the remotes and tries it. Surprisingly, the T.V. turns right on. "Hey," he calls out to her. "I got the T.V. to work." He nonchalantly scrolls through channels. "Casablanca is on. I heard it's one of Hugh Heffner's favorites."

"Is this just a fun fact…or do you want to throw a bathrobe on, and I'll put on a blonde wig, and we'll role-play like we're at the Playboy Mansion on movie night?" She says sarcastically from the other room.

"Well we are in a mansion," he jokes. "Just not the right one." He thinks about it, and then adds. "I don't want a blonde wig. I want the fro back."

"The fro ain't comin back." She re-emerges, a fancy looking camera in her hands. She's trying to figure out how to work it as she looks through the lens.

He studies her curiously. "What's that?"

"What's it look like?" She says cheekily, pointing the camera down on him as she climbs onto the bed. She places a leg on either side of him, and places her mouth on his as she moves to straddle him.

He smiles against her lips as she kisses him. "And what." Kiss. "Are you." Kiss. "Planning." Kiss. "On doing with it?"

She sits up a little bit and smiles slyly. "Forget watching a movie. Let's make one."

AJ's mouth drops a bit in disbelief. His brain doesn't know whether to be turned on or shocked. "Are you serious?"

"Haven't you ever filmed yourself before?"

"No," he answers honestly.

She tilts her head at him. "Haven't you ever wanted to?"

He doesn't answer her question, but a smirk comes to his face and he raises an eyebrow at her. "Have you done this before? Do you let him film you?"

"No," she says, leaving out the part about how he does try to often. She lowers her head and places a kiss on his lips. "But you just make me want to try new things." She sits up and starts scooting down the bed. "And I trust you." She locks eyes with him once she's at the edge of the bed. "Do you trust me?"

His eyes are glazed over with lust now, and he shakes his head at her, more so in awe than anything else. He stares back at her intensely. "Yes."

With that admission she presses a button and a little red light comes on. "Ok," she replies lowly. "Then strip for me."

AJ sits there for a moment, and for a second she thinks he's not going to do it, but then he gets off the bed. She follows his movement with the camera. His face never falters as he slowly pulls his shirt over his head. He throws it at her and it lands on the camera, momentarily covering the lens. She laughs and removes it. He smirks, and then just as slowly unbuckles his belt. When he gets the belt loose from the loop of his jeans, he doesn't throw it. Instead, he purposefully places it on the bed and locks eyes with her. "Don't touch it."

She doesn't. Not yet, anyway. But she just might.

He undoes the buttons, then pulls down the zipper. He glances into the lens as he eases his jeans down his thighs, legs, and then off. He's left only in his grey Calvin Klein briefs. He climbs back onto the bed, inching close and closer to her until he has her cowered back against the headboard. He hovers over top of her, acting as though he's about to go in for a kiss. Her eyes droop slightly and her lips part in anticipation. He snatches the camera out of her hands. She laughs, amused but not defeated, and fights to get it back. He keeps it out of her reach while holding on to it tight. Once Anjanae realizes that she's not getting it back, she goes right into actress mode. Her brown eyes look directly into the lens as she sits up and lets her hair down, curls falling around her shoulders. Next, she reaches for the hem of her tank top. AJ knows she isn't wearing a bra, and that as soon as she lifts it off her body, her pert breasts are going to be on full display. She makes a show of it, pulling the fabric slowly up and over her head. It lands somewhere in the background, instantly forgotten. She pushes him back with her hands and gets up. From the bed he films her as she walks over to the window, gloriously naked from the waist up, and opens the blinds to let the sun in.

"I want good lighting," she says casually.

AJ mentally thanks God that the houses are a good distance away from each other in the upscale subdivision, and prays that none of her neighbors own a pair of binoculars. But then she's reaching down and undoing the drawstring to her pajama bottoms.

"Because I want you to see everything."

The silk pants fall easily to the ground, revealing a pair of black lace panties. The light catches something embellished on them—crystals maybe, or diamonds—but he doesn't have time to decipher; because then she's shimmying out of them. Now she's completely naked. He doesn't know what to think when, before joining him on the bed, she slips on a pair of black stilettos. He's mesmerized, miles past speechless, but with the precession of a professional, he still keeps the focus right on her as she struts around the bed and comes to a stop in front of him.

She's looking at him intently. "Now what are you going to do with me?"

AJ leans back. "Come here," he commands lowly.

She looks down into the camera as she climbs on top of him. Soon the last remaining article of clothing hits the floor. And then it's all shared shots of cinematographically blended skin and entwined bodies; erotically unfolding over a background track of moans, sighs and screams.

~

Later in the week, AJ is back at the office. In an hour of down time between a dinner date and a sex date, he's occupying his favorite corner of the rec room couch, reading an Anne Lamott book. He's so engrossed in it that he hasn't noticed Dominque has sat down next to him.

"Aye," Dominique says, attempting to get his attention.

"Huh," AJ says, looking up mildly startled. "What happened?"

"Nothin…." Dominique starts, looking down at his hands then. "I just keep thinkin bout how dope that song you wrote was. I need ta get my demo tape together. And I was just wonderin…shit I was wonderin if you wanna work on it with me." He looks up with a dimpled-grin. "You write, I sing."

"You want me to write your songs? AJ asks, a little disbelieving.

"Co-write. But yeah. Maybe like eleven or twelve joints. Nothin major. And I'd give you credit for writing them. You know, like if I was to blow up off this tape or one of the songs got some play, you'd be compensated for ya publishing rights and everything."

"You know I've never written songs before, right? That was just a one-time thing…"

"It ain't gotta be a one-time thang, though. You ill. Ya pen game crazy." He looks at AJ imploringly. "So what chu say? Will you work on my project with me?"

AJ thinks about it. He did come to LA to write, screen write, granted, but he hadn't been doing much writing of any kind since he moved. And he did truly enjoy writing that one song. It had reignited a passion within him that had briefly gotten displaced since meeting Maggie. Until he could write what he wanted to write, he might as well make use of his talent. And he believed in Dominique and his dream.

"Yeah."

"Word?"

"Yeah," AJ nods with a smile. "Yeah, I'll work on your project with you."

"Cool," Dominique says, sitting back with a pleased grin. His thinking face comes on. "Now all we gotta do is find somewhere ta record. Someone ta produce the shit. Cause I don't wanna sing over no weak ass beat I found on the Internet. I want one of them heavy trap beats. I want the drums ta hit and the bass to bump and for one them lil engineers to press a bunch of buttons and synthesize my voice so it sounds real trill and shit. I want legit production." He looks over at AJ. "Whatchu think?"

"Do you really want my opinion?" AJ asks him with caution in his voice.

"Hell yeah, you my partner now. Give it to me straight."

"You don't need auto tune," AJ tells him. "Or a trap beat or to say pussy eighty-nine times like they do in most mainstream R&B songs. Those are ploys that people who can kind of sing use to grab attention. You can really sing. You don't have to rap the chorus or talk about money and cars on the bridge. Because I believe you can sit down and sing a real song. Something raw without all the other stuff getting in the way."

"So what you want me to do, sing over a piano and some strings and shit?" Dominique asks him facetiously. "Well that's fine and dandy, but who's gone play the piano and the harp and whatever other raw celestial instruments you got in mind?"

"I don't know about a harp, but I used to play piano."

Dominique is taken by surprise. "Swear?"

"My mom enrolled me in lessons when I was little. I played all throughout grade school; recitals, talent shows. I mean it's been over a decade since I've touched a piano, but I'm sure if I sat down at one some of it would come back to me. I also played the saxophone from sixth till twelfth grade in the school band. So if you wanted a "Turn The Page" or "Baker Street" kind of opening to a song, I could totally do that."

"Are them names of songs I'm spose to know, or…"

AJ thinks for a second. "And for a short time in middle school I played the guitar. My best friend at the time was obsessed with becoming a rock star so I taught myself how to play so he wouldn't have to be a one-man band. I wasn't super good at it or anything, but I could hit a few chords."

"Well, ain't you a jack of all trades," Dominique kids. "Okay then, AJ. Find you some instruments ta play and let's do the damn thang."

So AJ goes on the hunt for musical instruments. His Monday night regular, Mrs. Kelly, has three grand pianos in her Beverly Hills mansion. He knows they're for decoration and not for actual playing—he's sure the most action any of them get is when the maid flutters over them with her duster. They are all immaculate: the one in the parlor room, the one in the front room, and the one on the third-floor landing. After a late-night romp that had lapsed into Tuesday (during which she came three times and had two lines of coke and half a bottle of Cabernet) he casually dropped that he was a former pianist, and said that her Yamaha downstairs was perhaps the most pristine piano he had ever seen. She propped herself up on the pillow to look at him, the wrinkles under her eyes never matching the wild look in her eyes, and told him he should have it then. After all, she'd said, what use was it to her? She had two others anyway.

His thoughts exactly.

He told her that was very gracious, but that he couldn't take it from her.

She said nonsense; she'd have it sent over the next day.

And the next day a whole herd of movers heaved the glossy black Yamaha up four flights of stairs to his studio apartment. Jae poked his head in the door when he heard the commotion, saw what had been delivered, and shook his head. It took up a good chunk of the little room and would probably be considered an eyesore to those who couldn't appreciate its beauty. But AJ loved it, loved the flare of unconventionality it gave the little square he lived in. Over the next few

days he re-acquainted himself with the piano, re-teaching himself
how to play. He loved how the keys felt under his fingers. He loved how
the wordless melodies sounded in his ears. It gave him all kinds of ideas
for songs. Three days after it had been delivered, Anjanae came over.
She took one look at it and got a wily smile on her face.

He loved christening it.

Following the addition of the piano, he found a used Fender
guitar on eBay for a decent price, and visited a local music store where
he bought a brand new saxophone. Dominique came to his apartment
and they dabbled with some different sounds and songs, recording their
sessions with AJ's phone. But they both knew they needed a real studio
to record in to get it to sound how it needed to sound. They needed a real
producer to put all the collective parts together succinctly.

AJ found out about Turner Tevenot through one of his clients,
who just so happened to be Turner's mother. AJ had been "servicing"
Tracy semi-regularly since his second week on the job, and in passing
one night she mentioned to him that her son was an aspiring music
producer. This immediately piqued AJ's interest. AJ pillow-talked to her
about his friend who was an aspiring singer, and how that together they
had written some songs, and were currently looking to compose a mix
CD. She eagerly gave him her son's information and the link to his page.

It turned out that Turner had never actually produced anything,
but he did own every piece of top-notch equipment available, and kept it
all in an eight hundred-thousand-dollar recording studio bought and
furnished for him by his father after he'd woke up one morning and
announced that he wanted to be the next Scott Storch. It wasn't much
but it was the best option they had, so he and Dominique decided to
reach out to Turner anyway and see what assistance he could lend.

The first time AJ meets Turner he has to push back the thought
of a pink, ever so slightly discolored cesarean scar that he's ran his
tongue over on more than one occasion. Dominique stands next to him
on the doorstep of the studio with his hands in his pockets and a smirk
on his face, because he knows how AJ found Turner.

"Yo," Turner says with a grin when he opens the door to his
private Brentwood recording workshop. The little building that's built
into a hill is about two miles down the road from the mansion where his
mother is often left alone to her own devices while his father works and
while he, presumably, is hanging out here all day doing nothing.
"Dominique and AJ?"

"That's us," AJ says, cordially returning the smile. "Turner Tevenot, right?"

The young accolade-less producer outstretches his arms proudly, "The one and only."

Turner is tall, tan, and in shape. His shaggy blonde hair and orange skin give him a beachy look. His teeth are perfect when he smiles, probably veneers. He wears a purple t-shirt with the word Supreme printed ostentatiously all over it. His jeans are distressed and torn just enough to be trendy and the back pockets have a tacky set of wings across them. He's got a pair of Gucci flip-flops on that don't really match anything else, and a big gold watch covered in glittery diamonds. Before coming to LA, AJ didn't know any straight men who wore sparkly jewelry. AJ's assuming Turner is straight, anyway. At least that's what the blown-up picture of the half-naked Playmate hanging on the wall as soon as you walk in suggests.

"So," Turner says, leading them through the vestibule where there's a bathroom on one end, a kitchen on the other, and a lounge area with leather furniture in the middle. "You guys heard some of my beats on SoundClick and had to come see how I do what I do for yourself, huh?"

"Yeah," AJ says, not daring to look at Dominique. "Yeah, I heard a couple of your tracks on SoundClick and I told Nique that…well that we really ought to check you out for…for the demo tape we're trying to do."

"You two like a dynamic duo or something?" Turner asks, pointing between them. "Kinda like Macklemore and Ryan Lewis?"

"Nah," Dominique deadpans. "Not at all. Not even a little bit."

"I was just saying that cause–"

"Do I look like a corny ass white dude who's bout ta struggle rap bout some swap meets and tricycles?" Dominique asks him sternly, cutting him off midsentence. "I'm here to sing some real shit, you feel me? Not none of that weak shit. And AJ, I know he looks white on the outside, but he writes that heartfelt funky Motown fire. So if we're gonna work together Imma need you not ta patronize us like that ever again, you feel me?"

"No, I feel you, man, I feel you. My bad. For real. Didn't mean no disrespect."

"Um," AJ utters, wanting to diffuse the tension. "How about you show us around?"

"Sure. Of course. Right on." He leads them down two steps into the wood paneled studio. He has all of the equipment: the switchboard-looking thing, the keyboard-looking thing, monitors, mixing console, MacBook Pro, amplifiers, and everything else. There's cords plugged into cords plugged into walls. There are three different flat screen T.V.s mounted around the room. One has ESPN on mute, one has music videos running, and the last looks to have a pornography playing on it. On the other side of the room is the glass enclosed, soundproof booth, speakers coming out of the celling and a microphone standing up in the center.

"Got damn," Dominique mutters, looking around in awe. "This shit legit."

"Hell yeah, man," Turner replies, cheesing from ear-to-ear.

Aside from the T.V.s, posters hang on the walls in a rather juvenile fashion. Some professionally framed, some not. Marilyn Monroe, Scarface, Lil Wayne, Gucci Mane, and a blown-up picture of the cover to Future's *Dirty Sprite 2* album

"You know you in Southern California, right?" Dominique asks him rhetorically. "Where's the Pac posters at? The Eazy? The Korrupt? Snoop, Cube, Quik. I mean shit."

"Oh I like them dudes, too. Ice Cube is funny as hell in them movies with Kev–" He stops talking when he sees how Dominique is looking at him. "You guys want a drink or something? Here, sit down." He pulls out two plush swivel chairs and they sit. "I'll go get you all something." He disappears into the kitchen.

"Dude wack as fuck, I can already tell," Dominique says under his breath as he runs his hands over the buttons and knobs of the equipment in front of him. "I don't care if we do get a bargain cause you're breakin his moms off, I ain't finna let him fuck up my sound."

"Give it a chance," AJ tells him, and then adds in an extra-hushed tone. "And don't say anything about his mom while we're in here."

"I ain't," Dominique assures him.

Turner comes back with a silver tray of glasses filled with translucent burgundy liquid. "Ciroc and cranberry," he says with a smile, like he thinks he impresses somebody, sitting the tray down in front of them.

Dominique looks at him like he's stupid. "I only drink the brown."

"Oh. Well I got some Fireball in the fridge," Trevor offers.

"He'll be fine," AJ quickly interjects before Dominique can fire back at the poor guy again.

"Ok, cool," Tanner replies, sitting back and taking a sip of his beverage. "So are you two Cali natives, too? Or where are you all originally from?"

"Memphis," AJ replies.

Turner nods, not seeming impressed.

"Watts," Dominique says.

"Righteous," Turner replies, face lighting up. "You ever been shot?"

Dominique glances over at AJ with a smirk, like *can you believe this guy*, then looks back to Turner. "Ionno," he says with a little bit of menace in his voice. "You ever been shot?"

Turner looks down, face turning red. "Nah."

AJ takes notice in the school keychain loop lying discarded on the table. It's got a Mercedes fobble and key on it, but that's not what gets his attention. "You go to USC?" He asks Turner.

"Yeah, graduated last spring. I only went cause my mom wanted me to. School was never really my thing. Too much pointless work." He takes a drink of his diluted vodka and grimaces. "I would've rather gone to a party school, somewhere in like…I don't know…Panama City or South Beach." He thinks about it and nods with a stupid grin. "Yeah, that would have been lit. But you see my dad donates a lot of money to USC every year. Early acceptance was like a sure thing, so I thought…fuck it, why not? Wasn't doing anything else. Could still live at home."

AJ gets an odd pang in the pit of his stomach that he's not accustomed to. Jealousy. He can't help but to be jealous of Turner's educational resume. USC was AJ's dream school. It made it worse that Turner didn't even seem to appreciate the lauded establishment that he was literally handed the keys to without any effort given or resistance met. Not even the faintest worry of tuition or loans.

"Did my time, got a little anthropology degree," Turner continues nonchalantly. "Minored in some kind of business…I don't remember exactly what it was called. But at the end of the day your boy had to follow his dreams. Degrees don't give you happiness. Plus, I got too much talent to work a regular job. These hands were meant to make bangers."

He holds up his manicured hands as if to prove his point.

"Well how 'bout you throw one them bangers on," Dominique jests. "And we'll see if it's really all that."

Surprisingly it was.

Turner has a very attuned ear for what sounds right. And while he certainly could make those heavy trap beats that would blow your speakers out, he could also sew more low-key songs with his fancy equipment, the solemn and the sweet. Plus, he took direction well. If AJ explained to him the tone he wanted to set, Turner would set it. The three of them spent five hours together that afternoon, and many more hours over the days and weeks that followed.

Dominique warms up to Turner after a few visits, even giving him the nickname TT (for Turn Table Turner, even though that was technically three T's; two sounded better). Sometimes Dominique brings a big bag of weed to the studio. He buys it from one of his old buddies back in Watts and calls the thick green herb "OG Cali Kush." Turner got boyishly excited the first time Dominique showed up with some. AJ would patiently wait for the two of them to empty out and re-stuff a Swisher, and once they had both lit their respective blunts, they'd all get to work on the music. They always offer him some, but he always politely declines. AJ can count the number of times he's smoked marijuana on one hand without using all five fingers. He doesn't particularly enjoy not feeling like himself, preferring to think clearly and not through a filter. Since being out of college he seldom ever drinks, other than the occasional beer at home or glass of champagne at dinner, but never to the point of getting drunk. And he rarely takes an Advil for a headache, let alone anything stronger. So he sipped his water, pen in hand scribbling down new lyrics to the mood of the sample beats being played, occasionally picking up the sax or guitar if an instrumental layer was needed. Turner huffed, puffed, and choked with vigor on the strong weed he inhaled, pushing buttons and turning knobs with knowledge. Dominique blew smoke through his lips with expertise, until he set the blunt down, went in the booth, and blew them all away. Somehow all the smoking didn't affect Nique's voice, though he would lay off it on the days he really had to make the runs and hit the high notes. The three of them had enough creative chemistry to be a dream team, and while AJ didn't like to voice it for fear of spoiling it, he was pretty sure they were in the process of making something pretty special. Something that would make Dominique a star.

There is one person AJ talks about it to. Anjanae shares in his excitement. He plays her some snippets of a few unfinished songs, lets her read some of the words he writes, and delights in the smile they bring to her face. They had been growing closer. Sometimes it feels like she's really his and he's really hers, and that the world is theirs and that life is not as complicated as it seems. Sometimes it all seems so normal.

Like the night he and her double date with Jae and his crush.

Jae had cornered AJ in the hall the week before and begged him to be his wingman and to bring Anjanae along. Jae didn't have much experience dating, especially under his father's roof and his father's rules. And dating a non-Korean woman was damn near damning to Jae's father. But now that he had moved out, he could ask out the blue-eyed, blonde haired girl he had been a lab partner with in college and actively fawning over for four years. AJ had never seen Jae so nervous, and Jae was a naturally nervous person, so of course he agreed to assist.

Jae prepares a four-course meal in his apartment. AJ and Anjanae arrive a half hour early to help him set up. Anjanae brings an expensive bottle of Bordeaux that Jae questions her about, but AJ distracts him, fixing his collar, dabbing him with some cologne, and sticking a breath mint in his mouth despite Jae's protest that it will ruin the flavor of the meal. AJ tells him he has tasted his own food before and it doesn't matter. When the doorbell rings and Jae gets a panicked look on his face, AJ gives him a reassuring nod.

Mackenzie seems like a very sweet girl and AJ can tell Jae really likes her. It's all a little awkward at first, but because of his and Anjanae's easy back and forth banter, the other couple loosens up as well. And soon, over bacon wrapped filet mignon, grilled asparagus, and suspiciously expensive wine, they all fall into comfortable conversation with each other. When Mackenzie asks how he and Anjanae met, they recount their gas station story with secretive smiles meant only for the other on their faces. After Crème Brule for desert, they all retire to the living area half a foot away to play charades. Boys against girls.

"Ok, he's a rock icon," Anjanae says when it's her turn. She stands in front of them with her card. "He's got the moves…"

"Oh! Oh!" Mackenzie says excitedly, the name right on the tip of her tongue.

Anjanae gives her one more hint. "He can't get no–"

"Satisfaction! Mick Jagger!"

"Yes!"

Anjanae throws her card up in the air victoriously and prances back to the sidelines, high-fiving Mackenzie before plopping back down on the floor next to AJ.

"We're *killin* y'all," she says to him, cockily.

He laughs at her enthusiasm and kisses her on the cheek. "Just wait and watch," he tells her, and then looks to his partner. "Get up there, Jae."

Jae jumps up and takes center stage. AJ can tell by the way Mackenzie looks at Jae when he isn't looking that she really likes him, too. He's happy for Jae. And in that moment, sitting next to the girl he's crazy about, playing a silly game with friends, he's happy for himself.

"A famous singer," Jae says, looking down at his card. "Dead."

"That really narrows it down," he replies sarcastically.

"Really famous. Really dead," Jae reiterates, then looks at AJ and says mysteriously, "Or is he?"

"What?" Then he looks at the girls. "What is that supposed to mean?" He looks back at Jae and raises an eyebrow. "Tupac?"

"Tupac is a rapper, not a singer, AJ," Jae corrects, perturbed. "I said singer!"

"Well excuse me."

The girls start to giggle.

"He's got moves, too. Famous moves." Jae then tries to emulate said moves, gyrating his hips in a circle.

AJ covers his face with his hands. "Stop. Just stop."

Anjanae and Mackenzie have both fallen over and are in tears, laughing so hard they are snorting. But Jae cannot be deterred.

"There's a homestead in homage to him. Very touristy. Something…land."

"Disneyland?" AJ guesses. "Walt Disney?"

"Does Walt Disney freakin sing, AJ?" Jae chastises. "Jesus."

"I don't know," he replies innocently. "His movies were very musical."

"For God's sake, Andrew," Anjanae says, her teasing smile shimmering. "He's from the same city you are."

"You know who the hell he's talking about?"

"Two seconds!" Mackenzie says, holding up the stopwatch.

"Peanut butter and banana sandwiches he died on the commode," Jae rattles off quickly without pause.

AJ stutters, stammering, until the buzzer goes off.

"Time!" Mackenzie calls.

"Elvis Presley, fool!" Jae yells at him.

"Oh. Yeah. I probably should have known that."

They all start laughing again; Anjanae leans over and kisses him just to the left of his lips. Jae flops down on the couch next to Mackenzie with a defeated sigh. She scoots closer to him and Jae suddenly doesn't look so sad about losing anymore. After a while they start to look pretty cozy, and Anjanae and him decide to give them their space.

Once across the hall in his own apartment, reality slowly creeps back in. He closes the door behind them, Anjanae slips off her heels and he kicks off his shoes. Ritualistic settling. Like they are both home and that this is their house.

"Mackenzie seems like a really nice girl," she comments to him, moving towards the kitchenette.

"She did," he agrees, pulling his shirt loose from his pants and plopping down on the couch. "And Jae would appreciate your approval. He really likes you."

"I like Jae." She opens the fridge and pours herself and him a drink. "He's a little different," she adds with a smile. "But in a good way."

AJ laughs. "He's a mess. A very controlled mess. But I wouldn't want anyone else as a neighbor or best friend." He flashes her a good-natured grin. "And his approval of you means the utmost to me."

"Do you think he would like your girlfriend?"

The question comes out of the blue and leaves AJ thrown. She hands him his drink and retires to her chair on the other side of the little room.

"My what?" He stammers.

"Your girlfriend," she replies casually, relaxing into the chair and pulling her legs up. She doesn't sound nor seem mad, just curious. "From back home."

He still doesn't know what to say or what to make of her unexpected knowledge. Was he stupid to assume she wouldn't know? She wasn't stupid.

"You had her picture in a frame sitting on your bedside table the first time you brought me to your apartment," she answers his unasked question. "The next time I was here it was gone." She takes a sip of her drink. "Well," she adds. "It's not gone. It's turned face down behind your alarm clock."

"Anjie…"

"She's cute. I think it's the freckles that do it." She can tell that he's about to offer her an apology, but she doesn't want to want one, so she looks him in his eyes. "I'm not mad, Andrew. I mean…I'm married. I have a husband at home. You have a girlfriend in a different state. Neither seems to pose much relevance to our relationship." She shrugs. "It is what it is."

AJ looks down at his drink, swishes the liquid around in the glass, and then takes a sip. He wants to tell her a lot of things, to explain to her the things he only just recently learned himself. He wants to tell her the truth. How he secretly thinks of *her* as his girlfriend. How he needs and plans to formally break up with Grace, but being that he's been in a whirlwind ever since arriving to LA, he hasn't had a chance to end it the right way. He wants to do it right. He wants to do it all right. And he wants to tell Anjanae everything there is to know about how he feels. But instead, he decides to just answer her question.

"I don't know if Jae would like her," he tells her honestly. "She's kind of…being raised in the South and being mildly sheltered…I don't want to say…"

"Prejudice?"

"I'd go with *uninformed.*"

She smiles and takes a drink. "No, I don't think Jae would like her. He'd sniff that out pretty quick."

"Yeah," AJ says to himself.

"I'm assuming she thinks you're out here pumping gas…"

"She thinks I'm waitressing."

Anjanae gives him a look.

"Waitering. Waiting tables. Whatever. It's what I did back home and it's what she thinks I'm doing here as I wait for my *agent*, Maggie Hunter, to break me into the wonderful world of screenwriting."

She nods her head to herself. "Well." Takes a sip. "You certainly know how to compose a good story. I'd cut you a deal."

A beat passes where neither of them will say anything or look at the other.

"Why didn't you tell me you knew?" He breaks the silence quietly.

"Why didn't you tell me?"

He looks conflicted and goes to open his mouth but the words don't come out.

"Never mind," she says. She puts her drink down and stands. "It's not important." She slowly walks over to him.

He watches her with all the adoration and lust in the world as she lowers herself onto his lap, straddling him.

"And truthfully, I don't care," she adds.

They stare into each other's eyes, conveying all the lies and truths between them, until she breaks the spell and lowers her mouth to his.

An hour or so later she's quietly trying to dress while he sleeps. But he hears the familiar rustle of clothing going back over skin, and it awakes him from the short-lived slumber he had allowed himself to slip into. He opens his eyes to see her shadowy figure stumbling in the dark searching for her shoes.

"Stay," he says quietly.

She starts, but then goes back to looking for her shoes. "It's after midnight," she tells him in tone that's removed. "I need to get home."

Reality resets within him. He flips on the lamp by the bed for her. She finds her shoes, puts them on, and tucks her blouse neatly back into her pants. He watches as she crosses the little apartment and grabs her purse off the counter where she left it. Anjanae pauses at the door. She thinks about it, and then turns back for the bed. AJ looks up at her and she gives him a quick kiss that feels a lot like either an *I'm sorry*, or an *I forgive you* for the apology he didn't get to give.

"Goodnight," she tells him.

And then she leaves.

Some nights she doesn't leave, though. A couple weeks later she spends the night, as she has a few times by now. Julius is out of town again so she doesn't have a curfew and doesn't have to be back. AJ offered to come to her, but she wanted to come to him. He's beginning to think his simple studio is growing on her. Some nights it's not about sex at all. Some nights it's just about being in the private bubble they've created, where all their mutual denials and dreams of who they are and who they want to be seal them off from the world. This particular night they lay clothed together under his sheets; her back pressed against him, his arm around her midsection. She's wearing one of his University of Memphis t-shirts as a sleep shirt, and her hair is wrapped up in a scarf that she now keeps in his nightstand drawer. They had dozed off in this position over two hours ago, and he is in such a deep, tranquil sleep that it takes him quite some time to register that his phone is buzzing on the nightstand. He sits up and rubs his eyes. He sees Anjanae still asleep next to him, smiles, and then gingerly reaches over her to grab his phone. He didn't plan on answering it, he only wanted to stop its incessant noise, but when he sees whose number it is flashing across the screen, his conscience won't let him ignore it.

"Mom?" He says quietly, confused.

"Hey, baby!" His hears his mother says cheerfully.

He glances over at the bedside clock that reads 1:12 a.m. "It's one o'clock in the morning," he says softly into the phone. "Which means it's four o'clock in the morning there. What are you doing up?"

"Oh, I couldn't sleep," she says. "Up frettin' over you."

He laughs lightly. "Why are you frettin' over me?"

Anjanae stirs and then rolls over, eying him sleepily as she lies on her side.

His mom takes a deep breath on the other line. "I just get the feelin' that there's somethin you're not tellin' me. Cause you don't want me to worry."

"Like what?" AJ asks her.

"Like you're poor. Like you're out on the streets. Like you're drowning under the pressure while tryin to cling to a dream. Baby, I don't want you to be a starving artist."

"Mom," he says in a firm voice. "I have a job. I'm not just out here hopin' and dreamin' and clingin'."

Anjanae smiles. He rolls his eyes and shakes his head.

"I know, honey," his mom says. "But being a waiter out there isn't like being a waiter here at home. You can't shelter me. I'm aware that the cost of living in California is way higher than the average and that making ends meet is a constant struggle. I don't want you strugglin', Andrew." She takes a breath, continuing in a more serious tone. "Now listen, I would rather just have you come on home, but if you need money–"

"Mom," he says firmly again. "I don't need money. I'm fine."

"You promise you're not lyin to me?"

"I promise that I'm fine in the money department." He quickly changes the topic, because while that part wasn't a lie, he is withholding quite a bit of the truth. "Now, why don't you make yourself a nice hot cup of tea and take your frettin' self back to bed."

"Ain't no sense," she says with a sigh. "I'll no sooner get back in bed before your daddy's alarm will be goin off. He's just in there a sleepin' like a log. Ain't the least bit concerned that his son could be lyin out on a street corner shrivellin' up in the cracks like an un-watered sassafras."

Anjanae can hear her through the phone and has to bury her head in the pillow to stifle her laughter.

"Mom," AJ says, trying not to laugh, too. "For the last time. I'm watered. I'm fed. I'm fine. Now, is there anything else you want to talk about? Is everything ok at home?"

"Yes," she replies. "I just miss you."

"I miss you, too."

"I love you."

"I love you, too."

After a beat he hears his mom sigh. "Alright, well, I'll let you get back to sleep I guess." She pauses, and then adds definitively. "Goodnight, AJ."

"Goodnight, Mom." He hangs up and looks down at Anjanae. She's staring up at him with a big grin on her face

"Somebody's a momma's boy."

He lies back down, pulling her snug back into his arms. "I'm an only child. It's always been just her and me. She doesn't know how to deal."

"And your dad?" She murmurs against his chest where she rests her head.

"What?"

"You said it's always been just you and her…."

He's quiet for a moment. She idly runs her fingertips along his arm.

"He runs a dealership. Gone a lot. Business trips. You know, that kind of thing. My mom was a nurse for ten years, but when she had me she decided to be a stay at home mom. That's where he wanted her anyway—at home, I mean. Even though that's rarely where he was."

AJ's staring at the ceiling and Anjanae is staring at him. She studies him thoughtfully, then looks back down and treads cautiously.

"How does he feel about you leaving to live here?" She asks.

"We never really saw eye to eye. He had a spot saved for me at the dealership. I didn't take it. Therefore he takes me for some ungrateful son." He swallows, she watches his Adam's apple move with anguish up his throat and then back down. "So I'm sure he doesn't care about my wellbeing, whereabouts, and ways of making ends meet. He doesn't understand."

The *me* was silent, but she knows that's what he meant. She continues to stroke his skin with her feather light touch, allowing the silence to envelope them. A beat or two passes, and then he's turning on his side to face her.

"What about you?" Head propped up on his hand, chaotic curls falling into sleepy eyes. "What about your family?"

He can feel her tense against him. He thinks briefly that he shouldn't have asked, that the walls are on their way back up and the moment is over.

But then she surprises him.

"I've got a father who I can count the number of times I've seen on one hand," she tells him. "A half-brother and a half-sister that I barely know. I lived with my mother." She's face-to-face with him, but not looking.

AJ wants to take this easy; it's a rarity that she opens up to him in this way. Most of the things he's learned about her are limited to stray observations. That's not to say he's without knowledge; he's spent a fair amount of time observing her and could spend many hours more. Having her willingly share is an added bonus.

"Are you close with her?" He asks.

It's as though she has to think about it. "She worked three jobs most of my childhood to put food on the table. She doesn't work any of them anymore." She hesitates before continuing, it's the unspoken words between sentences that fill in the cold blanks. "We were close..." She's says after a while. AJ catches the past tense. "To some extent anyway...because we had to be. We were all that we had. We had to fend for ourselves, make a way." She smiles wryly then. "She was always entering me in these beauty pageants when I was kid. I won Little Miss Memphis twice, was top ten in the Tennessee trials, made the Southern Belle Annual annually. I *hated* it. But I did it for her because she did for me. I think she thought...." Anjanae's voice falls off insecurely. There's little smile of sadness and half a headshake. "I don't know what she thought."

AJ knows that to ask more now would be pushing her too far. He toys with the baby curls of hair at the nape of her neck. "You were Little Miss Memphis?"

She smiles proudly. "Circa 1994."

"Wow," he says idly. "I feel honored to have such a prominent presence in my apartment."

She swats at him and he laughs. They both laugh. And when it's quiet again, he asks her one more question that to him seems not too intrusive.

"Does she still live in Memphis?"

"Yes, but she's in the suburbs now." The lightness from the second before is gone. She swallows. "I send her a check once a month and hear from her about once a year. So I guess, to answer your question, no, we're not really close. Not anymore. We don't have to be."

The pain she wants to mask is present, in her voice, on her face. It pains him. After a beat he pulls her in close to him and kisses the top of her head. Their hands stroke and soothe each other until they fall back asleep a few minutes later. Her head is on his chest, her arms around him and his around her. They stay that way the entire night. And don't wake again until the room is bright with sun.

CHAPTER 13

Anjanae wakes up feeling refreshed, as she does most mornings that she wakes up in his arms. Julius' plane is scheduled to land at ten-thirty and AJ will be going to work later, but she can't bring herself to be bothered with all the inferior stuff. Not this second. Not while he's making her coffee with the little red Keurig he bought online upon her prompting, and then frying bacon and eggs in the little kitchenette, and then returning to the bed to have breakfast with her. Not while she's reveling in this feeling. He makes her *feel*. This feeling that she can't condense down to a word. This feeling that she has never felt before. But she feels good. Better than she's ever felt. She leaves his studio with a smile-laced kiss to his lips, and then skips down the four flights of stairs until she's in the restaurant. R&W isn't open for breakfast, but the cooks are already there getting ready for the lunch rush that will ensue in a couple of hours. Jae is in the dining room taking all the chairs off the tables. She swats him on the butt with her car keys as she passes by on her way to the door. He jumps and turns around to see who did it.

"Good morning, Sunray," she chides cheerfully.

"Real cute," Jae replies with an eye roll. "Get outta here with your bed-head."

Anjanae opens her mouth in an offended fashion. "I do not have bed-head."

"Mmhm."

"Whatever. You wished you looked this good in the morning."

"But I do," Jae says with a sassy smile.

She opens the glass door. "Next time have a low fat double pump latte waiting on me when I come down, ok?"

"This ain't Starbucks, boo-boo," he calls after her.

She laughs as she leaves. He shakes his head with a chuckle and goes back to removing chairs from tables.

Back upstairs, AJ takes a shower and gets dressed for the day. He's reveling in the same feeling Anjanae is and the smile plastered on his face feels permanent. So when he walks out of the bathroom and sees

Grace's name flashing across his vibrating phone that lies discarded on the floor, he's hesitant to answer. He hasn't talked to her in over a week outside of a few bland back and forth text messages. It was probably starting to look suspicious. He should come clean. Not about everything, of course, just the fact that he didn't think they should be together anymore. Hell, Grace was probably thinking the same thing. They had barely been communicating. She surely wasn't happy and this surely wasn't what she wanted. She was probably calling to have this exact talk with him. He convinces himself to answer.

"Hey," he says, trying not to give himself away.

"Hey," she replies in a voice louder than her norm. "I almost didn't think you was going to pick up."

He can hear a lot of noise in the background; the undecipherable sounds people talking and beeps and buzzes, what sounds like an automated intercom.

"Where are you?" He asks.

"Guess," she says, her unusually loud voice now tinged with restrained excitement that's bursting at the seams.

"I don't know," he replies back warily.

And then that thing in the background that sounded like an intercom? Well it's talking again, and this time he makes out the tail end of what it says. *Departing from gate thirteen at ten forty-five.*

The smile that felt permanent is long gone. His heart loges in his throat.

"Grace…"

"I'll give you a clue. I just got off a plane."

"You're…you just got *off* a plane? You're already here?"

"Yes! I'm in LAX right now as we speak! Are you just so surprised?"

"*So* surprised."

"I had a long weekend and thought I'd come see my man. Your birthday is this week, I figured this would be my present to you."

"So…uh…um…just how long do I have my present for?"

"Unfortunately only two days. I've gotta be back at work Monday night." He hears her heave a sigh. "I'm trying to get to baggage claim but this airport is so friggin big and busy. Once I get my stuff I'll catch a cab and be on my way to you."

"No!" The word rushes out and he quickly has to adjust is voice. "No, don't take a cab. They're dirty and that's extra money you don't need to spend. I'll come get you. It won't take me very long at all to get there."

He needed to buy himself time.

"Are you sure?"

"Yeah. I'm leaving right now. I'll be there in like thirty minutes."

"Ok, babe. I'll be standing outside the Southwest pick-up area. See you soon. Can't wait."

He hangs up and runs his hands over his face and then through his hair. They were not on the same page. They were not on the same page at all. But they were, actively at this moment, in the same state. In the same city.

Fuck, he thinks.

He quickly springs into action, pulling a flannel on over his undershirt and slipping shoes onto his feet. He fishes the framed picture of him and her from the back of his bedside drawer where he shoved it a couple of weeks ago. He resurrects it front and center on the desk and then opens his closet and grabs an armload of designer clothes and dress shoes. He doesn't have a clue what he's going to do with them—as he nimbly scoops his car keys off the counter with one free finger—but they certainly can't be hanging in his closet for Grace to see and question. He steps out into the hallway and shuts his door with his foot. Jae is just coming up the stairs.

"Hey, AJ," Jae says with a smile. "Forgot my phone. I'm meeting Mackenzie for lunch and I told her to pick where. Can't miss that text. Practically had to beg my father for an hour off so I could spend some time with my lady. *Real men do not take lunch breaks, Jae-sun. Lunch breaks are creation of lazy American.* Like, are American men not real men? I'm a man. I was technically born in America. And I damn sho ain't lazy."

AJ is only hearing every fifth word that's being said to him. He can feel a cold sweat breaking out at the back of his neck as he mentally composes two days worth of lies and alibis. He notices that Jae has stopped talking and is looking at him quizzically with his head cocked to one side.

"What's with all the suits and fancy clothes?"

"Listen, Jae, look, I'm real sorry about this, but I really need your help. My girlfriend just landed at the airport. I'm on my way to pick her up. And when I get back, I need for you to pretend that I work here. Just act like I'm a waiter and agree with whatever I say. Okay?"

Jae's expression is blank. "I thought Anjanae was your girlfriend...."

"Yeah. Well. She's...it's complicated, I–"

"I thought you worked at a gas station in Hollywood..."

"I'll explain later. I promise. Just do me this favor and follow my lead. Please. I'll tell you everything. I will. But I have to go right now. Do you have my back?"

For a second AJ thinks that he's going to say no. AJ wouldn't blame him. He hates that he has to ask Jae to lie for him. He hates that he's lied to Jae.

"Yeah," Jae consents skeptically after a beat. "I got your back."

"Great," AJ replies, relieved. He holds out his fancy clothes to Jae and dumps them in his arms. "Can you stash these in your apartment for a couple of days? Thank you so much, seriously."

He doesn't wait for a reply and rushes off down the stairs, leaving Jae standing there highly confused and speechless with an armful of name brand clothes that he knows his friend should not be able to afford.

AJ calls Maggie from his car as he speeds down the freeway.

"Yes, dear?" She answers.

"Hey," he says unsurely, tentatively. "I'm not going to be able to work tonight. I know it's our busy night and I know I didn't give appropriate notice but in my defense I didn't get appropriate notice and I know that's no excuse to miss wok I really am sorry for the inconvenience. It's my girlfriend." He catches his breath. "She's here for the weekend."

"Your girlfriend," Maggie finally says, faking intrigue with her voice but not necessarily sounding mad. "I wasn't aware you had one."

"Well, I do," he replies, unenthused. "Can you get someone to take my client tonight? She's only going to be here for two days."

Maggie sighs. "I suppose." And then she adds seriously, "Can you be sure she gets back on the plane no later than Monday?"

"Yes. I promise. She'll be gone Monday. Thank you. I appreciate it. Talk to you later." He curses under his breath as he hangs up. He's hit traffic now. His speedometer reads lower than ten miles per hour and he's got at least another five miles before his exit. He picks up his phone again and calls Anjanae. He hates that he has to do this. It rings three times.

"Miss me already?" She answers in a cheeky voice.

A sharp pang runs through his chest. "Anjie, I…uh, I know we had a picnic planned in Topanga park tomorrow but…but something's come up."

There's a pause. He can practically hear her drawing her conclusion.

"You have to work." It's not a question. It's a dry, simple statement. And he honestly doesn't know whether or not what he's about to tell her is going to displease her more than her assumption does.

"No. No, I don't have to work. Grace is in town. I swear I didn't know she was coming she just called and said she was at the airport and…fuck it's just a mess and I'm sorry. I just wanted to let you know. You know. So you knew." He knows he's rambling, and she's not interrupting him, so he keeps going. "Anyway, she's only going to be here for two days and then everything can just…."

"It's okay."

"What?"

"It's fine. Do what you have to do and call me when she's gone."

"You…are you sure you're okay?"

"I'm okay."

"I'm really sorry, Anjanae. I had no idea."

"AJ. It's fine."

"Ok. Ok, I'll talk to you later."

"Ok."

The line goes dead and he takes the phone away from his ear with a dejected sigh. He knows it's not ok, but there's nothing he can do right now besides put on his signal and take the next exit. As he takes the drive around to the airport, he glances at his watch and sees that it's a little before eleven. The irony isn't lost on him that Julius is somewhere in there, too. Of course, he probably flew in on the most expensive airline and Grace had flown in on one of the cheapest. And the two of them would never give the other a single glance or sense the common thread. Still. He creeps in a circle through the congestion until he's at the right pickup area and gets in the right lane, scanning all the unfamiliar faces standing on the curb with their suitcases until he spots her fair-skinned, freckled face. Her tangerine tinted hair is piled up on her head and she sports a comfortable ensemble of sweat wear. He recognizes the oversized hoodie she has on as his. She's careening her head and glancing about nervously. The second she spots him she breaks out grinning and starts waving frantically. He puts on a smile that feels a lot more forced than it should, pulls up and parks.

In the thirty-minute or so car ride, he lets her tell him all about life back in Memphis. He asks her questions about the hospital and their friends and his family and her family in order to keep the topic of conversation off of him and his life. Grace talks fast and enthusiastically, and he tries to concentrate on the things she's saying, but he keeps slipping back into the conflicted stream of consciousness going on in his head. He is happy to hear that things are going well for her and that she seems to like her new job. He's also glad to hear that she pays his mother regular visits; he knows she gets lonely. Grace tells him that she and his mother went shopping at the Oak Court mall and then out to eat at Olive Garden (his mom's all-time favorite restaurant) earlier in the week. She says that she's got his mom's birthday present to him in her suitcase; she was in on the secret and so excited that Grace was getting to see "their boy," instructing her to take lots of pictures while they're out and about. He asks her what she wants to see first, hoping he can coerce her into some sightseeing. But what she wants to do first is see his apartment. And to eat. At the place he works.

AJ holds the door to R&W Barbecue open for her, taking a deep breath as he does so. It's the noon hour now and the dining room is filled with the usual hustle and bustle, a collage of different ethnicities enjoying their midday meal.

"Come on. My favorite table is open," he says to her, taking her hand.

"We don't have to wait to be seated?" She asks skeptically.

"Pshh," he replies cooler than he feels. "I work here. It's no big deal."

He grabs two menus off the counter and pulls her across the restaurant to a vacant table. It's not his favorite table. In fact, he's not sure in all the times he's dined here that he has ever even sat there. But it's open, and for two, and in the back.

She sits down across from him. "So," she says, grimacing ever so slightly. "This is where you work?"

"Sure is."

She opens her menu, "So," she says again, still grimacing as she runs her fingers over the slightly sticky laminate. "Is this food like Chinese or Thai or…"

"It's Korean," he replies rhetorically. Then, fearing how he sounded, adds in a more upbeat tone, "It's really good. Better than the food at the Wing Shack. The cooks here are excellent." He gives her a bright, reassuring smile.

"I don't know," she muses, still not looking up from her menu. "Foreign food can be sketchy sometimes."

"I assure you won't get sick. I eat here at least once a day."

"I guess I'll just have to trust you," she says, and then looks up, giving him a bright smile back. Except hers is real.

Another pang to his chest.

He spots Jae out of the corner of his eye. He recalls Jae saying something about meeting Mackenzie for lunch, and realizes that he must have cancelled his date to play a lead role in his alibi. And then he feels even worse about himself. When Jae sees he's being looked at, he takes out a pad of paper and a pen, despite being a cook and not a waiter, and walks straight to their table.

AJ puts on a fake smile; Jae follows suit.

"Grace," he says, getting her attention. "This is my co-worker and friend, Jae. Jae, this my girlfriend, Grace."

Jae holds out his hand to Grace, keeping the fake smile plastered on his face. There's a very brief pause where Grace just stares at him, but then she's smiling brightly again and shaking his hand.

"Nice to meet you," she says politely.

"Same to you," Jae replies back with the same politeness. "AJ has told me so much about you."

There's half a second where Jae's glance meets AJ's.

"Oh," she giggles girlishly, cheeks turning rosy. "Only good things I hope."

"Only good things," Jae confirms. "Your boyfriend's a good guy. And a great worker. We were really short staffed when he showed up. A true life saver this one."

AJ hopes that Grace isn't perceptive enough to see through Jae's lies, and see that the restaurant is very well staffed and that there's not one other white waiter or waitress in attendance. Even though he feels like a jackass thinking it, he knows that she is quite gullible and is probably drinking everything said to her up as the truth.

After they eat he takes her up to his apartment upon her continuous requests to see it. She walks through the door, takes one look at the huge piano in the middle of the tiny room, and looks back at him with horror in her eyes.

"Why do you have that?"

"You know I used to play. I don't know…I thought I'd take it back up. It was cheap, used. I have a friend…he's a singer. We're recording some songs."

"Recording some songs?"

"Yeah."

"Ok," she says, a thin coat of chipper over the judgmental.

She goes back to looking around. He immediately notices the two coffee cups and plates he hadn't removed from the counter that morning. As she looks around the living area, he scoots them into the sink, hoping that if she sees them in there she'll just think he hasn't done dishes for a couple of days. She parks her suitcase right next to his bed, and smiles when she sees the picture of them on his bedside table. He watches as she flits from one end of the little room to the other, going through his stuff as girlfriends do. When she opens his closet he realizes that he wasn't able to grab all of his "work" clothes. One Tom Ford suite, a Calvin Klein shirt and slacks, and the Ferragamos remain. She eyes them frugally.

"When did you start dressing so snazzy?" She asks. "You've got like five hundred dollar's worth of clothes in here."

He doesn't dare correct her. But five hundred dollars doesn't even cover half the price of the shoes alone. He tells her that he wanted to have some nice pieces for when he meets with his agent and for when he networks with other writers in the business, which he tells her one simply has to do in LA to make it. Though he hasn't networked with anyone who has any other aspirations other than getting laid or getting paid.

He's able to convince Grace to let him take her sightseeing in Hollywood. They hunt down the stars of her favorite actors and actresses, see Grauman's, go to Madame Tussauds, shop at the souvenir stores, and take plenty of pictures together as a happy couple. She clings tightly to her Target purse, starts every time an impersonator grabs her arm, and appears generally overwhelmed by the crowds of people everywhere, but he manages to kill four hours with her, and by the time they get back to his apartment the sun has started to sink. He asks her if she'd like to go to LA Live that night. Maybe try to score some last-minute tickets to a show or a ballgame or whatever's going on at The Staples Center.

"Oh, I don't know, maybe," she says, not sounding like she wants to go out again. "I want to take a shower first, wash the airplane and Hollywood scent off of me."

"Go right ahead. Soap, shampoo, everything you need is in the bathroom," he quickly interjects before she can suggest that he join her. "While you're in there...how bout I make us some hot chocolate?"

She smiles big and brightly. "Sounds great."

He watches her grab a few toiletries out of her suitcase and then disappear into his bathroom. He hears the water turn on as articles of clothing fly out of the open door into the short hall. When he hears the squeal of the shower curtain being pulled back, he goes into the kitchenette and grabs two hot chocolate k-cups out of a drawer. Once the machine starts to do its thing, he exits his apartment and crosses the hall. He raps his fist against Jae's door and hopes that he's home. A second or two later Jae opens the door. His face is emotionless when he sees AJ, and he says nothing. AJ recognizes after a suspended silence that he's the one who knocked, therefore he's the one who needs to say something. He goes with the first rambling thought that comes to his mind.

"I'm going to break up with her. I planned on breaking up with her but then she just showed up and...and I don't want to ruin her trip, you know? I mean she was my girlfriend for years we've just...grown apart, you know? Emotionally. Literally. Anyway, I'm sorry to get you involved. I owe you one, really."

"I did an Internet search," Jae says flatly.

A lump forms in AJ's throat. He swallows.

"Your name is common, so I assumed it would do me no good to run it in Google. So I typed in *Anjanae* and *Los Angeles*. That's when I realized...I don't even know her last name. Still. Anjanae. That's not a very common name, is it?"

AJ feels his palms start to sweat, a knot twisting in his stomach.

"I got a couple different Facebook and Twitter hits for some girls that clearly weren't her. But then...as I'm scrolling through the random images of random people named Anjanae...I see someone who looks familiar. So I click on it, and low and behold, it's her. In a Moschino gown. On a red carpet. Arm and arm with a man who *isn't* you, but who also looks vaguely familiar. I think about it for a while, and then it dawns on me. This man is Julius Collins. The producer." Jae smiles then at AJ. It's not a friendly smile or a happy smile. "You see I use to be a bit of a movie buff," he tells him. "And any movie buff knows who Julius Collins is." The smile is gone again, replaced by a mocking look of concentration. "That particular picture was from the 2012 Oscars. Possibly they've since gotten divorced, I reasoned to myself. Or maybe they weren't even married to begin with. Maybe she was just his girlfriend for a brief moment in time and now she's your girlfriend, however the hell *that* works. So I go to Julius Collins's Wikipedia page and, sure enough, right there under spouse it says Anjanae Collins 2009 –present."

"I know it doesn't sound good, but I can explain…"

"Can you explain why I had to tell some random red-headed who's supposedly your real girlfriend that you work here as a waiter when you really don't?"

"I can if–"

"I don't know what exactly it is I'm helping you cover up, or who exactly you are, but you should know if this is like a drug thing, if you're part of some…I don't know…white Deep South drug cartel, I am *no*t down. I don't want any part of it. I have a future to think about and I will not let you fuck it up with whatever kind of Ponzi scheme you're running out of my family's building."

"I'm not part of a cartel. This is not a drug thing."

"I don't even know if your name is AJ Brooks."

"My name is AJ Brooks."

"How do I know that? The AJ Brooks I know is an aspiring screenwriter from Memphis who works third shift at a gas station to pay his rent. The AJ Brooks I know lives across the hall from me, dates a really awesome and seemingly regular girl, and is super down to earth and cool and someone I *had* considered a friend. But this guy I met today? Well he's one crafty mofo. He's juggling a rich married mistress, a down-home girlfriend, a huge…*pile*…of purple label suits, and God knows what other secrets while apparently not even holding down a job. I mean what am I supposed to think?"

"I am an aspiring screenwriter. I am from Memphis. And I do have a job. Just not at a gas station."

"Where then?" Jae asks, perturbed.

For a second AJ thinks he will lie again. But then he's saying the words.

"I'm a male escort."

Jae blinks fast a few times. "What…what does that even mean?"

"It means that I take women out on dates, accompany them to events, provide them with company, and…" He hesitates before owning up to the last part, taking a deep breath. "Sometimes have sex with them…for money."

Jae isn't blinking at all now. "Holy shit."

"I know. I know. I never intended any of it to happen," he starts to ramble once again. "The first day you met me, I thought I was going to meet with an agent. But she turned out not be an agent. But I needed a job and the money was good and it all just happened so fast...."

Jae's stare is blatant and bleak as his eyes burn a hole into him. "What the fuck are you doing?"

AJ looks down at the ground. "I don't know."

"So..." Jae says, still trying to wrap his mind around it all. "So Anjanae, she's just one of your...clients?"

"No," AJ says quickly, immediately looking back up. "No. She's not a client. I mean she *was* a client. That's how we met. But that was just the first time and I've since given her back the money."

"A hooker with cash back rewards," Jae mutters glibly.

"The point is," AJ interjects sternly, clearly. "She's not my client, she's not my dirty little secret. She's...It's real. What I have with Anjanae is real. I really love her."

He realizes after it's left his lips what he's just admitted, but he doesn't care. It's not like it's not the truth.

"She's married, AJ," Jae says somberly.

"She is. She is married."

The space between them returns to how it stared. Quiet. Neither saying a word in the aftermath of honesty.

"Listen," AJ finally says definitively. "I know I don't have a right to ask anything else of you, but please don't tell Mackenzie about any of this. Anjanae really likes her and...and she wouldn't want her to know."

"I'm not going to tell anyone," Jae says quietly.

"Thank you." AJ turns to go back to his own apartment, but he pauses. "And Jae...our relationship is real, too. I wasn't pretending to be your friend."

Jae simply nods, and then shuts the door.

Back in his studio the shower is still running. No sooner does he open the cabinet in search of the bag of mini marshmallows he bought the day before does he hear the water stop. In its absence there's silence that carries a feeling of dread because he knows he soon will have to fill it with words. He plops four or five of the sugary confections into each steaming mug while reliving the conversation he just had with Jae.

What the fuck are you doing?

He looks up to see Grace emerge from the bathroom. She's got one of his plush white towels wrapped around her body, her damp hair combed back. She crosses the room to stand in front of him. She smells like his soap and the shampoo that comes in a green bottle, the kind she used to wash her hair with at home. She must have brought some with her. From home. *His home.* He reminds himself of this. It was his home just three short months ago. Before everything went left. He attempts a warm smile for her.

"Cocoa?" He offers, holding out one of the mugs to her.

But she doesn't take it. Instead her thin pink lips quirk upward into a smirk, and her right hand goes to the knot that holds the towel secure. "I had something else in mind," she says softly with suggestion.

She wants to have sex. Of course she does, they haven't seen each other in three months. And, unless she is hiding something from him like he is hiding many things from her, she hasn't had sex in three months.

And he...

He sits the mug back down on the counter and her towel hits the floor. He tries to absorb the familiarity of her body with his eyes. From the strands of hair just around her face that are turning crimson as they dry, to her small sea foam eyes that are just a couple of shades lighter than his own, and the freckles around her nose that match the peppering of freckles across her chest. From there his eyes drop to her full breasts, travel across the planes of her milky skin, land on the scar to the left of her belly button where she got her appendix taken out the day after Christmas two years ago, past her sloping hips, to the crescent shaped birthmark on her left thigh that he immediately noticed the first time he ever saw her naked many moons ago, and then all the way down past her firm calves to her pink painted toes. He attempts to drink it all in, all the places he used to caress and cherish and tarnish. The last body he planned on having; the last person he planned on being with. *Just three months ago*, he reminds himself. Just three months ago he had a ring for her. A ring she never knew about. He tries to extricate himself from everything else she doesn't know about. He tries to empty his busy mind that's filled to the brim with thoughts of betrayal, so he can be present in this moment with her. So he can do this one last thing for her. The girl he was supposed to marry.

She puts a hand on his face; he puts a hand in her hair. They both draw each other near, who kisses who first is hard to tell, but lips part and tongues delve, nonetheless. It doesn't feel like being with someone that he was in a three-year relationship with. It feels like being with a client. Just like being with a client.

Luckily, AJ has gotten good at producing an erection in the presence of women when he isn't in to them or in the mood. He was an expert at creating an air of intimacy out of absolutely nothing. A professional at making each and every client he's with feel like he's making love to her, when in actuality there is no love to be had. A worker disguised as a lover who is driven to get the job done. And he always got it done. Often more than once. Often more than twice. That being said, *he* didn't always orgasm. Sometimes, once they had their fill of him, he would politely take his money and leave without finishing himself. His clients don't care if he comes, but Grace will probably find it suspicious if he doesn't. Sometimes his mind would unconsciously think about Anjanae when his body wanted to see it through. But that seemed wrong now. It seemed wrong altogether. He shouldn't be thinking about her while he was with someone else. Because every time he's with someone else, he feels like he's cheating on her.

And as he lays Grace, his girlfriend, down on the bed before him, he feels again like he's cheating on Anjanae.

Afterwards, in bed, he lies awake with Grace sound asleep at his side. A bed he had previously only shared with one person. He makes a mental note to wash the sheets and pillowcases after she leaves on Monday. He doesn't want her trace to linger after her presence is gone, a stray red hair or a different shampoo scent that will undoubtedly serve as a painful reminder to Anjanae that someone else has been here. He then wonders if she's lying awake, too. He wonders if she's lying next to her husband or if she's sleeping in one of the spare rooms. He wonders if she's angry with him, disappointed, unhappy. His thoughts are so all consuming they might as well be audible. He carefully scoots to the edge of the bed, quietly disentangling himself from the sheets and her. Grace snores softly as he pulls his boxers and sweats back on. He then goes out onto the fire escape, gently shutting the door behind him.

The September air is cool against his skin, refreshing as he takes in a lungful of it. He braces his hands along the brass railing and stares up at the sky that has gone dark on him, counting three, then four stars. Standing out there in the dusky twilight, he knows without any uncertainty that he is profoundly and painfully in love with Anjanae. It's sad and somewhat messed up that it took Grace coming to town for him to realize this. Although, if he's being honest with himself, he supposes he's known for some time now. It was his personal secret, something he had been trying to keep to himself—albeit probably not very well, he felt like he practically emanated it—because as Jae had recently reminded him, she is married. And because he's someone who doesn't know what the fuck he's doing anymore. And because this thing between them was probably far too complicated to ever work out in his favor. After all, he's a realist. But oh, she makes him feel like the optimist he isn't. She makes him believe in things that aren't quite tangible. He knows now that Anjanae is the first and only girl he has ever truly loved. It took meeting her for him to realize that the things he had mistaken for love in the past were actually just contentment, compatibleness, and general feelings of care. He wasn't one to ever throw the word around, but he had said it before, and this far exceeded that in every barely bearable but immeasurably magical way.

That's not to say he didn't care about Grace. He did care about Grace. He does care about Grace. And he doesn't want to hurt her. He wants her to be happy, he wants her to have the things that she wants. Her nursing career, a family, a simple life in a conservative suburb in Tennessee. Stability. This was someone he had spent countless hours, numerous holidays, nights, days, and years with. He wants the best for her. When they were in Hollywood earlier, she told him that the redbrick house on Rose Street with the white picket fence and the little shed was still for sale. A small part of him was happy to hear this. The other part of him wishes it had sold. So that she could be put out of her misery of imagining them living there together, and so that he wouldn't have it as an option in his mind when he's homesick for a home he doesn't have but could if he were to one day wake up and chose to move back to Memphis, make an honest living, and get married. Because like it or not, there's still a small corner of his soul that craves stability also.

The problem is, the rest of his soul wants something else entirely. He heaves a sigh and goes back inside.

The next morning, he wakes up and it's raining. It's the first time this has happened since he moved to LA. He and Grace decide to stay in for the afternoon. Quality time is what she says she wants, and who is he to deny her when she's flown this far to see him? They watch reruns of one of their favorite sitcoms while he opens his early birthday presents from her and his mom. Grace got him a sweater in his favorite color, royal blue, a little fuzzy teddy bear that has its arms wrapped around a ceramic coffee mug with hearts on it that is filled with an assortment of his favorite candies, and a silver Fossil watch. He tells her she didn't have to get him anything, and she says yes she did. He opens his mom's present next. She got him a leather wallet and filled all the slots inside with gift cards to every place he ever liked to eat. He smiles to himself and shakes his head, knowing the worried thought process that went behind her gift. He opens the card that came with it—one of those beautiful ten-dollar Hallmarks like she had been getting him since he was kid, never a ninety cent Wal-Mart card—and reads the heartfelt lines she wrote about how she couldn't ask for a better son and how she loves him so much. She signed her name and forged his father's. He suddenly notices a little flap insert on the other side of the card, and immediately hopes she hasn't given him any money. Instead, he pulls out a plane ticket to Memphis for December 23rd. His mouth opens but words don't come out. When he looks at Grace, she's smiling from ear-to-ear.

"She didn't want you to have to pay to come home for the holidays."

"Oh," he replies, still dumbfounded.

"You *are* going to come home for the holidays, aren't you?" She asks skeptically, smile dissipating.

"Of course," he says after the briefest of hesitations. "Where else would I go for the holidays?"

Her smile returns in full force. She leans in, wraps her arms around him, and gives him a big kiss that causes a pop when her lips separate from his. His mind flashes back to his last birthday. His parents had come over to their little duplex for supper. His mom brought a crockpot of her famous chili and the four of them ate at the tiny oak table, space heater running in the corner. He remembers it had been an unseasonably cool but sunny day. Later they'd all sat around the living room, cozied up with cups of cocoa. Grace had made him the chocolate cake he loved so much. His dad took one bite of it and told him that "He needed ta marry that girl." When he'd glanced over at his mom on the couch, she was subtly nodding her head. That day felt like it took place in a whole other time frame, way longer than a year ago.

That evening he decides he's going to take Grace to Beverly Hills for dinner. To his favorite restaurant on Rodeo. He tells her he's never been, but that he's heard great things. He's been there four times with two different women. If he can let strangers treat him to five-star meals, he can treat the girl who's given him three years of her life to one. He owes her at least that, because the redbrick house will probably sell and the ring he bought will probably remain in the box. He calls ahead and makes reservations. She puts on a Forever 21 dress and Deb heels. When she asks him if she looks fancy enough for Beverly Hills, he removes any waver from his voice and tells her that she does. Passing through the restaurant downstairs on their way out, he almost has a heart attack.

Maggie Hunter is standing near the backdoor in all her glamour and omnipotence. A million thoughts run through his head at the speed of light. She smiles when she sees him and walks over. Her hand is extending. He's rooted to the spot.

"You must be AJ's girlfriend," she says to Grace, pearly white teeth gleaming.

AJ watches in a slow-motion type horror as the two women shake hands. Grace looks confused, but she's going along with it, smiling genially.

"I'm Ms. Hunter. I own the restaurant."

He has to work to control his face, and he prays the actual owners aren't within earshot to hear her blatantly lying through her teeth.

"Mr. Reeh and Mr. Woo are responsible for running the kitchen, of course. I just do all the hiring and firing. Walk through a couple of times a week to make sure the place hasn't burned to the ground. General managerial stuff."

God, she's good at this, AJ thinks. Everything she says, she says with absolute conviction. It's scary and remarkable all at the same time.

"Oh," Grace replies, smiling back gullibly. "So you're AJ's boss?"

"That I am."

She flashes his girlfriend the smile. AJ swears he tastes blood in his mouth. Had he bitten his tongue? The inside of his lip maybe?

"Ok. I know who to call now if I want to make sure he's behaving," Grace says in a playful tone to the older woman.

Maggie laughs. It's fake but it sounds real. "Likewise. All I have to do is probably threaten to call you and he'll straighten right up."

Grace does her girlish giggle, seemingly smitten with Maggie.

"No, AJ's a great worker. He's been a wonderful asset to the team." Maggie pauses momentarily, a purposeful beat meant for him, and then adds. "Here at R&W Barbecue."

"Uh…um," AJ stumbles, finally finding his words. "We were just headed out. I'm taking her to 208 Rodeo for dinner, being that it's her last night in town and all." He cuts his eyes ever so slightly at Maggie.

"Oh, well isn't that lovely. I won't keep you then. You two have a wonderful evening."

"It was nice meeting you," Grace says as AJ ushers her towards the exit, one hand on her back and the other opening the door.

"You too," Maggie replies, her glance momentarily diverting down to Grace's ten-dollar pink pumps, and then back up again. "Love the shoes, by the way."

Grace's eyes light up. "Oh well thank you!"

AJ knows Maggie is patronizing her, however he won't spoil the compliment. He leads Grace out of his fake place of employment, and away from his real boss.

"See you back at work Monday!" He hears her call out after him.

Maggie lingers after the two lovebirds leave, taking a better look around at the shabby little establishment he apparently lives above. She wonders if Andrew is at all aware of how he is on the eyes and how much better he could do than some Raggedy-Ann replica. They didn't even look like they had an ounce of chemistry. Goodness, what was it with men needing to call someone, anyone, their girlfriend? The fear of being alone was something Maggie had never known, and she imagines AJ could live a lot looser of a life if he let it go. She's just about to leave when she notices a young Korean man glaring at her from across the restaurant. She puts her smile back on and heads his way. When he sees her coming over, he turns around and pretends to be busting a table.

"Are you a friend of AJ's?" She asks him.

"Maybe," he mumbles, not looking up from the rag in his hand that he's rubbing across an already clean table.

"Sit," she says in a cordially commanding tone, tapping a manicured nail on the wood. "Let's have a chat."

She slides into the booth before he can verbally decline. She watches as he glances around. The nearest tables are vacant; she wouldn't be eliciting a conversation with him if they weren't. But she can tell that he's a naturally jumpy person. She can also tell that he doesn't like her. Which is unfortunate, she thinks, because he doesn't even know her. He begrudgingly slides in across the table from her. His demeanor is stiffly awkward and his eyes are averted away from hers.

"Do you have Courvoisier here?" She asks, opening the menu on the table and pretending to peruse it.

"No," he says under his breath.

"Moet?"

"No."

"That's fine. I don't really need a drink anyway." She closes the menu and looks straight at him, but he still won't look at her. "You know who I am, don't you?"

He says nothing. But she thinks she notices the barest flicker of something pass across his tense facial features as he continuous to stare at the wall.

"You're a smart guy. I can tell. I'm very good at reading people, pegging them. I can gauge a person's potential the first time I meet them. And I can see you have a lot of potential in you."

He glances at her then, giving her a disparaging look. "You aren't about to offer me a job, are you?"

"No," she laughs airily. "I'm afraid not. You see, stereotypes are stereotypes for a reason...I realize, of course, that some white men can jump and some black men can't and not all Mexicans can fix a mean enchilada and that there are lesbians who wear beautiful dresses and so on and so forth, and the diplomatic democrat in me would *really* like to consider myself an equal opportunity employer...but I simply can't take a chance on certain labels being true. It's all about safe investments and traditional economics, you understand I'm sure."

Part of Jae wants to go off on her and set her straight, but another part of him is terribly jealous of how freely she feels she can speak.

"That's not to say I don't think you're very cute," she quickly adds upon taking in his offended expression. "I'm sure you do quite well for yourself."

He's looking right at her now. Glaring, in fact.

"You wouldn't take a job if I offered it to you anyway, would you?"

"No," he says straightforwardly. "I wouldn't."

"I know." She smiles. "A guy like you belongs on the other side of a business venture. What's your name?"

He hesitates before uttering, "Jae."

She nods. "I bet a guy like you doesn't like working for someone else. Working here. Not getting the respect you deserve. Not doing what you want. Feeling stagnant."

He's not saying anything, arms crossed and a scowling, but she can tell she's right. He's becoming easier and easier to read.

"What do you want, Jae?"

"To be a chef," he mutters after a moment, barely audible.

She nods again, considering this. "There's ways to make that happen. Most renowned chefs were once just line cooks, after all. But then they took chances."

She's met again with his silence.

"You seem like you're a good friend, Jae. A good friend who would never want to see AJ in any trouble, legal or otherwise. And trouble comes about when people talk about things that they shouldn't. You understand?"

"I'm not a snitch…"

She winks. "I knew you were smart." She scoots to the edge of the booth and stands. "You shouldn't judge him. It's just a job." She extends her hand to him then. But he refuses to shake it.

She laughs airily again. And then she leaves.

~

Anjanae doesn't know what she's doing. She parked catty-corner across the street from AJ's apartment building with her lights cut off. The lone sounds of her windshield wipers working against the onslaught of pouring rain slice through the lines of self-hate in her head. She's never been this type of girl, the type of girl that sits outside of a boy's house waiting and watching. She's always detested that type of pitiful girl. But she wants just a glimpse. Just a glimpse of Grace. The girl that he calls his girlfriend. The girl in the picture with her cheek pressed to his. Not a client, not a random woman he bedded, but someone he had actually shared a life with. *A love with*, she thinks. Back when she was just another unhappy housewife living on a hill and he was just a guy with a normal life in the outskirts of Memphis. Back when neither knew the other existed somewhere out there in the abyss. Before Maggie Hunter and all the women. Before his life changed and he changed hers. She knew he would take her out tonight, because she knows him. He would do it up big for her last night in town, a nice place in Beverly Hills more than likely, a candlelit dinner with fine wine and all the fixings. Because he was a gentleman, and, even more than that, a genuinely good person at heart. And she wishes so bad that he wasn't because maybe then it would be easier.

She's been parked there for over forty-five minutes. When she pulled up, sure enough, his car was missing from its usual space out front. The fluorescent lights from the restaurant's window glow in the dark of the night. It's getting cold in her car, she'd turned the heat off over fifteen minutes ago to conserve gas as though she were someone on a budget, and she's just considered the fact that she should leave for the fifteenth time when she catches movement out of the corner of her eye. She's mistaken someone else's vehicle for his at least six times since she's been parked, but this time it's it. The powder blue Escort comes up the road on the other side and whips nonchalantly into the closest vacant spot. She watches through the sheets of rain as the driver's side door opens first and he gets out. He's got something in his hand; looking down, preoccupied. An umbrella pops open and he rushes over to the passenger side to open her door for her. She gets out but it's hard to make out any of her features in the. She's maybe 5'7 in the shoes she has on. Not fat, not thin. Average. Straight crimson hair down her back. He holds the umbrella over their heads as they make a run for the door, laughing as they do so. They share a quick kiss as he recloses the umbrella, and then they go inside. Out of sight. Anjanae imagines against her will what they'll do next. She continues to stare emptily at the empty sidewalk where they had just been. Eventually she looks away, looking down, the diamond on her trembling finger catching what little light there is in the dark car. Hands shaking and heart racing from the rush of restrained emotion; hurt, not anger. But she doesn't cry. She twists the key in the ignition and drives away.

CHAPTER 14

The next night he calls her after he's put his girlfriend on a plane and more than likely spent the entire afternoon scouring his apartment as an apology for the last two days, and asks her to come over. She thinks to herself that Grace probably isn't even all the way to Memphis yet, but agrees anyway. When she arrives at his apartment she texts him and tells him to come outside. She waits against her car. The rain has stopped but the air is still misty with its remnants and the temperature is cooler than usual. She zips up the old jacket she'd thrown on and puts her hands in her pockets. The restaurant door swings open and he exits. His hair is damp and unruly from a recent shower and he's wearing a faded pair of jeans and the comfy University of Memphis sweatshirt she likes to wear from time to time. He smiles when he sees her. It's warm but tentative. She can tell he's worried. He worries a lot and she knows it. She worries, too.

"Hey," he says, leaning in to kiss her cheek. She lets him but doesn't return it. He backs up a bit, still smiling, hoping for the best. "I've already ordered your favorite and got us the window table. It should be ready soon. I thought we could have a quick dinner. I've got a client, but not till eleven. I just really wanted to see you."

She snorts. It's a derisive sound that's accompanied by a cold smirk and a single headshake.

"What's wrong?" He asks sincerely, like he doesn't know.

"What isn't wrong?" She shoots back. The smirk is wiped from her face and she implores of him with a stark stare. His face is apologetic, and she knows he doesn't want to hurt her, would never want to hurt her, but that doesn't erase what is. Her features soften and she takes a deep breath. "I know I said it was okay. I know. But nothing about any of this is okay. You have to know that."

He feels a sense of shame as he watches anger forge itself on her face.

"She gets the PG13 censored version of the movie. She gets to watch a fairytale. She gets to believe that it's all good, that you're all good. But me? I get the X-rated, uncut, uncensored version. I have to cover my eyes with my hands when it gets to parts I don't like. Because that's part of getting the full picture…instead of the wallet size that you can be proud of and show others. My movie isn't being edited to conform to a sheltered audience."

"Anjanae…" He says her name softy like a silent plea. A prayer. An apology.

"What if one day she loaded the wrong movie into the DVD player? What if she saw what I see? What if she knew what I know?" She's staring him dead in the eyes now. "Could she handle it? Would she still love you?"

"Anjie…"

She smiles sadly again and shakes her head. "Ignorance is bliss. It really is."

He looks torn, his mouth opens and closes but nothing come out. She turns around, opens the door, and gets back in her car without another word. She drives away, leaving him standing there alone with nothing to say to stop her.

Back home, Anjanae trudges up the steps of the spiraling staircase, down the long and empty hall before coming to a stop in the doorway of her bedroom. Julius lays on the bed in his pajamas, staring at the computer in his lap. He doesn't notice her standing there, he never does. She feels both worn down and broken; he might see it when he does finally look at her, but she doubts it. She stares at him for a while, this man that she married seven years ago. This man who once looked at her when she was nineteen like she was the most beautiful woman he had ever seen. This man who married *her*, a waitressing community college art student, and moved her into a mansion at just twenty. This man who had simultaneously given her a life and took her life a way. The man who told her she'd never have to worry or want for anything again. The man her mother dramatically proclaimed as a blessing sent from God thanks to her prayers. His spectacles have slipped low on his nose, but he seems not to mind. Every few seconds the pads of his fingers hit a few keys on the laptop. It's the only noise in the house, until words are suddenly coming out of her mouth.

"Do you love me?"

Julius looks up, taken aback by both her presence and her question.

"Or am I just another pretty possession to you?"

His eyebrows scrunch up at her in confusion. "Where is this coming from?"

She gives a little shrug, looking at the floor instead of him. "Sometimes I feel like I only exist to fill a void in others' lives."

Her husband studies her for a second. "You fill a very important void in my life," he tells her, and then goes back to looking at whatever work is on his computer. "You're my wife. Of course I love you."

It's not good enough. But she takes it.

She shrugs off her clothes and undergarments piece by piece. She doesn't look at him while she's doing so, but by the time she makes her way to the bed, she notices he's closed his computer and put it on the floor. She climbs onto the Egyptian cotton sheets, and then she has to look at him. Lust has replaced everything else in his eyes. The hungry way he looks at her body makes her feel too exposed and a bit embarrassed. They haven't had sex in over four months, and she knows he's more than ready to have her. He inches closer to her, the fading scent of his cologne that she never much cared for and his natural aroma invading her nostrils. She reaches for the hem of his t-shirt and pulls it over his head. He's a little more out of shape than he was the last time she saw him naked, but he doesn't seem the least bit self-conscious about it, smirking domineeringly at her and wasting no time pushing his bottoms and briefs down and off, the familiar tilt of his erection springing free.

She lets him touch her with his cold hands, fondle her in ways that feel medicinal instead of sensual. She touches him, too. Wrapping her hand around him, stroking once, twice, before he's gasping and grasping at her wrist, pushing her back against the bed. And then she lets him slide his body on top of hers. When he presses into her she winces at the infiltration, not the least bit aroused. But she tries to act as though she is. Tries to find even the mildest enjoyment in his back and forth motion, his pelvis that barley rubs her right, how he sloppily slobbers kisses on her neck as he pants. She realizes they haven't actually kissed at all during this encounter. She tries to imagine a time when sex with him wasn't a chore, though she knows while there were tolerable times, the chemistry was never there. She then thinks about someone she does have chemistry with, someone who can make her scream and shake and shatter. But no sooner does she start to work her imagination than does she feel his telltale tensing. He groans loudly into her ear, calling her baby, which she hates, and telling her something she already knows. There are a couple quicker, un-rhythmic thrusts, followed by a long and satisfied moan of pleasure from him. He jerks inside her. And then it's over. She's relieved. Yet not.

His weight is heavy on top of her where he rests as he catches his breath. All in all, it was only a few short minutes of exertion, she thinks to herself, waiting for the moment when their naked bodies are no longer touching, a shameful feeling washing over her in the aftermath. He recovers and rolls off of her. He flips the night light off and tells her goodnight, putting his back to her. A minute or so later he's snoring. Anjanae scoots as far over to the left side of the big bed as she can get, facing the balcony window and putting acreages of white sheet between them.

She does worry. And she does want for something else.

She worries that she will lead an unfulfilled life forever. She worries that at twenty-seven her life is all that it is every going to be. She worries that she sold herself short and will never be able to buy back who she was. She worries that the security she settled for is slowly killing her spirit. She's spent many a sleepless night over the last seven years ruminating on these fears, thought consuming nights that have been far worse than the nights she used to stay up worrying about if she was going to be able to make her rent or pay off her student loans, but as of late these fears have become more profound than usual. Up until recently she hadn't had a reminder of what could be in years. A reminder of who she was, who she really was, before she was a trophy collecting dust on the shelf. She had forgotten what living could feel like, how thrill tasted. She couldn't properly miss herself until she met herself again. He brought her back and brought out her true colors, hues and palettes she had never painted with before. And in re-finding herself and finding him, she had found something else. Something not everyone finds.

She wants AJ. She wants him more than she has ever wanted anything or anyone. She loves him more than she has ever loved another soul. And she loves his soul; it's the exterior things that make it complicated. Money, Maggie Hunter, women whose names she doesn't know, and Grace. Anjanae is the string that keeps AJ tethered to a sense of normalcy, the emotional anchor that keeps him grounded when other women are handing him hundred-dollar tips and slipping expensive presents and room keys into his back pocket, and she knows this. However, Anjanae also understands that while she's his tether and anchor here in Los Angeles, Grace is his security blanket back home. Back home, the last true place things ever really were normal for him. And while he never says it, she knows from time to time he flirts with the idea that he could go back. He never will, of course. And she will probably never tell him with words what he means to her, because while she holds his heart and mind in her hands, as he holds hers, his body belongs to others. And while she just gave her body to someone else who had, in a way, purchased her, she wishes despite herself that AJ were hers and only hers. The irony of it all makes her smile sadly against her pillow, eyes welling up with tears. The fact of the matter is they fill the same empty space in the other. The fear is that the same person that fills her with purpose has all the potential to emotionally drain her of everything she has. So, in retrospect, cold comfort is safer than the devastation of a burning fire. Logic tells her to put it out. Love tells her to let it consume her. Confliction is her bedfellow.

CHAPTER 15

Almost a week has passed since his falling out with Anjanae. He gave her a couple of days, then he texted her. And then he called her. And then he texted her again. All of which went unanswered. He misses her. He realizes that no more than a day has passed since they met that they hadn't talked to each other. Even if she had to sneak down to the first floor and lock herself in the guest bath, they talked. Sometime for hours. Three days rarely passed before they had to see each other, have each other. Sometimes for hours. God, he misses her. Seven days feels longer than it should. He can't forget the pained look on her face before she got in her car and drove away. He drove her away. And he knows it.

It's late on Sunday morning and he can't help but think that he almost always spends Sundays with her. Last night he spent three hours with a woman he had never met before. Brenda Éclair, a recently widowed beneficiary, flew down from Napa Valley to attend a fundraising dinner for a big-name charity for which she is a big-time supporter in the name of a big tax write off. Maggie's number was dialed; he was picked up at seven by a big black limo. High rolling women who grasped glasses of rosé and donated checks with a bunch of zeros at the end they'll never miss complimented Brenda on her younger new beaux. AJ smiled and shook hands and pretended like he had known the woman on his arm longer than the two minutes that he actually had. By some stroke of luck, he hadn't had sex with anyone in the ritzy room, not that he could recollect anyway, and Mrs. Éclair's sham was executed flawlessly. It was supposed to be a first-tier folder kind of night, just a date to a dinner, but Brenda decided it was time to cut out about an hour into the event, and the two of them spent the next two hours in her hotel room. Despite wishing he could have turned her down, he made good pay with the unexpected overtime. Afterwards, she tipped him with a rare ruby ring. He tried multiple times to give it back to her, but she wouldn't take it. She told him it was her late husband's and worth a small fortune. She'd been keeping it in a special compartment of her Hermes bag, waiting for the right time to re-gift it. His fingers, as she put it, were the perfect fit. She told him she had all of her husband's money and her own precious gems, so what use did she have for a man's ring? She didn't have a man. And he had shown her such a good time, she told him, that she thought he should have something special. So he slipped the ring and all of the money into his pocket and went his way. She said she might call Maggie and fly him up to her vineyard for a weekend sometime. To drink wine and fuck, he's sure, though she doesn't say that.

As he takes the side streets all the way to Hollywood to pick up his check, he can't help but to notice a huge purple van broken down on the side of the road. The skinny, dark haired boy popping the hood looks very familiar.

"What the…" AJ mutters to himself, making a U-turn and pulling up behind the monstrous eyesore of a vehicle. "Jae?" He says, getting out of his car.

Sure enough, it's Jae's head that shoots up from under the hood. "Oh. Hey," he says nonchalantly as he sees AJ approaching. "What are you doing?"

"What are *you* doing?" AJ counter-questions.

"I bought a van," Jae replies as though that were something completely in character for him to do. Jae was a firm believer in practicality. He drove a tiny neon green Prius that got fifty miles to the gallon. "I think it might be out of gas," he adds, slamming the hood back down. "It's kind of up in the air, though, seeing as the gauge and none of the lights on the dash really work."

"What possessed you to make this horrible decision?" AJ chides friendlily, albeit quite curious.

"Your boss."

AJ's jaw drops a bit. "You talked to Maggie? When did you talk to Maggie?" Outside of basic greetings when they run into each other in the hall, Jae hasn't said much to him in the last week. And AJ had no idea a conversation between Maggie and him had even taken place.

"It's been about a week."

"And she told you…she told you that you should buy a pretty purple van?"

"She told me that I should take my dreams into my own hands and go into business for myself. So, I'm opening a food truck."

AJ is stunned.

"What do you think?" Jae asks him.

"I think that's amazing."

"Yeah, me too. Don't worry, I've thought it through. Wrote out a budget. Got my finances together. I had money in a separate savings account for if I ever went to Med School, which my parents want me to do, but I'm clearly not going to. They conveniently forgot that I could access that account when I turned twenty-one. And. Well. I accessed it. I've got a patron who's a part time mechanic and he's offered to give the van a good run through and cut me a deal on what needs to be updated. Once I get it running good it's on like Donkey Kong. I'm going to serve a little bit of everything. Not the same old Korean stuff day in and day out. One week it might be soul food, then the next week seafood, then the next week Mexican. Take it all over LA. I was thinking that I'd pay Anjanae to paint a real pretty mural or something on it. You think she'd do that?"

"I don't know. I haven't really talked to her since…"

"Grace. Right. Sorry."

"It's cool. Hey, do you need a ride out of here?"

"Nah, ya boy got AllStar. I already called. They said it would be about twenty."

"Ok. Well, call me if for some reason they don't show up," AJ says, turning for his car. "I'll be around."

"You doing anything tonight?" Jae asks out of the blue, quickly adding, "And just so we're clear I wasn't being facetious just then. Not are you doing anything tonight as in like a rando rich chick. As in are you doing anything at all?

"Nope," AJ replies with a laugh. "I'm sure not."

"I bought some unprocessed chicken breasts and freshly shaven Parmesan at the Whole Foods yesterday. Mackenzie's out of town visiting family this weekend. You want to come over? I'll cook chicken parm."

AJ smiles. "Sounds good," he says, quite glad that he hasn't in fact ruined their friendship like he feared he had. "What time?"

"Six, ok?"

"I'll be there."

The office at 360 Hollywood Place is empty except for Maggie. She told him he could come pick up his check, that she'd be there. AJ does find it a little odd that she'd choose to be there on a Sunday instead of somewhere else. It's almost like she has trouble occupying her free time. It's almost like she fears solitude. It's almost like her empty office is more preferable than her empty apartment; the workspace she has over the home life she doesn't. These are, of course, just his stray observations, and he doesn't know if these things are true about her. He knocks on her door and she tells him to come in. He hands her the cash he made last night with Mrs. Éclair. She writes him a check for a week's worth of escapades, eying him as she passes the piece of paper to him.

"Do you ever spend any money on yourself, Andrew?"

"What?"

"You have on a Hanes t-shirt, Levi jeans, and a pair of ratty Chuck Taylor's. Don't get me wrong, you still look hot in your plain clothes, but the only time I see you wear designer labels is when you're going to meet a client and you're clothed in one of the ensembles I've provided you with. I know what I pay you. I know you can afford nice things."

"I'm saving," he says simply.

"Have you bought *anything* for yourself?"

He thinks about it. "A saxophone."

"A saxophone?" She snorts derisively. "You know, Andrew, you can still save *and* splurge a little from time to time. Most of the guys bought a new car within the first month of working for me, and it's been over three months and you're still driving that heinous little blue thing you pulled up in the first day. There must be things you've always wanted but never had the money for. All I'm saying is you have a steady stream of income now that's going to keep on flowing. Treat yourself once in a while. You deserve it."

AJ considers this. Are there things that he wants? Are there any *attainable* things that he wants?

Maggie smiles as she opens her desk drawer. "I got you something for your birthday."

"You didn't have to do that."

"I know."

She sits a square canister with a bow on it in front of him. He takes the lid off, and inside sees an exorbitant gold watch. It's a Rolex. She bought him a gold Rolex.

"When I got Dominique his I had them put diamonds around the face, but you don't really strike me as a diamond encrusted bezel kind of guy. If you do decide down the road that you'd like a little bling on it, I can call my jeweler up anytime and have him come over and get that done for you."

AJ has never seen an actual Rolex before; in magazines or on television, sure, but never up close and personal. He certainly never expected to see one on his wrist. He certainly had never known anyone who had a jeweler on speed dial. He certainly had never had anyone spend that kind of money on him and, quite frankly, he doesn't really know how to act.

"I...thank you."

She smiles her smile. "It's nothing."

And he knows that it really isn't. Not for her.

Both of their heads shoot up when they hear the front door open. The idea of someone who is not one of the boys coming through the door on a Sunday clearly startles them both, even if neither would admit it. They peer through the glass-enclosed office to see an older woman in designer garb and dark shades shuffle into the building. A lot of AJ's clients are in their fifties and sixties, but this woman had to be pushing eighty, wrinkly jowls sagging and Chanel scarf tied around her wigged-head.

"Goddammit," he hears Maggie mutter. She immediately pushes her chair back and goes to the door. "Mother," she says, her voice making a prompt shift to faux cheerfulness. "What are you doing here?"

She's speaking through her teeth, and all he can think as he stands there is that she has a mother. He didn't imagine her having a mother. It made her slightly more human. Slightly. And he can't help but stare.

"What do you mean what am I doin' here?" The older woman asks, and he picks up on a twangy accent of some kind. "It's your week ta get me."

"Is it really that time of year again already?" Maggie asks redundantly, masking her displeasure with a tone of disbelief.

Maggie's mother puts her hands on her hips. "It sure is."

"I'm sorry. It creeps up on me. I feel like a mother of a public school child in the summer. Normal nursing homes don't let out for vacation once a year."

"Well ya didn't put me in a normal home, now did ya?"

"You wouldn't be put in a normal home. You wanted one with a gym even though you don't exercise, and a pool even though you don't swim, and one that serves three-course meals three times a day..." Maggie's eyes drop to her mother's midsection. "At least you're taking advantage of one of the amenities I pay for."

"I'll have you know all my boyfriends love the way I look. They like a lil somethin' ta grab onto."

Maggie quickly holds up a hand. "I don't want to know."

"I'm just sayin'. Not everyone is into this whole twig thing you got goin' on. I know you're caught up in this here Hollywood lifestyle and all, but you are aware that you ain't gotta starve yourself if you're not one of the actresses or models…"

"I'm not a twig and I eat. You know, a phone call would have been nice. By the way, just how did you get here?"

"I caught a cab."

"You caught a cab? By yourself?"

"I had two tinis on the plane and was feelin' my oats."

"And you navigated the airport…all by yourself."

"I'm not a damn degenerate, Margaret. Now enough small talk. I wanna go to the Chinese place."

"You do know that Grauman's isn't a buffet, right?"

"You do know that I will still ring your little neck, right?"

Maggie lets out a disgruntled sigh. "Look, mother, I already have plans made for today and I can't break them. So here's what we're going to do. I'm going to leave you in the care of my capable assistant this afternoon. He'll take you wherever you want to go. Then the next two days I'm all yours. Deal?" She waits half a beat and then calls out to him. "Andrew!"

"What?" He perks up from the spot against the wall in her office where he's been eavesdropping. "No," he says quickly. He had planned to spend his day sulking in his studio, writing songs until six rolled around and he'd go across the hall to Jae's. He doesn't want to play nanny and chauffer to her elderly mother. "Today's my off day. I just came to get my check…"

She walks over to him, leaving her mother in the vestibule. "You'll get a nice little bonus if you do this, now come here." She takes him by the arm and leads him out front. Her mother doesn't look pleased with what she's being offered.

"Where's that Theo?" She asks, squinting her beady little eyes that look nothing like Maggie's at him. It's clear that she is used to Maggie leaving her in someone else's care, and AJ suddenly feels guilty for not wanting to be of help.

"He's on location," Maggie says with indifference, as if that's a valid explanation. On location where doing what, she doesn't bother to elaborate, and by her mother's blank expression and glassy eyes, it's safe to bet that she won't be thinking too long or hard about it. "But I promise Andrew is very attentive," she adds, looking at him then. "Andrew, this is my mother, Martha Hunter."

"Nice to meet you," AJ says, putting on a smile and politely reaching out to shake hands with her, despite being forced into the situation.

Martha leaves his hand hanging until he finally puts it down in defeat. She stares derisively at her daughter, letting her know she's not happy, then sighs in consent. "Alright then. Come on, Anthony," she says to him without even glancing in his general direction. She's shuffling back towards the door. "Them airplane peanuts wore off about an hour ago."

Maggie leans in while simultaneously reaching into her pocket. "She won't be able to get in and out of your little car, you'll have to take my Lincoln." She drops a set of keys into his hand and slips her black card into his back pocket. "Take her where she wants, buy her what she wants. FYI, she doesn't know my exact job title, so if for some reason she asks…well…you're creative. Make up something moderately modest for me, ok? She's in the middle stages of dementia, she won't remember what it is tomorrow." She pats him on the back and gives him a little push towards the door. "Thank you, dear."

AJ does a quick Google search of Chinese buffets in the area and goes with the one with the best reviews. On the ride to the restaurant Martha makes a number of crude comments, poking fun at the man selling homemade set props on the side of the road, and passing judgment on a homeless woman scouring a dumpster for food. She also chides her daughter for her taste in vehicles, redundantly asking him if she thought she was some kind of hip-hop artist. AJ wanted to be cute and say *no, but she is what many hip-hop artists think they are*. He bites his tongue, though.

They eat their lunch in mostly silence. AJ figures he made the right decision by the way Martha scarfs down three different styles of rice and shoves one crab rangoon after another into her red lipstick covered mouth. Grease coats her long fake nails and her fingers clink from all the rings she wears. There's one on almost every finger. She mixes gold with silver and sapphires with rubies. He briefly thinks about the deceased man's ring given to him the night before, and then rips the memory from his mind. He notices she also has an impressive, crystal clear diamond on one particular finger, along with a polished band. She doesn't resemble her daughter much in mannerisms or looks, but at certain angles he catches glimpses of their similarities. Martha doesn't ask him anything about Maggie or her life, so he doesn't have to lie.

Martha seems interested in only herself and the food in front of her. After she comes back to the table with her second plate, he decides to break the ice.

"So um…where do live, Mrs. Hunter?"

"New Orleans," she says, taking a hunk out of some kind of red meat on a stick, and suddenly the accent clicks in his brain.

"Oh really," he replies, genuinely intrigued. He has never once heard Maggie mention her mother or New Orleans, and her own accent definitely didn't match the two. He always pictured her being either a native Californian or from somewhere on the East Coast. New York. Maybe D.C. Not New Orleans.

"Sure thing. Lived in Louisiana my whole life. I come from the bayou, but I don't tell too many folks that cause, you know, people judge." She squeezes lemon juice onto an oyster and then sucks the whole thing into her mouth with a slurp. "My family ain't never had too much and I wasn't cut out for that lifestyle. You see, I always had an eye for the finer things in life," she says with a smile he immediately recognizes. It's funny how one feature can do so much for a person. AJ didn't think so before, but now he's quite sure Martha was once probably very pretty. A pretty person who knew what she wanted out of life. "In the summer when I was a teenager me and my girlfriends would take a bus into the city and hangout in the lobbies of all the fancy hotels. There was always some kind of open bar filled with business men and high rollers, and I always looked older than I really was."

AJ actually finds himself rapt with interest, a chance at stealing a peek into something he's sure Maggie herself would never divulge.

"That's where I met Margaret's daddy," she continues. "He was a young oil tycoon. Rich as sin. We got married just as soon as I turned eighteen and I moved on out to Southern Cross."

"Southern Cross?" AJ inquires curiously.

"His family's plantation."

"Oh…"

"The homestead is just sittin' there all empty now. It's all in Margaret's name. I half expected her to sell it by now but she ain't. Still the most beautiful place on earth if you ask me."

"Your husband…"AJ treads cautiously. "He passed?"

"Oh yes, he's been dead years now." She takes a sip of her iced tea, and then with a very familiar nonchalance adds, "Blew his brains out in his office with a .38. Maggie had already left for college, thank God."

AJ's mildly appalled. He didn't expect this twist in the story.

"She always did favor him. Determined, ambitious, and hardheaded as all get out. Not knowing what to do if she couldn't wield her power."

"What…I mean why do you think…"

"He went and offed himself?" She takes another sip of tea. "He made a few bad business choices, a few bad investments. Things went left fast."

AJ listens diligently. He can tell Martha likes being asked questions and he's more than interested in her ever-honest answers.

"He made a lot of money. He spent a lot of money. Shoot, we all did. It got to the point where we were running through the reserves before the new was hitting the account. We never thought there'd be a day when the money wasn't coming in. We got too comfortable. He got too cocky. He thought he could do anything, legal or illegal, because in his eyes he was untouchable. When you stay afloat on top for so long you forget how to tread when you start going under." She shrugs simply then. "He couldn't handle the hot water that he got himself into."

"So," AJ says carefully. "What happened after his death?"

Martha shakes her head. "I didn't know what I was gonna do. I thought I was fittin' to lose the house, the estate, everything. I mean I had become accustomed to a certain type of lifestyle, ya know what I mean? I thought I was gonna go from being an affluent housewife to a bag lady."

"But you didn't…"

"Well, Margaret's first year of school was already paid for and she had done won all these scholarships to fall back on, ya see. He had left me just enough money ta get by on until she graduated…and as soon as she did…she got a job in New York City workin' for some big wigs makin' real good money." Martha laughs wryly then. "I bout had a heart attack when she told me she was leavin' and comin' out here. I thought, *Oh Lord here, we go again.* But. Turns out. She can make more money here than she did there." She drains her glass loudly and then sits back. "I never did like visitin' her in New York anyhow. Too many people in too tight a space. Weather's a damn sight better here, too."

AJ takes Martha shopping, out for ice cream, and then returns her to Maggie. After he has dinner with Jae and returns to his own empty apartment, he lays awake thinking about what he's learned. When he does finally sleep, his dreams are fitful and cycle between faceless women handing him random rings, Anjanae smiling at him from afar, and a room splattered with the brains of someone who couldn't handle what they'd gotten themselves into.

CHAPTER 16

The first time Garrett walks into Richard Rodriguez's home he feels like he is officially privy to the world he has always wished to be. The mansion is meticulous and swanky, the type of place that would have instantly floored the average person, but to Garrett it's really no bigger or better than some of his clients' homes. Still, for Richard he acts like he has never seen crystal chandeliers or gold accents or entire rooms designed in all white, Grand pianos and Picassos and Dom Perignon bottles.

"Shall we go out onto the patio?" Richard asks accommodatingly. He wears a prideful smile as he watches Garrett take it all in.

"Sure," Garrett replies.

Richard leads him from the foyer, through the living area. Latin music plays lightly in the background of the otherwise quiet, artistically empty home. What furniture there is appears barely used, and the glossy marble floor (stained with Spanish style designs) doesn't have a scratch or a speck of dirt on it. A staircase winds through the middle of the room, up three stories. To the left, against the wall and under an antique mirror, there's a glass case filled with rows of gold Daytime Emmys. While Garrett stares at the trophies, Richard opens the set of French doors.

Once outside, Garrett can smell the ocean in the air, and if he cranes his head far enough to the left he can make out the beach through the Malibu mist. Richard has an elaborate in-ground pool, with a hot tub in an alcove and a swim up bar built into a wall made of stone. There are two separate fire pits, multiple lounge chairs, and an entire entertainment center. Garrett thinks of what Maggie had told him a few days ago. How she had read a blurb somewhere written by one of Richard's former maids who was pissed because she lost her job due to him no longer being able to afford her. He was supposedly running low on funds, but you couldn't tell it by the looks of his place. Garrett decides the maid was probably just bitter that she lost her job, and Maggie was probably bitter too, seeing as she was about to lose an employee.

"Have a seat," Richard says, pointing to the patio table that has a bottle of champagne, a box of cigars, and two glasses sitting on it. Garrett pulls out a chair and Richard pops the cork on the bottle and fills both glasses with the light beige, bubbly liquid. He then chooses one of the thick, brown cigars and pushes the box across the table to Garrett. "You want one?"

Garrett shakes his head. "No thanks," he says politely. He had spent the first two or three checks he ever earned from Maggie on his teeth. He had a mouth full of pearly white veneers, the definition of a perfect smile. He occasionally made an exception for coffee, but that was it.

"So I have some news," Richard says mysteriously, smile hinting at his lips. "News that I'm technically not supposed to know, but do, and now I'm going to share it with you. So you can be prepared." He swishes the expensive liquid around in his glass, takes a drink and swallows. "You're about to be offered a role. A real role, not just a few lines here and there whenever Antonio and his lover meet for secret breakfast at the diner. They've decided to broaden your character." Richard smiles his swarthy smile then and lights his cigar. "You got it, baby."

Garrett is flabbergasted. "How...how do you know that?"

"Jeff and I are pretty close." He puts the cigar in his mouth. "We were at the club the other day, playing a couple of rounds, and he told me Dave's plans for you. Dave's our showrunner." When Richard removes the cigar a plume of smoke wafts from his lips. "It only made sense for him to capitalize off of the attention you drew. After your first episode aired, Twitter blew up with people wanting to know who the new hottie in the diner scene was."

"Seriously?"

"What, you don't think you're hot enough to spark a flame on social media?"

Garrett shrugs, then smirks. "I mean...I do, but..."

Richard smiles like he's pleased by Garrett's response.

"I guess I just didn't expect it to happen so fast, that's all."

"I told you, it's the look. You either have it or you don't." Richard ashes his cigar over the glass tray, then looks back up at Garrett. "So listen, they're setting it up for you to be Kasey Frank's new love interest." He takes a cool drag. "I'm probably going to be getting back together with her mother." He pauses to puff a trail of smoke circles through his lips. "Not Kasey's real mother, of course, her mother on the show. Heather Agley."

Garrett nods.

"Come to think of it," Richard says. "They may just cast me a new lover altogether. One of those eager, fresh-faced, twenty-something starlets." He wags his eyebrows at the thought and Garrett laughs. "Doesn't sound so bad, huh?" He takes a short drag. "Not that I'm saying there's anything wrong with Heather Agley; she's a wonderful actress. But the woman is damn near fifty. I'd like something new to rub up against during all those arduous love scenes. Know what I mean?"

Garrett nods again and grins, not bothering to tell Richard that he's over fifty.

Richard reaches for his glass. "The last two seasons I've had to put up with Kasey Frank and all her shit." He takes a sip. "Which virtually took all the fun out of shooting with a half-naked naked woman. She's got a pretty decent body, I'll give her that, but the bitch is a bitch." He raises his glass towards Adam with a wink. "That's your problem now, though, buddy."

Garrett laughs meekly and takes a sip from his own glass. "I'd be lying if I said she didn't make me a bit nervous," he admits.

Richard relaxes back in his chair. "You just gotta know how to roll with the punches. She might show up in the morning refusing to act, running her mouth and acting like the uncouth piece of trailer trash that she is…then go on break and come back completely compliant, ready to submissively shoot whatever however. I think she may have some kind of untreated chemical imbalance." He takes a puff off his cigar. "But it's nothing that can't be wooed out of her. You're an attractive younger man, pay her a couple compliments and she'll be putty in your hands."

Garrett smiles. "I appreciate the pointers."

"I got your back, kid." He takes a drink and swallows. "I'm tellin you, Garrett, big changes are coming your way. Promoters, sponsors, advertisers, groupies…" He winks over the rim of his glass after that last one. "They're all coming your way. And if you ever have questions, ever want any advice on how to handle any of the above…don't ever hesitate to ask me. I've been through it all before, and I'm here to help."

Garrett shakes his head. "Why are you being so nice to me?"

"I see a lot of myself in you," Richard tells him honestly. "And I remember what is was like to be young and hungry in Hollywood, just on the cusp of success."

Garrett's face flushes pink at the compliment. He looks down to hide his grin.

"You told me the other day that you were from a small town in England, right?"

"Yes," Garrett replies. "North Oremsby, Middlesbrough. It's about four hours or so from London if that puts it into perspective. Not much of place, really."

"Raised by a single mother, correct?"

"Yes."

Richard nods, staring wistfully out at the Malibu hills in the distance. "I came from a small village town in central Mexico, not even a blip on the radar," he tells Garrett. "No father. Raised by a single mother, just like you."

Garrett stares at Richard with diligence.

"I always had big dreams, always had talent," Richard continues. "Even as a little kid in Mexico, I knew I was meant for more. My mother did, too. So when I was seven, she put my brother Ray and I on a bus to America. We had an uncle in San Antonio who let us live with him. He didn't know much about raising kids, so Ray and I basically raised ourselves. We taught ourselves English, got ourselves to school, even got our citizenship on our own. San Antonio was alright, but I still wanted more." He makes theatrical hand gestures as he speaks. "I wanted California. I wanted fame. I wanted to see my face on billboards and TV screens."

Garrett smiles as he listens, because these are the things he wants.

"So when I graduated high school, I decided I would move to Hollywood. My brother," he shakes his head. "He never had any interest in the entertainment industry, but he decided he would come with me. He could've been an actor; we were both blessed genetically. However, I was the one with the star complex, and he was the one with the hero complex. Ray's only a year older than me, but he's always felt like he had to look out for me, protect me." A wily smirk comes to his face. "I don't much blame him, I've always been a bit troublesome."

Garrett laughs.

"So there we were on a bus again—neither us of could afford a car—heading west. We lived on the street for about a week until we found a filthy apartment no bigger than a box…and then I started beating down the street. I went to every casting call that there was, fried hamburgers and worked retail in between auditions, and slept when I got the chance. But you know how that goes." He takes a drink. "I'm sure you've had your fair share of mildly demeaning odd jobs."

Garrett nods in agreement. *If you only knew*, he thinks.

"It took me from the time I was eighteen to the time I was twenty-three to get my break. Hell, I was used to struggle. The life I'd led made me tougher. Unlike a lot of the weak-minded Americans I waited in line to read lines with—that eventually threw away their dreams and moved back to Kansas or Michigan or wherever—I never gave up." He motions with his arms and looks around at his un-humble abode. "And look what I have now." He looks back at Garrett. "You could have it, too. You *will* have it, too." He finishes off his champagne. "Because like me, you believe it."

Garrett considers this. He does believe in himself. He believes that he is better than most of the aspiring actors he's met. He believes he is better than Middlesbrough, England and all his former friends back home. He believes that he is better than Maggie and her stupid job and all the many, many stupid women he has screwed for her. He truly believes that he is better than Theo and Rafael and Dominique and AJ and Austin. They would probably always need Maggie, and their dreams would probably never come true. Their stars simply didn't shine like his; they didn't have it. But he did. And he would have so much more than all of them. He was sure of it.

"I'm having a little get together tonight," Richard's voice interrupts his musings. "Drinks and hors d'oeuvres around the pool. Just some close friends and a few Playmates I met at the Mansion last month. You want to stay?"

Garrett grins. "Sounds fun." He excuses himself to go to the bathroom, where he'll call Maggie and inform her that he can't make his nine o'clock.

He might just fuck someone for free tonight.

~

It's been ten days now since AJ has spoken to Anjanae. He calls her once a day but never more than that, and she never answers. He still hasn't worn his new Rolex out in public, but he's tried it on for size a few times, admiring the sophisticated way it looks. He decided he would re-gift the ruby ring from Mrs. Éclair to Dominique. AJ's never wore rings before, he doesn't really plan to start, and Nique likes flashy things and the color red. When he offered it to him during a studio session, Dominique told him he'd be stupid not to sell it, and that his conscious wouldn't let him take it from him. So AJ took it to an upscale jeweler and almost lost consciousness when the man behind the counter offered him a cool $50,000 for it. He sold it despite the fact that it made him feel guilty. He reasoned that not much didn't these days.

AJ also took the time to mull over what Maggie said to him about spending some money. He thought about what he wanted—not jewelry, not clothes—and then made two big purchases in self-celebration of his twenty-third year on earth. He found a cherry red 1967 GTO online in San Louis Obispo. It was in mint condition; low miles, leather seats, convertible, garage kept. The next day that he had off, he drove up the coast to get it, taking Jae along with him to drive his Escort back. A couple of days later he dropped his next big sum of money. One of his clients was a former fashion designer for a big-name label who now made millions off of her millions by buying foreclosed houses, renovating them, and then flipping them. She pillow-talked to him in the Palisades about a house she had in Reseda, way out in the valley. He expressed interest, she offered him a hell of a deal, and he placed a down payment on it the very next morning.

Happy Birthday to me, he thinks glumly. Because his presents to himself are still not what will really bring him fulfillment or peace.

~

Garrett is in Richard's trailer getting primped by the hair and makeup artists before his next scene. Garrett doesn't have a trailer, being that he hasn't technically been offered the new slightly more permanent role Richard had suggested he'll get, plus Richard's trailer is nicer than most people's homes and he's been told that he's always welcome to get ready in there whenever he wants. A blonde woman in a black smock sprays his hair and then runs her manicured hands through it, fluffing lightly for effect. A man wearing tight jeans and black eyeliner dabs a Vaseline coated finger across Garrett's lips. He puckers and waits for him to finish, glancing in the mirror to see Richard coming to stand behind him, engrossed in his phone. The makeup man removes his finger and grabs a soft circular pad off of the vanity to blot Garrett's nose with.

"Anything good happening tonight?" Garrett asks Richard.

"Well," Richard says, looking up from his phone. "That one little sultry slut I've been talking to for the last few weeks…you know…fake blonde twenty-something with the big ass that you referred to as an Instagram model…"

"Oh yeah, that one," Garrett grins. "You need to hit that shit."

"I plan to. A girl like that will let you put it anywhere. Anyway, she's invited me to Greystone tonight. You heard of it?"

"Hell yeah I've heard of it."

"You ever been?"

"No. I think you have to know someone."

"Well you know someone now. I know it's a younger crowd and all but they're bound to let a living legend like me in." He winks. "Plus I'm pretty sure Insta-hottie has fucked a few ballplayers and rap singers so I'd say her name has always been on the list. Feel free to use either at the door. Oh, and I told her to bring some girlfriends that look like her, by the way."

"Nice," Garret grins.

The door to Richard's trailer opens and Dave Cobble, the soap's showrunner, sticks his head in. Dave only shows up on set a couple of days a week. He mainly runs things from his office in Los Feliz. A presence that is felt more than seen.

"Hill, can I see you in my office?"

"Sure, of course," Garrett quickly says, hopping up from the chair.

"Uh-oh," Richard teases.

Garrett winks at him over his shoulder, both secretly knowing he's about to get a part, and then Garrett exits the trailer and follows Dave across the lot to his on-set office. Dave sits down at his desk. Garrett takes his spot across from him, keeping his smile tame as he waits for the news to be delivered. Dave is not smiling. He sits back in his plush executive chair, crosses his legs, and then nonchalantly removes his glasses to shine them with the cloth square he keeps in shirt pocket.

"We're letting Richard go."

Garrett thinks he must have misheard him.

"What?" He asks to be sure.

"We're writing him out, killing him off," Dave clarifies coolly, breathing hot air onto his lenses, wiping them again and then returning them to his face. "He's had a great run, of course, a long run. But honestly, we've kept him way past his expiration date."

Garrett is flabbergasted. He wonders why Dave is even telling him this.

"We've decided we need a younger male heartthrob to hook a younger demographic of viewers. That's where you come in."

His eyes widen when he realizes what's happening. When he realizes that he's replacing Richard. Surpassing Richard. Eclipsing Richard's star with his. He's going to be the star. And it feels fucking amazing.

"This will be on a trial basis," Dave adds. "Being that you have next to no experience in the industry. If you do well, this character arc could turn into a more permanent role. A *lead* role. I have high hopes for you, Hill. I hope you won't disappoint."

"Of course," Garrett says quickly. "No, I assure you, I won't disappoint."

"Great. You're dismissed then."

"Thank you. Thank you, sir," Garrett says gleefully. Dave nods and Garrett stands to leave. He's got his hand on the doorknob when he's stopped.

"Oh, and Garrett…" Dave says.

He looks back.

"You understand that you should keep this between you and I for now, right? We don't want Rich to say…I don't know…try to break his contract and quit before we get the chance to wrap loose ends up. We want to keep things copasetic and quiet for the good of the show and the cast."

"Of course, sir."

When Garrett returns to the trailer, Richard is waiting for him with a big smile on his face. Garrett's heart beats fast but he doesn't feel the guilt that others might.

"Everything go how I said it would?" Richard asks him, grinning like a fool.

Garrett strips every trace of truth from his face. "Yeah," he replies smoothly. Then he smiles in Richard's face with the nerve of someone who's won. "Everything went exactly like you said it would."

Richard gives him a hearty pat on the back. "Good deal. Let's go shoot."

"Let's go shoot," Garrett agrees. Then the two walk to set together.

A week passes. Garrett goes to Greystone with Richard, drinks Rosé in V.I.P, and gets head from a bottle service girl in the bathroom.

Monday two more scenes get shot, two more scenes closer to the penultimate scene where the old star will die and the new star will take over. Tuesday Richard takes him to Benny Hana for dinner and drinks and they run into a well-known casting director, to whom Richard introduces him. Wednesday they both sit in a room and read the same script, only Garrett knows his is final and Rich's will have edits. Thursday night Richard calls and tells him he can't make it to a party he's been invited to, and says for him to go in his place. While there Garrett meets one of his favorite rappers and gets a hot model's number. Friday they're both back in the studio shooting.

After they wrap, Dave calls Richard into his office. Garrett decides it's best if he leaves before shit hits the fan. But about ten feet away from his car, he hears Richard's voice ricocheting through the lot. *That didn't take lo*ng, Garrett thinks to himself with an eye roll.

"Garrett!" His name is tinged with rage and disdain.

Garrett sighs, stops, and turns around. Richard is walking across the parking lot with purpose. The older man's once famous face is pinched, creating wrinkles across his slick, tan forehead and causing his jet black brows to point down at his prominent nose in a way that makes him look harsh and sinister.

"You opportunistic little ingrate," Richard spits, coming to a screeching halt less than an inch away from Garrett's face. "I took you under my wing, ran lines with you, gave you pointers, introduced you to people, let you into my house…the little one line no name boy in the background that nobody knew or noticed…and this is how you repay me?" His nostrils flare and sweat gathers on his upper lip. "You take my fucking *job*? Who the fuck do you think you are?"

"It's just business, Rich," Garrett says so calmly that it's condescending. "Nothing personal. You know how it goes."

Richard stares at him, the whites of his eyes wild. "Oh I do know how it goes," he says with a smile that is not one of happiness. "I've been in this game for over thirty years. Your pawn's been in play for two seconds. But hey, you're winning right now, right? So fuck who you fucked over to get here, right? Because this is what you wanted. This is your break." He pauses, still staring right at Garrett, and then continues in a more menacing tone. "But just remember, you ain't ever going to be in control of the board, boy. And now that you're on it…just know you can get checkmated as quick as the next." He starts to back away, shaking his finger as he does so. "And I promise you will. I promise."

"Ok, man," Garrett replies with aplomb as he slides into his car. Once the door is shut he has a chuckle. He hopes that when he's a washed up old hack he can fade away with a little more self-respect than Richie. If he's ever as pitiful as that sad sack, hanging on to one role for dear life, he hopes someone puts a bullet through his brain. How sad. He calls up the model he met earlier in the week and tells her drinks are on him tonight. He wants to celebrate his win.

Fuck that sore loser.

CHAPTER 17

AJ is waiting across the street from the restaurant in Santa Monica at eleven o'clock on Wednesday. He's leaned up against his new vintage drop-top GTO, arms crossed and sunglasses pulled down over his eyes. He watches as the restaurant doors swing open and three women walk out.

Anjanae immediately spots him standing there across the street, but pretends like she doesn't see him. Unfortunately, his good looks and bright red car make him hard to miss, and soon her two cohorts are pausing to ogle.

"Mm," Christine murmurs under her breath. "Look at that fine piece of real estate over there."

Annabelle peers at him over the rim of her sunglasses. "If he's real estate, I'd like to buy me some of that land."

Anjanae uncomfortably ignores them and pulls on her sunglasses. As they walk to their cars Annabelle whistles at AJ and Christine cackles girlishly.

"I'll see you hooches next week," Annabelle says as she unlocks her G-Wagon.

They all get into their respective cars. Anjanae watches in her rear-view mirror as the other two women drive off. She then puts her car into drive and acts as though she's leaving too, but really she's just circling the block. A few moments later she pulls up behind AJ's GTO and puts it in park. When she gets out she doesn't look the least bit thrilled to see him. Then again, her soul is hidden behind designer eyewear. AJ removes his own shades and sticks them in his pocket.

"You got your dream car," she says as she approaches him, her tone removed. "Must be makin' a killin'. Knockin' down them old women."

"This isn't even the half of it," he replies, choosing to ignore her snark. "I'm buying a house."

Anjanae snorts and shakes her head with a derisive smirk, looking away from him and crossing her arms defensively.

"We need to talk," he tells her.

"I don't want to talk."

"I assumed as much seeing as I've called your phone over a dozen times in the last two weeks and you haven't answered once."

"Yeah," she says flatly. "By the way, you need to stop doing that before my husband takes notice."

AJ shakes his head and walks past her to the parking meter by her car. She watches him curiously as he inserts quarters into it, one after another.

"What are you doing?" She asks tersely, lifting her shades up.

"We don't have to talk," he says, turning back towards her. "Let's just go for a ride." He looks her in her eyes and implores. "Take a ride with me."

She hesitates, staring at him with a look he can't read. Then with half an eye roll she consents, getting in without saying anything to him.

She doesn't say anything to him. They ride along in silence. Every so many minutes he takes his eyes off the road to look over at her. She's got her stiletto-clad feet propped on the dash, her demeanor still very much aloof. She won't look at him; at least he doesn't catch her looking at him. After quite a few miles on the expressway he exits off onto a highway. The scenery has become a lot less metropolitan, both the ocean and the city long gone in the rearview. The neighborhood they're in now is very middle class. A sign along the road says *Welcome to Reseda*.

"I thought buying a house in the valley would be a good move for my sanity," he tells her, though he already knows she won't respond. "I thought, when I go home, I want to be away from everything. The city, work…I want to be separated from all of that. For a few hours out of the day I want to feel normal."

He's met with the silence he expected.

"Plus, property is cheaper out here," he adds.

"I wonder why," she says snidely then, under her breath.

He turns onto a residential road with an uphill slope. The houses are modest but fairly nice. He pulls into the driveway of the last house on the left. Once he shuts off the engine, he looks over at her.

"This is mine."

She's looking at the very ordinary two-story bungalow in front of her, expression still unreadable. After a beat, she gets out of the car walks to the front door. He watches her, then follows.

He takes out his new key and unlocks the front door, letting her step in before him. He watches her as she stands in one spot and looks around, arms crossed again. The living room isn't much; an empty space void of furniture, bare white walls, and a stucco celling with a basic

wood-paneled fan mounted in the middle. Sun streams in through
the curtain-less window, illuminating the dust settling on the faded oak
floor.

"I know it doesn't look very homey right now," he says to her. "I
just got the keys two days ago, haven't really had a chance to move any
of my stuff in yet. But I have big plans for it."

She wordlessly walks to the nearby kitchen. The sounds of her
heels change as she steps off of wood onto outdated linoleum. The plain
refrigerator and cabinets are nothing special, but there's a big farm sink
by a window that looks out onto the front porch. She idly stares at the
glider swing built for two and the potted peonies that line the deck
railing. She wonders if the real estate agent put the flowers there or if he
did. They look well-watered and healthy, and she imagines he'd take
good care of plants, even though she's never known him to own any.
Out on the sidewalk that goes by the driveway, a little boy is walking a
dog. It's not a small yappy dog or an exotic dog or even a purebred dog.
In fact, she thinks it's a mutt. A golden retriever mixed with a collie, if
she had to guess. Though she's not sure why she cares. An older couple
riding their bikes passes the boy and his dog. There's waving, mouths
smiling and moving, communal familiarity.

"First thing I think I'm going to do is rip up these floors and put
hardwood in here. Redo the cabinets and counter tops. Replace the
fridge. Get a nice stainless steel one. Maybe black since it shows less
smudges."

She's on the move again, peeking into the small, attached
laundry room, and then turning to head up the stairs. He follows her.

"I'm actually going to keep my apartment in Koreatown. It's
cheap and it'll be a convenient place to crash for when I work really la–"
He catches himself. "For when I really don't feel like driving all the way
out here."

She reaches the top floor and stops to let her eyes adjust to the
dark. The electric is off, and without any windows in the hallway it's not
near as bright as the bottom floor.

"I think it will be a good little starter home," he continues to
ramble. "Two bedrooms, two bathrooms, a two-car garage in the
basement…"

She goes into the first bedroom on the left. She can tell instantly
it's the master. It's empty just like all the other rooms, but it's spacious
and sunny and has the view he told her he would get. He hangs back in
the doorway and watches as she slides back the glass door and steps out

onto the private balcony. The backside of the house is built on an incline, and the balcony looks out over a ravine of trees and foliage. She rests her hands on the railing and breathes in the September air while taking it all in. He comes to stand beside her.

"You would find the only hill in an entirely flat neighborhood," she says idly without looking at him. It's the first thing she's said since they arrived.

"I still wanted you to feel somewhat at home when you come to visit."

He looks at her, and after a moment a small smile curls the corners of her lips like he knew it would. He smiles too, then faces forward again. The only sounds around them are those of nature. Birds chirping, light breeze rustling the tree branches. The commotion from the main highway is muffled, the quite street offering a reprieve from any unnecessary noise. It's optimum seclusion trumping opulence, and they both revel in it as they take in the view together

"I missed you," she admits out of the blue.

He turns to face her, surprised by her omission.

"I missed you a lot more than I wanted to," she continues, looking down. "It hurt a lot more…trying to get over you hurt a lot more than being with you when things weren't perfect…aren't perfect. And I know it was only two weeks…but in those two weeks I did a lot of thinking." She looks up at him then. "And I think that there is nothing in life that's perfect. And I don't think I want to go back to how my life was before you were in it."

"I know that I don't want to go back to how my life was before you were in it," AJ replies with conviction. "I know my life has had a lot of changes recently. I know some of those changes aren't ideal. There's a lot of times where I don't know what I want out of life or even what I'm doing with my life anymore, but I do know that I want you. I don't regret anything…any choice I made that led me to meeting you. I will never regret meeting you. And I hope you don't regret me. I know our situation isn't ideal. And I know *I'm* not ideal. An–"

She closes the distance between them in an instance, takes his face in her hands, and kisses him.

He takes her hand in his and leads her back inside, over to the chair in the corner of an otherwise empty bedroom. The previous inhabitants who took most of their other furniture with them must have left it behind. There's not a bed or a couch in the entire house. AJ would have laid her on the floor, but he doesn't have a blanket or a sheet to put between her and the cold hard planks. They undress each other slowly, and then he sits down on the abandoned beige chair and pulls her onto his lap. In actuality it's the perfect position, ideal for the desired closeness they both so desperately need in that moment. She sinks down onto him, arms wrapping around his neck to interlock behind his head. Everything touches everything, from within and out. Both of his hands rove over her body comfortingly, from her shoulders to the small of her back, holding her closer still. It's not a position for fast or hard movement, but he's deeper in her than he's ever been. When he hits a certain place, her head falls back, and he blazes her neck and chest with his mouth. She recovers from the initial feel, and resumes riding him. Everything in his peripheral vision condenses down to the smooth brown skin of her shoulder blade. Every little lift and grind of her hips is enough to keep them both hanging there in the most glorious limbo of limbs and sensation, as he lightly rocks them back and forth and together. He relishes every second of the slow burning fire, the pleasure that's so pure that it's near pain, and it's written on her face, too. Eyes squeezed shut. He grabs a handful of her hair and pulls her head back so he can see her, telling her to open them. And she does.

She comes hard. He follows shortly after.

When AJ takes her back to her car in Santa Monica, she pulls a small gift bag from her backseat that was carefully hidden under two coats she'd probably never need in Southern California. He's taken by surprise when she hands the bag to him.

"Your birthday present," she says. "I bought it before…everything."

"You didn't have to get me anything," he tells her, staring into her eyes earnestly.

She smiles softly. "I wanted to."

He smiles back, then reaches into the bag past the tissue paper. He retrieves a classic moleskin notebook, a vintage quill tip pen, and two jars of ink in both black and blue. His smile grows.

"It's perfect," he says, and when he looks back up his eyes are filled with genuine appreciation. "Thank you so much."

She smiles and nods. "You're welcome."

They stand there on the street as cars zip by them. Neither making a move to leave. Neither looking away from the other's eyes.

"I love you, Anjanae."

"I love you, too."

PART TWO

CHAPTER 18

Maggie doesn't believe in love. She definitely doesn't believe in monogamy. How could she? She'd ruined that farce for herself a long time ago, hadn't she? She wasn't interested in marriage, and commitment was contingent upon things she knew she could never relinquish. So, naturally, she had been single for quite some time. She reasoned that love was for the optimistic and the open; she was realistic and closed off. Her former lovers found her hard to get to know, and that's just how she liked it. Men would still come on to her often, but it often felt like most of them weren't worth the effort. Which often meant she spent her nights alone. She accepted it as collateral for not being a fool.

Yes, she was in a bit of a drought. Which was ironic seeing as she had a small cadre of highly capable, well trained, satisfactory guaranteed young men at her disposal. But Maggie never had sex with any of her employees. Past or present. The thought had never even crossed her mind. That was a man's mistake, fucking the help. She was a professional. Sure, they were fun to look at—she'd hand-picked them after all—but younger guys weren't really her thing. She liked distinguished older men, always had. But as she got older she realized that when she spotted one of these men, they were a lot closer to her age than they used to be. She could choose to let this make her feel old. Make her have a midlife crisis. Take up a frivolous hobby, get a Ferrari, get collagen injections, fuck a man half her age. She could be like the women she catered to, but then she couldn't be herself. The prideful, smart, successful woman that loved herself. She didn't need someone else to. So she placed romance on the back burner in order to first and foremost focus on capital gain.

The best drug dealers were not drug users.

In truth, Maggie didn't date much even before she was who she became. She'd always been highly fastidious and perpetually hard to impress, even as a young girl. She didn't lose her virginity until the summer before she left for college. She went to a private high school and had spent those four years studying fiercely, never seeing the draw that her girlfriends did in the preppy, pimply-faced, polo-wearing boys. To her they were just a distraction, and not a worthy one. She was much too focused for all that giggly schoolgirl shit. During her summer breaks in high school Maggie left the comfort of the suburbs two days a week to volunteer at an outreach program in downtown New Orleans, helping to build houses in impoverished communities. It looked good on her transcript, that's why she did it. That last summer while working downtown, she met a boy from the ninth ward named Tremaine. He wasn't that much older than her, only by a few years, but he had a certain air of experience and charisma those boys at her private school never had. He made her laugh, charmed her, and ultimately won her over in a way she hadn't been before. They'd sneak around; have sex in the backseat of his Buick or her dad's Jag that she drove to work, under the bridge near the outreach sight, vacant lots, basically anywhere they could. She didn't regret the fling one bit, but when summer ended, it ended. As bittersweet as it was at the time, she had always understood that getting an education and having a future was more important than puppy love and sentimental feelings. So she told Tremaine goodbye and left for the West Coast.

Her first real boyfriend came along her first semester at Berkeley. Paul was a professor. Not her professor, though, so it didn't have as much taboo and cliché attached to it as it did when *other* girls did it, so she told herself. He taught both classic literature and advanced philosophy, two completely futile classes she'd never take, so they never had to worry about the administration being peeved over any kind of favoritism. It wasn't like he was an old man, but he was in his mid-thirties, which was a fifteen-year age gap between him and her eighteen-year-old self. They met at the Coffee Shoppe where she started her days, much earlier than most students. He was always there when the café opened at six, just like her. One day he offered to buy her drink, and when she told him a large black coffee with no cream or sugar, she got an eyebrow raise. The next morning, they shared a paper. The next a booth. The next they woke up together and had coffee in bed. Paul was a recent divorcee who had lost his house in the settlement and moved into an apartment conveniently located just off campus. It was obvious to her that she was his early midlife crisis, but that didn't stop her from letting him obsess and dote over her. When her father had died, he insisted he fly to New Orleans with her. Her mother had almost died herself when they got off the plane together. Oh, she was pissed. Not that her gold digging mother had any right to judge her for dating an older man, but her disapproving anger pleased Maggie just as much as Paul's experienced hands and knowledgeable head did. She stayed with him for almost three years, but when she completed her undergraduate degree a year early and got accepted into one of the most prestigious business programs in the country, she decided it was time to move on in more ways than one. He immediately proposed they do the whole long-distance thing, however that idea didn't appeal to her at all. Quite frankly, she had grown tired of the worshipping attentiveness he paid her, and outgrown the fawning student role that was the fix to his fetish to be admired. Quite frankly she *didn't* admire him. Because if you can't do, you teach. So she left him and moved across the country to Boston.

At MIT she decided she would try to date someone her own age. Ben was twenty-two and a Business major too. He was a very nice boy, with a very bright future, from a very esteemed family from Connecticut. However, the frat shenanigans that infatuated college age boys infatuated Ben, despite being in a serious grad program and not at some undergraduate party school. Other than the obvious lack of maturity, he wasn't particularly mind blowing in the bedroom either. She'd tried to teach him things, but for someone with such a high IQ he wasn't a very quick learner. About six months into the relationship she began cheating on him with her married boss.

Mark was forty and part owner of the start-up company where she was interning between juggling a full course load of classes. The first few months she worked there, her relationship with him was strictly professional and platonic. Well, maybe not completely platonic. Maggie didn't miss how his eyes occasionally lingered on hers, and how sometimes their flirty exchanges left his ears red. There were a lot of college girls who worked there, many of whom could have proved tempting to a man in an unsatisfactory marriage, but he managed not to fall victim to their firm bodies and bright eyes. Maggie, however, knew how to keep the ball rolling with brief but purposeful glances and suggestive half-smiles; all done with a subtleness she knew drove him crazy. She let the tension build until it broke one night in the break room after everyone else had left. She knew that very night, as she climbed on top of the conference table littered with documents, she had him wrapped around her finger. To her knowledge they flew under the radar of everyone else who worked there, no thanks to him. She crafted his alibis, planned their meetings, and suppressed his idiocrasy. He threatened multiple times to leave his wife for her. In turn, she told him he was foolish, mainly because she didn't want to have to remind him that his wife actually wanted him, while she just wanted a momentary stress reliever from her tedious schedule. The sex was good, but she found fault in almost all his other aspects. He was a cheater. He was weak minded. And it was almost sad that it had taken him nearly twenty years after graduating to start making real moves, and when he finally did he couldn't do it alone. He had to have partners with more funds than him, and recruit college students with more knowledge than him, and take out bank loans that he'd probably never be able to pay off because said business was very small and was probably never going to be very big; she could tell just by how he ran it. When she'd told him one day she was going to run her own business, he'd laughed at her like she was simply some idealistic girl. He doubted her, and that was perhaps his most undesirable attribute, next to the acute Bostonian accent that she could tolerate just long enough to get him somewhere private and silence him. She ended things with him and Ben (who never did find out what she'd been doing behind his back) in one fell swoop.

She graduated top of her class at MIT. She applied only to positions on Wall Street, and most made her very appealing offers based solely on her impressive college credentials. She reviewed her options, narrowed them down, and countered back like her father had taught her. She held out and got even better offers before taking the best one. She stayed single her first few years in New York, focusing on her career and moving up the corporate ladder faster than her counterparts. The nice thing about New York was you could meet interesting new people every day to have non-meaningful relations with—should the urge hit and you feel so inclined—and be practically guaranteed to never run into that person again. It was perfect for that particular part of her life. You could go to a different restaurant or bar or club every night, and you could go to all of these places alone and not be judged because New York was full of independent loners roaming the city by themselves. You could give someone a fake name, a fake number. No name, no number. It was so fabulously freeing. And while some did get her number and did get to know her in limited primal ways, she didn't allow herself to be labeled a *girlfriend* again until she was nearly thirty.

Eduard was an Armenian investment banker from a competing company. He was in his late forties, pushing fifty, and well renowned by Wall Street standards. They met in a boardroom vying on each of their corporations' behalf for an important client's business. Maggie won. She could tell Eduard was impressed by her drive, and perhaps by her ability to beat him at a game he thought he'd mastered, despite her relatively young age and the fact that she was a woman in a predominately male dominated occupation. Sure enough, the next morning there was an email from him in her inbox. In it, he confirmed what she'd assumed, and followed up by asking if he could take her out sometime. She accepted his offer. He took her on three swanky dates before she allowed him to accompany her up to her thirty-third street apartment—practicing decorum again seeing as her veil of anonymity had been thwarted—and after a month or so of spending time, they decided to make it official.

They stayed together for a little over three years. After the one-year mark, he suggested she move in with him. Against her better judgment, she did. Oh, sure it was an all right relationship. They went on nice vacations (the South of France, Greece, Egypt), dined well, went to plays, and were invited to all the best formal events in town. It was all very domesticated and normal and healthy, until it was grating and stifling and insufferable. He became very clingy, to the point where she felt like she couldn't turn around or breathe without him being there. When she wanted some alone time or to go somewhere by herself, there were always questions. And when he wasn't hounding her about something insignificant, he was dropping not so subtle hints at her. About marriage. About children. He was in his early fifties and had never had children because he had always been too consumed by his career; it's what ended his first marriage a decade before. But now that he was closing in on retirement and had accomplished all that he'd set out to accomplish, he suddenly realized that he wanted some. Two. Three. Hell, maybe a whole quartet. To hell with her career. To hell with what she wanted to accomplish. That was the other thing (besides the clinginess and the questions and the persisting); he had ceased to care about what she wanted. He didn't want to hear about her day, what she did, what she managed to accomplish. So much as one word about it would set him off. Suddenly, what had first attracted him to her was now what he abhorred about her. She held a higher title than he had at her age, she was making way more money than any of the women at his company were, she was making more money *for* her company than he was for his, and while he was cutting back on his hours at the office, she was adding to hers. At that moment, she was more successful. To say it put him off was putting it lightly. He didn't understand why she still even *needed* to work. She had landed a wealthy man, after all. His salary, and eventually 401k, would more than maintain their lifestyle. He didn't understand why she couldn't just be happy being a housewife and birthing his babies. And that's when she realized he didn't understand her. She evaded his questions until she couldn't any longer. He took her to her favorite Italian restaurant one night, where he proceeded to get down on one knee, present to her one of the biggest diamonds she'd ever seen, and ask the ultimate question. There wasn't any indecision to her answer. She said no, and that was that.

The year following her breakup with Eduard was tiresome and not at all as freeing as she'd thought it would be. Sure, she was happy to be free from him, but it seemed like everything else was chambering her, like she was treading through quicksand in her high heels trying not to get sucked under by the corporate depression she felt was soon to engulf her. In lieu of her ruining his life and wasting his time (his words, not hers) she didn't fight him for the apartment. She could have taken it from him if she wanted (even though it was technically his to start with) but she'd lost her lust for arguing. Therefore, she had to find a new place to live, which in Manhattan is the epitome of trying. She settled out of fatigue for a halfway decent one-bedroom that wasn't rent controlled, furnished, or worth the outlandish price she was paying for it. It was also a bit more of a trek to work than her apartment with Eduard had been, meaning she had to walk several more blocks, and New York had been in the midst of what felt like the worst winter to date since she'd lived there. Speaking of work, she had been fighting for a raise for a year but her boss wasn't budging. And when a higher paying positioned opened up, he chose some *man* who had only been with the company a year to fill it instead of her. She knew she could leave and go to another company, she had the decorated resume, but the idea of going through the same old rigmarole in simply a different building or a different floor only served to depress her more. Yes, she made six figures and had a fairly secure job, but when she compared that to what she could do, she was disappointed. Her father was running his own business before his thirtieth birthday, and here she was almost thirty-five, still working for someone else and fighting for respect and recognition amongst her peers. Her father always preached the liberty of working for one's self. She wanted that. She wanted to be admired and revered, maybe even a little feared. She wanted control. She wanted *to* control. But for the time being, she was still working for the man.

During this period of mild melancholia, she met Theo, perhaps her most meaningful relationship. She had to pass him every day on her way to and from work. It was such an ugly sight, a beautiful man peddling fake purses out of a trash bag. One day, feeling particularly philanthropic, she decided she would help him get a job. A nearby upscale restaurant was hiring. She ate there often; always leaving gracious tips, well-liked by the manager. Her letter of recommendation went over well and he got the position. He was so appreciative. In fact,

she didn't know if a man had ever looked at her with such
admiration as Theo. Of course, it was obvious to her that he was quite
gay and not to mention quite a bit younger than her, but that didn't
matter. She wasn't looking for sexual companionship. Maggie didn't
have many friends. There were a few women from work she'd go out for
drinks with, attend Pilates and spin classes with. She knew basic things
about these women; what their husbands did, the amount of kids they
had, how they liked their wine spritzers, but nothing overly personal.
She wasn't interested enough in these women to learn more; their
storylines weren't compelling and their springs weren't deep. Maggie
was, however, interested in Mister Theo. Like her, he didn't seem to
have too many people in his life, and they both relished taking their
lunch breaks together, having long talks while enjoying the special of
the day.

She was fascinated by the things he'd done, enamored by the life
he'd lived and his will to stay above water. He told her about his rough
upbringing, about being homeless off and on for seven years. He told her
about how, before she got him the job at the restaurant, he had not only
been selling fraudulent and stolen merchandise, but sex as well. He
explained to her how, when he was seventeen, he worked at a popular
but dodgy gay club in Greenwich Village. He lied to the club manager
about his age, hoping to get hired on as part of the wait staff, but was
instead hired on as part of the male entertainment. He usually just
stripped, but occasionally he'd get dressed up and do the drag show, too.
He told her he got solicited regularly and how sometimes, for a little
extra money, he'd take these men up on their offers. One night he got
caught giving a blow job in the bathroom and was fired on the premise
that prostitution was strictly prohibited, even though he knew good and
well he wasn't the only dancer there doing it. So without a job, he
continued to do it. He told her how he took to hanging out in sketchy
places in attempts of finding immoral men. How he'd take cues from the
working girls and the transvestites, see what they were doing and where
they were going, sometimes even stealing their Johns right out from
under them. Out of curiosity, she asked him one day how much he made
when he was doing all this, and was startled to find out just how low a
strikingly good-looking man was giving himself up for. It hardly seemed
right, doing these debasing things in backseats, seedy motels, and side
alleys for such a small price. On another day, purely out curiosity again,
she asked him if he'd ever had a pimp. He told her there were a few
instances where a sleaze ball had seen him on the street doing his thing

and tried to recruit him, but he always decided to remain on his own. This is when she told him jokingly that with her business savvy she could have made him a whole lot more money. They both had a good laugh over this, and she secretly tucked the thought into the back of her mind.

The thought stayed in the back of her mind for a while, festering. They say idle hands are the devil's workshop, and with no one or nothing to occupy her nights the wheels of her imagination spun in the worst ways. One of her favorite restaurants at the time was a little out of the way place in a grimy part of Chelsea that most wouldn't feel comfortable visiting after dark. It stayed open late, had the best chicken Parmesan in the city, and served a wide array of top shelf liquor for a fraction of the price of her favorite Upper Eastside establishments. She'd go alone after late nights at the office and eat at either the bar or the little table by the back window she claimed as hers. After she finished her meal she'd linger—some nights sipping Moet, other nights Courvoisier—and people watch. The window faced the alley, and around nine thirty, the girls and the men posing as girls would start to come out. That particular street was a prime location for prostitution, partially secluded and somewhere between rich and poor. She'd watch cars pull up and dim their lights, watch leather and rayon clad women get in and then reemerge a few minutes later with a wad of money. Sometimes she'd watch them prance across the street on half broken heels to the motel, looking over their shoulders every few steps. Sometimes she'd see a man standing in the shadows, keeping a watchful eye on the liaisons, giving quiet direction, and reaping what his women sewed. She wondered to herself why sex workers were always straight women and gay men. She wondered why there wasn't a market for straight men. She wondered what it would be like if women were the target clientele. She thought of how different it could be if women were the customers and not the servers. *Higher standards, higher income.* She thought of how different it could be if a woman was running the show instead of a man. *Higher standards, higher income.*

Soon, she was crunching numbers and figuring wages. She wanted to have it all laid out perfectly on paper before she proposed her master plan to Theo. She had invested well her entire life; her stocks solid, her savings plentiful. She knew how to manage her own money without a middleman; handle her own assets without hiring a third person. She could cover up a fraudulent cash flow; she could evade taxes. She could do it. There was more than one night while concocting this scheme where she considered the fact that she might be crazy. A very small part of her felt like she was making a horrible mistake, forsaking a life of stability on a whim to make herself wealthier. A very small part of her doubted whether Theo would go along with her idea. But for as sorry as she felt for him and the hard knock life he'd led, she got the feeling he felt sorrier for her and the unfulfilling life she was leading. She hated people feeling sorry for her more than just about anything, but if she could exploit his genuine sympathy to get them both better lives, she would. The bigger part of her knew that she would be successful in whatever endeavor, regardless of how ludicrous, because of this sheer gumption. The next thing she knew she was leaving her letter of resignation on her boss' desk, and having a sit-down conversation with Theo. She told him all he had to do was trust her.

He trusted her. Two weeks later they were on a first-class flight to Los Angeles, where the rich lived and the desperate flocked. The perfect combination, she thought. Maggie knew she could have stayed in New York and formed her "startup," but the truth? She wanted a new life to start from scratch. A new start in a new city where nobody knew her, where the weather was always nice and there was a plethora of young, beautiful, broke men for her picking. Within the course of a year she had garnered a nice client list, recruited a roster of six sexy employees, and was enjoying a comfortably plush life. She hadn't expected it to all come together so quickly, but it did, and she felt like a natural in her new role. It was around her one-year mark in LA that she met David, the first and last man she'd dated since coming to California.

David was a sixty-year-old man who went to the tanning bed twice a week, got hair treatments monthly, and wrote golf retreats off as business ventures. She knew from the start she could never take a man like him seriously, but his lifestyle was thankfully much more interesting than him, so she entertained the notion he had of her. They met in the Gucci store at the Beverly Center. He approached her, dropping his name and a few others in flirtation to impress her. She wasn't, but pretended she was. She told him she was an accountant who had recently been transferred to her company's Los Angeles office. She told him she was from New York (leaving out by way of New Orleans) because she knew a cocky Californian man like him would probably be turned on by thinking that he was conquering one of those tough East Coast broads. He was a board member of The Academy, as in *I'd like to thank*, and had been born and raised in Beverly Hills with a silver spoon in his mouth that later turned into a key in his hand. That key worked a lot of industry doors. He knew damn near everybody in the business and while she was with him, they attended many a soiree. He practically turned her into a socialite, and she quickly learned it was much more fun being one of those in LA than it was New York. She rubbed elbows and kissed cheeks with Hollywood elite while listening to him go on about his brilliant accountant girlfriend. She got the feeling she was an anomaly to his normality, which was much less educated, and it was obvious he was quite smitten with her. Of course, this was all just recreation for her; she had no real interest in being in the industry. Still, it was fun to be able to say you had been to the Oscars and such. After nine months she decided to break things off. At this point in her life it was more important than ever to keep people at an arm's length. And while it probably would have taken him at least ninety more months to figure out her actual job title, she was tired of feigning interest in a one-dimensional old man who had never actually worked a day in his life. The breakup was very amicable, no hard feelings to be had. She even ended up advising some actors on their investments based on David's praise of her aptitude; which he really knew nothing about, but God bless the poor dumb thing. To this day she was still sent invitations to award shows and events. She took Theo.

While David went back to dating barely legal models and actresses, Maggie went back to being alone. Which was better for her, she told herself. For over eight years she hadn't had a steady man in her life, a real relationship, or even a long-term friend with benefits. She had mildly reverted back to her mid-twenties Manhattan ways, picking strangers up for one night only affairs. But it just didn't feel the same mid-forties in Los Angeles. Still, at the end of the day she had some of the same wants and needs as everyone else, and when she felt like it, she'd allow herself to be wooed over white wine at a bar in a neighborhood the wasn't hers. Such instances led to quickies in bathrooms and check-ins to the nearest hotel, clothes being ripped off with haste or pulled to the side in impatience, hot air and heavy breathing, clumsy hands that didn't know her body and the sloppy kisses of someone she'd never see again. She never took them back to her apartment, rarely giving them her real name. These liaisons were seldom satisfactory, so she limited them to a minimum, relying mainly on the top of the line devices she bought for herself. On rare nights of honesty, when she'd soothed herself to near sleep and lay in bed alone, appeased but not satisfied, tumbler of brown liquor to keep her warm, she'd admit that things were only this way because of who she was as a person. She was a lot, and she knew that. She had never met a man that could handle her, *really* handle her. She'd never met her equal. Her match. Her soulmate. An arguer. An asserter. A self-secure passionate person who wasn't afraid to take the backseat from time to time, but who also wouldn't balk when met with her resistance. Yes, these were the things she wanted in a man.

But by no means did she need one.

And she hadn't had one…in a *very* long time.

CHAPTER 19

Maggie is walking down Rodeo Drive with one of her fake friends. Leah Taylor is a well-renowned makeup artist to the stars, and wife of International male model and occasional actor, Tom Taylor. Leah's younger sister, Jessica, is the lingerie model who dated David right before Maggie did. Leah had always hated her sister, so she immediately befriended Maggie out of spite towards Jessica. But that was Hollyweird for you. Maggie had always heard the bad blood was formed out of jealously because Leah was never pretty enough to be a model herself, but she didn't know this for a fact. Leah had certainly had many things tightened, reduced, removed and redistributed elsewhere in an attempt to look like the star she was not. Maggie imagined that making beautiful people more beautiful day in and day out had taken a toll on her ego. Poor thing.

Both women wear chicly simple dresses, high heels, and sunglasses. Their arms are weighed today with multiple shopping bags as they stroll the sumptuous street, catching up with each other.

"Anyway, Tom thinks that I should cater to him like I cater to my clients. I do make-up for a living; I spend all day listening to bitches bitch while I make them pretty. For God's sake, I don't want to come home and hear it from my husband. He's so needy."

"He was in the chair when you met him. Maybe he thinks you're going to trade him in for a newer model," Maggie says cheekily. "Double entendre intended."

"I've never thought about that," Leah muses.

Maggie can see it pleases her to think her husband might be jealous, that he's needy because that's his way of coping with his secret fear that she will leave him for someone better. Of course this isn't the case. He's needy because he's a man. But Maggie doesn't tell her that. Maggie just tells her what she wants to hear.

"Enough about me, though," Leash says. "How are things going in the financial advising business?"

"Oh you know, so-so," Maggie replies coolly. "We live in a town where everybody loves money just a little less than they love spending it. Most of my clients have more than they know what to do with; I'm just trying to get them to invest it wisely."

"You know, I have some bonds but I really need to get my stocks up, and my advisor is such a stick in the mud to talk to. I need some insider info; what's on the up and up?"

Maggie opens her mouth to reply but is suddenly distracted by the sight of two familiar men having lunch outside a little bistro up the street; a white-haired man in a checkered shirt and some kind of hat resembling a beret, and a black man in a snug sweater with a shirt underneath buttoned up to the collar. They both look very dignified as they discuss something tedious. They are, after all, both prominent producers. They are Charlie Bradford and Julius Collins. Maggie has known both of them for close to nine years. They were friends of her ex's and therefore, by proxy, friends of hers. They all ran in the same elite social circle.

"Is that Leah Taylor and Maggie Hunter?" Charlie calls out with a leer when he spots them.

Julius turns and peers over the rim of his low-sitting specks. "Why I do believe it is."

The two women smile politely and make their way up onto the deck.

"Why good afternoon ladies," Julius says cordially. "Come. Lunch with us."

Maggie and Leah grab a chair and take a seat.

"Waiter," Julius snaps his fingers.

And a waiter is immediately there. "Yes, Mr. Collins?"

"Get two drinks for these here two fine women," Julius tells him.

"Of course, sir."

"Moet et Chandon," Maggie says.

"Of course, ma'am."

"Is it too late for a Mimosa?" Leah wonders aloud.

"It's never too late for mimosa," Charlie chimes in.

"That's right," Julius concurs with a smile.

"Alright then," Leah says. "You've persuaded me. I'll have a mimosa."

"Yes, ma'am. I'll be right back with your drinks." And then he scurries off to do what he's been told.

Maggie remembers how Julius' wife's name had been on her schedule not that long ago. She'd had two dates with Andrew back in late May. Rough patch, Maggie had assumed, since she hadn't called back in three months. She stares across the table at him. An Audemars

Piguet watch takes up his entire wrist, and she wonders derisively if that flouncy sweater he's wearing is Coogie or Ralph Lauren.

"I believe that I read a new Julius Collins' motion picture is in the works," she says to him with reserved ostentatiousness. "Another box office hit, I'm sure."

"Yes, it's coming along quite nicely. We're set to wrap shooting next month."

"Charlie here hasn't had a box office hit since…what was the year? 1999?" Leah teases the older gentleman.

"2003," he corrects her. "If I remember correctly that was your husband's last hit, too."

"Yes, but he's a model. Acting is just his side gig. He doesn't have to be successful at it."

"How is Thomas enjoying that retirement he was forced into," Charlie chides.

Leah just rolls her eyes.

"Models expire by thirty," Charlie explains to Maggie, though she knows. "Actors by forty. Us producers, we can go on forever."

"Because no one is forced to stare at your ugly mugs," Leah mutters under her breath.

Charlie sits back in his seat and roars with laughter.

"Oh, your words, Leah," Julius says with a smirk. "They burn so."

"I don't need to make another hit as long as I live," Charlie informs her, taking a drink of his midafternoon cocktail. "I've had plenty of trophies."

"Are we talking globes or wives?" Maggie asks facetiously.

Charlie winks at her. "Both."

They all four have a chuckle. The waiter drops off the rest of the drinks.

"How about we just say cheers to being successful," Julius suggests. "All four of us, in all our endeavors…whatever they may be."

"I can toast to that," Maggie says.

"I guess I can, too," Leah agrees.

They all raise their glasses and clink them together.

"And cheers to trophies," Julius adds. "On shelves and on arms."

Maggie glances off to the side as she takes a long swig of champagne.

~

Later that night, Maggie sits in a booth at a Burbank sports bar waiting for Garrett to show up. She hasn't been this far out of the city limits in a while. She's neither seen nor heard from her little narcissistic, blue-eyed, blonde haired employee in a while either. She'd taken to leaving voices messages on his phone regarding where to meet a client, and nine times out of ten she'd get a brief text message back hours later saying he couldn't make it. He hadn't been to the office, hadn't even collected his last check. She finally got him on the line and *told* him that they needed to have a talk. He agreed to come, not that he had a choice. She was already going out of her way for him, offering to meet him at some out of the way place a mile from the studio where the soap is shot. As it is, he's twenty-minutes late. She orders a second glass of wine for herself and a glass of sparkling water for him and stares a hole into the door. Finally, he waltzes in, dressed in a loudly printed Versace jacket with the hood pulled over his gold mop of hair, a gold chain around his neck, skinny pewter pants, and studded Louboutin loafers, looking like the most even mix of metrosexual and wannabe G she's ever seen.

"What's up," he says, plopping down across the table from her with the overly pleased golden retriever puppy look she's beginning to despise.

"You've worked one night in the last two weeks," she answers flatly. "I've called, you don't answer. I've summoned you to the office, you don't come."

Garrett leans forward. "I just don't think it's a good look for me to be hanging out around the office anymore, that's all."

"You act like my office is a shanty pink building across the street from an airport with a sign made of fizzled out fluorescent bulbs."

He takes a drink of his sparkling water, smiling to appease. "All I'm saying is, given my new celebrity status, I need to be careful of where I'm seen."

"Now that you bring it up," she says, air of pompous ridicule in her voice. "I really do wish that these windows had blinds. I can barely make out your fetching features for all the flashing cameras."

He rolls his eyes.

She takes a drink of wine. "You're hardly a paparazzi magnet yet. You've appeared in a few episodes of a daytime soap. Let's not get ahead of ourselves."

"Yeah," he says, taking a defensive tone. "And I'd like to keep appearing in episodes if that's all right with you."

"If you want to quit, Garrett, just say so."

"I don't want to quit."

"You clearly have other means of income now, and I would hate to come between you and the image you have of yourself, so just say the word and I'll take you off the schedule and payroll effective immediately."

"No," he says quickly. "Don't take me off. I still need the extra money." The truth? Ever since he had been cast he had been spending money left and right, trying to keep up with his new television friends. He had been going out almost every night, paying for bottles so he could pop champagne in VIP, and buying drinks for girls that weren't buying him. There had been multiple trips to Rodeo Drive to cash an entire check and then some on a new wardrobe, so when the paparazzi did start following him, they wouldn't catch him slipping. "I'll get you a copy of my shooting schedule," he tells her. "So you'll know in advance when I can work and when I can't. And I promise, I'll answer your calls as long as I'm not on set."

"Are you sure you want to keep doing this?" She asks just to be arrogant. "Because I can replace you easily. It's not a problem."

"I'm sure. I don't want to quit. At least not yet."

She cuts her eyes at him.

"I want to make sure they don't kill me off in the winter finale," he admits.

"Are you serious?"

"I know I just got made a series regular and that they're telling me I'm the next new male lead and everything, but anything can happen for ratings. I'd like to hold on to my safety blanket a bit longer if that's all right. Till January. Then you can replace me."

She's looking at him, smirking. "You know that's your conscience talking." She nods with her eyes as she takes a drink. "Cause of what you did to Rich."

Garrett sighs. "I didn't do anything to Rich, the producers sacked him." He glances at his watch, a brand new Bulgari. "I've got an eight p.m. call time. Are we good here?"

"Yes. We're good. Go. Cheerio." She shoos him out of the booth, watching him walk out of the restaurant and cross the parking lot to his pristine little Audi two-seater. She remembers when he was driving a supped up Civic that backfired all the time and had peeling paint and a mismatching door. That was before she came into his life and rearranged it, upgrading everything he had and knew to new. Now after all she had done for him, he wanted to leave. She shakes her head as she looks back away from the window.

There's a man at the bar staring at her. She doesn't miss it. Unfortunately for him, she thinks, the only thing on her mind is business. And he's much too old for her to employ. She pretends like she doesn't see him, takes out her phone, and continues to nurse her glass of wine. The man finishes his drink in one tilt, gets up, walks straight to her booth, and boldly slides in right across from her. Maggie doesn't startle. After a second she coolly glances up from her phone, and looks at him like he must be out of his mind. His smile is swarthy and his eyes are charming.

"Hello, I'm Alejandro Suarez," he says self-assuredly. "But most people call me Ali." He extends an arm to shake her hand.

She leaves his hand hanging. "Hello 'Alejandro most people call me Ali'. What are you doing in my booth?"

He lowers his hand and smirks. "I apologize for my forwardness. I've just always been a man who goes after what he wants."

She tilts her head, deciding to play along. "And why would you want me?"

"You caught my eye the moment I walked in the door. You have a certain air about you that can't be ignored."

"Is that right?"

He nods.

She could admit to herself that he *is* an attractive man. Distinguished. Early fifties. He has a tan complexion, a full head of dark hair that is graying just around the edges, and facial features that were slightly weathered in a ruggedly handsome way. His broad shoulders are encased beneath a stylish suit jacket and his wrist has an understated gold Rolex around it. She smiles.

"Tell me, Alejandro most people call me Ali, do you usually get what you want?"

"Sometimes."

They hold each other's gaze; both generally intrigued by the other.

"I can leave if you want me to," he says after a beat. "It was rude of me to just sit down without invitation."

"Yes it was," she replies. "But since you've already gone and made yourself comfortable…you might as well stay."

He smiles. "Good." He glances at her now almost empty glass and sits back. "Can I buy you a drink?"

"I'm fine. Thank you, though." In her mind she's smiling smugly, enjoying watching him watch her put him through his paces.

He studies her and shakes his head. "You're difficult."

"That's really dependent upon who's working the puzzle."

He smirks. "I'm good at putting pieces together."

"I'm sure you are."

"You shouldn't underestimate me."

"I wouldn't dream of it."

He sits back in the booth and crosses one leg over the other in a way that only well aged, sophisticatedly secure men do. "You know you haven't told me your name yet..."

"I know," she replies back coolly.

He tilts his head at her and gives her a look. A look she's sure works well for him. Still. He's not backing down, and she was maybe just a little bit glad.

"Maggie Hunter," she relents.

"Tell me, Maggie Hunter, I'm not going to get you in trouble with your boyfriend, am I?"

She looks down and smiles then. When she looks back up she meets his eyes purposefully. "If you think you're going to flatter me by suggesting that I'm in a relationship with a man half my age you've got the wrong woman."

"Who's flattering? I can estimate your age just as easily as I can estimate his. I'd say it doesn't matter how much younger than you he is. I'd say you're a woman who is used to getting what she wants, numbers be damned."

She stares at him. She can vaguely smell his cologne, tempered by the day and their distance. It registers in her mind as something she's spritzed on a tester at Bloomingdales in consideration to buy for one of the boys. She had ultimately decided it wouldn't suit any of them. But it suits him. She looks back down.

"You know," she tells him, running a manicured finger around the stem of her wine glass. "As two people who are used to getting what they want, this is a very dangerous game to play." Her eyes flick up to his. "Because someone has to lose."

"I'm willing to take my chances."

He has some gumption. She shakes her head with the slightest of smiles.

"So he's not your boyfriend?" Ali presses again.

"No." She swallows the last sip of wine. "He's not."

Ali's smile is a smug one, not unlike hers. "Good to know."
He admires her for a moment more and then begins to move towards the
edge of the booth. "Well as thrilling as this has been, I must get going.
Prior engagements call." He looks at her hopefully. "Could I get your
number?"

"You won't catch me."

"Pardon?" He asks, taken aback.

"You said as thrilling as this has been. It's only thrilling because
it's the chase. And I'm here to tell you I don't get caught." She pauses,
then adds, "And I don't give my number out to strangers."

He flashes her his pearly white teeth. "Well, if it's any
consolation, I'd really like for us to not be strangers."

She keeps a stiff smirk on her lips, not acceding.

He shrugs coolly. "That's fine. I'll just get it from the book."

She raises an eyebrow condescendingly. "You really think I'm in
any book."

He meets her gaze again, shakes his head, smiles and sighs. "I'm
about to go really old fashioned on you." He pulls a pen out of his
pocket and clicks it on.

"Do you always carry a pen on you?" She chides.

He winks as he reaches across the table to grab a napkin. "I stay
prepared."

She cracks a small smile as he neatly writes his number on the
napkin. He clicks the pen when he's done, shoving it back down in his
pocket, then stands. He takes out his wallet and throws some money on
the table to cover her drink.

"I don't need you to pay for my drink," she tells him.

"And I don't need you to need me." He flashes her the smile *and*
the look then, simultaneously. "I just want you to want me."

She rolls her eyes. He starts for the door then stops.

"You should know I'm not threatened by you." He looks over his
shoulder at her. "That's why I left you my number. Call me or don't call
me. The ball is in your court. Regardless, it was a pleasure meeting you,
Miss Maggie Hunter."

She nods cordially. He leaves.

Leaving her, for the first time in a very long time, wanting
maybe just a little bit more.

CHAPTER 20

Six days have elapsed since Maggie met Mr. Alejandro Suarez. She sits in her apartment and stares at the wrinkled napkin with a number written on it in slightly smeared blue ink for the sixth night in a row, trying to decipher if the last number is a three or a five. The amount of control she's able to exercise never ceases to impress her, because she's thought about dialing the number at least twice a day since she got it. She reminisces on the way he looked at her that night at the bar, and decides that the last digit is a five. The next thing she knows her thumb is pressing the numbers. She listens to the sound of ringing, part of her hoping he picks up and the other part hoping it was a three.

"Hello?"

He doesn't say his name, but she knows it's him. She may have only met the man once, but his voice has stored itself in her mind. Baritone. Smooth.

"I'm not calling you," she tells him.

There's silence for a second while he registers what's happening and who's calling. But then she can practically hear him smile through the phone.

"It sure sounds like you are," he replies cheekily.

"Yes but I'm not calling to ask you out or anything like that. I've been invited to this fundraiser dinner Saturday night, one of those tedious events that I'd prefer to skip, but it would be disrespectful for me not to show up and tacky for me to show up alone. You see, I have this plus one and I need a date. Not a date as in a *date* date. I just need an escort." She hears what she's said and quickly backtracks. "No. Not an escort. That wasn't the right word. Let me rephr–"

"You're really not good at this," Ali interjects.

"I'm good at everything."

"Humility?"

His sarcasm makes her smile, but she masks it in her voice. "Funny."

"What time is the dinner?"

"Eight."

"I'll pick you up at seven-thirty," he says without dither, not missing a beat.

"Who said I wanted you to pick me up?"

"Do you want me to meet you there?"

"No," she relents after a purposeful pause, a slight sigh at the end for effect. "I suppose you can pick me up. I'll text you my address."

"Ok," he replies. It's the deep and silky tone that he's taking with her now. "I will see you Saturday night then."

"Mmhm," she mumbles in a removed fashion to let him know that she agrees to the plan, but that she isn't all smiley and smitten over it.

She hangs up before he can say anything more.

Maggie sits there for a minute afterwards and stares at her phone. Then she shakes her head. Then she smiles.

~

When Saturday night rolls around, the bellman holds the door open for her when he sees her coming. The elegant red dress and strappy heels she's wearing would make it hard for anyone to miss her. She thanks him as she exits her building, slipping her phone into her clutch. When she looks back up, she spots Ali. He's standing in front of a newer model dark grey Cadillac sedan, wearing a nice suit and a confident smile. Maggie tries not to act impressed as she approaches, but she is. He opens the passenger side door without a word and she slides in.

"You look nice," he tells her once he pulls out onto the road, glancing over at her with a little smile.

"You do, too."

Ali chuckles. "You sound surprised."

"Well when you meet a person at a bar the important details aren't usually exchanged. Like whether or not they own a suit or drive a respectable car."

"Suits," Ali tells her. "Plural. I own more than one."

"That's good to know."

"It's good to know that my car is respectable," he says, and then adds cutely, "I would hate for it to be disrespectful."

'Seriously," she tells him. "The type of car a man drives says a lot about him."

He lifts a dark brow as he navigates traffic. "And what does my car say about me?

"It's new and very clean, so that says you care about your appearance. It's a sedan, so that says you're secure. You don't need some two-door sports car or big burley truck to feel like a man." She watches as a smile makes its way across his face as she speaks. "Grey says practical. Cadillac says classic..."

"So I'm a pretty, well-endowed, sensible classic," he replies.

"You added a few choice words, but yes, that is what your car says. Now," she adds, returning his cheekiness, "Whether it's telling me the truth or not..."

"I guess you'll just have to find out."

He turns to look at her and his eyes twinkle with the kind of trouble she wouldn't mind getting in to.

Later at the benefit dinner, Maggie and Ali are seated at their designated table. Maggie doesn't personally know any of the other attendees; she knows she was invited because of her former relationship with David, but thankfully he's not in attendance. The other occupants of their table are up mingling around as the event winds down, but she and Ali don't feel like they need to do that. They're doing fine just enjoying each other's company.

"So, do you live in Burbank?" Maggie asks, taking a final bite of her dessert and pushing her plate away.

"Hm?" He asks, looking a bit confused.

"I met you at a bar in Burbank. I just wondered if that's where you lived."

"Oh, no. I wouldn't want to be that far out. I live in Downtown LA, recently renovated loft. But I've got a house in Burbank right now."

"A loft in Downtown and a house in Burbank," she says amusedly, taking a sip of champagne. "How high-end and low-key."

Ali chuckles. "I should have elaborated. I'm a realtor. I currently have a property in Burbank that I'm showing. I'm afraid I only have one abode."

"A realtor," she says. She unconsciously glances at his Rolex; it's different from the one she saw on his wrist at the bar. "Is that a lucrative profession?"

"In Los Angeles?" He smiles. "Yes, it can be very lucrative. But I've been in the business for years, worked my way up. Most of the houses I sell now are 40,000 square feet or more with price tags starting around 1 million and going skyward. You can make very good commission if you know what you're doing."

"You must know what you're doing."

"What can I say, I pick my properties and I have an eye for potential."

They hold each other's gaze. He picks up his glass and takes a drink.

"Plus, it's about understanding the market," he continues. "Knowing when it's up, when it's down. I know when to hold and I know when to fold."

She smiles.

"What do you do?" He asks her.

"I'm an agent," she replies without waver.

"Oh. Like a talent agent?"

"Yes," she says, taking another sip of champagne. "I manage a lot of talent."

"Anyone I know?" He asks her curiously.

Maggie sits back and smirks. "Now you know I can't divulge that kind of information about my clients."

Ali looks down and smiles. "No, I understand. I deal with 'the stars', too." He takes a drink and swallows. "You know that's something we have in common. Our careers."

"How so?"

He looks back up at her. "We both have to exercise discretion. And we're both in sales."

Maggie quirks an eyebrow at him, perplexed and unsure of where this is going.

"I sell houses and you sell dreams," he says.

She chuckles, relaxing then, and takes a sip from her glass. "Yes, well, I suppose that is true."

Afterwards, Ali escorts Maggie to the entrance of her building. They stop in front of the door, both wearing genuine smiles; she tries to hide hers, but it's there.

"Well. Thank you for accompanying me tonight. I know it was probably quite a bore."

"I had a great time," he tells her, and he sounds sincere.

She looks him in the eyes. "I suppose it wasn't too bad of a night."

"So," he says then. "Have I proven myself? Am I worthy to promote from *not a date* to a date?"

Maggie smirks to herself, looks down, and then turns for the door. He waits. She stops, and glances back over her shoulder. "Call me," is all she says.

Ali smiles, pleased. He watches as the bellman opens the door.

"Welcome back, Ms. Hunter," the little man with a top hat says to her as she waltzes through the door into her building.

"Goodnight, Ms. Hunter!" Ali calls after her sassily. She looks back one more time, rolls her eyes, and then disappears. He laughs to himself, runs a hand over his face, shakes his head with a smile, and gets back into his Cadillac.

CHAPTER 21

Austin was once the weakest link in Maggie's lineup, but he has since stepped up to the plate and is now hitting homeruns. In the beginning she thought he might not work out, but he had proved her wrong. He had proved to be just as valuable as the others. He had garnered a string of women who now considered themselves his regulars, and these women never complain, so Maggie assumes he has improved upon his technique and honed his craft like she had advised him to do. He is really doing quite well for himself, there are more and more women calling and requesting him after meeting him out and about. Austin is neither the brightest book on the shelf nor the meanest conversationalist, but she thinks his silly lopsided grin and good looks get him far enough. Perhaps his unpretentious nature, boyish simplicity, and witlessness are oddly endearing to these wealthy older women. Whatever it is, she is glad she had kept him around long enough to mold him into the man she knew he could be. A man that women want weekly.

Austin knows Maggie doubted him. Hell, she made him doubt himself. No one had ever told him he was bad in bed before. He had never really considered the possibility, and when he did it made him oddly self-conscious. Austin had never had anything to be self-conscious about before. He has washboard abs, muscular arms, and a big dick. What more did he need? *Back in Ohio*, he thinks, *nothin*. He hadn't strutted around his hometown like he was hot shit (he wasn't naturally prone to being an asshole), but he was a good-looking guy. He had been popular. Lots of friends. Star athlete in a small Midwest town. He had always scored easily. Girls would hang out in the stands at practice, in the bleachers at games, after school at his dad's garage, at the drag strip on the weekends. They'd blow up his phone, flirt in the hallways; he never had to do anything, they were just there. The preps, the cheerleaders, and the good-ole-boy chasers. There had always been girls around him who were down to have some fun. He'd had a couple girlfriends, a few flings. And he'd never considered the fact that when they were *having fun*, that maybe they weren't having as much fun as he was. Maybe he hadn't cared. But Maggie made him care. And she made him see the difference between girls and grown women. He'd had to step up his game.

She told him to stop watching porn and start reading paperbacks. So he read women's fiction, non-fiction guides, online articles, feminist blogs, and deviant message board threads for hours on end. She told him to ask questions. So he did, every single time he was with a woman. What do you like? Like this? Like that? How? Up more? To the left? More? Less? So many questions it made him feel silly.

But then it got better. Direction slowly decreased and the results slowly increased. He looked for different signs. Less screaming and moaning, more shaking and trembling. Austin soon found that you didn't *hear* results; you felt them. And it felt good. It felt good to know he was responsible for such reactions, that he was providing such strong pleasure for someone else. Of course, there were still moans and screams, but they weren't of the counterfeit variety, and he took pleasure in being able to know the difference now.

He is doing well. Maggie's checks never bounce, and all the zeros have him continuously perfecting his craft. He is constantly working on getting more clients and working over the ones he already has. He's put his ideas about acting to the side because, honestly, he doesn't need the money a guest spot or a commercial could get him. His looks have landed him a better gig. In the three months he's been working for Maggie, he's bought a brand new, fully loaded F-150, and rents an apartment by the beach. It is a great thing, having sex for a living, but after a while he misses basic companionship. The little things you take for granted in a relationship until you don't have them. Before, the main draw in any relationship with the opposite sex had been sex. But now, all he has is sex. Fancy dinners and sex. No one to just sit on the couch and watch movies with. No one to get burgers and fries at one o'clock in the morning or take a walk on the beach with. No one in the passenger seat of truck. No one on the left side of his bed. Sure, he has his guy friends. He and AJ hang out from time to time. He occasionally gets together for a beer with a couple of the guys from the airport he used to work with. But it isn't the same as having that one person. Maybe, just maybe, he misses having a lady in his life to spend quality time with, time that doesn't have a price tag attached to it.

As it is, Austin has a standing Tuesday afternoon appointment in Mrs. Vernon's third floor master bedroom. Mrs. Vernon had formerly been Brent's client before he quit. She had been described to him by

Maggie as a stuck-up, hateful old widow who holed up in the house her husband bought, and ran the restaurants he founded from the comfort of her bed, bath, and cabana. It was true, she did have a sour attitude at first, but she warmed up to him quickly, and ever since the ice melted she's been sweet as can be. Every Tuesday at twelve, three more times a month than she had been seeing Brent. An hour and a half later Austin slips out while she sleeps, taking the winding grand staircase down to the main level. He tucks his crisp white shirt back into his black slacks as he goes, discarded blazer thrown over one shoulder. The mansion is empty as always, the only background noise is that of a vacuum running. He reaches the bottom and fishes his keys out of his pocket. The vacuum cuts off. He's just about to reach for the door when…

"Hey!"

Austin spins around to see a young Hispanic woman who couldn't be more than nineteen or twenty. She's petite with long black hair that's pulled back in a messy ponytail, and she wears an unmistakable maid's uniform.

"Yes?"

She looks around as if to make sure they really are alone, and then faces him again. "Your boss, how much does he pay?"

He looks down to smirk, then looks back up. "She," he corrects.

Her eyes widen in surprise. "Really?"

"Really. And she only employs men."

She quirks an eyebrow. "Are you sure?"

Austin sighs and takes a tentative step towards her. "Look…you don't wanna do this. It'll be worse for you than it is for me. Different standards. As a woman…this ain't what you wanna do. I promise."

"You don't know *what* I want to do. What I want to do is whatever will make me some fast money," she tells him defiantly. And then, fearing that she's spooked him, adds in a milder tone. "I am tired of working for Mrs. Vernon…"

"Why? You live here, right?" He crosses his arms and looks around as if to prove his point. "Pretty nice digs if you ask me."

She stands there defensively with her arms crossed, looking down at the vacuum cord she had pulled out of the wall a couple minutes before.

"I mean you basically have an entire mansion to yourself," he continues when he sees her dejection. "It's you and her, and she rarely leaves the East Wing."

She cracks a small smile but it's very brief. "I am tired of it," she tells him. "You don't know what she is like."

He tilts his head at her.

She glances up. "Ok. Maybe you do. But you don't have to live with her. You get to go home after you finish your...*job*."

"I know she can be demanding and all, but she's ain't my worst client by far."

They stand there silently for a moment. He watches her watch him from under her dark lashes. She's tough with her self-imposed walls, brashly bold, and befittingly beautiful. He wants to get to know her.

"I'm Austin, by the way," he says, reaching out his hand to her.

She just stares at him. "That hand has been on places of my boss that I do not care to touch. Sorry."

He retracts his hand with a defeated smile. "Understandable."

"I'm Hermosa," she relents after a second.

"Beautiful."

"Thank you."

"No," he laughs nervously. "I mean that's what it means. Your name." And then he immediately feels stupid, because of course she knows what her name means. He curses himself in his head. Why hadn't he just let her think that he'd called her beautiful? It's not like he doesn't think that she is.

"Oh," she says quietly, cheeks flushing.

"I uh...took a couple of years of Spanish in high school," he stammers, bashfully touching his hand to the back of his neck. "It was mandatory, I think."

"Mm," she mutters, unimpressed.

"So...are you from Mexico?"

She raises an eyebrow. "Because we all jump over the same fence, right?"

"Oh...no..." he quickly backtracks, more flustered now than ever. "I didn't mean–"

"I'm from El Salvador," she says with an amused smile, deciding to drop the offended act, satisfied with how much she's making him squirm. "But East LA's been my home since I was seven. Well, until I started work here."

He swallows timidly. "I know it's none of my business, but I'm guessing that your family came here for a better life." He shakes his head. "You won't find it down that road."

She looks at him. It's hard to tell whether she likes what he's saying or if she's offended, so he just keeps talking because he feels like he has to say these things. So she knows. Knows that she doesn't have to sacrifice herself.

"You may not be workin' your dream job. You may not be makin' that much money. But you live in Beverley Hills. It may not be your house, but it's a start. You don't gotta pay rent...you can save a little, maybe go to school. Figure out what you really want to do. Don't sell yourself short."

"I know my worth, okay, Captain Save-A-Maid?" She declares disparagingly. Then she looks down again. "You ain't have to try to rescue me ever. I'm cool."

"I know. I was just saying it's not a good career path, that's all," he replies innocently. "Plus," he adds. "You'll still be wearing a maid's uniform. You'll just be doing a whole lot worse things in it than mopping and dusting."

He watches as a little smirk takes form on her lips.

He smiles at her. Then leaves.

Over the next month they run into each other in the hallways of Mrs. Vernon's house every Tuesday afternoon. Austin thinks it's purposeful on both sides. They exchange quick barbs and flirtatious glances; it's the best part of his week. He thinks about asking her out all the time, but it always feels inappropriate with her boss, who he just fucked, sleeping upstairs. Still, he always looks for her when he's leaving. Until one week she's not there. And then the next week she's not there. He hopes she didn't decide to do what she was thinking about doing. He hopes she's okay. And he hopes one day maybe he will see her again under different circumstances.

CHAPTER 22

Five days after their first date, Maggie and Ali have their second. He takes her to a swanky Italian restaurant. One he had no way of knowing she loves. And she doesn't let him know. She sips her wine and eats her baked ziti like it's not one of her top five favorite meals. Her pride won't let her act impressed. Even though he looks dashing with his dark hair slicked back and yet another stylish suit on. Even though she knows that with both their meals, and the aged bottle of wine imported straight from Italy he sprang for, the bill will be upwards of two hundred dollars. Even though he never misses a beat or breaks a sweat. Over the decadent piece of chocolate cake he ordered and insisted they share, she notices his eyes starting to darken.

"Don't give me that look," she warns him, snagging a bite of cake off his plate.

"What look?" He asks lowly.

"This is our first date," she reminds him.

"Second," he corrects her.

"That one didn't count," she informs him.

"Maybe not for you…" Lecherous eyes linger on hers, smirk full of suggestion.

"I'm not inviting you up to my place tonight," she tells him matter-of-factly.

"I don't want you to invite me up to your place tonight."

"Good."

"Your place is fifteen miles and thirty floors away. That supply-closet over there is twelve steps."

She smiles as she reaches for her glass of wine. "You must be out of your mind."

Two minutes later, after the only other table in their section clears, they come crashing into the tight, dark closet. His mouth is fused to hers as he backs her further in, shrugging off his suit jacket as he does so. Without breaking contact with his lips, Maggie sides-steps past a mop and over dustbin until her back hits the wall. His hands slide down her ribcage, hers in his hair. Ali breaks apart from her mouth to ravage her neck, biting, sucking and licking all the right pulse points. Her nimble fingers unbutton his shirt in no time, and then she's pushing it off his shoulders. He pulls her blouse free from her pants and, in the urgency of the moment, rips it open, sending buttons flying. Maggie pauses her ministrations to meet his eyes, breathing raggedly.

"You owe me a blouse," she says, thinking briefly in the back of her mind that she'll have to wear his suit jacket out of the restaurant.

"Ok."

She shrugs it off and his mouth is immediately exploring all the newly exposed skin. She makes quick work of his belt, getting his pants open at the same second his hand is slipping under the waistband of hers. She shifts against him at the first contact of his fingers, and he grins against her lips. She detaches her mouth from his to breath, kissing his neck, his shoulders, letting out a muffled moan against his skin. He circles, rubs, probes, and curls a few more times and then withdraws his hand, pushing her pants and panties the rest of the way down. She shimmies and steps out of them both. Without warning he promptly hoists her up, turns around with her, and pins her to the adjacent wall. Her legs wrap around him and he enters her with one swift motion, one hand clamping over her mouth in order to stop the rest of the restaurant from knowing what they're doing.

Maggie no longer cares.

~

Monday morning Maggie steps off the elevator in her apartment building and walks through the lobby on her way to the door. The front desk attendant spots her and waves.

"Ms. Hunter! Wait, I have a package that was left for you!"

She stops in her tracks, looking confused, and turns back for the desk. He hands her a Neiman Marcus box with a big bow around it. She takes it from him.

"Thank you," she replies, looking even more confused now.

Once at work she sits down at her desk and slowly undoes the bow. She looks the box over twice but there's not a name anywhere suggesting who it's from. She takes off the lid and unfolds the paper to reveal a brand new Burberry blouse identical to the one Ali had ruined. Same light blush color, same fabric, same gold buttons, same size. She's amazed, and she smiles against her will.

"You have an admirer..."

She spins around to see AJ standing in the doorway. She puts the blouse back down and wipes the smile off her face. "Don't act so surprised."

He smirks knowingly. "I'm not."

"Don't give me that look."

"I'm not," he replies coyly.

"Go do somebody," she tells him dismissively.

He turns to leave with a laugh. Once she's sure he's gone, Maggie sits down at her desk and takes out the white phone. She dials. He picks up on the second ring.

"Good morning, Maggie Hunter," Ali answers seductively.

She instinctively fights the urge to smile again, even though he can't see her.

"How did you know what size I am? And, what's more, how did you know what designer it was and where to get it?"

"There you go underestimating me again," he replies in a cheeky tone.

"It's just that most men aren't proficient in the arts of size gauging and designer differentiating," she says, and then playfully adds, "at least not most straight men."

Ali chuckles. "Well now you have me questioning my prowess. Did I give you the false impression that I was gay the other night?"

"No," she says lowly. "No, you didn't."

"Didn't think so," he replies in an equally low voice. "I guess you'll just have to settle for the fact that I'm not most men."

"That's what most men say."

"Touché." She can hear his swarthy smile through the phone. "I'll call you later, okay? Maybe we can get drinks tonight after work or something."

"Maybe. Goodbye."

"Goodbye, Maggie."

She hangs up with a smile on her face and decides, being that she's having such a good day, that she'll treat herself to lunch at the little café down the street. She grabs her purse and walks back out into the rec room. Dominique is sprawled out on the couch drinking a beer and watching one of the *Real Housewives* series, reserving one square cushion for AJ, who is engrossed in some book, per usual.

"Aye," Dominique says, looking over the back of the couch at her. "You made a mistake and gave me an extra hundred dollars this week."

"Oh, just keep it," she says, not really caring.

"Damn," he replies, surprised. "You in an exceptionally good mood today."

"Somebody bought her a fancy blouse and put it in a box with a pretty little bow on it," AJ says without looking up from his book.

Maggie shoots him a look. AJ glances up at her with an innocent smile and then goes back to reading. Theo comes out of the bathroom.

"Somebody bought you a fancy blouse?" He asks, intrigued.

"Let's not make a big deal about it," she says, fishing for her keys.

"A man?" Theo questions.

"No, a woman," she says sarcastically.

"Well I don't know," Theo replies. "You haven't dated anyone in a minute. I thought maybe you had made that switch."

"And I'm not dating anyone now. It was a date. One date."

"One date and he's buying you blouses?" Theo comments with skepticism.

"He sounds like he trickin' off," Dominique assesses. "You gotta watch those. Tryin ta buy ya love in advance so you won't be disappointed when you find out he ain't got nothin ta offer in the bedroom."

"That's not it," Maggie says under her breath.

Dominique gets a big shit-eating grin on his face. "Aww hell," he says, slapping AJ on the shoulder. "She done took a lova."

AJ smirks and nods in agreement.

"I have not taken a lover," she states matter-of-factly.

"Stop lyin'," Dominique tells her, taking a sip of beer. "You need ta bring him on over so we can check him out though."

"Have I ever introduced you to anyone in my personal life, Dominique?" She asks him rhetorically.

"I had to spend one very long afternoon with your mother," AJ mutters under his breath as he continues to read.

"Oh come on," Dominique says to her. "Ya men need ta meet ya man."

"Yes, and explaining you all to him sounds like such a fun discussion."

"Didn't you already have that blouse?" Theo asks from her office, holding up her blush colored present.

Maggie sighs. "I love you guys. I really do. But what is my number one rule? Keep business and personal separate. I'm a firm believer in adhering to that. You don't need to be privy to every little detail of my life." She snatches the blouse back from Theo, puts it in her purse, and heads for the door. "No offense."

AJ can tell she's smitten with this new special person in her life. It makes her seem almost human. Almost.

CHAPTER 23

AJ is steadily racking in the money. His clients are loyal to him in the way that junkies are to heroin, and they seem to tip better than his co-workers' women do. In a span of a few short months he's bought his dream car and a house in the valley. Despite the money he remains modest, humble, and hopelessly in love with Anjanae. But despite that love, there is still work to be done.

Tracy Tevenot and her husband Francis have a marriage that runs hot and cold like the weather in the Midwest, where Tracy used to live before hitting the marital jackpot. One week she would be a happily married housewife, and the next she'd be handcuffed to her headboard by a hooker (re: him). She and her husband go through bouts of separation, so AJ never knows from one week to the next whether she'll be on his schedule or not, although she usually never goes over two weeks without needing a "separation." Francis would go spend some time at the beach house in Malibu, and while he was gone AJ would pay a visit to the Brentwood estate he'd left unattended. AJ knows Tracy would never actually go through with a real divorce, because despite not being any fun Francis is loaded. If AJ has learned anything since coming to LA it is that being rich is more important than being fun, and being comfortable is more important than being happy. Because when you've got money, you can buy a good time. AJ knows that without Francis and his money Tracy would be just another uneducated, ex-bartender from the hills of Kentucky. Twenty years ago she mixed an excellent drink for a very wealthy Parisian who was in town for the Derby and wound up set for life. She told AJ this one night after she had mixed herself an excellent drink out at the pool bar. She proceeded to strip and skinny dip, putting on a show he didn't ask for, until he finally joined her in the water to do what she paid him to.

Tracy possesses the bitter resentment of a woman duped into signing a prenuptial agreement, and is often half in the bottle when AJ comes over. AJ knows that though her husband is a fine wine connoisseur (the type who swishes the shit around in his mouth and has a temperature-controlled cellar the size of most people's houses) Tracy actually hates wine. Of course, she has to drink the fancy stuff at special events and dinner parties, because you can't be a socialite and drink shine. AJ knows that she claims to be a size two, but is really an eight (he has removed enough well-tailored pants and designer jeans by this point to know the difference). AJ knows that she fancies herself a sex expert because she had recently read *Fifty Shades* like every other woman her age, drinking up the nonsense posing as erotica like water. She likes for AJ to do the things that this Christian character did to Anastasia: blindfold her, tie her up, and give her a good paddling. He, of course, obliges, which sometimes makes it hard for him to look Turner in the eye whenever he goes to the studio with Dominique. AJ knows the book Tracy so adores isn't an actual manual for real BDSM, and he only knows this for sure because he knows Janet Halliday.

Janet Halliday is a respected oral surgeon with her own money, living in the Pacific Palisades with her optometrist husband, Jack, with whom she has an open marriage. They entered into this arrangement a few years prior upon realizing that they really didn't do it for each other anymore, sexually. They loved each other in every other way; they simply didn't share the same kinks. For instance, Jack gets turned on by blonde twenty-somethings, which Janet ceased being twenty years ago. On the other hand, whips, chains, and safe words are more Janet's thing. But unlike Tracy, Janet doesn't wish to be dominated. No, Janet wants to dominate. And AJ lets her. AJ lets her do damn near anything she wants.

AJ knows Janet worries about image. None of her peers know about her proclivities, none of her friends know about her fetishes. She doesn't have dyed black hair or a leather wardrobe; in fact, she's actually a conservative Catholic. White coat, white teeth, demure cross necklace and honey colored hair. Her kind face is palatable for billboards, and if you find yourself in West LA, you will surely see it on billboards advertising her private practice. AJ knows that her one main rule in the open arrangement she and her husband have is that patients are strictly off limits, as well as anyone else who knows them or may know them. Her husband likes to go to dive bars in Hollywood (far from their elite West End circle) to find his partners. But Janet prefers the discretion of a professional.

AJ thinks sometimes that Janet might hate men. At least that's what it feels like in those seconds before the safe word slips out of his mouth against his will. At first he had naively thought that he wouldn't need one, *a word*, but that was before he saw a real BDSM mater in her zone. She doesn't tie him up; she chains him up. The steel restraints are so tight they tear into his wrists, and that's without straining against them, which he always ends up doing anyway. Sometimes he's gagged.

Sometimes bondages are wrapped around parts of him *other* than just his arms and legs. He has to ask permission for every move he makes, not that he *can* move, and she verbally demeans him while making demands. He pleases her and gets punished in return. She tortures him until he's in physical pain and pleading, and still she won't stop until she hears the word. But after it's done, she's so polite. She puts her clothes back on, kisses him gently on the cheek, hands him his money and thanks him for his time.

Sometimes he wonders if she became a dentist just so she could pull teeth. The thrill of inflicting pain neatly tucked into a respectable profession. Crafty.

AJ knows that Janet is probably the client that bothers Anjanae the most, because while he never says anything about any of his women to her, Janet's evidence is very visible. He occasionally comes out with scratches and hickeys from the others, but after he sees Janet, it's bruises and burns and cuts. He knows Anjanae sees it all, and while she never says anything, he can see in her eyes that it's a painful reminder of what he does. And he hates it.

He sees Fereshteh Abdollah every other week, usually on Tuesday nights, but there is the occasional Friday morning when she wants to start her weekend off right. On his third visit she greeted him with a surprising, "Hello, AJ, so happy to see you," the first English words he had ever heard her utter. Come to find out, she took ESL classes twice a week. Ironically, AJ had ordered a language learning DVD online and checked out a few books from the library (once a quick Google search of some phrases he remembered her using informed him that she was, in fact, speaking Farsi) after his first appointment with her in order to attempt to communicate better. She picked up English much faster than he picked up Farsi, but the intellectual in him still enjoys learning new things. By his sixth visit, Fereshteh could hold a decent conversation in English. And, as it turned out, she was a good conversationalist. Her husband hadn't been a sultan, as Dominique had predicted, but he had been a man of great wealth and clout in their home city of Tehran. Fereshteh explained to AJ that her late husband had always treated her well and provided for her immensely. But the marriage had been out of arrangement, not love. She was given to him at sixteen without much of a choice. And though her husband was a good man to her and their son, she knew the rest of the world, perhaps the rest of even their own country, wouldn't see him as such. He made lucrative money in the oil industry and invested it in ways that would make him more, thus involving him in the dark side of Iranian politics. He was gone often on business that was she not to inquire about, and she was perpetually lonely as a kept wife in a palace. Then, when she was twenty-five, she met a young American soldier.

There was a base not far from the park where she took her son, one of the only places she was actually allowed to go to alone. That's where it started. He spoke Farsi fluently, therefore she never had to learn his language. He treated her in ways that made her rethink how good she thought she'd had it before. He actually talked to her about things; and the sex, to her pleasant surprise, was much more two-sided. She kept the affair under wraps for close to a year until he went back to America. He wanted her to come back with him, but she feared the repercussions too much to even consider it. That had been twenty years ago, but she never forgot the feeling. Two years ago her husband suffered a massive heart attack and died, and after some time to think about it, she saw no reason to stay in Iran. Her only son had been living in America for three years, attending medical school at UCLA. And since meeting that American soldier long ago, she had longed for the sense of freeness he possessed. So with all the money that had been left to her, she left for LA. She told AJ she called Maggie because she was tired of feeling lonely, and she wanted to recreate what she once had. She explained later when he asked that she hadn't meant to be discriminatory when she made her request to Maggie. When she said "a white man" she simply meant an American. This made him laugh.

Katharine Kelly likes a glass of Pinot and a line of coke before, and two extra-long cigarettes afterwards. Sometimes she calls an hour ahead and has Maggie tell him to stop at the gas station and pick her up a pack of Virginia Slims on his way over. Thankfully she never asks him to make a run for her other party favors, and thankfully she stopped asking him if he wanted any after the second or third time he politely declined. With such substantially freed inhibitions, she's a very compliant participant and quite open minded. She doesn't care how he takes her, just as long as he gets the job done in the end. Depending on whether she does a little more powder in-between position changes, she'd be up for a round two, in which case he makes twice as much. Mrs. Kelly has a standing Monday night appointment. She never asks to go out; it's always strictly sex. And AJ would argue against any pathologist, psychologist, or poll collector who claims that a woman's sex drive wanes with age, because he's pretty sure the woman is pushing seventy-five and not a week goes by that she doesn't want it.

AJ has never runs into anyone else in Mrs. Kelly's mansion, other than the occasional maid who always diverts her eyes with quickness. There's a picture of a distinguished, white-haired man hanging on the wall going up the stairs next to the portrait of Mrs. Kelly and a vintage Van Gogh. There's a framed photograph of the same man and Mrs. Kelly and a few kids he's also never seen sitting on her vanity in the bedroom. She wears a ring and has a married prefix. AJ doesn't know if that husband's dead, alive, traveling, or simply asleep in another room on a separate floor. He doesn't ask and she doesn't tell. It all works out quite well.

He sees Vera Van Buren every Thursday evening. She preferred him to Garrett, so she never switched back after the night that he had filled in for his coworker. AJ genuinely likes Vera as a person, and if he were to pick a favorite client, it would probably be her. She's always polite to him and, most of all, *much* more realistic than many of the other wealthy widows and bored housewives he sees. She understands their arrangement and has no problem admitting she simply wants company occasionally—a date to dinner and, every now and then, an orgasm. He goes with her to her favorite restaurants, sometimes a movie premier, and every third Thursday she asks him to accompany her back home where he works his magic on her. She is the only client who really expresses an interest in his life, often asking him about his plans, ambitions, and Anjanae. She is the only client—hell, one of the only people—who knows about him and Anjanae. Vera also gives him honest guidance when she feels he needs it, advises on him art-related endeavors, and teaches him how to say certain sexy things in French.

Other than the regulars, there are also the intermittent wildcards. If his schedule wasn't particularly full a certain week, he'd go to the bar of an upscale restaurant, sit down on a stool, and wait for a lonely lady to sidle up next to him. It never takes long and he never has to flirt shamelessly like other men who occupy bars to pick up women for mere recreation. All AJ has to do is give a woman a look. He'd heard Maggie say on more than one occasion that he had expressive eyes; she was always using different decorative words and colors to describe them. He'd always just considered them green, but whatever the case, they worked in his favor. A subtle glance cast the line. A well-received

compliment, reciprocated introduction, and charismatic smile hook
the target; a few short minutes of enticing conversation, perfectly
feigned interest, and subtle eye undressing reel them in. By the time
someone asks someone else if they want "to get out of here," it is time to
come clean.

AJ always puts it delicately: he has a way with words and can explain
the situation in a way that doesn't make it sound so appalling and illicit.
It is always risky business dealing with someone who isn't a regular
client, and who might be offended by such a proposition. But AJ is
confident in his prowess.

Nine times out of ten they still want it, even though they have to pay.

Sometimes he slips them the number to the black phone. However, as a
rule of thumb, with such random encounters it is best to simply seal the
deal that night, in which case they never get Maggie's number and
would never see him again. He would just be fleeting fling, a pleasant
memory in their mind that they could replay on less memorable nights
when they wanted to relive the thrill.

Luckily, nice restaurants are usually only a short cab ride away from
nice hotels; though there are dalliances in bathrooms and back alleys for
the women who can't wait, the same ones who, after his admittance of
occupation, start pulling on his pants while still in public.

Other times AJ gets picked up while shopping by women who are
interested in purchasing more than the merchandise. Almost every time
he goes on Rodeo Drive or Melrose he gets approached by couture
wearing cougars smelling of alimony and Number 5 who know exactly
what they want. The sight of a very attractive, very young man who can
afford Louis Vuitton is like an aphrodisiac to these types of women. If
they are lucky, they get to find out how just how he can afford such
things.

AJ quickly learned that he was always on the clock, even when he
thought he wasn't. He could walk down the street and lure a woman into
his web without any intention. It is as if he can turn around at any given
moment and catch someone objectifying him; going for coffee at the
little café by his apartment alone on Sunday mornings, perusing the

farmers market with Jae on Wednesday afternoons. Sometimes he thinks this must be how women feel all the time. Sometimes he thinks it must just be him. That he must be radiating sex so resiliently now he's become an inadvertent self-advertisement. He doesn't *want* to have to stop during his free time and do business, but Maggie's aura looms there right over his shoulder at all times, telling him to act on all viable opportunities in the name of opulence. So he does. If he's with Jae when a woman enters his zone, Jae will knowingly (albeit, somewhat disapprovingly) turn his head while the coy transaction and number exchange takes place. If he's with one of the other guys (usually Austin or Nique) and a woman shows interest in them, they'll both vie for her business. And in the end, to the mild frustration of his coworkers, he's typically the one who walks away with a new client. The only time he is not focused on this aspect of his life, the only time his mind is quieted of Maggie and money and job-related maneuvers, is when he's with Anjanae or writing. Otherwise, if he has the time and thinks he can make a new client out of a total stranger, he will strike up a conversation. Only if he thinks she can afford him.

~

Then there were the one-off requests. Like the woman with the dying wish.

It came about one night somewhat unexpectedly. Maggie told AJ she'd received a call to send an escort to the bar at the Beverly Wilshire. She then turned to Garrett and told him another woman had requested a man to meet in her in the lobby of the same hotel at the same time. The two boys both thought it a little suspicious, but trusted that Maggie knew what she was doing.

She did.

Being that the bar was located in the lobby, the two ended up waiting on their dates together. So there they were, in a room filled with business people and industry folks schmoozing over pricy cocktails, trying to pinpoint which two were there to fuck them by the hour. It was 9:20 p.m. and they had been there over thirty minutes. Garrett had just made the comment to AJ that he was about to dip if his date didn't show up in the next five minutes; he had lines to rehearse and better things to be doing, so he said. They were both sitting at the sidebar sipping club soda, one stool separating them as to not look too suspicious. AJ was about to tell him to stop bitching when a woman got up from the main bar, walked around the corner, and sat down in the open seat between them. Neither AJ nor Garrett made a move or said a thing, unsure whether she was a client or not. She looked to her right at AJ and smiled, then turned to the left and gave Garrett the same smile. That's when they realized what their arrangement for the night was.

Claire was forty-nine, terminally ill, and terribly rich. It started as a small malignant mole on her back that progressed to stage four and spread to her brain before she found out. A persistent headache and vision that blurred sporadically, that's what led her to the doctor. The scan showed an inoperable tumor and the oncologist told her ten months. Meaning she wasn't expected to make it to fifty. Her fiftieth birthday was the coming Tuesday and she wanted to treat herself to an early birthday present. Yes, she had made it three months past her expiration date, she was happy, but she knew that this would be her last birthday. She was having more bad days now than she was good. It was okay, though; she had gotten past the denial stage a long time ago. Plus, today was a good day, and the first rule of cancer is you never let a good day go to waste.

She confided in the boys before they departed up to her suite that she had wasted twenty years of her life that was now being cut short married to a selfish man who was a lousy lover, and how while she was with him she'd often fantasize scenarios like being with younger men and having a three-way where she was the main focus. She had always been scared to leave him because she had a huge inheritance and he hadn't signed a prenup. But once she was given her diagnosis, she gave up fear and started living differently. She hired the best attorney available, got a divorce, moved from cold Chicago to warm California, quit her tiresome job, and traveled.

Her husband had been very controlling and never let her go anywhere alone. In a six-month span she had been to Rome, Paris, Berlin, Cairo, Cape Town, Melbourne, New Zealand, and Fiji. She had sightseen, skydived, and swam with dolphins. But there was still one thing left on her bucket list. Sure she could have picked any random man in the many foreign lands she had visited, or even here in Los Angles, but what she didn't have time for was mediocrity. You never knew what you were getting till you got it, and she wasn't allowing another man to waste a second of what she had left. Plus, her travels had been about traveling. This was about *this*. And she wanted the best experience money could buy. She wanted to be catered to. She wanted her mind to be blown. She wanted them.

AJ had never had a threesome before. Not one that involved two girls, much less one that involved two guys. He knew it happened. He'd heard his college buddies brag about bagging two girls at once, or the drunken thrill of tag teaming a girl with a frat friend. Being the serial monogamist he'd been, it had just never appealed to him. It always seemed like a rather awkward set-up, one that would be somewhat unfulfilling, especially for the woman or women involved. He didn't want it to be awkward or unfulfilling for a client. A dying client.

He considered the fact that he may be too sober to do this.

He pushed his glass of ginger ale aside and ordered a bourbon that he quickly threw back before the three of them left the bar together. He wondered to himself if Garrett had ever done this before, and tried to gauge his coworker's reaction as the blinking numbers ticked towards the top floor. There was a middle-aged couple on the elevator with them, so they had to keep it cool. Garrett was hard to read; he didn't look necessarily thrilled, but he didn't appear nervous either. The couple got off on the thirty-fifth floor, and as soon as they did AJ watched as Garrett moved towards Claire. He gave him a look that said he should too, and so he did. *Clearly the fantasy starts here*, he thought. There were subtle kisses and touches until the doors opened and they were walking out onto a deserted floor. And then she was sliding her card into the door and it was clicking. And he was standing in a penthouse suite not unlike the ones he'd been in before; in fact, he may have very well been in this one before, with strawberries and champagne and chocolate on a cart by the bed. And then it almost felt like any other night. But then they were all undressing.

AJ wasn't used to seeing other men completely naked; pornos he had watched in his teen years or in the P.E locker rooms of high school, sure, but never in such close proximity. He diverted his eyes away from Garrett the best he could, focusing them instead on the woman between them. Claire was attractive and her nude body was one to be respected. AJ couldn't help but think to that for as sick as she was and for all the stress she must be under, she took great care of herself. She was thin, but the tone to her arms, calves, and back suggested she worked out. *Her nimbleness suggested the same.* She was fair skinned with a light dusting of freckles over her breasts that were not fake but still fairly firm for her age. Her hair was the color of cornfields, straight and flowing all the way down to the slight swell of her hips. He knew she mustn't have had chemo. Her eyes were cornflower blue, devoid of all fear and indecision. He had stared into a lot of eyes by this point, and never had he seen the exact glint she had in hers. Confidence. Readiness. Completeness. He pushed the thoughts of death and dying and the fact that another man's dick was mere inches from his out of his mind, as he pushed her back against the pillows and went to work.

Surprisingly, he and Garrett worked quite well together. The bottle of champagne surely helped, adding to the fluent fluidity the three of them spoke without words. It was like a well-synchronized song and dance that AJ's sure most wouldn't have been able to pull off as smoothly. Thankfully she didn't ask for him and Garrett to kiss or touch each other. If she had, he doesn't know what he would have done. The most personal it ever got was when one of their mouths went where the other had just been, but under the veil of protection, even that didn't seem overly homosexual, especially with a little liquor in their systems. They didn't leave an inch of her untouched...licked, fucked. One of them would go here, the other would go there, simultaneously stimulating her from different angles. She came three times with each of them, accumulating to six total for her. Both of them took one for themselves only after they were sure she was sated beyond repair.

Afterwards she paid them their fees and tipped graciously. It was the most money AJ had ever made in a night. On the ride back down in the elevator he and Garrett didn't look at each other. They strolled through the empty lobby, hoping the night desk attendants and concierge didn't find them too conspicuous looking, rumpled clothing and messy manes. Only after they entered the parking garage did they dare glance in the other's direction.

"See you at the office," Garrett said, fishing his keys from his pocket.

"Yeah," AJ reverberated. "See ya at the office."

It's as if they both suddenly realized how ridiculous they sounded, talking about *see ya at the office* like they have office jobs. They both snorted under their breaths.

"Blimey, that bitch boss of ours right set us up, didn't she?" Garrett remarked with a smirk on his face. "Good work tonight, though, mate, really," he added, holding a closed fist out to AJ.

"Thanks, man," AJ replied facetiously, bumping fists with him. "Same to you."

They laughed it off, got in their expensive cars, and went their separate ways.

AJ has trouble sleeping that night. He crashes at his apartment as he does when his *shift* runs into the wee hours of the morning. Every so many nights out of any given week he'll find himself incapable of turning his mind off. He'll lie awake, a continuous reel of women replaying in his head, punctuated by slides of Anjanae and Memphis and all his unfulfilled dreams. He'll toss and turn in a cold sweat that feels an awful lot like guilt, until he admits defeat and gets up.

The next day, already dressed for his evening date, he sits on the plush office couch trying finish a song he'd promised Dominique he'd have done and ready for him to record Monday. Theo walks in, seeing him staring absently at the wall across for him, pen in his hand and blank notepad on the table.

"You look mildly traumatized," Theo assesses, stopping at the bar cart to pour himself a drink.

"I ran a train on a terminally ill heiress with Garrett last night," he says without looking away from the wall. "Well," he adds dryly, "I don't know if train is the right term. That makes it sound cheap and unsatisfactory. It was a very expensive and she was very satisfied."

Theo glances at him out of the side of his eye. "You want a drink?"

"No, I'm fine." He looks way from the wall, leans back against the couch, and unscrews the lid off his bottle of water. "That was one of the things on her bucket list. Having a three way with two younger men." He takes a swig and swallows. "I was a part of someone's bucket list."

"Yeah," Theo says, coming to sit on the couch with his glass of Grand Marnier. "I know." He takes a sip. "Maggie was afraid if she told you all what the plan was that you two wouldn't agree to do it."

AJ smirks to himself and shakes his head.

"You know," Theo adds. "Because you have morals and Garrett thinks he's Liam Hemsworth now."

AJ laughs it off again, picks up his pen, and starts to write.

CHAPTER 24

The truth is AJ does have morals, and this isn't at all how he'd been before. That's not to say that he'd been a prude. He had always been very open-minded when it came to the subject of sex, and he was, after all, creatively inclined. Spreading it around had simply never appealed to him as it did to most men. He had never slept with more than one girl during the same period of time. He had never strung multiple girls along at once. That wasn't him. He hadn't been lying to Anjanae when he told her that he had only been with five women prior to taking the job with Maggie. In college he knew guys whose numbers were in the thirties and forties, and he'd wondered how there was enough hours in the day for a person that young to have accumulated that many notches in his bedpost. Needless to say, he doesn't wonder anymore.

AJ lost his virginity at seventeen to a senior girl named Lauren. He was a junior taking twelfth grade English; she sat in front of him. She was popular, but unlike most of the in-crowd at his high school (of which he was not in), she had always been nice to him. They had a friendly rapport in class; she was very pretty and also very personable, and not nearly as shallow as the group of girls she hung around with. He kept his crush on her to himself, but at the beginning of second semester when she confided in him that her grades were slipping, he offered to help her study. He'd go over to her house after school and go over test questions with her, talk about her college plans that her friends weren't interested in, and listen to her vent about her football player ex-boyfriend who had dumped her for a cheerleader. Eventually one thing led to another and they wound up in her bed one afternoon while her parents were at work. He had been terribly nervous, especially knowing that she'd had sex before, and stopped a few times to ask if what he was doing was okay. He was ecstatic when after the first time she still wanted to see him and, even more amazingly, wanted to do it again. So that summer he made a point of exploring every inch of her body whenever he could. One particular night, after he had made her come back to back for the first time in the back of his car, she confessed that no one else had ever managed to make it happen once, let alone twice (this was a confession he came to hear from more than one woman). She told him that her previous boyfriends had only been concerned about what they could get from her, how frequent they could get it, and how quickly they could get it. AJ wasn't surprised. He was a guy who had heard guys talk all his life—locker rooms, classrooms; friends, non-friends—and he knew how most of them approached sex. However, he had a different outlook. He aimed to please, and he wanted to be as proficient in the act as he could be. When the summer ended, Lauren went away to college. They kept in touch for a while, but ultimately it brought an end to their fling.

Returning to high school his senior year, AJ had wrongfully assumed that Lauren was just a fluke, and that he'd be resigned to celibacy once more. That was until someone told him a sophomore girl had a crush on him. He and Hannah were both in the band; she played the flute and he played the sax. One fall day after their first competition of the season, he decided he would ask her out. She said yes. Hannah was technically his first real girlfriend. He took her to homecoming and prom, let her wear his class ring and band jacket, and snuck around with her in backseats and behind buildings; the typical cheesy teen romance routine. They dated for ten months before they both decided that they would be better suited as friends, and amicably broke up.

His freshman year of college AJ tried the whole "casual hook-up" thing. He lived just off campus in a cramped and crappy apartment that he shared with two other guys. It was the textbook definition of a bachelor pad, and under that roof being single was highly promoted. His roommates were very much into the frat lifestyle, AJ not so much. Most of the nights that parties were going on at his place, he would leave and go find a quiet place somewhere on campus to study or read. However, occasionally he would stay for the party and indulge, and on two different occasions he had a one-night-stand. They actually weren't one-night stands, because he didn't limit them to the single inebriated experience, and treated them much differently than his roomies treated their trysts. It was more of a friends with benefits situation. He'd have coffee or lunch with them, maybe a movie, and whenever they called and asked him to "come over" he'd willingly oblige (really this should have been a sign of things to come). He hooked-up with Rachel pretty much all of fall semester, up until she flunked out of college and moved back home to Chattanooga, and he hooked up with Emily for a good portion of Spring semester, until her ex-boyfriend showed up at her dorm one day and proposed to her.

Sophomore year he met Grace. They had both math and English together. One class was immediately after the other in buildings at opposite ends of campus. Seeing as they had to make the trek together, they started to make conversation. Then they began sitting next to each other. He was impressed by how quickly she could solve an equation and make sense out of a bunch of numbers; he was horrible at math. She on the other hand found difficulty in writing term papers and assembling essays. In his mind he heard the saying about how opposites attract. Once they started studying together it didn't take long for them to become a couple. Neither of them made things difficult, there were never any games and everything was easy. They were both compatible, both driven. He admired her will to be a nurse. She liked the poetry he wrote her. His parents loved her and her parents loved him. After a year of being together his family started asking him in hushed voices when he was going to pop the question, they *loved* her. AJ knew this was how things went where he was from. A good chunk of his friends from his little high school in the suburbs of Memphis were already married and on their second child. Grace came from a small rural town about thirty minutes away, and most of her friends were married with children at twenty-two as well. He knew what was expected of him, and he saw no reason to fear it. It was hard for him to find fault in their relationship. Their arguments were few and far between, their lines of communication worked, and their eyes didn't stray. Without much thought to it, he began thinking of her as his future fiancé, his future wife. They moved in together on their two-year anniversary and things continued on smoothly for another year. It wasn't until graduation drew nearer that their differences started becoming clearer to him, the cracks in their foundation more prominent. He considered the fact that they might have mistaken complacency for compatibility. And it wasn't until Maggie offered him an opportunity—an out—that he considered he might want something else more than he wanted her. That he might actually want to pursue his passions more than he wanted to settle.

Of course, that opportunity wasn't what he thought it was. And nothing since then had gone as planned. But there was one good thing that came out of it.

His house in Reseda is decorated in her artwork. There are two framed paintings hanging on the wall between the living room and the kitchen, and one in his bedroom. Those pieces mean a lot to him, but his favorite creation is probably the mural she did on one entire wall of the basement. He told her to do what she wanted, and he loved what she did. Any time they have an extended amount of time to spend together—like when he has a couple days off in a row at the same time Julius is out of town shooting—they'll hole up in the valley. She comes over in the evening and they cook together, attempting to recreate a recipe one of them found online, which usually ends in a huge humorous mess and them ordering a pizza. He lights the fireplace when the sun goes down and they sip on wine or some of the peach brandy he knows she likes (that he now keeps). No T.V. playing in the background, no phones in hands. They keep each other up late, tangled limbs and strewn pillows, and wake up after the sun has risen, usually to start the day the same way they ended the previous. Sometimes they have breakfast in bed and coffee on the front porch, other times they go to the diner down the road and order what has become their usual. In the late morning she likes to paint out on the back deck in the sun, while he writes in the little nook just off the bedroom that he's transformed into his office. They'll go on afternoon walks around the neighborhood, or to matinee movies at the Cineplex in Chatsworth. Sometimes they just stay in and sit on the couch, one reading the paper and one reading a book and vice versa, not needing words. Other times there are a lot of words, when they get into deep discussions and healthy debates over news headlines, current events, or whatever may be on their minds at the time. And then, of course, there's more sex.

AJ knows just about everyone on the street now. Nancy and Fred Bridgestone live next door to him on the right, a retired couple in their late sixties who have two grown children who've since moved out. Nancy and Fred ride their bikes at least five miles every day. Fred is on the town board and also helps out at the nearby soup kitchen a few days a week. Nancy teaches Zumba on Tuesdays and volunteers at the local library on Thursdays. They both garden avidly, and are constantly bringing AJ an array of fresh fruits and vegetables. His neighbors on the left are Jack and Miranda Tyler. Jack sells medical equipment for a big-name manufacturer and Miranda is a dental hygienist. They have a thirteen-year-old daughter named Rebecca, a ten-year-old son named Toby, and a golden retriever mix named Duke. The kids and dog come over to AJ's often. He lets Toby teach him how to play video games while Rebecca scours his book collection. Both kids and the dog are crazy about Anjanae; Rebecca admires her and Toby has a crush on her, which his sister makes fun of him for till the otherwise very self-assured little boy turns completely red in the face. Whenever Anjanae comes over she brings back issues of Vogue for her and Rebecca to go through. She usually brings something special for Toby, too, like candy or comic books, and has even been known to stop and get specialty treats from a dog bakery in Beverly Hills for Duke. Across the street from AJ is Eileen and Trevor Farley, a young couple who just welcomed their first born, Sophie, into the family a few weeks ago. AJ was outside watering his flowers the day they brought her home from the hospital, and got to see her all brand new and baby scented.

A little further down the street are Carla and Antonio Gonzalez. Their seven-year-old son, Ricky, is a young pianist prodigy. AJ has never heard anyone play like him, and knows the kid will probably be world renowned in no time. Ricky's seventeen-year-old brother, Carlos, has been in some trouble at school: smoking weed in the parking lot, talking back to teachers, typical teen stuff. AJ has talked to Carlos enough to know the tough act is just a front; he is actually very smart. Carlos confided in AJ that he had applied to film school at USC but didn't want to tell his parents unless he got in. At the end of the cul-de-sac is Jesse, a recent divorcee in his late thirties. Jesse is a top-notch mechanic who has been featured in a quite a few automotive magazines. From time to time he and AJ hang out at each other's garage, drink a few beers, and talk cars. Jesse gets his fifteen-year-old daughter, Bridgette, every other weekend. Jesse doesn't know it, but Bridgette has secretly been seeing Carlos for at least three months. AJ thought about telling him once, but decided ultimately that he wasn't one who needed be ratting out anybody on the block, especially given the secrets he's hiding from them.

AJ loves his neighbors, but more than that he loves the normalcy they create for him. He inadvertently bought a house in a close-knit community, but he couldn't be happier. Backyard barbecues and birthday parties are just what he needs to even out all the other stuff he's been doing. Nobody from work has been to his place in the valley, not Austin, not Dominique. Jae comes over from time to time, sometimes with Mackenzie; they bring the food truck and everybody in the neighborhood has a good time eating and conversing. Other than Jae nobody knows about AJ's secret life in suburbia. He supposes that Maggie knows, because there is nothing that she doesn't know, but she doesn't make it aware and has thankfully never shown up out of the blue. His neighbors of course all naturally think Anjanae is his girlfriend, constant comments being made about what a beautiful couple they make. They just smile, not dare correcting a soul. He's led his neighbors to believe that she's a graphic designer who lives in Silverlake, and that he writes instruction manuals for many of the world's favorite devices, something he does both from home and at an office in Downtown LA. When asked, they can both elaborate on the spot about what their faux professions entail in great detail. After all, they are well-practiced liars, never lying to anyone more than they lie to themselves. But it's okay. Because when they play pretend, no one is ever a gigolo or a housewife. When they pretend, they are themselves.

Of course, sometimes the fantasy blurs the lines of reality in his head. Sometimes when he sees her interacting with Rebecca and Toby, or holding Eileen and Trevor's baby, he foolishly wonders what it would be like to have children with her. He envisions a caramel complexioned little baby with curls, smiling from the apples of its cheeks like her. Sometimes when he wakes up in the morning and she's still lying in the bed next to him, he wistfully wonders what it would be like to start every day this way for the rest of his life. He envisions them watching the sunrise at seventy from a wraparound porch, rocking chairs and hot coffee. But then he catches himself. Then he reminds himself that they are both tied to two other people by a powerful vice called monetary manipulation, and bonds like that are hard to break free from. As it is, conversations about Maggie Hunter and Julius Collins have become mute over the last month. It's fortunate but unfortunate, out of sight but never out of mind. Even if they don't talk about them, he knows. He knows she wants to ask him to quit. Just like he wants to ask her to ask for a divorce. But neither does. Neither wants to break the spell they're both under, neither wants to ruin the moment they're both in. The simplest moments are the most special to them. When they're pretending everything is fine, everything is fine. So why face the truth when you can…

"Close your eyes."

With his hands on her shoulders, AJ carefully guides her across the basement garage. It's concrete clad and unfinished, still filled with cardboard boxes of stuff he still hasn't found time to unpack between juggling his two personas and living in two places. The wall across from him is an intricate skyscape from the observatory. He had taken her for a sunset picnic at Griffith Park one evening a few weeks back when Julius thought she was at a diner with Christine. With a hood pulled over her head and one of her husband's fancy cameras in her hands, she took a picture from the perfect vantage point at the perfect time. He remembers how all the colors in the sky blended at the bottom of the kaleidoscope, settling into a mauve horizon, slowly sinking away. How the falling of night melted the lines and contoured the corners, the faint hills and valleys below, a million little lights shimmering off in the distant city, and stars that were just beginning to burn where it was already black. She got the photo developed, blew it up in her mind, and over the course of the next weekend recreated it on his basement wall.

"Are they closed?" He asks, smiling.

"Yes," she giggles. "They're closed."

He keeps gently pushing her forward, guiding her towards the back where there's something covered with a tarp. "Do you remember the other day when you told me you had never learned how to ride a bike?"

"Yes…"

"Well I was talking to Nancy and Fred yesterday and it just so happened to come up in conversation."

"I told you that in confidence, you know," she says sarcastically, eyes still shut as she puts one foot in front of the other, trusting he's not going to let her trip.

"They thought that was just preposterous, and I agreed, but told them I didn't have a bike to teach you on. And that's when they said they had a spare bike. Technically it's their son's, but he's at college and I don't think he's going to be coming back for it anytime soon. Anyway, they offered to let me borrow it." He stops her in front of the covered mass in the corner. "Open your eyes," he instructs her excitedly, pulling the tarp off of it.

Anjanae opens her eyes. She's face to face with a dark blue mountain bike. He watches her as she stares at it despairingly.

"It doesn't have training wheels," she observes.

"Well no. Their son is twenty."

"This is a man's bike."

"It's okay." He smiles at her. "It doesn't know you're not man. Go ahead and get on, we'll practice in the driveway first and then maybe we'll take it down the road."

She throws him a look over her shoulder. "Hell, why don't you just drop me off on the shoulder of the 405. I'm sure I'll be fine."

He lets up the garage door, smirking over his shoulder, and the afternoon sun pours in. "Now that's the adventurous spirit I was hoping to spark."

She warily approaches the bike. Her hands tentatively go the handlebars. She awkwardly attempts to straddle it, but backs out at the last minute, sending the bike crashing to the floor with a thud. "Dammit!" She curses. "You could have at least held onto it while I got on, AJ."

"Just sit down. You act like you're mounting a wild mustang that's going to take off before you get your leg thrown over the saddle."

"Might as well be, it's just every bit as dangerous." She backs away from it and crosses her arms obstinately.

"Here," AJ reaches up to the rack above her head, grabbing a shiny red helmet. "I got this from them, too."

She makes no move to take the helmet from him and stares at it there in his hands like it personally offended her. "Oh, I'm not putting that on my head."

AJ rubs a hand over his face as he sighs, shaking his head at the highly difficult woman he's in love with. She just smiles.

Fifteen minutes later and he's managed to get her out of the garage and few meters up the road. She got on and stayed on this time, peddling up and down the driveway and then making a few laps around the circle of the cul-de-sac. Her balance is naturally good, which is all that riding a bike really is. Even though she doubted it, he knew she'd be ok. It's a beautiful early October day, sixty something and sunny, as always. There's not another way he'd rather be spending it.

"Now what?" She asks him. She's parked at the top of their street, feet braced on the pavement with him standing next to her, as he's been this whole time.

"Coast down the hill."

She looks down the road and then at him. "You are crazy. I've been on a bike for all of two minutes and you want me to ride down a freaking hill?"

"You don't have to steer or pedal. The only people who drive on this road are the people who live on it. And it's the middle of the day. They're all at work. There's nothing or no one for you to hit. Just coast."

She pouts at him. "I don't wanna coast."

"Anjanae…"

"Andrew…"

"Do you want me to go stand at the bottom?"

"No, I want you to run alongside the bike."

He tilts his head and gives her a look.

"Fine," she consents with a forced frown, putting her feet back on the pedals. "But just know that if I die you're the one who is going to have to find some way to explain this to my husband."

"What, our salacious biking endeavors?"

She shoots him a derisive glance before she takes off, cautiously pedaling until she reaches the incline and gravity takes over. AJ watches as she glides down the hill, wind blowing through her hair. Despite her speed, she maintains control, just like he knew she would. When she gets stopped at the bottom, she hops off and immediately turns around with a huge smile plastered across her face.

"I just rode a bike!" She yells up to him.

He grins. "Yes you did!"

"Down a hill!" She yells back, breathless because she's pushing the bike back up the hill at a run now.

"I know."

"It was a steep hill, too, wasn't it?"

"Very steep." She makes it to him and he throws his arms around her, enthusiastically kissing her forehead as she laughs. "I am very proud."

CHAPTER 25

Maggie likes Ali's loft the first time she sees it. It's about a week after he ripped her old blouse and bought her a new one. He takes her out to dinner and then to a show at the Hollywood Bowl. Afterwards he asks her to accompany him back to his place for a nightcap. She smirks at the suggestion, but assents. Because she *would* like to have sex with him again, maybe more traditionally this time, like in a bed, and she's reluctant to invite him to her place. And also because she likes him, if she's being honest with herself, and she really doesn't want to end the night so soon. His building has an old-school elevator that lends to a romantic feeling, though she doesn't know why, and when they reach the top he unlocks a door that looks more like it leads to a huge freezer than an apartment.

It's all clean lines and open air, high industrial ceilings and exposed brick.

"I know it's a little empty," he tells her. "I moved in six months ago but still haven't got all my stuff shifted over." He looks around as if taking it in from an objective eye for the first time. "...Or done much furnishing."

"I like it," she reassures him.

The natural light is amazing; a continuous window takes up one entire side of the apartment. Walls don't separate rooms, other than the bathroom, though a claw foot tub sits out in the open (again, *the air of romance*, she thinks). It's true that there isn't much furniture. There's his bed, a glass desk without a drawer, one cotemporary looking swivel chair, and a mahogany armoire. A record player sits in one corner atop a cart filled with vinyl 75s. An open liquor cabinet sits in another corner, filled with glass bottles of only the best (*he knows what he's doing*, she thinks with a sneer). Despite the absence of furniture, his kitchen is fabulous. Beautiful marble countertops, a wraparound bar, and no table. The refrigerator is see-thru, the stovetop is futuristic, and there are double ovens in the wall. Above all else, his loft is neat. No scattered papers, discarded clothing, or dirt. And that's rare for a man. She respects it.

"Would you like a drink?" He asks.

"Why not?"

He pours them both a cognac, draws them a bath, and puts on a bluesy jazz album. It would have been cheesy if he hadn't done it so well. So smooth. The air is thick and smells of the lavender salts he put in the tub and the liquor they sip while his deliciously rough hands slip below the bubbles. After the water turns cold and their skin has puckered and pruned, they move to the bed. After sex, she lingers for the allotted amount of time that she gives herself for such occasions, and then gets up and begins to collect her clothes.

"You know you can stay," he tells her huskily. "If you want to, that is."

"I know," she replies indifferently, sliding her new black lace underwear back up her legs.

"Ok," he says simply.

She makes the mistake of looking back at him, his exposed upper body, his sexy five o'clock shadow, and his bedroom eyes begging her to come back to him without the use of pity or words. It's late and she doesn't really feel like catching a cab, so she reasons there's no harm in saving herself some trouble.

"Fine," she consents, crawling back under the sheets with him.

In the middle of the night she startles awake and contemplates fleeing, but blissful slumber soon overtakes her again and the thought is vanquished.

The next morning, she awakes to him dressing. He tells her that he has an early showing, but that she can stay as long as she likes. He tells her there are cinnamon rolls in the oven and coffee in the pot. He comes back to the bed to give her a quick kiss; he's freshly shaven and smells of cleanliness and the cologne she likes. He tells her to simply lock up when she leaves and he'll call her later, and then he leaves. *God,* she thinks to herself, *he trusts me way more than he should.* She texts Theo (on the white phone, she had tactically left the black one behind) giving him the address and telling him to come get her in a half hour. God forbid she call a cab or take the metro. She then stretches languidly and slowly separates herself from the warm bed, slipping into his equally warm robe that she finds hanging on the bathroom door. She wraps the plush oversized garment around her, knotting the belt at her waist in a show of decency, though no one is there, and makes her way into the kitchen. The coffee he made is strong and bitter, just the way she likes it. And as she nibbles on a roll, she can't help but start opening cabinets. Nothing to see (glasses, plates, a few pieces of fine china, and matching copper pots and pans) but it feeds to the incessant urge she has to find flaw in him. To vet him, per say. So she decides in her spare time she will scour his apartment for traces of secret wives, other lovers, and bad habits.

There's really little for her to go through; the loft is barren of nooks, crannies and hiding places. The laptop that was sitting on the glass desk the night before is gone; he must have taken it with him to work, and she did vaguely recall seeing a briefcase in his hand. She starts with the lone piece of furniture. Sitting in front of the armoire are three pairs of dress shoes: oxfords, wingtips, and loafers, plus a pair of running shoes. She opens the swing-out doors. Suit jackets, blazers, and shirts hang inside. An assortment of neckties hangs on a hook on the inside of the left door. On the right side, a small holder with three Swiss watches in it: gold, silver, and a vintage looking leather one. There are three drawers below; one for socks and underwear, one for pants, and one for comfort clothes like t-shirts, jeans, and sweats. She carefully snoops through each, coming up with only one hidden gem: an old black and white photo of a dark-haired woman with her arms around a little dark-haired boy. She can't tell where they are, but they both look happy. She flips it over and in his distinctive writing reads *Me and Madre 1959*. She smiles and puts it back where she found it, closing the doors and moving on.

In the bathroom all she finds are his personal products (cologne, aftershave, razors, soap, and shampoo) and a practically full bottle of aspirin. She shakes some of the pills out in her hand to make sure they are actually aspirin, and they are. There are no feminine products of any kind stashed away or accidently left behind by a previous flame. Nothing at all.

She pours herself a second cup of coffee and sits down in front of his record player to take a look at his collection of music. He has eclectic tastes: classic rock, Motown soul, funky jazz, and Latin classics. Good taste, though. She didn't notice before now, but there is a small stack of books to the left of the record rack; Maya Angelo, F. Scott Fitzgerald, Jonathan Franzen, Stephen King, Gillian Flynn, and Emerson. Again, eclectic, but good.

She gets back up, pausing momentarily at his nightstand. A Tiffany lamp sits atop it along with a box of Kleenex and a tube of Burt's Bees lip balm. She opens the drawer to find a pack of throat lozenges, a box of condoms she briefly saw last night, and a set of nail clippers. Safe sex, good hygiene, and preventative measures against snoring—she couldn't fault him for any of that.

Satisfied with her search, she sheds his robe, puts her own clothes back on, takes a cinnamon roll to go, locks up, and leaves. She feels no shame as she does the walk of shame out of his building and onto the street. Theo is waiting around the corner in his BMW where she told him to be. When she slides into the passenger seat she can feel him smirking without even looking.

"You're glowing," he says.

"Shut up," she tells him.

~

The first time she lets Ali spend the night at her apartment, she's a nervous wreck. Her, Maggie Hunter, who is never a nervous wreck. She stays up half the night watching him, although he doesn't make a move. Not that she really has anything to worry about should he attempt to peruse her apartment without her knowledge like she did his. She left her laptop locked up in her office at work, and the black phone is in a small safe tucked under her bed, the key to which isn't even in the zip code. She took care of both those things earlier in the day, knowing ahead of time he was coming over. Other than that, her apartment is void of personal items that relate to her profession, her *real* profession. And other than that, her apartment looks like a regular apartment where a regular person lives. Well, maybe that's pushing it. The apartment is technically a penthouse condo, and it's filled with her fancy furniture, name brand appliances, and designer clothes. But he already knows she's high maintenance. He knows her. Kind of.

As she lays perfectly still watching him sleep, she begins to take notice of all the perfect imperfections that make up this man, this man that she has let into her life. She stares at his bare back, her white sheets settled around his waist. Without even flexing, the muscles of his broad shoulders are traceable to the eye. And with her eyes she traces every line and indentation of his naturally tan skin from the top of his spine to the dip of his lower back where the cotton falls. The smooth plane of his back is almost without blemish, save for the birthmark at the base of his neck and the pair of bright red claw marks she left right down the center. She catches herself smiling when she thinks about how they got there. His jet-black hair sticks up in spurts on his head; sticking to the spare pillow she previously wrapped herself around when she slept. She realizes then that nobody else has ever been in this bed with her. A new wave of panic wants to crash ashore, but the rhythmic sound of his breathing is oddly lulling, and the warmth of his body heat keeps the fear at bay. The red numbers on her alarm clock tell her it's a quarter past three. She rolls over and settles into her sheets. A minute or two later she feels him stir and her heart skips a beat, put then he's scooting up against her and wrapping his arms around her. And for the second time in mere minutes, she catches herself smiling.

It's a process, but over the next few weeks it gets easier and easier for her to share her space with him. She actually starts looking forward to him coming over. To him talking back to her in that heady baritone voice whenever she starts to get smart, to him sexing her on of every piece of furniture she owns when she gives him that look, to him cooking for her. Yes, he cooks for her, using things in her kitchen she had never used, serving up delectable authentic Spanish dishes, and then cleaning up his mess afterwards. He caters to her and makes her feel comfortable. So, the Wednesday afternoon he called her at twelve and told her that he was passing through Hollywood on his way to a showing and had a big takeout bag from her favorite Chinese restaurant, she didn't even break a sweat when she invited him to come have lunch at her office. Dominique and Andrew were the only ones there, they had been playing her some of their little songs they'd made before they each had to go pay a visit to their respective Wednesday clients. She told them that she had a *friend* coming for lunch, to which they both grinned like fools, and that it was time to play pretend. When Ali walked through the door, Dominique promptly told him that he was about to be an R&B superstar thanks to her, and played him two songs before she shooed him away. Before the boys left, she introduced AJ to him as a writer, not a lie, and told him that she had just secured him a job on a new Netflix series, big lie. Ali ate it all up as truth, and then they ate their lunch.

A few evenings later he takes her to dinner at a new upscale restaurant on Melrose. As they wait to be seated, Maggie looks around at all the other happy couples in the room waiting. All the other women who are lucky enough to have a man to take them to the grand opening of a five-star restaurant on a Saturday night without having to pay someone like her to make it happen. There's an old grey-haired couple holding hands in their vintage couture, a sugar daddy-looking fellow in a three-piece suit with his beautiful blonde twenty-something, and a brunette woman with her arm looped in a redheaded man's arm. The brunette woman is fairly attractive, mid-thirties maybe. Her long hair is pulled back in a sleek ponytail and she has a becoming beauty mark on the left side of her mouth. Suddenly Maggie realizes that the woman is staring at Ali, and she briefly wonders if she should feel jealous. But then the woman is turning to her date and saying something to him in his ear, and then they are both looking at Ali and smiling and waving. This catches Ali's attention and Maggie watches as a smile comes to his face. He immediately takes her hand and leads her towards them.

"Maggie, I'd like you to meet my co-worker Kayla and her husband Ben." He pauses and then says, "Guys, this my girlfriend, Maggie."

Girlfriend.

He just called her his girlfriend.

She waits for the dread that word typically evokes to hit her, but it doesn't.

Kayla and Ben are smiling and reaching out to shake her hand. "Nice to meet you," they both say in unison.

She smiles back and shakes their hands earnestly. "Nice to meet you, too."

Ali is smiling too when he looks at her. "Kayla has been with our little group of realtors for about as long as I have. We're kind of the OG's," he jokes with the grin she adores. "Ben here is an architect and does some of our renovations for us."

"Oh, well you two must have been meant for each other then," Maggie says, looking between Kayla and Ben. "The builder and the seller."

"Yes, it was something like fate I suppose," Ben laughs.

Kayla laughs, too. "Well I can certainly tell you Maggie, in all the years I've known Ali, I've never seen him glow so much. You must be a very special lady."

Maggie smiles, blushes against her will, and thanks her. Waiters come to seat them; they exchanged nice-to-meet-yous one last time, and are ushered off in two separate directions. At an intimate table for two in the back, she and Ali look over the menu while sharing a luscious bottle of wine he had picked with admirable expertise. Without looking up from her menu, she addresses the topic on her mind.

"So. Girlfriend."

"Oh," he says, looking up immediately. "Should I not have said that?" He asks in an apologetic voice, genuinely concerned that he's crossed a line with her. "I just thought…we've been seeing each other for a while now." He waits for her to say something but she doesn't. "I'm sorry, I should have talked to you before defining our relationship."

"Yes, you should have."

"So…" he treads tentatively. "Not girlfriend yet?"

"I don't know," she says coyly. She briefly glances over the rim of her menu to flash him a flirtatious look, and then goes back to reading the entrees. "I'll have to get back with you."

He smiles saucily and goes back to reading his own menu. "Okay, baby. Take your time. Take all the sexy time you need."

Back in her apartment that night, after they've brushed their teeth, put their pajamas on, and pulled back the sheets, Maggie and Ali lay on their sides staring at each other but not speaking. She reaches to run her manicured nails through his dark hair, searching for the perfectly mixed grey strands. He growls in appreciation of the sensation. Their eyes are locked on each other's.

"I guess I can be your girlfriend," she says lowly after a moment, so close that her breath falls against his lips.

He raises an eyebrow in amusement. "You guess?"

A small smile curls her lips. "Yes."

They lie that way for a while, breathing each other's air, idly stroking each other's skin. Staring. Captivated. Content.

"You want to have committed sex?" He whispers in his baritone.

She smirks. "Is it any different than platonic sex?"

He grins against her mouth. "Oh yes," he replies, rolling her onto her back.

"I don't know," she murmurs in between kisses. "I rather enjoyed the platonic sex."

"I know." His eyes twinkle naughtily as his hands bring her satin slip up and over her head, tossing it to the floor and kissing her senseless.

He proceeds to make love to her so thoroughly that afterwards she sleeps, probably for the first time since she was a child, through the entire night.

CHAPTER 26

As he often does, one afternoon Austin is strolling around the Promenade alone. Not having a typical nine to five leads to a lot of free time during the middle of the day. He typically goes for a run on the beach when he wakes up, sometimes stopping to workout with the juiceheads and yoga fanatics on muscle beach. He returns to his apartment, showers, makes a power smoothie and an egg white omelet, and looks for things to do. After flipping back and forth between ESPN and ESPN 2, and playing few levels of Black Ops on his new Xbox, he gets bored. And when he's bored he'll sometimes walk down to 4th Street, do some shopping, and get a bite to eat. This afternoon he has a Banana Republic bag in one hand and a California Pizza Kitchen takeout box in the other. As he walks down the sidewalk he passes one of the little trendy outdoor-seating-only eateries.

"Austin!"

He turns around and is surprised to see Hermosa standing there, waving at him with a smile. She's got on a white button-up shirt that's tucked into black slacks, and a clip on her collar with the restaurant's name and her name on it.

"Hey!" He says, big grin coming to his face. He walks over and the next thing he knows they're hugging. He's not sure who initiated it, but it seemed like the natural thing to do. He can feel her breasts pressing against his chest through the lightweight material of her shirt and his, and his hands feel like they've always belonged on the small of her back. He releases her before his mind travels too far down the thought path that it's on.

"Sit," she says, pointing to a table for two. "I'm on break."

He does as he's told, happily. "It's great to see you," he says. "How long have you been workin' here?"

"Bout a month," she replies. "Still not a dream job, but I make pretty good tips. Got an efficiency apartment over in Marina Del Ray. It's not much but it's kind of close and rent is really cheap. I also applied to Santa Monica Community College." She can't help the smile that takes over her face completely. "I start in January."

"That's great, Hermosa," Austin tells her, smiling at her smile.

"I know. And while I was there last week filling out forms and all that, I checked out the job openings they had on campus, and applied for a part time position in the library. I got the call last night that I got it."

"Wow," he says, sitting back in his chair to better look at her. "Way to stay on your grind, girl."

She laughs. It's a girlishly cute and genuine sound

"I'm happy for you," he says sincerely. "I'm happy you got out of Mrs. Vernon's house and are making it happen for yourself."

"Me too."

"It was shady of you to just quit and disappear without even tellin' me goodbye, though," he says playfully, feigning hurt. "I've been wonderin if I'd ever see you again."

"Oh whatever," she replies dismissively. "You don't think about me."

"I do think about you," he says seriously.

He's met with silence. She suddenly looks like a deer in the headlights. She suddenly looks bashful.

"So like anyway…" She says finally, diverting her eyes from his and purposefully taking a tougher tone. "Anything new happening in your life?"

"Nope. Same old same old." He looks bashful now, too, and pauses to think about what he's about to say. "I actually live super close. The grey and white apartments across the street from the beach. I was wonderin…well I was wonderin if when you get off work tonight you'd like to go to dinner with me."

"Are you trying to make a client out of me?" She asks, that familiar saucy spark returning to her eyes. "I know I got two jobs now but you're still not in my price range, Papi."

"No," he says quickly, and then laughs. "No. I'll pay for you. I mean I'll pay for your meal." He shakes his head and hopes to stop stumbling. "You know what I mean. There's this really nice place nearby. Five-star. Steaks the size of your head and like a huge ass wine list. If you like wine. Or steak. If not they got a whole bunch of other really good stuff. Great desserts. I can make us reservations."

Her face is soft and somewhat remorseful. "I'm sure you're a really good guy and all that," she says empathetically. "But your job is just too weird." She softens the blow with humor and a smile. "I'm sorta like a catch if you ain't noticed. I can't call myself dating a dude who I know is sleeping with other women." And then adds sincerely, "No offense, because I do like you as a person."

"No. None taken," he replies with a small smile, trying not to look too dejected. "I completely understand."

"But we can still be friends," she says quickly. "If you want."

"Yeah. I'd like that very much."

"Ok," she smiles. "Cool."

"So..." he says after a beat, deciding to perhaps push his luck. "Friends don't go on dates but they can hang out, right? Go on the pier; get a corndog, maybe a lemon shake up. Nothing super romantic."

She raises an eyebrow skeptically. "The pier?"

"I've lived in Santa Monica almost three months and have never been on the Ferris wheel. I'm scared to ride it by myself. I hear it lights up at night."

She's silent while she sizes him up, smirk on her lips. "Ok," she consents after five or six seconds. "I get off at 7:30. I'll meet you on the pier at a quarter till." She gets up and pushes her chair in. "I gotta get back to work. You are distracting me."

Austin smiles in satisfaction of her sarcastic response. "See you then!" He calls after her.

~

Three weeks later he and Hermosa are walking down the beach together. It's early afternoon, the sun is high in the sky, and they both have the entire day off. Her long black hair is down and pushed back by a sparkly headband. She's got on a floral crop-top and torn denim shorts, sandals in her hand and toes in the sand. All that toned, tan skin has his mind running wild. He thinks of how if she were his girl he'd take her by the hand, lead her to some private alcove, lay her down right there in the sand, and have his way with her. Or let her have her way with him. Whatever she wanted, he would do. But she's not his girl. They're just friends. And he respects those boundaries too much to even reach for her hand, even though he wants to. He doesn't consider the fact that he may be doing the same thing to her mind that she is to his; he's got his shirt off and it's tucked in to the back pocket of his board shorts.

Hermosa shakes her head and laughs as he does backflips down the shoreline. He does about six or seven in a row and lands perfectly on his feet, immediately dropping down to the ground to go after something he spotted in the sand. She thinks he might have a mild form of adult A.D.H.D but she hasn't brought it to his attention because she finds his distractibility strangely cute.

"Hey, Mo!" He calls to her. "Look what I found." He turns around holding up something small in his hand that she can't see from a distance. But she can see that he's beaming from ear to ear. "Seashell," he says.

"Yeah, goober. We're on the beach. There's like a shit ton of sea shells."

"But this one is pink."

"Oooh," she says, interested now. "Give it to me."

She catches up to him and he hands it to her to her. He watches her look it over, examining all its nooks and lines. He can tell she likes it.

"See," he says. "It's special. Now who's a goober? Goober. You're startin to take on my country slang. Next thing ya know you'll be sayin America without no A."

She looks up at him, giving him a cocky look. "Would you rather me call you el tonto?" She asks, flirtatious glint her eyes. "Or el stupido." She slips the shell into her pocket and moves past him to continue walking. He follows her. "Or el ganso?"

"You're so mean to me," he tells her.

"I say it all with love."

"And I love the way you say it." He winks at her over his shoulder and she rolls her eyes. A volleyball rolls into their path and he picks it up, looking around for where it came from. About thirty or so feet away a group of teenagers are congregated around a net.

"Hey, bro!" One of them calls to him. "Over here!"

Austin holds the ball in his left palm, rears back his right arm, and serves it with a firm punt of his fist. The ball goes flying across the beach where one of the boys spikes it and puts it back into play.

"Nice!" One of the boys yells back to him.

"Thanks, man," Austin replies with a wave and then continues walking.

Hermosa has become distracted by his body. His athletic, sweaty body. Muscles everywhere. His back, his legs, his stomach, his chest. And those arms. *Why does he have to look like that*, she thinks to herself.

"What cha looking at?" He asks her with his silly little lopsided grin.

"Nothing," she snaps back sternly, looking away.

"Just friends, right?"

"Just friends," she reiterates, more as a reminder to herself than to him.

They walk along in silence for a moment, seagulls fly overhead and a group of suntan scented children run by with a beach ball, shrieking excitedly as their mothers call to them from a beach towel nearby.

"Are you hungry?" He asks her. "This sea air is making me hungry."

"Ocean."

"You know what I mean. Let's go to Bubba Gump's."

"Ok, Forrest," she teases. "But remember you gotta put your shirt back on. We don't want to be denied entrance like last time."

He sticks his tongue out at her. "I'll race you to the boardwalk. Whoever loses has to buy lunch."

"Oh, you're on."

They both take off running across the sand. He's stays ahead of her all the way to the pier, but pretends to get winded at the last minute and lets her win.

CHAPTER 27

Three of Anjanae's paintings get accepted into an art show in late November. Julius is out of town working on the night of the event, but sends two dozen red roses to the Downtown LA gallery where the show is being held in his absence. AJ specifically asks for the night off, even though it's a Friday and Maggie protests. He has to be there. And he is. Even though nobody there knows what he is to her, even though he has to hang back and make supportive eyes at her from a distance. He makes conversation with people he doesn't know as he makes his way around the perimeter, taking in all the exhibits and the ambiance. The room is filled with art enthusiasts, art dealers, high rollers, socialites, and of course the artists themselves. Paintings hang on the white walls, sculptures sit up on white blocks, and intricate creations made from odd things are roped off in the four corners of the room. Christine and Annabelle are in attendance, guzzling the free champagne. Some of Julius's producer friends are also present; their wives *ooh* and *ahh* and pretend to have interest in what they're looking at. AJ watches with a smile as people who *do* have interest in what they're looking at come up to her, complimenting and congratulating. She made those paintings at his house; he'd witnessed the magic with his own eyes. At one point in the evening he catches her alone.

"You're doing amazing," he says quietly, coming to stand beside her.

"I feel amazing," she whispers back.

He sees her smile out of the corner of his eye. His fingers reach to briefly graze hers in one of their many wordless forms of communication. And then he moves on to the next exhibit to keep with the inconspicuousness.

All three of her pieces sell for very profitable prices. They leave separately and meet back up at the mansion where they celebrate in private.

A few nights later they sit on the floor of his studio, eating carryout and listening to some records they found in the bargain bin at some mom and pop music store the week before. He picks up his moleskin notebook off the piano bench behind him, turning to the page he'd dog-eared. AJ lets her read some of his stuff sometimes. Not everything, though; some is far too personal and she'd instantly see that she was the muse behind it. But this particular song is one he wants to share with her. He wrote it late one night, earlier in the week. No one else had seen it yet. Turner hadn't put the lyrics to music, and Dominique hadn't sung the words. They would, though, they definitely would. AJ felt like this was one of the best songs he had written yet, but self-consciousness and doubt still plague him, even as pride fills him. He knows she'll keep it honest with him. She had pointed out certain lines to him before that she thought didn't mesh quite right, suggested he move the hook, change a word or two. He cherishes her opinion and considers all that she says. So he passes her the notebook. She instinctively turns down the music and turns to the dog-eared page.

He watches her quietly as she reads it. Diligent eyes that move across the page in time, concentrative frown on her face as she absorbs his ideas like the parchment he wrote them upon.

"What do you think?" He asks after a moment.

She continues to stare at the paper. "What a shame it would be if you were selling trucks somewhere in Tennessee right now," she says simply, closing the notebook. And then she looks up at him, smiling both with her eyes and her face.

Amazed. He's always amazed, both with her and by her. A grin breaks out on his face and he pulls her to him, wrapping his arms snuggly around her and planting a single kiss to the top of her head.

"What if I leave him?" She says against his chest. It's muffled in the fabric of his sweatshirt and he can't be sure that heard her right.

"What?" He asks, pulling away a bit.

She tilts her head up, looking right at him. "What if I leave him? What if I've been stashing money without him knowing? What if I keep stashing money, and sell some of my stuff, and then ask for a divorce? What if I run?"

He blinks, letting her suggestion sink in. "Then I'd run with you."

"You'd leave Maggie?"

He doesn't miss that she didn't ask if he'd leave Grace, because they both know that's not who he belongs to.

"Yes," he replies. "I'd quit." He pulls her back into his arms. She rests her head on his chest; he rests his head on hers.

"Then let's run," she says quietly. "I'll save a little more money. You save a little more money. And we'll make a clean break."

"Ok," he says into her hair. "When?"

She thinks about it for a second. "The beginning of the new year," she says finally. "January. We'll live in Reseda…get regular jobs…write, paint, and be the people our neighbors already think we are."

He smiles. "That sounds like a plan."

She leans back to look up at him again. "You promise?"

He finds her pinky and wraps his around it. "Promise."

CHAPTER 28

Julius has the day off. He's officially finished filming, he's back home in Bel-Air, and he's got the rough cut of his new movie on a disc. He wants nothing more than to sit down and watch it. He'll have a big advanced private screening for all his lucky friends and cohorts here in a couple months or so, but for now he wants to absorb his visionary brilliance alone in the comfort of his bedroom. But he can't find the remote to the damn flat screen. He feels around in the comforter, looks behind things, and then notices that Anjanae's sock draw is sitting ajar. Perhaps it fell off the dresser into a pile of Gold Toes, he thinks to himself, mentally chastising her for opening things and not closing them.

He gropes around in the heap of socks, and suddenly his hand makes contact with something hard at the bottom of the pile, far in the back of the drawer. But it's not the remote. He pulls out a square see-thru case with a plain DVD in it. There's nothing written on the case, no indication of what's on the disc, and he doesn't recognize it as something of his own. Curious indeed. Naturally, he takes the CD out of the case and loads it into the DVD player, spotting the remote across the room on the chase lounge as he does so.

He presses play and watches as a young man's face appears. A boy. A white boy with thick hair and green eyes. He couldn't be more than twenty-three, twenty-four at the most. He's taking off his clothes. *What the fuck is this*, he thinks. The camera pans out and his stomach churns as he realizes with unsettling certainty that the backdrop to this home movie is his home. His bedroom. He hears a familiar giggle.

She wouldn't.

Someone with brown skin enters the scene; he can see her arms as she scoots towards the boy, getting closer. There's a fight for the camera. The boy gets it, he thinks. There's a flash of color as the room shifts behind the lens, and then there's his wife, staring into the camera like a seductress. She peels off her shirt and is braless beneath it. His pulse picks up as he watches her get off the bed, open the blinds, and strut around the room. *The panties she has on...did he get them for her for Christmas or was it Valentine's Day?* His mind muddles and he can't focus. The camera, however, keeps perfect focus as she slips on a pair of Louboutins. *He got those for her for Valentine's Day and the panties were special ordered from a boutique in Paris for her last Christmas.*

He should stop watching.

His wife has returned to the bed and is straddling the boy now. Underwear comes off. Hands are touching, touching in places they shouldn't be. They forget the camera for a heated moment and the lens is jostled and pointed at pillows, all he can hear is heady hums, both male and female. The man re-steadies the camera, re-steadies it right upon his wife's face as she...well her face is scrunching and she's biting her lip with a smile, and he knows...from the groan that leaves the boy's mouth and the gasp that leaves hers, that she is officially committing adultery. He doesn't miss the fact that he didn't see a condom or hear a wrapper being torn, and his blood boils.

He should stop watching.

The boy keeps the focus on Anjanae as she rides him, rolling her hips and bouncing up and down with skill. She could always move, Julius thinks to himself, such natural rhythm. He used to enjoy it thoroughly and now somebody else was. About that time the boy slowly pans the camera down her body to where they're connected. And he is forced to watch another man slide in and out of his wife. He should look away. He could turn it off and put an end to his misery, but he can't. His eyes are glued to the screen in horror. The boy's right hand slips down and he hears his wife whimper. The picture dissolves into shimmering skin as she leans into him and the view is obscured. Julius doesn't know what is being done to her, but he can hear her mewling in the background. More wet sounds, rustling sheets, and then a long feminine sigh. He's pretty sure he knows what has just happened, and it infuriates him how quickly someone else made it happen. He barely registers through the red coating his vision that the camera is being moved, being placed on a tripod at the end of the bed. He briefly looks away when the boy comes back into frame, fully erect penis on display as he climbs back onto the bed where his satiated looking wife beckons him with her eyes. He flips Anjanae over onto her stomach. And like the willing little whore that she is, she rises up on all fours and puts an arch in her back. If he weren't so angry, so blindly angry, he'd be turned on. It's so enticingly erotic, the way she throws her perfect ass in a circle and looks back over her shoulder at the boy and the camera. But it only serves to make him want to strangle her more. He re-enters her, giving one of her delectable cheeks a smack once he's settled in to the hilt. They take turns in this position, her throwing it back and him giving her deep strokes. So deep that her head drops to the pillow and she screams, *screams* into it, fists knotting in the sheets. That bastard, that little white bastard. He did seem to know what he was doing. Julius couldn't deny that.

He wonders in that moment if he can find him. If he can track him down, kill him, and get away with it. Probably not. But possibly.

The boy pulls out, puts her on her back, and slides back in without more than two seconds elapsing. Her legs immediately go to wrap high up around his waist. One leg gets thrown over the boy's shoulder, the sharp heel of her stiletto digging into his upper back. Face to face now they're kissing, tongues in mouths and hands in hair. Licking, biting, and sucking on necks, ears and arteries, hips gyrating leisurely. The way they move together in tandem lets him know that they've screwed before; probably many times before, probably many times after. They're too acquainted with each other's bodies, too in tune, too trusting. If this had just been some awkward five-minute fuck he might have been able to gloss over it, turn the other cheek like wives do when faced with their husbands' indiscretions. If this had just been a one-night stand, he might have been able to grant her a pass, because hell, he'd had some one-night stands on her. But it was clear that this was not a one-night stand. This was her fucking and getting fucked by her lover, in *his* bed, and filming it with *his* camera.

This was unforgivable.

He's shocked when he sees Anjanae reach down and grab her lover's firm ass with both hands. Her lover obliges, going deeper. She's making sounds he's never heard her make before. Strangled sobs and desperate moans. Her hands are on his back now, nails digging in and clawing streaks in his skin. And then she comes again. The boy's thrusts lose rhythm, and Julius soon hears his wife's lover's low growl of pleasure. He pulls out and comes on the sheets. His five hundred thread count

Egyptian cotton sheets. Julius would have rather he came on her. What audacity.

He hears them both giggle and laugh in the aftermath as they try to catch their breath. And then the camera is shut off and everything goes black.

He resolves right then and there to make her a bitter, divorced, bag lady. She had signed the prenup so her dumbass won't get a penny; she'll be poorer than she was when he met her. He'll get the best divorce attorney that money can buy. He'll take back her handbags and her shoes and her jewelry so she can't pawn a thing. Revoke the keys to her Range Rover. He thrills at the thought of her homeless on the street in rags, hair nappy and skin marred with grime. What did she have to fall back on? What skills did she have? Besides the obvious. She would have nothing. If she wanted to not end up sleeping on a park bench and diving in dumpsters she would have to work some menial job as a cashier or a store clerk, which would probably only afford her one of those bedbug infested apartments near skid row. He knew it would be tortuous for her to go from the lap of luxury to that. He hoped white boy was worth it. Like he'd want her if she didn't look how she looked and have what she has now. He hopes the tainted memory of hot sex will be enough to keep her warm at night when the heat goes out in her scuzzy building and her cheap landlord doesn't give a fuck about her comfort. Her days of comfort were about to be over.

Oh, she was going to come to regret this.

His mind races with ways he can spring it on her and how he will do it. She's gone now and he doesn't know when she will be back. *Probably out riding pink dick as we speak,* he thinks as a new wave of disdain washes over him. Did he have time to throw all her stuff out on the lawn, turn on the sprinklers, and make a public show of her indecency for their neighbors before she got home? He stops himself. He wasn't going to throw her shit out on the lawn; he wasn't going to give her shit. He could cut her clothes up, pour bleach on her designer purses, and carve obscenities into the soles and sides of her stilettos with a switchblade. And *then* throw them out on the lawn and turn the sprinklers on. If he moved fast he might be able to get it all done before she gets back. He stops himself again.

He was a smarter man than this. He needed to think more clearly and not let anger cloud his judgment. For he knew that vindication was a dish best served with smile-laced silence. He would play the fool that his wife so obviously thought he was. Until the perfect moment presented itself, and *then* he would let her in on the secret that she was about to be an ex-wife. First thing first he needed to find out who this boy was. Because if he could destroy whatever this cocksure young man had going for him, he would do so in an instant. If he was aspiring to be anything in the business, which he more than likely was, Julius had enough pull to make sure that dream never came to fruition. He wasn't out for blood. He was out for futures.

He quickly makes a few calls and acquires the number of a well-respected private investigator, has a brief conversation with the man, and then messages him a picture of Anjanae, her car, and her license plate number. He put her sock drawer back to how he found it, makes a copy of the movie, and is in the living room reading a book when she walks through the front door fifteen minutes later. When she passes by him he takes her hand in his and gives the back of it a single kiss, looks up into her eyes with a smile, and asks if Italian sounds okay for dinner. She says it does. He tells her the chef will be over in a half hour to prepare it. She says okay, that she's going to go shower first, and then goes upstairs. Julius wipes his lips off with his sleeve from where he'd kissed her skin, and then with a sinister smirk texts the P.I. again to tell him the name of the little bistro in Santa Monica where she has brunch every Wednesday morning.

CHAPTER 29

Private Investigator Freddie Fontana may be somewhat of a sleazy looking fellow, but he is excellent at his job. A week later he reports back to Julius with a file folder full of photos. They're at the dining room table of Julius's mansion; he'd called Freddie over right after his slut of a wife had left in a pair of ass hugging skinny jeans and an off-the-shoulder top. And as the lanky, plainly dressed P.I. with the tinted glasses who reeks of cheap cigarettes lays each picture out on the table, he sets the scene from when and where he took it.

"His name is Andrew James Brooks. Goes by AJ," Freddie states.

The first photo is of them standing on a sidewalk in front of the Range Rover he paid for, smiling at each other all sentimentally as they speak, enjoying what they think is a private moment. Stupid them. Julius can't think of two people he hates more at the moment. That thought is interrupted when Freddie lays down another picture on top of the one Julius had been vehemently glaring at. The new picture is of them in a restaurant booth. They sit on the same side, huddled up against each other like some silly lovestruck teenagers.

"Monday she met him for lunch at this Korean Barbecue place," Freddie explains. "Which, being a public place and all, was convenient for me because I could pretend to be a patron and got to overhear some of their conversations. They definitely interact like a couple, I'll tell you that. After their meal they went upstairs."

"Upstairs?"

"He lives above the restaurant in a studio apartment," Freddie replies, laying down a picture that looks it was shot at an upward angle from a fire escape or something below. The shadowy figure of his wife stands with her back to the window in only a bra. Of course Julius had already seen much worse. "Fourth floor."

"Classy."

"He also has a house in Reseda. When you were in New York Wednesday she spent the night there. I did a property search and it's a recent purchase, within the last three months. He got a hell of a deal on it, too. $80,000 for any property in California is a steal, even for the valley. He's of course making payments, but that's still a big investment for a twenty-three-year-old. He is twenty-three by the way, I know you were curious."

"Who are these people?" Julius asks, looking at the most recent picture that's been put in front of him. Anjanae and the boy are outside, dressed in very casual attire, sweatshirts and jeans. And an older man and woman are talking to them.

"His neighbors. Thursday morning they went on a walk. Ran into a few people while they were out, all of whom seemed to know them. Very friendly. Very familiar. I seriously doubt they know she's married."

Julius shakes his head, not knowing how to take it. "So she spent pretty much every day but Tuesday with him?"

"Yes, Tuesday he had other plans."

Julius eyes him curiously.

"The day started off normal enough. He went to lunch at a little soup and sandwich place with a guy friend, this Korean kid named Jae. Afterwards he went to a bookstore, bought a few things, went to Whole Foods, got groceries, and then went back to his apartment. But then about seven o'clock he exits his building in a real spiffy get-up. I follow him to Canon Drive where he has dinner with this woman." He lies down a picture of AJ seated at a table with a woman in a silver dress. "Snazzy place, snazzy woman. Older woman. I considered the possibility that she might be his mother, a relative, but it was clearly a date. Very romantic, hands on legs, sultry looks, that type of thing. After their meal they left in a limo and I assume went back to her place. I couldn't follow them all the way; private drives, gates and shit."

This pleases Julius greatly. He's going to get to tell his wife that she is not her lover's only woman. Tell her that she's not special at all to this boy. He's fucking someone else. And he's taking his white woman to five-star restaurants while her dumbass is getting cheap Korean food. He can't wait to see the look on her face.

"So he has another lover?" He asks almost giddily, just to be sure. "He's a player. Probably doesn't really even care about her."

"I don't know if he's a player, but he is something." Freddie smiles. "This is where things get really interesting. Friday afternoon I follow him to the Beverley Wilshire. He goes up to room 1711 where a *different* woman lets him in. The do not disturb sign immediately goes on the door, but I could still hear the moans from the hallway. Anyway he stays for about an hour, leaves the room stuffing a wad of money into his pants pocket, clothes all creased and crumpled."

The dots are connecting in Julius's head and he looks repulsed.

"So he gets in his car and goes straight to this office looking place in Hollywood. He's about to go in, but then this woman comes out."

Freddie lays down the last picture and Julius's heart stops.

He knows this woman.

She's a friend of his.

Or so he had thought.

"The kid reaches into his pocket and takes out the wad of money, hands it right to her. Then he gets back in his car, she gets into a white Mercedes, and they both go their separate ways," Freddie concludes.

Julius sits there in silence trying to process what he's learned, and then trying to make sense of what he's processed.

"At least now we know how he affords an apartment, a house, and a mint condition muscle car. Assuming he gets to keep some of his earnings, he did hand her the whole bankroll. Speaking of her, I surveyed the office building she was seen coming out of and it appears like she's got quite a few good looking gents on her payroll. I gotta tell ya, it's been awhile since I've come across a madam, and never one that strictly pimps men. This has been a more interesting job call than I thought it would be. As far as your wife, judging by how close she seemed to the boy, I'd say she knows what he does and just accepts it for what it is."

"You think she's fully aware?" Julius asks him seriously.

"I think so. The good news is I have never witnessed an exchanging of money between your wife and him. So at least she's not spending the allowance you give her on male hookers. The bad news is she does definitely seem to be in a serious relationship with one. I'd probably go get my shit checked out sooner than later if I was you, but that's just me. You might be burnin before long."

But Julius is burning. His veins feel like they're filled with fire, flowing lava right under his skin, making his pulse hammer violently in his ears. His is face hot from the radiation of vitriol within him and he has to fight to keep a cool façade even though he feels like he's incinerating from the inside out.

He swallows and speaks calmly. "Do you have the address for that place in Hollywood where he gave the woman the money?"

"Yeah, should still have it in my phone." Freddie takes out his Samsung, presses a few buttons, and then writes the address on the back of the last photo. "There you go, all yours."

"Thanks." Julius takes out his wallet and awards Freddie with a very generous disbursement, more than he even asked for, and then shakes his hand.

"Pleasure doing business with you, Mr. Julius," Freddie replies with a greasy smile, easily accepting the extra cash. "It's all in your hands now." They both stand up. "Though if you're feeling homicidal I'd suggest you do like OJ and wear a glove. Actually, I'd suggest you were a glove in any and all settings and situations for a while, but again, that's just me. Safe sex and safe crimes are always a good idea."

"Mmhm," Julius mutters as he ushers him to the door.

"You got my number if you ever need me again."

"Let's certainly hope that I don't."

After Freddie leaves and the door is closed, Julius immediately goes upstairs to make the rewrites to his revenge to include one more person. He makes a copy of the sex-tape, sticks it in an envelope, and then calls up his assistant to make a personal delivery for him. Julius then gets a gallon of bleach and a pair of scissors.

~

About two o'clock in the afternoon an awkward looking little man with hipster glasses walks through Maggie's office door without invitation.

She looks up from her computer at him. "Who the hell are you?"

"I'm Mr. Collins' assistant," he stammers nervously, face flushing.

"Mr. Collins?" She questions.

"Yes, he wanted me to hand deliver this to you." He holds out a generic yellow office envelope to her. She hesitates before taking it, eyeing him up and down in a way that makes him squirm more.

"What is it?" She asks, looking it over but not opening it.

"I don't know, ma'am. He just told me to be sure you got it." And with that he quickly scurries out the door before she can press him any further.

She shakes her head at the silliness of it all, and then tears open the package. Inside is a white CD envelope with a CD in it. She takes out the CD. Written upon on it in black Sharpie ink are the words *I Know What You Do*.

"What the fuck," she mutters to herself in confusion, screwing her face up at the disc. She knows the only way to figure out what it all means is to see what's on it, for which she has no clue. So she loads it into her computer and waits.

The first thing she sees is AJ's face.

~

Anjanae realizes there's something off when she gets about halfway up the driveway. There are things on the lawn, like someone had snuck onto their property and littered everywhere. She squints as she gets closer, trying to discern what the objects are. Undistinguishable shreds of different colors. And then there's something stuck in the branches of a nearby tree. And then she's close enough to see that it's her favorite pink Moschino dress. Except it has a huge white splash right down the center. A huge white splash that wasn't there before. A huge white splash that makes it look like bleach had been thr–

Panic blooms in the pit of her stomach.

She pulls up to the house, throws the car into park, and jumps out. Her stuff. All of her stuff. Everything. Everything is everywhere. She doesn't know where to start or what is what. Tops that have been cut up, dresses that have been torn beyond repair, shoes halfway across the yard. The few paintings she had kept there, now crumpled up into little balls of ink splattered paper peppering the green grass along with the shredded fragments of credit cards. A grey Hermes purse with bleach stained spots all over it comes flying out of the top floor window, sailing sadly to the ground. A red stiletto is thrown next; it hits the windshield of her car, bounces, and lands next to her. She quickly picks it up, hoping to salvage something, but then sees that he's carved *slut* in great big letters across the side. He throws its mate and she has to duck. She looks up at the window where his malevolent face appears. He's got her grandmother's pearl necklace in his hands, one of the only nice things that her family had ever had. Her mother had been so angry when it was left to her, but she had cherished it deeply.

"Julius," she says, voice breathless. "What…what are you doing?"

"Destroying all your shit so in case we get a stupid judge who decides to award you some of your possessions, you won't have anything worth possessing to possess," he tells her with a worrying amount of aplomb. And then yanks on the strand, sending pearls flying.

"Are *you* possessed?" She yells up at him. "Stop! Why are you doing this?"

"Two letters," he answers simply. "I'll give you a hint. First you should buy a vowel and then a consonant."

Her heart quickens with realization. *How does he know his name, how does he know his name*? "I...look..." She stutters helplessly. "I can explain whatever...whatever it is you...you think you know. Just come down so we can...so we can talk about it, okay? I..."

"I'm sorry, dear, that wasn't the answer I was looking for. You lose final jeopardy." He leans back inside the window and then reappears a moment later with her MacBook in his hands

"Julius!" She shrieks. "Come down here. Don't –"

But he does, and she watches in horror as her laptop does summersaults in the air. She tries to catch it but he's thrown it too far and she is resigned to listen to its tragic thud as it hits the pavement of the driveway, screen separating from keyboard and shattering. She stares at the mess surrounding her in disbelief. She's in a state of shock, she wants to pick up the pieces of her belongings, but she can't move. She doesn't even realize that her things have stopped raining from the sky until she hears the front door being opened. She immediately snaps out of it.

"Julius," she utters in an apologetic tone, taking a tentative step toward him.

"You must be a special kind of self-conscious."

"What?" She asks meekly, taking a step back now because the look in his eyes is frightfully cruel.

"Shacking up with a gigolo. What kind of pathetic excuse for a woman falls for someone who they know fucks other women?"

"I don't know what you're talking about," she lies, trying to make it sound true even though her voice falters and quivers.

"The proof was in the performance, darling."

She swallows and takes another step back as he inches closer.

"Oh yeah," he leers. "I found your little home movie. You found yourself a white boy who actually knows how to throw. Good for you. Too bad he's only going to get to exercise those skills on men now, seeing as he's going to be spending the next few years in jail. Prostitution is illegal, you know. Keep that in mind in case you have to take it up in order to support yourself here in the very near future. Not getting caught is key."

"Julius…"

"Do you know the number of women he screws in weeks' time? Because I do. And you kiss him on the mouth." He chuckles patronizingly. "Well that's enough to make me want to puke and throw you into a pool of disinfectant. You are cheating on a man-made millionaire with a morally bankrupt sad little boy who lets some woman in an office dictate his day-to-day and make money off his dick. You're supposed to fuck up, honey, not down. For God's sake that's the first commandment in Gold Digger 101. Did you miss a day of class?"

"Stop," she seethes quietly. He's right up on her now, and she's cowering backwards.

"Give me your keys."

"No." She puts her hands behind her back in an attempt to keep him from getting them. Both the keys to the house and the Range Rover are on her fobble.

"*Give* me your keys, Anjanae," he says more menacingly this time, grabbing her arm forcefully.

"No," she says defiantly, yanking her arm back out of his grasp.

But he just grabs it again. She puts up a fight, but he's stronger and wrestles the keys out of her grip, snatching them away from her.

"Give them back!"

He opens the passenger side door of her car, takes out her purse, and throws it at her. Then, with her car and house keys in his hand, he turns and heads back up the walkway to the front door.

"Julius," she says with a sob, chasing after him. "Julius you can't do this. You can't do this to me. You can't just put me out," she pleads desperately. "You have to let me get my stuff."

"You don't have stuff. *I* have stuff. Some of which was on temporary loan to you up until you decided to break your vows and is now all over the front yard." He spins around to face her again, his cold eyes boring into her. "By all means collect the scraps and go find yourself a sensational seamstress to sew it all back together again but your humpty dumpty whore ass has got me confused with someone else if you think I give a one-fourth of a fuck about you ever having *stuff* again."

Tears are streaming down her face against her will. Not because she's sorry for what she did, she's not. AJ is the love of her life without a shadow of a doubt and Julius Collins was never and will never be worth her tears. She should have never married him; it had all been a terrible mistake on her part. She's crying because he's stripped her of everything she has including her pride. The designer clothes don't matter anymore, not compared to the loss of her family heirlooms and her artwork. The simple comforts like her favorite Santa Monica Community College sleep shirt, her toothbrush, a few spare pairs of socks and underwear. He's left her with absolutely nothing but the clothes on her back and the few things she has in her handbag. And of course the moderate amount of money she had put in the secret account she'd started a month or so ago. She was glad she had thought to do that, but in hindsight, she should have thought to do more sooner. And she suddenly becomes aware of just how dependent she had actually been on a man, and an intense wave of self-disgust washes over her.

"I've cancelled all the cards you currently have in your billfold and took your name off the joint account, so I hope you have change on you. I left your phone on but I will be cutting it off tomorrow. Call yourself a cab and get the fuck off of my property before I turn the sprinklers on."

With that he slams the door in her face.

Anjanae turns her back on her husband, on the mansion, on her old life, and takes off down the driveway on foot. She doesn't look back, not even once, all the way down to the bottom.

Sitting on the ground outside of the gate as she waits on the cab, she tries to call AJ. But his phone is dead.

CHAPTER 30

"Theo, call Andrew from your phone, he's not answering me," Maggie snaps. She's pacing the floor in a manic fashion with the white phone clutched in her hands.

"Does it ring?" Theo asks.

"No, it just goes straight to his damn voice mailbox."

"Then it's either turned off or dead."

"He's going to be dead," she mutters under her breath.

Theo, Dominique, and Garrett are all lounging in the rec room. They were previously watching a ball game, but they can't help but to be distracted by her now. The three of them watch her trek from one end of the room to the other in no less than four strides each time. She pivots, stomps off in the opposite direction, then repeats, never ceasing. The sound of her heels on the wood floor is deafening and the anxiety emanating off her is a cause of concern for them all. This was not her usual cool, collected, calm demeanor at all.

"The fuck wrong with you?" Dominique asks her.

The front door swings open and AJ walks right into the den of fire unbeknownst to him. Maggie stops in her tracks and casts her blazing eyes upon him. The three boys watch from the couch, waiting to see what happens.

"Andrew, how nice of you to join us." She's speaking in that artificially sweet voice and it carries the worrisome tang of a worked nerve that's about to split. "Tell me, I thought you wanted to be a writer. Be behind the scenes. Not in front of the camera. Right?"

"Right," AJ replies, confused.

She lets out a brittle laugh, and then she's in motion again, storming the floor. The rampant and rapid *click click click* of her heels resuming.

"Maggie," Theo says gently. "What is wrong?"

"Andrew made a forty-seven-minute-long self-starring sex tape with Julius Collins' wife," she spits.

Everybody is silent. Then three heads turn to look at AJ.

"That's where all the damn R&B love songs was comin from!" Dominique exclaims in realization. "He had the fever!"

"What?" AJ says, stunned. "Did it get stolen from her house?" He racks his mind; worry lines forming on his face. "I read in the paper the other day that there's been a string of break-ins in Bel-Air. Crap." He looks up at Maggie. "But look," he says quickly. "You don't have to worry about it. It's between her and I. We're a…we're in a…" He stumbles over definitions. "She doesn't pay me. She's not a client."

"I noticed," Maggie says tersely. "Seeing as I've only had her down for two times and those were months ago. She's been getting freebies."

"She's my–"

"She's your what?" She cuts him off. "Your girlfriend is in Memphis. You only get one girlfriend, wife, or homie-lover-friend. Everybody else has to pay. You have been screwing this girl off the books for months now."

"Is that why you're mad?" AJ asks her, face screwing up. "Because I thought you'd be happy that she…that *this*…wasn't connected to you or the business."

"When you work for me you are my business," she reprimands him. "Everything you do is my business, therefore everything you do comes back to me. I am *mad* because Julius was a friend of mine–"

"So you pimp me out to his wife?" He asks, cutting her off this time.

"Business and personal. Andrew. That is your problem. You obviously cannot separate the two. And you didn't let me finish. Notice how I use the past tense: Julius *was* a friend of mine. A friend who had his assistant hand deliver me an explicit DVD today and now we are adversaries."

AJ realizes what this means. "Nobody broke into the house."

"Nobody broke into the house."

"Well," he says after a moment. "At least it's not leaked on the Internet then."

"No, but my name is probably about to be leaked to the press. By one of the most elite and well-respected men in Hollywood."

"We made it months ago," AJ says, not knowing what else to say.

"Why," Maggie grapples, pinching the bridge of her nose. "Why would you do something so stupid and reckless?"

"We were bored and–"

"If you're bored you come to me and I will put you to work."

"We just wanted to try something new," AJ rambles nervously. "Neither of us had ever thought of doing something like that before, let alone actually doing it. We're both kind of introverts–"

"This is not introversion!" Maggie yells, holding up the tape.

"Perversion maybe," Theo comments from the couch.

AJ shoots him a look.

"I don't know," Theo says, holding up his hands. "I haven't seen it."

"Well I have," Maggie states flatly. "And it's enough to make a man more than a little enraged."

"You watched it?" AJ exclaims, face flushing.

"Of course I watched it. I'd put it on the Internet and market it myself if the person who gave it to me wasn't threatening to put us all away."

"Shoot, I wanna see it," Dominique says.

"You're not seeing it," AJ tells him.

"Why?" Dominique chides. "You embarrassed of your performance?"

"It's forty-seven minutes long, do you think I'm embarrassed of my performance? I don't want you to see her naked, stupid."

"She's naked?" Dominique exclaims.

"You would think someone in the sex industry would know how these types of things work," Theo remarks off-handedly.

"And what's more," Maggie starts in again. "After you made it, you let *her* keep it."

"I just thought that was the polite thing to do. Plus, she said he was too old to know how to work a DVD player if he ever did find it..."

Maggie takes a deep breath and looks down, hand on forehead. "I like you, Andrew. I really do. But sometimes I think you might be stupid. Not *stupid* stupid like Austin, but the kind that smart people are." She takes her hand off her head and raises her voice. "He makes movies for a living! If he knows how to shoot them I'm damn sure he knows how to load them."

"Good thing he ain't load and shoot for real though..." Dominique inserts.

"If he just wanted to kill him that would be one thing," Maggie says, and AJ gives her a side eye. "But Julius Collins is a crafty man. He is going to drag this out and drag us all down."

"You know," Dominique says, not really realizing the magnitude of things. "One day Imma have ta tell my fans when they ask that my first songs was about Julius Collins' wife who my co-writer was breakin off back in the day."

Garrett, who has been being quiet all this time, but who looks more than a little pissed, turns to Dominique. "You do realize this means we'll all go to jail, right?"

Dominique gets a scared look on his face then, looking from Garrett to Maggie to Theo. "You'll talk to em, Theo, won't you? You'll tell em we don't get down like that. You won't let em get us."

"Act like you've been to jail before, boy," Theo tells him, annoyed. "Did you get raped then?"

"No. But it's been a long time," Dominique says, remembering the days before he met Maggie when he was selling weed and shit and had done a few stints in county. That was before he learned how to move stealthily and also before he had anything to lose. "I've been spoiled. And pampered. They'll sense the softness and try to take me down. I don't wanna go down, Theo!"

"We all shouldn't have to suffer for his stupidity," Garrett says then, glaring right at AJ. "I mean you don't see anyone else getting caught up in their clients' personal lives, now do you?"

"She's not my client," AJ says firmly.

"I don't give a rat's ass what she is to you, she's nothing to me other than some unhappy housewife whose philandering is threating my future." He cocks his head to the side and leers extra hard at his co-worker. "And I'll be dammed if I let some messy whore who can't keep her knickers up ruin my chance at success."

AJ lunges at Garrett with his fists clenched. But Theo jumps up and grabs him, holding him back. Garrett just scoffs and shakes his head, then turns and heads towards the door.

"I don't know about the rest you twits," Garrett says. "But I've got a life outside of this shit. I've got big opportunities. I've got clout in this city."

"You got a reoccurring role on a soap opera, chill," Dominique tells him.

"I'm a series regular," he replies back through clenched teeth.

"Garrett," Theo says in a calming voice, still keeping AJ wrangled. "Maggie will take care of this."

"She better," he says, giving Maggie a derisive backwards glance. "That's all I'm saying." And with that he walks out the door with a slam.

~

After Theo lets him go, AJ leaves. He immediately takes out his phone to call Anjanae as soon as he's outside. That's when he realizes that it's dead, and he curses. He lets it charge while he drives, and as soon as it gets to five percent he calls her.

"Hello," she answers, sounding calm but depleted.

"I know everything. Are you ok? What happened?"

"He cut up my clothes, bleached my bags, carved obscenities into my shoes, took the keys to my car and kicked me out of the house."

"Oh my God," AJ murmurs. "I'm so sorry, Anjanae. I...he didn't put his hands on you, did he?"

"No. Not really. He had to fight me for the keys but he didn't hit me. He just...took everything."

"Where are you?"

"I'm at a cheap motel off of Vermont. The Blue Bay...Blue Lagoon...I don't know...something along those lines."

"You don't need to stay at a motel. You can stay with me. I'll come get you right now."

"No. It's better if you stay away from me for a while. I think he's been tracking you and I don't know what he's going to do. He said...he said something about sending you to jail, AJ. If you want to get out of town I understand."

"I'm not going anywhere. I'm not leaving you. At least let me bring you dinner and some money so you can get some things."

"I'm fine. He thought he cancelled all my credit cards, but he forgot one. I charged the room to it. Plus, I've got like forty dollars' worth of cash on me and probably close to another five or ten if I empty all the change out of the bottom of my purse. And then there's the money in the secret account, but I don't want to touch that until I have to. I can survive on fifty dollars for a while, I can make it stretch. I haven't been rich that long."

"Maggie is going to make this right, Anjie," he tells her. "She's going to talk to him. She knows him. I'm not going to go to jail; she's not going to let that happen. She'll get him to calm down, and once he calms down, you and me...we can be together. It will all get sorted out. Ok?"

"Ok," she says, no other choice but to believe him.

"If you need anything call me."

"I will."

"I love you."

"I love you, too."

CHAPTER 31

That night Maggie can't stop pacing. She can't sit. She can't be still. She has to come up with a way to deter Julius from his vindication. She's called him three times and each time he'd stayed on the line just long enough to assure her in a threatening tone that her time was coming, and then hung up on her without letting her get a word in. Every time she hears a siren in the background from the busy streets below, or footsteps in the hall that in reality belong to her neighbors, she thinks, *this is it*. Every time a plane flies over, or a door slams, or Ali drops something, she startles.

Ali.

Ali's standing in her kitchen with tomatoes and peppers in one pan sautéing and corn tortillas frying in another, watching her wring her hands and move from one piece of furniture to another.

"Everything okay, babe?" He asks, concerned and totally in the dark.

Ali.

He'd planned to come over and cook for her before the shit hit the fan. She had considered cancelling on him, telling him she was sick. But then she decided he might be the perfect distraction. Something inside of her yearned for his comfort, his protection in the face of the imminent fate she faced. It was a foreign feeling to her, but she welcomes it. And even though she can't tell him the truth, can't tell him what's really wrong, she is glad that he's there. His mere presence soothes.

"Yeah," she says with a small smile, stripping the fretfulness from her voice. "Everything's fine."

"You sure?" He's moving between the two skillets with ease, lifting one from the burner and flipping its contents with a fluent shift of his wrist. He sits it back down and then presses a spatula to the tortillas, a searing sound filling the room. He looks both so sexy and so comfortable in her kitchen. It makes her happier than she ever expected it to.

"I'm sure. Just a stressful day at the office."

"Ok," he accepts her answer, smiling softly. "You want me to make you a margarita? I brought the mix over and I think we still got some Patron left in the fridge from the last time."

She smiles. "That sounds great."

Ali.

She considers the fact that she might be about to lose him. If Julius really does turn her in to the police, if she really does get arrested, charged, thrown behind bars...that would be it. It would be over. He would know the truth about what she really does, and she really couldn't expect him to visit her in jail, especially not after a lie like that. She catches herself already mentally mourning the loss of him. Out of all that she has to lose—her freedom, her money—she almost feels like she would miss him the most. She thinks she might love him. And she considers coming clean to him right then and there before the hurricane hits. But then she stops herself.

It's not over yet. Her white flag is not flying. She hasn't given up. She doesn't give up. And she will not go down without a fight.

"I'm going to step out into the hall and make a phone call real quick," she tells him, standing up and walking towards the door. "Business."

"Ok," he replies, dumping ice into her blender. "Dinner should be ready in about five to ten minutes."

"Ok," she says, exiting her apartment and shutting the door behind her. She walks to the end of the vacant hall. And then she calls Julius Collins one last time.

She convinces him to meet her. After dinner she leaves Ali in her apartment, telling him that one of the stuck-up starlets she represents wants to negotiate her contract. He buys it, and at the best table in the dimly lit backroom of a five-star restaurant over two cognacs and two cigars, Maggie negotiates with Julius.

"So what kind of fine bargaining devices do you have up your sleeve to coerce me into not leaking your name and those pictures to the press," he asks her with a sly smirk. "I'm going to do it. I just want to watch you wriggle for a while. I was hoping you'd offer me a few freebies from one your hookers, but then I learned you only hired men. So that's sadly off the table. No offense to them, I'm sure they can suck a mean dick. Male mouths just aren't my style. Of course, you could always get on your knees for the cause."

"Why do you have to be vulgar?"

"Why do *I* have to be vulgar? I'm not the one convincing young men to throw dick for dollars they don't get to keep. You do not sew, you just reap."

"Oh you're so poetic," she chastises with an eye-roll and a sip of cognac.

"No, I'm honest. I make an honest living. We may both be ostentatious millionaires, but I made my millions myself. I work hard for my money; you make other people work for yours. You ain't doin' a damn thing but counting it." He laughs. "An investment banker. Or was it a financial advisor? Everybody thinks you're such an elegant, educated lady. You ain't nothin but a crafty, calculating cunt."

She takes a drag, blowing a plume of smoke in his direction. "How much money do you want for your silence?"

He laughs. "You're not pandering to a regular person here, dear. Didn't I just tell you that I am a millionaire? You can't persuade me with your spare change."

"You may not need money, but I know you're motivated by it. And I may not have turned out to be the financial advisor you thought I was, but at one point that is how I made my living, and I have the degrees, multiple, to prove it. I have the credentials, qualifications, and know-how to flip your money five different ways. Reductions, evasions, investments, and write-offs. Those are champagne solutions, right?" She puts the expensive cigar back between her lips and takes a puff. "Am I pandering to the correct tax bracket now?"

Julius smirks hard at her over the rim of his tumbler as he takes a big gulp.

"Listen," she says, exhaling another string of elegant smoke circles. "I won't argue with you that I'm a crafty, calculating you-know-what, but I'm a crafty calculating you-know what who's flown under radars and dodged agency speculation for over a decade, all the while piling up unaccounted for money like it's nothing. I can make your millions billions."

He's quiet. Contemplative. Considering, maybe.

"While I'm at it," she continues, dead set on sealing the deal. "I want to remind you that it's *your* image that will be collateral if you choose to out me. Because tabloids don't care about who's fucking who, they just care about what your name is. And out of everyone involved in this unfortunate little fiasco, yours is the only familiar name. They don't know who Andrew is. They don't know who I am. But Julius Collins? That's the producer of someone's favorite movie. The creator of that one film that won all of the awards. The visionary icon that all the A-listers love to work with. But after this, you'll forever be memorialized as that old black director guy whose wife was fucking a young white gigolo. He must be an absent husband, they'll say. A lousy lover. An unlikable person. With a new movie coming out, that's a shifty light to be painted in. Of course some say all publicity is good publicity, but I get the feeling you're not one of those people. Are you?"

Silence. One second. Two. And then...

"I want fifteen percent of whatever that boy makes."

This surprises her. She almost doesn't know what to say. It's a pleasant surprise though, and she can't help but to smile at his practical sense of orneriness.

"Just him. I don't care about your other employees; keep all their proceeds. But I want a cut of everything he does. Everyone he does. Every client. Every date. Fifteen percent of all the earnings he makes through you are mine."

"Ok," she says simply.

"And then I want you to handle my finances for free for the rest of your life," he continues. "And if you so much as mess up my money by $1,000 dollars I'll have you killed. I don't know how yet, but I will. And if the IRS ever comes after me, I will deny that I knew what you were doing so fiercely that they should want to give me an Oscar for my performance. I promise, don't try me."

"Ok."

"And I want you to keep him away from Anjanae. I want you to personally make sure that all contact he has with her is severed."

"Ok."

"Alright," he says definitively, draining his glass.

"So we have a deal?" She asks to make sure, holding her hand out to him. "This is our little secret?"

He takes her hand and they firmly shake. "Deal."

Maggie picks up the tab, clearly pleased with herself, and then goes to find Andrew.

Julius goes to find Anjanae.

~

The Blue Lagoon motel doesn't put peepholes in their doors. So when someone knocks at a quarter past midnight, Anjanae hopefully assumes that it is AJ. After all, he's the only one who knows where she is. But when she opens the door, there stands her husband. Ex-husband.

Soon to be ex-husband. Estranged husband. Whatever he is to her now, he's standing in front of her. She doesn't know how he found her or if she should be scared or not. He doesn't look happy, but he doesn't look angry either. And there's more morose on his face than remorse. He smells like cigar smoke and alcohol. She instinctively crosses her arms over her chest, feeling too exposed in the men's Clippers t-shirt she bought on sale for a $1.25 at the convenient store down the street to sleep in. She doesn't speak; she waits for him to.

"I'm no longer leaving you," he states plainly. "You messed up. You made a mistake. A mistake that I do not forgive you for, but maybe one day I will. Regardless, you're still my wife."

She just stares at him.

"And I admit I may have overreacted. I'll replace everything that was in your closet. Brand new everything. We'll go shopping this weekend. I'm leaving your Range outside, there's an overnight bag in the back. I'll take a cab home."

Still silent. Still staring.

"I've been looking at condos on the Upper East Side recently. Ever since spending so much time there while filming this last project, I've come to realize I really like New York. I've come to realize I prefer it to LA, actually. And I think you will too. I think a change of scenery will be good for us. New start, new city."

She doesn't have words. He wants to continue to keep her, *keep* being the key word. He wants her to be kept. And, what's more, kept in another city all the way across the country. Where is her say? Gone out the window with everything else? She thinks that he has *her* confused with someone who still wants to be with him, but she doesn't say this.

"Anyway," he says definitively. "Come home when you're ready." He tosses her keys on the motel bed, and then he leaves.

After he's gone Anjanae sits on the bed and stares at the keys. A smile slowly takes form on her face, because she doesn't need those keys anymore. It took losing them to realize that. She's free now, and she's not going to be caged again. She knows who she is now. She knows what she wants now. She takes out her phone and texts AJ, telling him to meet her at Topanga Park in the morning. And then she sleeps peacefully.

CHAPTER 32

He sees her before she sees him. She's sitting under a purple jacaranda tree at the top of the trail on the east side of the park where she told him she'd be. The cool December sun shines through the limbs and makes her glow. In a plain t-shirt that hangs ever so slightly off one shoulder, with her curly natural hair pulled up, faded jeans and sneakers on she's just as beautiful as she always was and always will be to him. And when she spots him and smiles with such happiness, an ache runs right through the center of his soul.

AJ has already chosen his fate.

"Hey," she says cheerily, getting up and walking to him.

"Hey," he replies, returning her smile, trying to not let his voice fail him.

"So get this," she says, as though she's about to share some juicy gossip. "He came to my motel room last night. Told me he wasn't leaving me anymore, that I could come back home. Oh, but wait," she adds, that cocky but cute little grin of hers on her lips. "This is where it really gets good. I can come home, but I won't be staying there for very long because he wants for us to move to New York. He wants for us to 'start over' as a 'happy couple' on the Upper East Side." She snorts. "Can you believe that?"

"Wow," AJ says quietly, nails digging into the back of his hand she can't see.

"I know right? But in reality this was a blessing. It may have forced our plan into action a little early, but I'm ready. I was going to leave him anyway, and you were going to quit anyway, and now we can just go ahead with our plans. Our plans together." She smiles great big up at him. "I'm ready."

"I think you should go to New York."

"What?" The question leaves her lips like a breath delivered from a punch to the gut. She's taken completely aback and left bereft.

"I think you should stay with him. Or if not him, go be with someone better."

"Oh."

The disappointment in the utterance of that single, quiet word deflates any and all emotional walls he had attempted to construct going into this conversation.

She's looking at the ground because he knows she can't bear to look at him. In that moment she looks so young, so innocent and so completely vulnerable. They sway in their spots until he finally finds the courage to open his mouth and speak again.

"Only a questionable person would do what I do. Someone normal, someone worthy…they wouldn't.…" His voice falls off and falters as he fights the inevitable end that has arrived. He swallows. "What I'm trying to say is you deserve better. I don't." He shakes his head. "I don't deserve you."

Her eyes are on him now. Eyes that he's looked into a million times when they were just molasses rims around onyx orbs when she was on the brink of oblivion, or sparkling topaz gems lighting up when she laughed, or halos the hue of honey when she was deep in thought. Looking into them now, they are simply big brown whorls imploring him without pride not to leave her. He's looking away now.

He shakes his head ardently. "I don't believe he deserves you either but…" It takes him a beat to extract himself from the emotion of the moment, to take the intimacy out of the equation and to do what has to be done, like he's been taught. He looks up then and locks eyes with her. "But that's life. And life is unfair." He shakes his head once more, solemn and slow. "You can't save me. I can't save you. We each have to do what we have to do."

She looks down, silently accepting the finality of it.

"You have to leave," he continues somberly. "And I understand. I just hope.…" He searches for her eyes, but she will no longer look at him. "I hope you understand why I have to let you leave."

She doesn't say anything at first, but after a beat she sniffs and nods. "Ok. Well," she fishes out her car keys, still not looking at him. "I should get going." The detachment in her voice is deep, the coldness palpable.

He hates himself and loves her and if he could just convey it so he knew she knew maybe it would ease some of the pain.

"Anjanae, I–"

"Don't," she tells him sternly, brokenly. "Please don't."

And he doesn't. He lets her go, like he said he would, and she takes the opportunity. He watches her walk away from him. She disappears down the path, gets in her car and drives off. He hangs his head and heads off in the opposite direction, tortured and torn.

~

Maggie is elated and smug. The way she was able to divert that potential crisis, well she'd executed it just beautifully. She mentally praises herself for her smarts and her savvy and her impeccable business skills. Her self-inflated ego makes her float, unsinkable she feels. She peers outside of her office door into the rec room. Garrett is the only one there; he came by to pick up his check and got distracted by a movie she had playing on the big screen. He'd been on the couch for the last hour with his Louboutin loafers propped up on the ottoman in the middle.

"Hill, dear," she beckons him.

"Yes, darling," he replies in his cocky little British accent, getting up and sauntering towards to her. He does the hair flip halfway there, and she thinks to herself that he looks to be in a good enough mood to cooperate.

"A new client just called and she wants someone right now. She's just down the road at the Loews in the Panorama Suite." She eyes him with a coy smile. "Seeing as we're drawing in close to the end of the year and your quitting date, I thought you'd like to rack in a little last minute money before you leave."

"Yeah, I spose I can do that," he replies coolly, running a hand through his blonde hair. "Do her, I mean," he adds, blue eyes twinkling. He turns to look at himself in the full-length mirror. "Am I bespoke enough for the bedroom?"

"If you were any more bespoke I wouldn't know what to do with myself."

"Alright then. Hit record for me, aye," he says, pointing at the television on his way to the door. "I'll be back in an hour."

∼

Meanwhile, Dominique is cruising through his old neighborhood midafternoon in pursuit of some good weed before he has to get back to Beverley Hills for a date. He whips his ride into the gas station's lot and parks by the dumpsters where Trell told him to meet him. He leaves the car running, cuts the radio, and cracks the window. A few minutes later he sees Trell rounds the corner on foot, do-rag over his messy braids, over-sized hoodie, baggie jeans, and Nikes that had seen better days. Dominique thinks to himself that his old friend needs to find himself a higher paying clientele. Maybe start slinging in a richer zip code.

"What up, five," Trell says with a greasy smile as he approaches the car, hanging his head into the window.

"Just coolin," Dominique replies. "Whatchu got fa me?"

"Shit, you already know." Trell and Nique interlock hands, and when they release Nique has a baggie and Trell has a wad of money.

"My man," Dominique says happily, looking over the bulbs of purple tinted herbs in the Ziploc.

"I told you I got you," Trell says, clearly proud of his product. "Imma have to dip though. I got a junkie to serve next door. He's buyin a quarter brick."

Dominique knows this means Trell is about to sell a pretty good amount of cocaine, which will undoubtedly make him more money than the little bag of weed he just sold him.

"Make that money then. I'll catch you later."

"Aight. Later, bruh."

Dominique watches Trell saunter off across the lot towards the discount convenient store next door where some shanty cars are parked. Dominique then pulls out a pack of papers and a clipboard that he keeps in his console for such occasions, and then proceeds to roll himself a joint. Before he lights it he glances up to see where Trell went. In the midst of jalopies his old friend is standing outside of a very nice Cadillac, talking to the driver who is still inside. The sleek dark grey sedan looks very familiar to Dominique, but he can't place why. But then the driver gets out, and he has to chuckle. It was Ali, his boss's boyfriend, dressed in his fancy business clothes about to clasp hands with a Watts drug dealer. He wonders to himself with a smirk if Ms. Hunter knows her new boo is a cokehead. Hell, he thinks, reaching for his lighter, she might be a cokehead herself for all he knew. She did like to keep her personal life and proclivities private.

But then the situation takes a sharp turn.

Ali is grabbing Trell's arm. He's spinning him around, manhandling him as he fights to get away. He throws him up against the hood of the car. It's a swift, clearly practiced dance, all happening in less than two seconds. Trell is pressed against the grey paint with his hands pinned behind his back. And then Dominique watches in horror as Ali slaps a set of handcuffs on the young man's wrists, shuffles him to the door, and shoves him into the back of the Cadillac.

Oh fuck.

Ali goes back around to the driver's side, and as he does so, Dominique swears his eyes flick across the lot to where he is. Probably recognizing the brightly painted Impala from his girlfriend's office. Scratch that. His *suspect's* office.

Oh fuck.

Dominique throws his unlit joint, his lighter, and his clipboard across the car, puts it into gear, and peels out of the parking lot so fast that the marks would probably still be there three months later.

~

A brunette lets Garrett into her hotel room. The suite has spectacular views of Hollywood. The woman isn't too bad to look at either. In fact, compared to some of his other clients, she's really quite attractive. She's not old, that's a perk, and through the clothes she still wears she looks to be pretty toned-up, nice arms in a sleeveless top. Plus, she has a sexy little beauty mole just to the left of her full lips. He thinks this will be easy money.

"What did you say your name was, darling?" Garrett asks, stepping closer to her after she's closed the door, giving her his well-practiced bedroom eyes.

She raises an eyebrow rascally, smirk on her lips. "I didn't."

He smiles, her attitude turning him on. "Well I guess it really doesn't matter."

"I guess not," she replies, voice low and silky. She walks over to the table and takes a few big bills out from under her purse and then struts back to him. "Here's your money, before I forget."

She holds it out to him. He takes it.

"Thanks, babe," he says, slipping the cash into his pocket. "You want a little bubbly before we get started?" He asks her, turning to the in-suite bar.

"What I want is you," she says forwardly, making him turn back around.

"I'm all yours," he tells her, closing the distance between them. "At least for the next hour anyway." He flashes her his pretty boy smile and puts his hands on her waist, promptly pulling her against him.

"Perfect," she mutters with a smile against his mouth.

As they kiss Garrett shrugs off his blazer and breaks apart from her just long enough to pull his shirt over his head and then goes right back to making out with her. Every time he tries to undo her pants or unbutton her shirt she smacks his hands away. But she is slowly backing him towards the bed. And when they get there, she pushes him down onto the mattress and straddles him, pinning his hands over his head and smiling down wickedly at him. *She's a feisty one*, he thinks to himself with an excited grin, wondering what she'll do next. Many of his clients have fetishes and kinks of different sorts, so he doesn't think anything of it when she takes out a pair of handcuffs from her back pocket.

CHAPTER 33

AJ is at the office, about to start getting ready for the night's jaunt when his phone begins to buzz in his pocket. In the back of his mind he hopes that it's Anjanae calling to tell him she's not getting back with Julius like he told her to. But he knows that's just wishful thinking, and he needs to stop. It's his fault they're over. He made his choice. He chose this. He pulls his cell out and sees that it's Dominique.

"What's up," AJ answers casually. "You know you made the boss mad, right? You stood up your five o'clock, she called Ms. Hunter pissed off and–"

"AJ, listen to me," Dominique cuts him off, speaking in a steady tone that has an eerily foreign tinge of seriousness to it. "Don't react. Don't say nothin. Just walk out the door."

AJ's brow furrows, he doesn't have a clue as to what Dominique is talking about.

"I'm about two minutes out," Dominique continues, voice low. "Imma slow down when I hit the block and you jump in on the run."

AJ snorts at what he perceives as silliness. "And where is it we're going?"

"Mexico."

"You went to the hood and they laced your blunt again, didn't they?" AJ jokes.

"He's a cop."

Silence. The line reverberates in AJ's ear. Everything dissolves and refocuses.

"Who's a cop?"

"Ali. He's a fucking cop. She's been fucking a fucking cop." Dominique is speaking in quick spurts now, panic coating every syllable.

"Are you...are you sure?" AJ asks. Because he can't comprehend that Maggie could be capable of being duped, that this could really actually be happening, even as his heartbeat begins to quicken and the hairs on the back of his neck stand up.

"Bruh I swear. I just saw dude arrest someone with my own eyes. And he saw my ass, too. We're hit like dog shit." AJ hears Dominique take a ragged breath; he must have turned the radio off because in the background all he can make out are the audible sounds of a car speeding down the highway. "He knows," Dominique says after a beat. "This wasn't just no accidental shit with him and her. He's been stakin' her shit *out*.

"Oh my God," AJ says under his breath in awe, reality and all its ramifications hitting him square in the face. This was bad. This was worse than Julius. This wasn't a scorned husband. This was a cop. A cop that had been practically living with Maggie for three months, staking her out, just like Nique said. God knows what he knew. God knows what kind of proof he had collected in that amount of time.

"We gotta bounce, you feel me? Like not now but *right* now."

"We can't just leave and throw everyone else to the dogs without any kind of warning," AJ reasons.

"This on her, AJ. You sleep with a dog your gonna get bit."

"Yeah but she didn't know that the dog was a pig."

Dominique takes an annoyed breath. "This the same woman who was ready ta sell your ass downstream if it meant saving her own ass just two days ago. This is her problem. Why can't you just turn your back, walk away, and let it all go up in flames behind you?"

AJ doesn't say anything, but he looks over with confliction at Maggie's office where he can see her through the glass, typing away at her computer, oblivious to the bomb that was about to detonate in her face.

"I'm almost there," Dominique says. "Is you ridin or nah?"

The other line is still for a full second, and Dominique hopes against all odds that his friend choses sense over conscience.

"Nah," AJ finally says. And then he hangs up.

In the car Dominique glares down at his phone and curses. "Dammit, AJ."

AJ opens her office door. Burnt notes of magnolia and her omnipotent perfume flood his senses like they did the first time he ever set foot in the room. She's still perched at her throne like a proud queen, and he's still on the other side, but this time she's the one in the dark. She glances up from her computer to smile at him. He knows he has to speak before she looks back away and he loses his nerve.

"We've got a problem."

He meets her gaze with all seriousness. Maggie searches his eyes, and what she sees makes her suddenly concerned. She watches him swallow, and waits.

"Dominique just saw..." He falters, recollects, and continues on in a more even tone. "Dominique just saw Ali. Arresting somebody."

Her face is devoid of all emotion.

"He's an undercover cop," AJ adds; just to be sure she's following.

She doesn't react theatrically. She doesn't question. She just coolly turns in her chair, opens her cabinet, and takes out a bottle cognac. AJ watches as she fills a glass tumbler with the brown liquid, and then proceeds to promptly throw it back in one tilt without even grimacing. She refills the glass immediately, but this time she sits it back down on her desk, and opens her drawer. She takes out the black phone, sends one last mass text to all its contacts, and then drops it into the full tumbler of liquor. She finally turns to face him again. Her nonchalance is as chilling as ever.

"Call Theo," is all she says.

AJ nods and quickly goes over to the corner with his phone to make the call. When he's not looking at her, Maggie wrings her hands. The average woman probably would have questioned such accusations against their lover. *Oh no. Not him. He wouldn't do me like that.* But Maggie didn't put anything past anyone. Why should she question the claim when she didn't question the man? She took everything Ali had said at face value. He had said he was a real estate agent; she believed him. Why hadn't she dug more? She was usually warier. More thorough. More investigative. He had thoroughly investigated her. Right? That's what he had been doing after all, wasn't it? This hadn't been a romance; this had been an investigation. Still, what did he have on her at the end of the day? She lied about her life, most of what she had divulged to him had been fibs. She hadn't been *that* stupid. But she *had* let him into her house, into her workplace—under false pretenses, of course. Still. What all had she let slip? What all had he picked up on his own, unsupervised, as she slept. Dammit. Dammit, dammit, dammit.

She had met her match indeed. They had both been lying to each other the whole time. The only difference was he knew she was lying.

"He's on his way."

AJ's voice snaps her out of it. He's standing in front of her desk, slipping his phone back into his pocket. The door swings open and both their heads shoot up. They're relived to see that it's just Dominique.

"Just so yanno," Dominique addresses AJ, panting to catch his breath. "When we all get thrown in the pen and I gotta pretend that I'm in a monogamous relationship with you in order to keep the boys off me…I'm tellin' em you're the bottom."

"Fine."

Austin strolls by, sees them, and stops. He slouches in the doorway, one hand on each wall, smiling obliviously. "What kind of pow-wow are y'all havin' in here?"

"Don't worry about it," Maggie tells him. "Go lock the front door."

"Why?"

"Don't worry about it," she reiterates with a hand motion. "Just do it."

Austin shrugs with a sigh. "Fine." He turns to go. "I've got a nine o'clock ta get to anyway."

"No!" The word flies out of her mouth so quick and so unusually frantic, it causes Austin to stop dead in his tracks. "All services are suspended until further notice," says more neutrally. "Nobody is going anywhere."

Austin's scared now. He stands still in the doorway, not moving.

"Your angels is waiting, Charlie," Dominique says to Maggie, searing her with his pissed-off gaze. "What be the plan?"

"Theo's on his way," she replies.

Dominique's face screws up. "And what's he gonna do? Screw Ali into submission like Ali did you?"

Maggie stares at him coldly, but doesn't respond.

"Plus," he continues. "Do you really think it smart for us all ta be gathered here?" He's still leering at her. "I mean," he scoffs. "If ole boy comes ta get us, he's gonna get us all."

"Let him come get us," she tells him. She opens the bottom drawer of her desk, and surprises them all when she takes out a revolver. The boys watch with wide eyes as she expertly loads and cocks it.

"What you finna do with that?" Dominique asks, jaw practically on the floor. He looks over at AJ. "You know she had a piece in there this whole time?"

AJ just shakes his head in dismay.

Dominique turns to Maggie again. "You gonna kill a cop now?"

She shrugs.

Dominique rubs his face with his hands. "You just tryin go straight to the chair, ain't chu?"

The white phone goes off on Maggie's desk. All four of them stare fixatedly at it, an 800 number flashing across the screen. One ring. Two rings. Three rings. Four. She snatches the phone off her desk, simultaneously putting the call on speaker as she picks up.

"You have a collect call from a Los Angeles County Correctional Facility," an automated voice says. "To speak to…" The recording cuts, there's a second of silence, and then Garrett's unnerved voice comes across the line. "Itwasasetup," he manages to jumble out quickly before the automated recording returns. "To accept charges please press–"

Maggie hangs up.

"Oh crap," Austin murmurs under his breath.

"Yeah," AJ says.

"Yeah," Dominique concurs.

Theo comes walking through the open office door. He looks cool and collected as usual, taking his Ray Ban sunglasses off and wiping them on the hem of his satin shirt, clearly unaware of what he's walking into. Everyone is still so shell-shocked they don't even bother to acknowledge him.

"What's goin on?" He asks, slipping his shades into his pocket and finally looking up. "AJ said it was urgent." His eyes land on Maggie. Immediately he diverts his gaze over to AJ and Dominique. "Why she got the piece out?"

"We've got a bit of a problem…" AJ offers as calmly as he can.

"Ali's on his way," Maggie says casually then, out of the blue. She sounds totally removed from the situation and, perhaps, reality. She balances the revolver in her hand. "When he walks through that door…I'm going to shoot him."

"Okay." Theo says. "Yeah." He swallows, slightly shaking his head. "I'd say that constitutes a problem." He glances at AJ over his shoulder and mouths *what the fuck* as he makes his way over to Maggie's desk. He squats down in front of her, looking her in her eyes earnestly. "Maggie, ok, listen. Can you calmly tell me what went wrong today?" He places a hand on her knee. "Why do you want to murder Ali? You love Ali. Did he cheat on you?"

She snorts derisively. "I wish it were that innocent."

"You mean you wish we was that innocent," Dominique mutters under his breath, arms crossed against his chest.

Theo continues to study Maggie's face. "Did he put his hands on you?" He asks her seriously. "Because if he did, I will go find him right now and personally teach his ass a lesson."

"You'll get arrested," she says simply.

"Please," Theo scoffs. "He ain't gonna do nothin."

"No," she reiterates. "He will literally arrest you."

Confusion etches across Theo's face. Maggie pats his hand that's on her knee and offers him a disturbed little smile, but no real explanation. He stays on the ground, but looks back over his shoulder again at AJ for answers.

"It turns out Ali is an undercover cop," AJ tells him. "Dominique saw him about an hour ago arresting someone. Ali saw him, too." He takes a breath. "And Garrett is in jail. He was set up. This has all apparently been one expertly planned, drawn out sting operation. If I had to guess, I'd say it's about to come to a head."

Theo continues to stare at AJ even after he's stopped talking. AJ knows Theo's trying to muster up a coherent response and a brave face that will make it seem like it isn't as bad as it really is. But AJ knows they're screwed.

After a beat Theo nods silently, focusing his attention back on Maggie. He takes his pocket square out and unfolds it in his hand. "First you need to hand me the gun," he tells her. "You don't need to be charged with pimping *and* possessing."

Maggie's emotionless eyes bore into Theo. At first he thinks she isn't going to give it up, but then she accedes, slowly placing the revolver into Theo's linen covered hand. Theo closes his hand around the weapon, caressing the prints off of it with the cloth as if she'd already killed someone with it. For all he knows she could have. He stands up, walks over to the window, opens it, and throws the gun out into the bushes. As he recloses the window and secures it, Rafael walks in.

"What's going on," he asks Maggie, closing the door behind him. "I am with a client and she gets a text on her phone from you that says 911. What does this mean?"

"Emergency, stupid," Dominique mumbles under his breath.

"Do not get an attitude with me Domonique. I have had a long day."

"It's about to get a whole lot longer, homie."

There's a commotion outside. The unmistakable sound of a door forcibly being jarred open. And then the sounds of footsteps. Multiple sets of feet rushing. The boys are frozen in place, not a single one of them making a sound.

"This is the police!" A man's voice bellows from the front of the building. They are maybe five, five and a half steps away.

"Lie like your life depends on it," Maggie tells them. "Because it does."

And then her door flies open.

~

All of them are escorted out of 360 Hollywood Place in handcuffs and taken in to the police station where they are each questioned separately by a detective and an officer; neither of them are Ali, but none of them are confused as to who got them there. After the private interrogations, the boys are all thrown into a public holding cell on the men's side, and Maggie is put in a public holding cell on the women's side. They are each allotted one call, and when it's Maggie's turn, she dial's the front desk of her apartment complex and asks to speak to the bellman, Barney. She tells the clueless little old man who she's made small talk with every morning for the last decade of her life where she has a spare key hidden, and then, once he's in her condo, where she has money hidden. She can tell he wants to ask questions, but he doesn't, and agrees to do what she's asked with the type of bashful obedience she loves. The next morning the money is brought and they are all bonded out. Before they leave they are informed that a court date has been set for the following morning. But for now, they have a few more hours before they have to face their fate.

CHAPTER 34

The guys are standing on the sidewalk outside of the jail in their crumpled clothes from the day before. They look exhausted with bags under their eyes, smelling of sweat and stale air. The morning sun makes them squint, and each of them appears more confused about the current state of their life than the next.

"How are we spose to get home?" Austin asks.

"Walk," Dominique answers sarcastically.

"Seriously?" Austin questions with naivety.

Dominique snorts under his breath. "Lightweight."

"Excuse me," Austin retaliates. "But I've never spent a night in jail before."

"We'll have to call a cab," Theo says, pulling out his phone.

"What happened to Rafael?" AJ asks. "He never came back last night after they took him to questioning and they didn't release him with us this morning?"

"I'd say he's totally screwed," Theo replies, looking at AJ. "You know he's undocumented, right? He'll be sent back to Cuba regardless of what happens to us."

"They still got Garrett, too," Austin adds.

"Yeah but he wasn't taken in with us," Theo tells him. "He was arrested literally on the job."

"Two down four to go," Dominique mutters glumly. "Countin our dumbass boss. You think she got bonded out?"

"How the fuck do you think *we* got bonded out," Theo mumbles, about to dial the number for a cab service when a Lincoln town car pulls up to the block. They all eye it strangely. The backdoor opens, and there sits Maggie.

"Get in," she tells them.

They hesitate only briefly before quickly doing as they're told.

Fifteen minutes later the town car pulls up to 360 Hollywood Place and they all file out. Theo is the last one out and slams the door shut behind him.

"Ok. So what's the game plan?" He asks.

"We need to call a meeting as soon as possible," Maggie replies, pulling the office keys out of her purse. "Our clients are our first priority and they need to be kept abreast as details develop."

They all cut through the alley to the back lot where their cars are, not even bothering to go inside the office and see how bad the police had ransacked it.

"You ruined the phone with all the numbers in it," AJ reminds her. "How are you going to get ahold of everyone?"

"I have everything on a flash drive at my storage unit in Van Nuys," she informs him.

"You have a storage unit in Van Nuys?"

"Why are you still surprised by anything she says, Andrew?" Theo asks rhetorically.

"I mean…she has a whole unit for *one* flash drive?" AJ ponders aloud.

"Of course not," Maggie injects. "I filled it with a bunch of unassuming junk posing as personal belongings and placed the flash drive inconspicuously amongst it."

"Of course," AJ says under his breath.

"Her mind is sociopath status," Dominique tells him.

"I backed it up last month," Maggie says as she unlocks her Mercedes. "So all but the newest clients' contacts should be on there." She opens the door and slides onto the red leather driver's seat. "I'm going out to the valley to retrieve it. You all go home. Shower. Eat. Meet back here in two hours and we'll go from there."

AJ showers but he can't eat. He sits on his bed with his stomach in knots and stares down at his phone in his hand. He dials Grace's number, and as he does so, he doesn't even know why. It rings a long time, but she eventually picks up.

"What?" She asks flatly when she answers.

He's taken aback by her unusual coldness. "What do you mean what?"

"I'm asking what do you want. It can't be bail money cause you're not callin from an 800 number. So are you just callin to fulfill your monthly check-in so you can not feel like the shitty boyfriend that you really are, or are you callin to finally break up with me? Or do you still want me to play the part of your girlfriend? Do you still want me to play the fool? What do you want from me, Andrew?"

"You…you saw?" He stutters. "You know?"

"Oh yeah," she replies tersely.

Static silence. He can't speak. He has no words. He has no idea how she found out he was arrested, and now he's in fear that the rest of his family will find out too.

"I wouldn't worry too much if I were you," she says finally, cattily. "It was a quick clip caught by a pedestrian and posted on an online LA magazine website, and your back was to the camera. Lucky for me I know the back of your head like the back of my hand. As it turns out, I'm just one of many who probably do."

"Grace…"

"I subscribed to a bunch of free LA publications when you moved so I could stay in the loop of your life. Have topics of conversation ready for when you called. I read and stream LA news more than I do Memphis news. This one particular online publication I came across four or five months ago had a weekly drug bust and brothel round up. I thought it was funny," she chuckles dryly. "Never in my life did I imagine I'd see my boyfriend on there."

"Grace…"

"It was the woman that caught my eye in the clip," she continues, ignoring him. "I recognized her immediately. Your boss from the restaurant you supposedly worked at. But she's your pimp, right? Am I usin the right terminology?"

"I'm sorry. I didn't want for you to find out like this. My intentions were never to hurt anyone. I–"

"You disgust me. Actually, you know what, disgust isn't even the word. Repulse. You *repulse* me."

He takes it. He deserves it.

"I will never *ever* be able to look at you the same again."

"I know," he says quietly, and then takes a deep breath. "Grace…please just…just don't tell my mom. Please."

"I won't tell her. Not for your sake, but for hers. She doesn't deserve that kind of disappointment. But if it stays in the press she will find out. If you go to jail she's going to know. Are you going to jail?"

"If we lose our trial," he says simply, the possibility ever real.

"Well if you do lose…I don't want a collect call, I don't want jail mail. I don't want so much as to hear one thing from you or about you. Ok?"

He focuses on the floor. "Ok," he replies, the tightness in his throat threatening to choke him, to make him physically ill.

She hangs up.

And in two days he had lost the only two women in his life other than his mother who had ever really loved him, by no fault but his own.

~

On her way home from Van Nuys with her flash drive Maggie can't stop replaying scenes from the night before in her head. The cops who'd interrogated her kept throwing around the name "Officer Rodriguez," *According to Officer Rodriguez. A statement made by Officer Rodriguez.* Officer Rodriguez was undoubtedly Ali.

In the dirty public cell amidst prostitutes, drug addicts, and the lowest forms of female humanity (of which she did not consider herself a part of), she mentally repeated the name to herself. *Rodriguez. Rodriguez.* Sure, that was a common last name, but she only personally knew of one other person with it, and the dots immediately started connecting on their own. Richard Rodriguez. The soap star. The soap star whose job Garrett had stolen. Garrett, who she had a meeting with at the sports bar in Burbank the same night she met Ali. Right before she met Ali. Minutes before. She hadn't caught his eye, Garrett had. He had been following Garrett and found her. She had just been a piece of the puzzle. And oh, what a serious piece she had been, literally, metaphorically, and philosophically. What a thrill it must have been for a police officer to inadvertently come across her. He'd prolonged the pleasure for three months while working the locks to Pandora's box unbeknownst to her. She'd thought she had it thoroughly hidden, but he knew where it was the whole time, just waiting for the perfect moment to throw open the lid and let the secrets fly.

Officer Rodriguez, LAPD

Before she can take a shower, eat, pee, or call her clients she has to type those words into Google. She's glad she'd left her laptop at home the day before, because she's sure if she'd had it at the office it would have been confiscated, and by some stroke of luck the feds hadn't showed up at her apartment yet. Not that there was anything related to her business on her computer. All the precautions she took that ended up not mattering.

Officer Rodriguez, LAPD

And there he is. In uniform, badge and all. Raymond Rodriguez. *Alias Ali Suarez,* she thinks to herself. She reads his bio on the LAPD website. He is the commanding officer of the gang and narcotics division and has had held that position for the last ten years. Decorated, heroic; lovely pieces praising him for all that he has done to clean up the streets. A well-respected cop in the days of disingenuous cops. *Ha.* And while hers was not a gang or drug related infraction, she assumed her illegal activities were just as every bit as enticing. What had assumedly started as him helping to extricate petty revenge on his brother's behalf simply because he had the power, resources, connections, and knowledge to do so, had more than likely morphed into a case that, as a cop, he couldn't put down until justice was served.

She continues to Google him.

Raymond Rodriguez. According to his Facebook *Ray* lives in Los Feliz, not Downtown LA. There are pictures of his Cadillac sitting in front of a modest Spanish style home. Pictures of him and friends in the backyard barbecuing with the same house in the background. A house she had never seen. The loft had been both a prop and a stage, and what an act he had put on there. He'd really gone the extra mile. Hell, he was a better actor than his brother. And then there are the pictures of him and Rich. Casual pictures of them hanging out as brothers do, pictures of them on a trip to their home country of Mexico the summer before, pictures of them in matching suits on a red carpet, presumably at one of Rich's events. Looking at them together she doesn't see how she missed it. They aren't identical, but there is obviously a very close resemblance. Why hadn't she seen it? Why hadn't she seen any of this? Is she stupid? When had she become so stupid? How could she be so stupid?

Before she gets off the internet she makes the choice to Google her office's address. And there it is. Three hits pop up that had been made in the last day. One is for a blog site she has never heard of. They have a seven second clip of the raid and arrest. It was fast, but she was recognizable. When she sees that the second hit is for *The Los Angeles Times* her heart summersaults then sinks. Two brief lines about a possible high-end male escort service in Hollywood. The third and final hit is from a news station forty-five minutes ago, it turns out Chanel Five acquired the video from the less popular site. The comment section is open. So far there have only been four commenters: one spammer asking the readers if they wanted a fast and easy way to make money, one person spewing their personal disgust for the human race and what it's become, one person speculating if there is a black book and what celebrities might be in it, and one person who said they recognized the woman as someone they knew from functions and events, and even though they never knew what she did for a living, they couldn't believe that she'd be a madam. And then they dropped her name right there in the comment section. For the world to see.

Maggie clears her search bar, closes her computer, and pours herself a drink.

And then another.

And then another.

CHAPTER 35

One of Theo's longtime clients has a house way out in Mount Washington. A place she considers secure enough for them all to meet. Her apartment and the boys' apartments are possibly all compromised, but her clients still have their anonymity. So her and her four free employees pile into AJ's little, old, ugly, serendipitously inconspicuous Ford Escort and head to the hideout.

She'd called all her clients. Most show up. The elaborate parlor of Mrs. Eversledge's secluded mansion is filled with well-to-do middle-aged women, along with some that are older and some that are younger, and a few men of varying ages. Most wear the same worried expression, though some appear indifferent. They are all gathered around a Versailles dining table at which AJ, Dominique, Theo, and Austin sit. Troy Langham comes through the door at the last minute looking ruffled. He attempts to blend in with the back of the room, but heads turn to look at him nonetheless.

"That dude's a big-time movie star," Dominique whispers to AJ, who's sitting next to him. "What he doin' here?"

They look over at Theo, who shifts slightly in his seat and glances off to the side.

"Oh," Dominique replies, realizing. "Well damn. Go on then, T."

"Maggie, are you going to tell us what all this 911 fuss is about and why we are risking complications of asbestos exposure to meet you here in this filthy facility?" Mrs. Lombardy, a white haired, pearl wearing woman asks. "I drove clear across the county to be here. You know I don't typically leave the hills..."

"Did you watch Channel Five news this morning?" Kasey Franks asks the older woman in a patronizingly catty tone.

"Oh who has time for that?" Mrs. Lombardy replies flippantly.

"For someone who doesn't ever leave the hills I would think you do," Kasey says snidely.

"And for someone half my age I would think you wouldn't have to pay for it just yet," Mrs. Lombardy retorts.

"Excuse me?" Kasey exclaims with offense, the gold bracelets on her arm jingling as her hand goes to her chest. "Pay for what? What exactly are you insinuating?"

"Oh please. Cut the charades, honey," Mrs. Lombardy tells her. "Why do you think we're all here?"

Kasey Franks flushes and a few other women stare at the ground in embarrassment.

"I've got a standing hair appointment in Westwood to get to," Mrs. Daniel's says, looking right at Maggie. "Can we get this public shaming over with?"

"I was simply waiting for everyone to get here," Maggie says, taking a deep breath. "But I suppose we can go ahead and start. And, no offense, but you're not in the *public* eye just yet. Unfortunately, that all may be about to change. That's why I've called you all here today."

"What are you saying?" Mrs. Bronstein asks.

"We were part of a sting operation last night…"

Everyone is locked in on her with unparalleled focus, besides the boys, who are all looking at their hands in their laps. They know how the story goes.

"We were taken into custody," Maggie continues. "Held for a few hours, interrogated and released. However, we are still under investigation. They're trying to build a case against us."

"This was not supposed to happen," Mrs. Halliday chimes in. "Your services were supposed to be the safest and securest. I don't pay for the utmost privacy to end up getting treated like a common Jon."

"Janet, I have been doing this for a decade and this is the first time anything like this has happened. I have been doing everything I can to insure each and every one of your all's anonymity from day one."

"All I'm saying is you better not let our names get released," Mrs. Halliday tells her, crossing her arms. "You better protect us."

"Do you know what you're going to do?" Mrs. Bronstein interrogates her. "Do you know how you are going to handle all of this?"

"I haven't really had the chance to sit down and divulge a plan just yet but–"

"Well you better figure it out fast," Troy tells her with a cold sternness from the back wall. "I have reputation. And it doesn't need to be tainted by all of…*this*," he seethes with disgust.

Theo sets his jaw and flexes his fist under the table.

"I have a movie coming out," Troy continues. "And a life and a–"

"Wife," Kasey Franks interjects.

"Just like you have a husband," Troy reminds her.

Kasey turns to look at Maggie. "I want to know if I get the same guy he gets because I am not down with that cross-contamination shit…"

"Oh don't act like you're any better than me, Kasey," Troy tells her. "This will destroy your career as quick as it will destroy mine."

"How exactly did this happen, Maggie?" Kasey asks her, ignoring Troy.

"Actually, Kasey, it was all started by one of your former co-workers."

Kasey looks highly confused.

"He was seeking vindication from one of my employees who he believes is responsible for his shine being stolen," Maggie explains. "He had my employee followed and then professionally set up. Garrett was caught red handed. He's currently in jail as we speak."

"Oh my goodness!" Mrs. Lombardy gasps suddenly. "They've got Garrett."

"Garrett *Hill* works for you?" Kasey asks in disbelief.

"Yes."

"Well I'll pay to have him sprung," Mrs. Lombardy says without hesitation.

"And who's going to pay to have you *sprung*?" Mrs. Bronstein asks her facetiously.

"They all sprung," Dominique mutters under his breath.

"I'm not going to have to be sprung because Maggie isn't going to let us all go down with the ship." Mrs. Lombardy looks right at her then. "Right, Maggie?"

Everyone is looking at her now.

An hour later the clients have gone on with their day and the boys and Maggie have returned to 360 Hollywood place. They are putting it back together to how it was before it was raided, wiping sweat from their foreheads and trying to not to think about their fate.

"What does it look like?" Theo asks her, sitting the last piece of overturned furniture back up and then pulling his keys out of his pocket.

"Court in the morning," Maggie replies, putting the pillows back onto the couch. "Nine-thirty sharp. I've opted for a joint trial so we can all be together."

"How sweet," Dominique says.

"It's going to be a bench trial," she explains further. "No jury, just a judge. That way we can get this shit-show over faster and get back to regular scheduled programming. This whole thing is thoroughly ridiculous"

"Do you know who's presiding?" Theo asks then.

"Judge Rosemary Esque," Maggie replies. "She's a little old lady. I'm sure she won't want to waste her time on a case that clearly should have never been. I suspect she'll throw it out in relatively quick order," she states confidently.

Too confidently, AJ thinks.

The next morning, they all file into the courthouse in their prim and proper attire. There are no lawyers present; Maggie didn't want one and Ray (Ali) didn't need one. Garrett is paraded out in a jumpsuit and shackles, seated near them but not next to them. The back is open for spectators; Richard Rodriguez is in the last row smirking devilishly. AJ takes note in how Ray never looks back at his brother, but every so many seconds he'll steal a peak at Maggie. However, Maggie won't even so much as glance in his general direction. AJ thinks that Ray doesn't look like he's happy or pleased to have done this to them. He doesn't appear vindictively overjoyed or cockily smug about what has transpired like Rich. But still. He did this to them. To her.

They all swear on the bible. They all plead not guilty.

AJ, Dominique, Austin, Theo, and Garrett to different counts of prostitution. Maggie to pandering and promotion of prostitution. Rafael is not present, as an Inadmissible Alien he was deported back to Cuba where he will face his fate there. The plaintiff introduces Rosemary Esque, and AJ watches as the petite woman crosses the room, exuding a palpable sense of self-pride and power as she does so. She is probably pushing seventy but her spirited ways and kept-up appearance doesn't reflect that. Her hair is cut short, styled trendily, and dyed a respectable blondish brown color. She sports a stern demeanor and, at times, a pinched face, but through the course of the hour he'd catch her smiling with her eyes at certain things being said that amused her. Fiery eyes. A spitfire, if he had to choose one word to describe her, and she didn't take Maggie's shit. Not at all.

"Officer Rodriguez, what originally led you to suspect that a high-end male escort service was being run out of 360 Hollywood Place?" She asks.

"I got an anonymous tip," Ray starts.

"Bullshit it was from your brother," Maggie interjects without thought.

"Ms. Hunter," Judge Esque warns scolding, cutting her eyes at her.

Maggie looks away, arms crossed defensively. AJ suspects his boss has been drinking, he's sitting right next to her and can smell it on her breath. He knows in this state she'll be quick to throw salt, and that's not good.

"Continue, Officer Rodriguez," Judge Esque tells Ray.

"I got an anonymous tip from a citizen who suspected someone they knew was involved in illegal activity." He pauses, and then in part to cover his own ass adds, "The assumption was drugs."

"Bullshit," Maggie mutters, under her breath this time.

"But of course it turned out not to be drugs," Ray continues calmly. "I was tailing Mr. Hill—that's who I was tipped off about. Mr. Hill did lead me to Ms. Hunter, and I did introduce myself to her under the pretense of interest in a romantic relationship, using the fake name Ali Suarez. You see your honor…in my field I do a lot of undercover work."

"Literally," Maggie says aloud, unable to keep her mouth shut. "Tell me your honor, is it typical for an officer to sleep with the suspect they're pursuing and write it off as *undercover* work?"

"Ms. Hunter if you speak out one more time when I haven't called on you I will have you escorted out of this courtroom and then who's going to plead your case, hmm?" Judge Esque asks with a snarky bite, staring right at Maggie till Maggie looks away again. Judge Esque then turns to look at Ray. "Officer Rodriguez, did you have a sexual relationship with the suspect?"

"I did not."

"Liar," Maggie seethes.

"Ms. Hunter, do you have any proof that you and Officer Rodriguez had sexual intercourse?"

Maggie doesn't say anything. Because she doesn't have any proof. She has nothing. Her silence and flushing face speak for itself. AJ can see Dominique's leg jostling under the table out of the corner of his eye. He hears Theo crack his knuckles and Austin take a ragged breath. He bites his lip till he tastes blood.

"Officer Rodriguez," Judge Esque inquires. "What *was* the extent of your relationship with Ms. Hunter?"

"Friendly," he replies. "I have been in her place of residence as well as her office on a couple different occasions. We did go out, dates if you want to call them that. I had to be somewhat close to her in order to gain information. Evidence wasn't just lying out on the table; she had a very covert operation going on. This was a case I knew was going to take time and trust to crack. It wasn't like in my typical line of work with the narcotics division where I could pose as a buyer, ask for a bag of crack, exchange my money for their drugs and immediately make an arrest without any more proof needed."

"When you found out this particular crime wasn't within your wheel house, why didn't you turn it over to your fellow officers in the prostitution division?" Judge Esque asks.

"Before I was head of the gang and narcotics division I worked in all areas, was involved in all kinds of cases and arrests. Even though I specialize in drug and gang related issues, I do have experience in most all areas of police work, including prostitution and brothel busts," Ray explains with cool conciseness. "I thought it would be best and most successful for me to see the case through seeing as I had already formed an acquaintanceship with the suspect. No sense in introducing someone else and risk throwing the whole operation off balance. Though I did turn it over to the proper officers when the time came. They made the arrests."

Judge Esque nods and then looks down momentarily at her podium. When she looks back up, her eyes are on Maggie.

"Ms. Hunter, do I see here that you are counter suing Officer Rodriguez for slander and defamation?"

"Yes, your honor."

"You are aware Ms. Hunter that most people would be inclined to believe Officer Rodriguez over you. This is a well-respected, high-ranking LAPD officer who has been with the precinct for years. And you are, well, a bit of an enigma at the moment. You are proclaiming to be innocent while alleging that Officer Rodriguez is slandering your name and defaming your character. But what reason or benefit would Officer Rodriguez gain from accusing you of pandering and these young men of prostitution?"

"I don't know. You'd have to ask him that," she says with cold coy.

"If you are innocent and have nothing to hide, then why did you destroy your cellular device moments before being arrested?"

"I dropped it," Maggie replies simply.

"In a glass of alcohol?" Judge Esque questions with a skeptical smirk.

"You've never dropped your phone before?"

"According to the police records you had a second undamaged phone on your person that was confiscated and searched."

"And was anything found on it?" Maggie asks jestingly with too much nerve.

"Why do you have two phones?" Judge Esque asks, ignoring Maggie's question.

"You don't know anyone who has two phones?"

"Kingpins and hit men," Judge Esque replies without missing a beat, waiting for Maggie to finish her eye roll before continuing. "Listen, you have a nice little flock of good-looking young men that you supposedly represent. They hang out at your office; you supply liquor for them, gym equipment, an entire game room. You've got personal shower stalls in the bathroom. Rodriguez reports that they come and go as they please all day every day. I've got to tell you, Ms. Hunter…in my experience this is not at all indicative of a normal agent client relationship. Suspiciously enough, you don't represent any women, and out of the five guys on your little roster, only one has an acting credit of any kind to his name. Only one is working. The others can't account for any gig you've landed them, nor provide other sources of income or work history for the last six months or more. If you were me, what would this look like to you?"

"It takes years sometimes to break someone into the business. More often than not it's not just going to magically happen overnight so the fact that they do not have a paid gig in what they aspire to be is not all disconcerting to me. As for their work history outside of the business?" Maggie shrugs nonchalantly. "I don't request they disclose that. I don't know how they get by and I don't ask. Which explains my shock to learn Mr. Hill was caught accepting money for sex."

AJ discreetly glances over at Garrett in his orange jumpsuit. His face is bright red and his fists are clenched as he stares at the floor in abject anger.

"I had no idea and had nothing to do with that," Maggie continues. "Aside from him, a lot of these millennials still have the unbiblical cord attached and get sent money from their parents every month to pay their rent. It's not uncommon."

"Do you know what the Merriam-Webster definition of a panderer is, Ms. Hunter?" Judge Esque asks, taking out a big dictionary from under her podium and flipping to a pre-marked page.

Maggie blinks twice. "No," she replies with indifference.

"A go-between in love intrigues," she reads aloud. "Someone who caters to or exploits the weakness in others." She closes the book and looks back up at Maggie. "Does that sound like you?"

Silence. The tang of metallic terror coats AJ's mouth. The lump in his throat feels like it's tripled in size and the knot in his stomach twists twice as tight. His nails involuntarily dig into his palms to combat the waves of anxiety pulsing though him.

"No," Maggie finally replies, the single syllable dipped in disdain.

"Do you have any other talent that you represent who are actually employed in the business and can attest to you being their agent?" Judge Esque asks her seriously. "Because otherwise, if being an agent to a bunch of non-working actors and singers is all you do, I don't know how you're not poor. You don't look poor," she infers, looking Maggie up and down in her designer wear. "Tell me, Ms. Hunter, if we were to take a look into your bank account right now…would it reflect that of an insufficient agent? Or a highly paid madam?"

Maggie is reduced to silence once more. She's in the metaphorical corner. There's a rock. There's a hard place. And for the first time in her life she doesn't know how to side step out.

"I'd be very concerned if I were you," Judge Esque tells her definitively. "I'm going to request a subpoena for your bank records and tax returns. That's assuming that you file taxes, which I get the sneaking suspicion you don't. Depending on how that comes back, the water you're about to be in is going to be a whole hell of a lot hotter than these boys you represent. Prostitution and pandering typically only gets you a couple of years in county. But money laundering is a federal crime and will be punished as such."

Maggie swallows harshly and nods.

"Court is adjourned," Judge Esque announces. "We'll resume Friday at 9 a.m."

~

Afterwards, AJ returns to 360 Hollywood Place to pick up the stuff he's left there over the last six months: a spare toothbrush and a stick of deodorant in the bathroom, a pair of sneakers in the gym. He's decided he's not going to call his mom till he's actually in jail. So Friday. He's not sure that she will pick up for an 800 number, and if she does she'll probably hang up as soon as she hears that it's from correctional facility. Because she doesn't know anyone who would be in a correctional facility. She'll think someone's made a mistake, dialed the wrong number. Because her son would never be incarcerated. Because her son didn't have any attributes of a criminal. He hates to have to tell her she's wrong. If she doesn't answer he'll write her. He's better with written words anyway. Maybe he can express his remorse with a letter that will let her know he never meant for things to go this far, that he never meant to let her down like this.

AJ sees Maggie in her office through the glass. She didn't go home after court, and she sits at her desk with a glass full of brown liquid in the circle of her hands. The black revolver sits atop a file folder about a ruler's length away from the bottle of Cognac she's been pouring from. He realizes she had to have purposefully gone out and dug it from the bushes where Theo had thrown it. He knows she must know he's standing outside the door, but her eyes make no notice of him. She stares vacantly across the room at a wall, either deep in thought or somewhere off in space, the only movement she makes is to raise the glass to her lips every few seconds.

He leaves to make his eight o'clock.

~

AJ is dressing in the mirror after the act. Mrs. Van Buren is sitting on the bed in her silk robe sipping a glass of white wine.

"I wish there was something I could do," she says sympathetically.

"I'm afraid it's in the judge's hands from here on out," AJ replies, buckling his belt.

"Did I see that Judge Esque is presiding?"

"Yup," he says, pulling his shirt on. "And I get the vibe she's not the most empathetic or merciful lady."

"She is a tough one," Mrs. Van Buren agrees. "We have a slight rapport. She's bought a few pieces from the gallery."

AJ looks suddenly pensive as he does the buttons on his shirt. "Big pieces?"

"I suppose." She takes a small sip of wine. "Why do you ask?"

He turns to face her. "If your employees delivered to her then you would have her address on file, correct?"

Her eyes light up with realization and her lips quirk into a smirk. "What are you thinking?"

"That I've lost my mind."

~

AJ returns to 360 Hollywood Place immediately after he leaves Vera's and lets himself into Maggie's office without knocking.

"I've got an idea," he proclaims.

And that's when he sees her. She's moved from the swivel chair to the couch and is sprawled out across it with one hand over her head in a distressed pose. Her other hand dangles off the couch, loosely grasping the neck of the now more than half empty cognac bottle. His heart skips a beat when he sees that the revolver has made it to the couch with her, right next to her so that the back of it touches her cloth covered hip. Something someone shared with him not that long ago unconsciously resurfaces in his mind, an eerie notion of a dark story from the past reflected in the present setting.

"For a screenplay?" She asks glibly, not removing her hand to look at him. "Is it based on the true torrid tragedy known as my life? Because plots don't get much thicker than this, baby." She raises the bottle to her lips and takes a long swig, not grimacing at all as she swallows the liquid that surely burns. "Perhaps you'll have time to write it as we serve out our sentences. Call it Memoirs of a Misguided Madame. Should I die before you get it made, I want Diane Lane to play me."

AJ ignores her dramatic theatrics.

"Actually, Diane's too nice of a lady to play me. Imma need Glenn Close or Judith Light." She takes another big gulp and then proceeds to ramble on. "Actually all three of those women are too old to play me. I know I'm well into my forties but my forty is most people's twenty. Don't you think? I think you should get a fresh-faced newcomer to play me. One who hasn't had much fame. Make a bitch rich. Someone should benefit from my bereavement."

"I've got Judge Esque's home address," AJ says.

Maggie lifts her hand off her face and peeks over at him. "What," she says flippantly. "Are you gonna go knock her off?"

"I'm not a killer. I'm a lover."

She sits up and studies him seriously. He sees the wheels turning as she mentally weighs the possible outcomes of what he's suggesting. And then he watches as that sly sparkle slowly starts to return to her eyes.

CHAPTER 36

The next night AJ pulls into the driveway of a fairly nice Bungalow in a Silverlake subdivision, parking behind a Lexus sedan. He gets out and walks up the shrub-lined drive, looking over his shoulder every so many seconds.

"What are you doing. What are you doing," he mutters to himself under his breath, still in disbelief of the amount of gumption he seems to have.

He opts for the side entrance as opposed to the front door. Despite that probably being the creepier choice, there is less of a chance of being seen by her neighbors this way, should she let him in. He looks up at the night sky and takes a deep breath before rapping his fist against the door. A beat passes and then he sees the kitchen light come on. Rosemary Esque clutches her nightgown as she approaches. She can see him just as he can see her, through the glass slit at the top of the door, and she squints in confusion. Still, she undoes the deadbolt and lock, opening the door just wide enough to speak to him. He knows it's not because she's scared, she doesn't strike him as the type to spook easily. She looks more annoyed than anything. Annoyed and wound tight.

"Can I help you?"

"Yes…I umm…" He swallows nervously, his voice wasn't coming out as cool as he wanted it to. "I'm sorry to just show up at your house like this but I…well my name is Andrew Brooks. I'm one of the guys from the Maggie Hunter ca –"

"I know who you are," she cuts him off curtly.

"Oh. Ok," he stammers. "Well –"

"You are aware that this is highly inappropriate, right?" She asks him rhetorically, blatant gaze hoping to make him feel embarrassment for his foolishness. "You showing up here at my house is not appropriate, and, if I'm being frank, is a move that would typically warrant a 911 call from most judges."

"I know. I know. But I had to."

Rosemary cocks her head to the side, intrigued by his boldness.

"I had to tell you that this is a mistake," AJ continues. "That this…whole thing…is all just one big misunderstanding."

She starts to close the door in his face.

"No!" He utters quickly. "Wait! Please…"

She stops but looks more vexed than ever, putting her hand on her hip while she waits for him to speak his peace.

"Look," he says with earnest plea in his voice. "The others and I, we just got caught up in someone else's vendetta. We're just characters with fictional plot twists inserted into a scene in someone else's story. Emphasis on the word fictional. We're not these people." He looks her in the eyes with all seriousness, as though he truly believes the lie he and her both know he's telling. "I swear," he adds desperately.

For a moment she just stares at him. And then she lets out a sigh. "So you're saying you're not male prostitutes…"

"No," he replies with a chuckle for effect. At least he thinks it's for effect, he really has no idea what he's doing at this point or why he's even here, but he continues on with the charade anyway. "I'm just a young man from Memphis, Tennessee who moved out here six months ago to pursue screenwriting. Dominique Davis is a singer. Austin Edwards is an actor. Theo Lewis, he's been a personal assistant for years."

"And who's Maggie Hunter?"

"A talent agent in Hollywood," he replies simply.

Rosemary quirks a brow and smirks ever so slightly. "Then who's the criminal in this equation?"

AJ shrugs. "Only one person was caught red handed."

"And I'm supposed to believe he was a free agent…"

"That is what I'd like for you to believe, yes," he replies, catching his second wind of boldness. Because he's picking up on the subtle shifts in her demeanor, reading her like he was back in the courtroom, catching how she smiles with her eyes and nothing else. And her eyes are right on him now. And he can tell he amuses her. There's amusement in those eyes, amusement and maybe a little something else he'd like to visit if he could just…

"I'm going to need proof," she says then.

"Would you settle for persuasion?"

Static silence. He keeps his confident stance as they stand there locked in on each other. The barest glimmer of something passes across her serious gaze, and in that moment he knows he's won his case. A dog barks down the road. A car passes.

"Can I come in?" He asks her with a charming smile.

She hesitates but doesn't say no.

"Just to talk," he reassures her, though he knows she still knows he's still lying.

Three seconds pass, and then she's moving aside for him to enter.

Judge Rosemary Esque's nightgown is of a generic fabric, somewhere between the palettes of deep red and burgundy. It hits a little past her knees and is cinched around the center to keep it from falling off of her petite form. Her choice in sleepwear isn't sexy but it's not grandmotherly either. He's sure a proud woman like her would have probably prepared if she'd known what was coming. But he had to catch her off guard, didn't he?

She pads bare foot across her kitchen to take refuge behind the dining room table, putting distance between them in her state of primary denial that he knows will soon pass. He leans back against the granite island on the other side of the room and watches her watch him. She's got her arms resting atop the back of the chair she's hiding behind, keeping an eye on him like he's prey that could get away, all the while debating the repercussions of pouncing in her mind. He knows.

"You've got a nice house," AJ tells her absently as he looks around. "Big. Empty." And then he purposefully looks back to her. "Do you ever get lonely?"

"Excuse me?"

She's trying to sound offended. Trying.

"I read that your husband is an investment banker in New York City. That you all do the whole split coast living thing." AJ puts his hands in his pockets and leaves his post against the island. He casually makes his way around the room, pretending to take in the beauty of cabinets and light fixtures and other things he could give a shit less about. "I read that he's rumored to have a penchant for young female business students who need help with tuition. Of course that's all philanthropic, I'm sure."

He stops to watch expectantly as a perturbed—though be it amused—smirk forms on her face. He smiles and starts walking again.

"I read that you started out as a family court judge in New York in 1979 after a very successful stint as a top-notch attorney," he continues. "Worked your way up, and by the 1990s you were overseeing some pretty big trials. Moved to California in 2003 to lead a calmer life. Some speculated you had gone into retirement, but you hadn't. Turned around and started working for the Los Angeles county court in 2004. I read an article where you were quoted saying you couldn't retire because you wouldn't know what to do with yourself, being that you have an extremely intense work ethic. I suppose that's why I also read that you're worth more than him."

Her smirk fades, but her eyes remain locked on his.

"It takes a certain type of man to handle women more successful than themselves." He pauses. Raises an eyebrow at her. "Can he handle it? Does he handle it?"

Rosemary breaks his gaze after a beat, the green eyes getting to her.

"Because I read that he's busy overcompensating for his many failed business ventures—coping six figure cars and playing sugar daddy to some twenty something's—to ever be here to…handle…it."

"You've certainly read a lot, haven't you?" She says to him in a dry tone.

"How good at my job would I be if I didn't do my research?" He asks her cheekily.

"And what is that job title again?" She asks him back, replicating his cheekiness.

"Writer," he replies with ease. "And as a writer it's second nature to do research. So when I found out you were the one presiding over my case, I naturally wanted to know more about you."

She narrows her eyes at him. "Just what kind of writer are you, Mr. Brooks?"

"Romance," he replies cutely. "And you can call me AJ."

Quiet. He's making her lose her words, the woman who reduced his boss—a woman who *never* loses her words—to silence in the courtroom. AJ's confidence continues to rise as it has been steadily doing since he got in the door. Because the fact of the matter is these women can specialize in whatever the hell they want, be it justice or corruption, but he specializes in clouding minds and running trains of thought off track.

He takes two steps closer to the table. "Wikipedia said your husband was born in 1936. So…seventy-eight, right?"

She keeps a firm stance and cool stare. "Yes."

AJ nods contemplatively. "Mm."

"What?"

"Nothing," he replies innocently. "I'm just wondering."

"About?" She inquires.

He flashes her a smile. "Don't ask unless you really want to know."

She strives to maintain a poker face, but breaks eye contact yet again. "I need a drink," she says with a flustered chuckle.

She leaves her post behind the table and starts to make her way to the fridge, a tactical error on her part. She has to pass him, and as she does he snatches her up. Body to body she's rendered powerless and practically crumples in surrender, clinging to him as he captures her mouth with his. AJ kisses her with a fervor and passion that she clearly isn't accustomed to, and when he breaks apart from her lips she is left panting. He meets her eyes earnestly and in the sincerest voice possible says...

"I'll leave if you want me to."

Ninety-five minutes later Rosemary is pulling her robe back on over naked skin that's flushed from satisfaction. The sheets on her bed are thoroughly rumpled.

"Do I have to pay you now?" She coyly asks him, voice husky from exertion.

"No," AJ says with his back to her as he pulls up his jeans. He looks over his shoulder at her, feigning confusion as he does buttons. "Because that would make me a prostitute." He grabs his shirt off the floor. "Which I'm not." He pulls it on. "And you a customer, which you're not." He locks eyes with her then. "Right?"

Rosemary eyes him up and down, partly in appraisal of his body, partly in appraisal of his competence. She cocks her head to the side and meets his eyes.

"Right," she says with a sly smile.

He winks at her. "Just as long as we both know our roles." He sits back down on the bed just long enough to pull his shoes on, and then he's headed to the door. Before he walks out he looks back at her one last time. "Goodnight, Judge Esque," he says politely.

"Goodnight, AJ. See you in the morning."

AJ walks through the front door of his apartment twenty minutes later, feeling both broken up and worn down. The confidence he had earlier in the night was lost somewhere on the ride home. In a final attempt to remove his mind from his reality, he sits down at his desk and picks up his pen. That's when he notices just how bad his hands are shaking; trembling so frantically he can barely grip the quill tip between his fingers. He tosses the pen across the desk and stands back up, runs both hands through his hair, paces one direction, turns, paces the other, and then takes out his phone. He dials Theo's number. It rings multiple times and eventually goes to voicemail.

"I think…I think I may have just incriminated myself," he speaks into the phone, each syllable quivering. "I was trying to make it better but…but everything's bad. Everything's wrong. We're not going to win. We're not going to–"

He snaps himself out of it and deletes the voice message before putting down his phone. He knows he's not in the mental space to be making calls. He knows he's lost, loosing, and destined to lose. There's nothing anyone can do.

He walks into the bathroom. He turns the sink on. Leans down. Splashes cold water on his face. When he comes back up, he catches a glimpse of himself in the mirror.

He doesn't like the person he sees even a little bit.

He walks back out and flops down on his bed, defeated. He stares up at the ceiling, hands over mouth, with a look of deity seeking desperation. The phone starts to ring. For a second or two he doesn't care, but that generic AT&T generated melody has a hold on him. Then again, maybe it's money that has the hold on him. Maybe it's hope. He glances at the screen. It's Maggie. He rolls his eyes, but answers despite the fact. Because the noose is too tight not to.

"What?"

"Well," she starts with baited breath. "How did it go?"

"I took care of it."

"How did you take care of it?" She asks, still doubtful.

"I took care of it real good," he replies facetiously.

"Good." She lets out a little breath. "Good."

There's a pause between when she should have said thank you, but won't, and when she will continue to press her luck. He waits for it like a pro.

"Look, I know it's late," she starts. "But Mrs. Kelly called and she wants to *see you* one last time before we *go to jail*." She accentuates the certain phrases with the sort of tired theatrics that only a person who knows they're in the clear tries.

"I thought you said we weren't going to jail," he dryly amuses her.

"That's what you tell me."

Her voice is low and he knows she's smiling.

But he's not.

"Fine," he says in perhaps the harshest tone he's ever taken with her. "I don't care," he quickly reverts back to monotone submission. "Tell her I'll be there in an hour."

"Thank you, dear."

She hangs up. AJ slowly blows air threw his lips and then begrudgingly peels himself off of the bed.

Fifty minutes later he's in another bedroom. Mrs. Kelly is outfitted in her signature satin negligee, walking about the room in her usual ditzy, semi-stoned state with a glass of chardonnay in hand. AJ is undressing over by the bed.

"I apologize for having you out so late the night before your court date," she laments on her way to the dresser. "I don't want to put a damper on your spirits, but realistically speaking, you could go to jail tomorrow. And I could die before you get out." She refills her glass to the brim with the sparkling liquid. "You might not be aware because the work feels so real, but I'm an older woman, Andrew. I have to act on my impulses seeing as I could go at any moment."

"I understand," he says. "It's ok."

He's down to his Calvin Klein's now. She takes a long drink.

"It's just…when Caleb got fired…I had doubts that anyone else would be able to adequately fill his spot." She sits her chardonnay down on the dresser. "But as it turns out," she starts to say as she reaches into her clutch. "You fill it much better."

She looks over at him and smiles predatorily before turning her attention back to the possessions laid out on the vanity. He watches her take out her little vial, roll up one of her many hundred-dollar bills, and ready herself.

"Can I have some?"

Her head snaps around in surprise to look at him. But the shock in her eyes is replaced by mischief in no time.

Once he has her naked on the bed, AJ licks a slow, sensuous trail from her lower back to her neck. He flips her over and starts the process over, from top to bottom this time. He kisses between her breasts, down her stomach. He pauses his ministrations and reaches for the vial. Meticulously he arranges a perfect, powdery white line just under her navel. Then he rolls up part of his profit paid in advance and puts it to his nose. Starting at one end, he snorts all the way to the other.

CHAPTER 37

The next morning the boys are gathered outside the courthouse waiting for Maggie to arrive. Dominique is standing with his head down and his hands in his pockets, being unusually quiet. He's thinking about all those long hours in the studio, all those amazing songs, and that almost finished mixtape that nothing will ever come of now. Austin is pacing solemnly up and down the sidewalk. He's thinking about how he's going to explain all this to his pops without forever ruining their father son relationship, and how the leeway he was just starting to make with Hermosa was going to be all but lost.

AJ, on the other hand, appears thoroughly unaffected in his pink button-up dress shirt and black slacks. He's coolly leaning up against the stair railing that leads into the building, strumming his fingers rapidly against the steel rail to a song and beat that he's just made up in his head. He's thinking that he hopes Rosemary (he can refer to her by her first name now, right? he thinks so) doesn't take too long so he can get back home and get this future Grammy award winning hit down on paper. He compulsively touches his face as if to just make sure that it's still there.

Theo strolls around the corner of the building, dressed extra dapperly. He looks like the picture of collectedness, but sheer fear is emanating from him like a bad cologne.

"You all ready for this?" He asks them.

Austin stops pacing. "I think I'm bout to sweat though my shirt," he says almost breathlessly, wringing his hands. "That's not gonna be a good look," he rambles nervously. "Neither are the bags under my eyes. I was so nervous I could barely sleep."

"I didn't sleep at all," AJ says from his spot against the rail, not sounding at all upset about it. "I was up *all* night."

Dominique looks at him weirdly. "Doin' what?"

AJ smirks. "A farewell tour."

At that moment a regal town car pulls up to the curb. Maggie gets out wearing a bright red dress and matching six-inch stilettoes. She's got her flawless blonde hair down and her dark shades on, looking remarkably well rested and unruffled.

"Let's go, folks," she says as she struts right past them, not showing even an inkling of doubt in her demeanor. "Show time."

The four of them follow her up the steps into the courthouse.

The set-up inside the courtroom is the same from earlier in the week. Richard is in the gallery again, leering like a Disney villain. Vera is there to show support this time. None of their other clients dare show their face, even though Maggie never did let their names be known. At the defendant's table Austin, Theo, Maggie, AJ, and Dominique are seated side by side in a row respectively. At the plaintiff's table are Officer Raymond Rodriguez and the arresting officer from the night of the raid. Garrett is pranced out and seated off to the side. When Judge Esque makes her entrance, Maggie and AJ exchange the subtlest of glances.

"It's unfortunate you all had to get up early, get all dressed up, and gather here, because this is going to be a rather quick verdict," she states as she takes her place behind the podium.

You could hear a pin drop and AJ can practically hear Dominique's heart thumping to the left of him. He wants to tell him everything's going to be just fine.

Judge Esque looks down at her podium. "Upon further consideration I have decided to suspend my request for subpoena of Ms. Hunter's bank records and tax history on account of insufficient evidence, lack of trustworthy evidence, and what I consider to be entrapment of the defendant by the plaintiff."

All the boys beside AJ look between each other with baited breath, they think they know what this means, but they're afraid to let the air out of their chests just yet.

"So," Judge Esque continues, taking a breath. "In the case of Maggie Hunter vs. Los Angeles County I find the defendant not guilty of pandering."

Maggie doesn't sigh, squeal, or cheer. She doesn't seem surprised by the verdict. Despite being guilty as sin. Despite coming so close to losing. It's as though she never had a doubt what the outcome would be. Too proud to even smile.

"In the case of Austin Edwards vs. Los Angeles County I find the defendant not guilty of prostitution."

Austin lets out an audible sigh, bowing his head in thanks to God.

"In the case of Theo Lewis vs. Los Angeles County I find the defendant not guilty of prostitution."

Theo doesn't make noise, but he can't keep the huge grateful grin off his face.

"In the case of Dominique Davis vs. Los Angeles County I find the defendant not guilty of prostitution."

Dominique laughs, almost hysterical with relief, clasping a hand over his mouth.

"In the case of Andrew Brooks vs. Los Angeles County I find the defendant not guilty of prostitution."

AJ is quiet. Unsurprised. Much like Maggie.

Judge Esque pauses before reading the last verdict, the brief silence spelling out a shift in winds. AJ glances over at his orange jumpsuit clad coworker to catch his reaction.

"In the case of Garrett Hill vs. Los Angeles County I find the defendant guilty of prostitution in the first degree by Act in Furtherance."

The look on Garrett's face is one of horror and confusion, eyes wide and mouth agape. AJ doesn't look back, but he's sure Richard is in the stands grinning.

"No," Garrett says out loud. "No, no, no!"

"I hereby sentence the defendant to two years in a Los Angeles County correctional facility with no parole," Judge Esque speaks over him.

"That's fucking bullshit!" Garrett yells, the confusion on his face quickly being replaced by outright outrage. "The whole lot of them did the same bloody thing as me, by what kind of daft logic do they get off and I get charged? Hm? Tell me!"

The officer in charge of Garrett attempts to rein him in.

"They were not caught accepting money for sex, Mr. Hill," Judge Esque tells him with placating aplomb. "Will you please escort Mr. Hill out of my courtroom," she says to the officer.

The uniformed man nods and shuffles Garrett out of the room cursing and spitting.

The room is silent once more, somberly so.

"Let's continue, shall we?" Judge Esque says, breaking up the awkwardness of the moment. "In conclusion," she proceeds, looking back down at her podium. "Following false accusations, Officer Raymond Rodriguez will be placed on probationary unpaid leave from the Los Angeles County police department until further notice for using professional privileges to fulfill personal needs." She looks up at the undercover officer of the hour then and adds. "Pending defamation and perjury charges will be addressed in court at a later date."

AJ glances over at the plaintiff's table. Ali looks dejected, but he's taking it in stride. He notices that Maggie still won't look at her former flame, but she is smiling fervently to herself now. And then she leans in to whisper in his ear.

"You're better than a lawyer," she tells him.

AJ stays facing forward, expression never faltering. "I probably get more people off," he replies lowly.

Judge Esque bangs her gavel and court is dismissed. They all stand up. His remaining coworkers are smiling from ear to ear and bumping fists, congratulating each other on a win they're not privy to knowing how they pulled off. AJ looks back at the crowd and locks eyes with Vera. They exchange knowing smirks. And then he pops his collar and follows is crew out of the courthouse.

Maggie descends the outside steps with a self-assured smile, her men trailing behind her looking equally as happy. She pays no attention to the reporters who were hoping for her fall and a juicy black book reveal as she passes by them.

"Maggie…" she hears Ray calling to her.

She keeps walking.

"Baby..."

She stops dead in her tracks and snaps her head around to see him chasing after her. He catches up to her, looking ever so slightly apologetic.

"I just…" Ray starts unsurely. "I wanted you to know that despite everything that transpired between us…despite all the lies…my feelings for you were not a lie. Falling for you was not part of the plan, but I did. I really did."

"Touching," Maggie replies, and then turns around and starts walking again.

"You know what," Ray snaps at her in anger. "You can cut me some slack. I just lost my job, possibly my whole career, over this mess. My brother's mess. And *your* mess."

She turns back around. "I told you this was a dangerous game to play, did I not?" She looks up into his eyes with a pompously pleased look. "What did I say?"

He looks away from her. She smiles.

"Somebody has to lose," she reminds him coolly with a smart aleck smirk. "So don't be sore about it, Ray. *Baby.*"

He has nothing to say. Satisfied, she turns her back on him.

"You can't say you weren't warned," she says definitively over her shoulder.

He's left to watch her and her four disciples file into the back of a town car and drive away from the courthouse in victory.

~

"So back to the office tomorrow?" Austin asks in the car.

"No," Maggie says. "We won but it's still smart for us to lay low for a while."

"So what's the plan?" Theo questions.

"I thought we'd take the first flight out to New Orleans in the morning, spend the holidays at Southern Cross."

"What's Southern Cross?" Austin asks.

"A plantation."

"Oh no," Dominique replies. "I don't do random plantations. I gotta respect my roots."

"It's not a random plantation," she informs him. "It's my home."

Dominique looks confused. "So whatchu sayin? You from the N.O.?"

Maggie nods.

"Huh. Shoulda known you was a spicy little Cajun. Be real," he says sarcastically. "You put some of that voodoo on Miss Judge Lady."

"Of course not," she says. "Who needs magic when you have tricks?"

~

Back at his apartment AJ is packing a suitcase when his phone rings. He picks it up with a sigh.

"Hey, mom," he answers.

"So guess who I ran into at the grocery this morning?"

"Who?" He entertains her.

"Grace."

AJ doesn't say anything and continues to pack.

"She said you two broke up…"

"We did."

"Now why would you go and do that? That was spose to be my future daughter-in-law. Do you got another woman or somethin?"

He stares at the calendar hanging on his wall. The dates of December stare back at him, almost every square filled with a different woman's name. Written work reminders.

"No mom," he says reassuringly as he rips the page off the wall. "I don't have another woman."

"Then what is it?" She asks, confused, concerned.

"We're just two different people in two different places. That's all."

There's silence on the other end for a beat or two, and then he hears his mom sigh. "Well Christmas is in a few days...you'll be comin' home, right?"

"I meant to call," he says regretfully. "But I had a very busy week."

"You're not comin home..."

"I have to work."

"What?" He can hear the upset and disappointment in her voice.

"I'm sorry."

"Andrew...is everything okay?"

"Everything's fine."

"You promise you're not lyin' to me?"

"I promise," he lies.

"So you're just gonna stay in LA and have Christmas alone?"

"Yup," he lies again.

~

We will now begin boarding first class for flight 686 with non-stop service to New Orleans.

The voice cuts through Terminal 1 in LAX. AJ, Austin, Dominique, Theo and Maggie board the plane and take their seats in the coveted and comfortable first rows.

Maggie sits next to AJ. He's on her right side, right where she wants him.

To be continued....

If you enjoyed *Dial 323 LOVE*, drop a review on Goodreads or Amazon, and pre-order the second book in the series, *Descension*. Available soon!

Thank you for reading my words.
- C.M. Arnold

Acknowledgments

I'd like to give a huge shout out and a major thank you to my editor, Jeff Ford, and my cover designer, Alexandria Pavek. You have both been so patient with my high-maintenance, perpetually persnickety ass.

To Alex. I think it was 2016 when I first reached out to you about doing some book covers. Two years ago. That's how many changes of heart I've had. *So…don't hate me…but I've decided to change the title. Actually, never mind. Actually, yes, change it. You know what, I'll let you know by Sunday if you should change it. Okay, now I have to change my pen name because a porn star already has it. Can he be holding a glass of bourbon instead of smoking? I don't think he smokes, not yet anyway. I've decided to hold off on publishing for a while; can you put the covers on the backburner? Okay, I've decided I'm getting close to being ready to publish now; do you have time to deal with me? Okie dokie then, dust off them covers. I've decided to change the title back to the original. I've decided to drop the pen name and use my real name. Nope, woops, initials. Initials! Does that silhouette look a little Trump-y? No? Just me? Can you change it anyway? It's just…I can't have a silhouette on my cover looking like Trump even if it's just in my head. Highlight this number. No, highlight that number. Actually, you were right, the way you highlighted it looks best. Okay, so here's what the spine depth needs to be. Woops, I had my gutters set wrong. Here's the new spine depth. Woops, I had my margins set wrong. Here's the new, new spine depth. Would you believe I had the whole damn thing double-spaced and never knew it? Don't kill me, it's gonna be a drastically different spine depth now. Jpegs, PDFs, and bleeds…oh my.* You have done everything I've asked of you, Alex, and done it well. You interpret what I describe even when I'm probably making little to no sense. You bring my ideas to life, and new and improved ideas to the table. You have been nothing but courteous, kind, and professional with me. It's been a pleasure working with you, and may we continue to collaborate in the future.

To Jeff. You know I'd be up a creek without you. Remember when I thought I could do this without hiring an editor? Yeah, that was real funny, wasn't it? I mean…the suits and suites alone. I literally should have titled the series Suits & Suites. If you ever take up teaching, have a course called Suits & Suites, please. I'm quite (not to be confused with

quiet) confident nobody, and I mean NOBODY uses the words suit
and suite more than me. Almost every page someone is taking off a suit
in a suite, their partner following suit. And I fucked it up almost every
time. And you fixed it every time. Then there was barley and barely.
Carton and cartoon (Heh. That was a good one. If you hadn't been
paying such close attention to that particular Book 2 scene I dare say you
would have missed it *wink*wink*). Tenses going every which way.
And various other misuses, mishaps, and mistakes of varying degrees.
You pointed out discrepancies I hadn't caught, controlled my tangents,
and made me aware when I was oblivious. You not only fixed this book
(3xs), you made me a better writer. And, hey, I ain't tryin' ta toot my
own horn or anything…but I know I made you a better editor. If you
could handle me…and trust me I know I was hard to handle at
times…you can handle any editing clients that come after me. Of which
I'm sure there will be many because you're a great editor. That said,
you're not only a great editor, but also a great friend. And the best
cheerleader I've ever had. Thank you.

P.S. You haven't proof read this section so it's probably riddled with
mistakes.